JESTERS INCOGNITO

HARRISON WHEELER

To Chester

Jesters Incognito

Summary: In the legendary city of Roxy, an 18-year-old cab driver starts an underground group of entertainers to overthrow a mercenary media king.

ISBN-13 (book) 978-1478321323
ISBN-10 (book) 1478321326

ISBN (ebook) 978-1-623-09483-6

[1.Speculative-Fiction. 2.Science-Fiction. 3.Humour-Fiction 4. Social Media-Fiction 5. Entertainment - Fiction]

Front and back cover design: Harrison Wheeler
Illustrations: Harrison Wheeler

ABOUT THE AUTHOR

Harrison Wheeler is a writer of speculative fiction for Young Adult readers, and a cartoonist for anyone with the capacity to see. Despite the Noize, Harrison has continually cultivated his passion for creativity in music, theatre, comedy, and storytelling over the years, and this book stands as the exclamatory flag on his visionary moon.

FOR MORE ON THE AUTHOR AND MULTIMEDIA EXTRAS VISIT:

www.harrisonwheeler.ca

Acknowledgments

To my editors, Ryan Murphy, Eric Daigle, Scott Spencer & Susan Wheeler. Vibrant souls and mighty wordsmith super talents, all.

To the legion of formidable foolish friends who have filled my well, worldwide. You know who you are.

To the strangers who unknowingly entertain me on LifeTV.

To Sammy, the queen of my kingdom.

Thank you.

Contents

1. A series of 65 bite-sized chapters, arranged numerically and in logical narrative sequence.

2. A Glossary of Terms resides at story's end, following the epilogue.

3. Illustrations peppered throughout. Surprise!

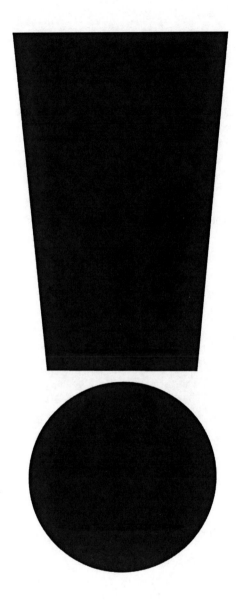

PROLOGUE

The corridor at work was pin-drop silent, as always.

Samantha was too miserable to notice the lively designs from the orange lighting off the metallic walls. She had been emotionally overcast for so long, and it didn't help that the elevator was slow. Again.

Stupid elevator. Stupid work. Stupid life, she thought.

The elevator was empty when it arrived. It was the first time in weeks Samantha had peace and quiet. Finally, a win.

Although. She felt disappointed. She knew her associate would never ride the elevator with her again. He was annoying. And bizarre. But entertaining. She knew she'd have a hard time killing him.

Samantha arrived at her floor and left the elevator. Just about. Before she stepped out, she saw a box, pitch black, the size of half a shoebox beneath the console of buttons.

Thick white exclamation marks painted every side. *What now*, she wondered.

Samantha brought the box home before opening it. The tiny card attached read:

Samantha,

Don't let the Doldrums get you down. Do something. Do it for no reason. Surprise yourself.

Foxtails and moonpies, Jester

CHAPTER ONE: A JESTER'S GESTURE

Let me begin by saying that I pity clowns.

Their tired balloon-animal routines fail at amusing even the most premature newborn baby, and those who aren't bored of clowns are usually just scared of them, thanks to the abundance of cheesy 80s horror movies. What's more, one of the most notable of their clan, whose name I needn't mention, tarnished the clown image forever after he endorsed artificial hamburgers worldwide.

They're far from funny, their costumes are tasteless, and most of the clowns I've met have a drinking problem. Clowns are sad and misdirected. It's a shame, really, all that wasted talent.

Jesters, on the other hand, are largely misunderstood as silly, wannabe clown knock-offs. This could not be any further from the truth. In contrast to being a clown, being a jester is not about getting cheap laughs. We want to get a rise out of people, sure, but it's more than that for jesters. Much more. Why else were we advisors to kings in ancient courts?

About a year after I decided to become a jester, I drove my taxi across the city on a regular night shift. It was dusk on another eerily quiet Saturday summer evening.

"Car 89, back in." I radioed.

"Copy 89." dispatch radioed back. "Who's in 89?"

“It’s Vincent,” I replied. “Vincent Meistersinger. I’m always in 89.”

A pause on the radio. “Ya, thought so.” Another pause. “We had lots of calls about you already tonight. Know anything about that?” dispatch asked, his voice dripping with insinuation.

“Nope,” I lied.

Of course I knew about the calls.

So I had a zest for mobile entertainment, is that really such a crime? Sadly, the answer is yes. But, come on, I gave my passengers something to talk about. So I stapled miniature colour prints of surrealist paintings to the ceiling, so what? So I taped the daily comics to the back of the passenger’s seat, so what? So I always had a new collection of figurines on the dash and good music on the radio, too. Good music never hurt anyone. Besides, it’s my cab!

“Of course they don’t. That’s why they’re calling us all the time to complain about you.”

“Complaints are compliments if you stand on your head. None so deaf as those who won’t hear, as they say.”

I could almost hear dispatch rolling his eyes over the air. “Just drive the cab, ok buddy? Or Shmitty’s going to want a word with you.”

Shmitty’s Cabs is the name of the company I drove for. Shmitty, its owner, always worked hard at making his drivers hate him. I needn’t tell you our nickname for him.

I made sure to crank the music on my radio nice and loud before I hung up on dispatch. Some early ska music, just to let them know how little I appreciated being reprimanded over the air.

Call it strange, or eccentric, call it perpendicular, I don't really care; I had my own agenda for taxiing. Not only was I looking for rides, I was looking for an audience. You see, I enjoy being a memorable stranger in other people's plots.

Two old ladies hailed me after their trip to the supermarket. They were in good spirits, polite and giggly, happy to be out on the town. Once they were stuffed into the back seats, groceries and all, I took the opportunity to talk to them about evolution. Why not?

"Be honest with me ladies, who looks more like a monkey, me or you?" I asked. They were completely taken aback.

"What in the world are you talking about? We're not monkeys!" the stern, thin one said.

"I beg to differ ma'am. It is a weird topic to follow a routine shopping trip I suppose, but I couldn't help but think about monkeys when I saw all the bananas you bought." The two of them looked at the yellow bunch of bananas sticking out of their brown paper grocery bag, and then back at me.

"And supporter of the evolutionary theory or not," I continued, "You have to admit that all of us look pretty monkey like. If we didn't have any clothes on, none of us I mean, worldwide, we'd be nothing much more than a bunch of glorified pink apes riding elevators and holding press conferences, y'know? I bet if we didn't walk around in shoes all the time we'd be picking pennies off the street with our toes!"

Through the rearview mirror I could see the stern one was still fuming. The other, chubbier one sat back and stared out the window in deep thought. She was watching the passersby and considering them as pink apes, I knew it.

Jesting is an art, no question about it. We playfully participate in conversation without divulging our true opinion on the subject matter. Sometimes we resort to silliness, and most of the time people aren't aware we jest them at all. That's when we know we're doing it right.

The chubby woman smiled politely; her eyes were playful. "Are you an evolutionist?" she asked.

"I'm an absurdist, ma'am," I answered. "But let's suppose evolution is true; what about the monkeys today? Why can't we see them evolving? Are they still evolving?"

Silence in the backseat. And then, a little giggle.

"They're probably sitting in the zoos watching all of us," said the chubby one still looking out the window. "Us pink monkeys with clothes and technology strapped to our bodies, and thinking to themselves…"

"Don't encourage the young man, Lucy," the stern one interrupted. "We don't know who he is."

"Exactly" I continued on Lucy's willingness, ignoring the other's bad vibes. "They're thinking, 'I'm going to get me a driver's license, round up some of my crew, and then we're going to buy some pants that'll hang super low like all the cool kids I see!"

"Like a monkey!" Lucy exclaimed, lifting off the seat in a thrill.

The laugh we shared was a burst of colourful voices in the cab, especially gratifying when I caught a glimpse of the stern one crack a smile. They got out of my cab looking lighter on their feet. The chubby one shuffled back to my window.

"How old are you kiddo?"

"I've made 18 laps around the sun, ma'am."

"Well you sure are a funny monkey for your age!" she laughed, rustling up my mess of hair.

Success! What a buzz! I was hooked on 'being a jester'! Life was no longer a monotonous routine to be endured! No sir! It was a buffet of absurdity to be indulged upon! I love to be the one to discreetly hijack a person's day, just to ignite a reaction in them. It stirs the juices, you know? A contradiction here, an insult there - let's celebrate the oddities of this pinball game called life! And the best payoff is that you never know the outcome. That's why it feels so great! Every encounter is a surprise!

I picked up a few other rides after the little old ladies, most of whom had their heads buried too deep in their power phones for me to be able to talk them up. A high school student complained she couldn't text with her friends because her thumbs had swollen from texting too much. I assured her those thumbs would come in handy if she ever found herself in need of a ride on the side of a highway, but she didn't hear me, still trying to text as though her life depended on it. Then a businesswoman spent the entire ride shouting at her husband over Vidchat for not recording her favourite TV show, 'Triple Threat or Death Threat'. I tried explaining to her that that show was more real than most people realized, but she didn't hear me.

Society is too distracted to enjoy a good jest anymore.

And then there was the chef who stumbled into my cab on his way home after his bistro closed. He was a round man with enough stains on his jacket to pass as a Jackson Pollack canvass. I took a different approach with him.

"Hi there monsieur chef, how are you tonight?" I asked.

"I'm drunk like a skunk," he replied, slurring his syllables. His eyes swam around in his skull like a couple of lost fish. "We had a party of 400 tonight, and if I see another crème de mousse I'm going to puke. Just get me to 98 Homewood before I pass out, ok?"

"Done!" I said. "What kind of music you like?"

The chef's brow furrowed as he tried to figure out why I was asking the question. He looked like he would lose balance sitting down, which I'd never seen before.

"Any style of music. Just so you can enjoy the trip. What's your fave?"

"I don't know," he said, dismissively.

"Funk?" I suggested.

"Whatever!"

"Perfect! A man after my own heart!" I jumped out of the car and opened the trunk. I had stashed a bunch of different hats and wigs and simple costume accents in the trunk of my cab. Jewelry, shades, fake teeth, make-up, and feathers. I threw on a costume that complimented the customer's taste in music, and got back in the cab as a different character. Bizarre? A little.

Before the chef knew it, I was behind the wheel sporting a sequence vest and oversized disco shades cranking some funk tunes out of my cab's stereo. I could have been an alien, judging by the look on the chef's face.

"Best thang 'bout the funk be the bass line," I shouted over the music, doing my best 1970s jive-speak. "I'm drivin' the speed limit, yessir legit, but that bass line make it feel like we travelin' at light speed baby!"

Eleven minutes later, I left the chef standing in his driveway with a baffled expression on his face as I sped off with my music cranked as high as my radio would go. I wish I could have been at his kitchen table the next morning when he tried to convince his wife that it had happened.

Full time taxi driver, part time jester. That was life at the beginning of it all. The two professions complemented each other nicely. I got paid to drive, which paid my rent (most of the time), and as a sweet bonus, driving cab was the best job in the world to practice 'jesting' techniques. Because I never knew who, or what, the next ride would be, my finely tuned wit and artistic sensibilities stayed sharp. As a jester you need to be quicker than two snaps of a swizzle stick. And we all know how fast that is.

I parked my taxi outside the train station on my fifteen-minute break, sipping a coffee while jotting ideas in my sketchbook. With my seat reclined and my left leg dangling out of the window and the other propped on the steering wheel, I took stock of the jesting I had done that evening. Quick sketches of the characters I picked up in my taxi filled the page, and I scribbled pieces of the conversations we had too, the juicy bits, next to my cartoon recreations. Sketchbooks, like the one you are reading now, have always been my creative warehouse.

My eyes moved to the side-view mirror, showcasing seven or eight Dynamitaxis dotted white behind me. They made my black checkerboard cab look ancient, but I think it's the old-school charm that people liked. Behind the last of us in the line-up sat one black, dome-shaped car idling. A thin, swift silver bumper ran around the bottom of the entire vehicle, and two tiny blue lights glowed barely visible through its tinted windshield, pulsing like a dull lighthouse warning light in a thickened fog.

It was the Noize.

Were they following me?

My phone vibrated on top the cab's dash, startling me. A text from my friend, Breakfast. He drove taxi, too.

>dude. 90.3. killer europe beats

In English, his text means he suggested I turn on the college radio station and listen to some exciting European music. I knew it would be DJ music, seeing as Breakfast is a Deejay. DJ Breakfast. His real name is Myles, which I only ever use when we're arguing, but he loves breakfast so much he'd eat it every meal of the day. So those who know him well, call him Breakfast.

I tuned in to 90.3 FM. Sure enough, a DJ was spinning some dub tunes together; slow bass lines syncopating sparse drums. It was in fact a very cool vibe for the midnight crowd Uptown. It rippled through the night in a layer of slow motion sound with a full moon, flashlight white, puncturing the metal skyline. A couple of kids wearing ball caps were up way past their bedtime; who knows what they were up to. They were punk music, I thought. An elegant white car pulled up next to me and a buxom blonde stepped out and ran across the street, smoking a cigarette. She was some big band charts; some sexy saxophone lines maybe.

Everyone's got their own vibe. Scientific fact.

I texted Breakfast back.

<*Me likes the beats.*

>That's the tempo life should be lived.

<*You said it.*

Looking back into my side-view mirror again, I saw that the Noize had vanished from sight, like a ghost. It's hard not to feel paranoid with them patrolling the city, hiding behind their cloaking shields.

<Noize is out tonight.

>Oh ya. I love those guys.

<Shaddup. U wouldn't luv'em if you got caught.

>Never gunna happen. Hey, I got the new soundbomber. U gotta c this thing. Xplodes!

<Sweet! Show me at the meeting. You coming to Cosmos tonight?

Cosmos was our greasy spoon hang out of choice. The food knocks you out but keeps you coming back for more. Never say no to Cosmos.

>I can't make Cosmos 2nite.

<What? Again? Dude.

>I know, I know. Xtra work @ station.

<Ok. Just stay out of trouble.

>Roger that.

<K I should split bro. Waiting 2 meet a potential new member.

>Nice. Da more da merrier. Tell them we're a blood-drinking vampire anarchist satan-worshiping cult.

<You forgot werewolf-hunting Sasquatch believers.

>And the discounts. Make sure to mention the discounts.

<HA. 10% off of slippers at Cost'mo.

>Right. Mandatory slipper-wearing at our cult. No slippers, no satan.

<L8r bro.

>Out.

I keep curious company. By no means am I the only jester in town.

CHAPTER TWO: INTERVIEW WITH A CABBIE

Downing the rest of my coffee, I sunk deeper into the seat and waited to see if my guest was going to show for our appointment. I turned up the music and continued watching the slow motion comings and goings of midnight through my windshield. A tall trench-coated man stood inside a bus shelter on the far side of the taxi stand, his unamused expression illuminated by the soft glow from a Digi-Poster in front of him. He double-clicked the various videos and pop-up menus within the poster, commercials and useless factoids no doubt, but eventually found something adequate and sat down to enjoy it. His expression unchanged.

What a farce, I thought. Digitally enhanced or digitally entranced? The programming showing live through my windshield was infinitely more entertaining.

The interior light of my cab abruptly flipped on as the right rear door opened and a young woman hopped inside, jolting me out of bystander mode.

"So, you're a jester," she said, enthusiastically. Her voice had a beautiful tone. Bubbly. Bright. She wore a white summer dress and a single brown bracelet to match her long auburn locks.

"And you're LaRose?" She nodded. "Well then it's true I'm a jester. Truer than steel, truer than blue, and truer than the ripe smell of curry and sweat in here from the driver before me." I pulled away from the train station and drove in a circle around the surrounding neighbourhood.

"You're hair is enormous," LaRose remarked, candidly.

"I like to think it's full bodied."

"Uh-uh. Your head looks like an ice-cream cone with a huge scoop of vanilla on top. And cotton candy on top of that."

"I see you don't lack candour. Shall we return to the topic of jesters? You'd like to become one, I presume?"

"Oh yeah, for sure. But you don't want people to know, is that right?"

"You got it. Surprise is a jester's calling card."

"Hmm. And we keep our day job."

"That's the point. Perform secretly, as it were. If people think we're all just regular employees…"

"How many are there?"

"Fifty. Fifty one if you're in. I assume you miss having an audience eating out of your hands just as much as we did."

LaRose looked out the open window with a blissful smile on her face. It was so obvious she was a performer, just by the way she carried herself. Musical theatre, maybe.

"And so what is a 'jest' exactly?" she asked, coming out of her trance. "Are you suggesting door to door stand-up comedy? You'd be less liked than Jehovah's Witnesses!"

"One jester I know does that, actually. He has a great time! Just be a jester at your own discretion. If not comedy, then how 'bout a quirky little story? For the heck of it! An observation? How about just some devil's advocate jesting to spice things up a little?"

"I like the idea so far," she said.

"Well, you come highly recommended. What do you do, anyway?"

"I used to sing."

"You mean you *are* a singer."

"I guess you're right."

"A jester's always right," I proclaimed, sticking my finger into the air, pointedly. "Unless we're wrong, in which case we're still right in being wrong. Bah! But seriously, think of the priceless looks on people's faces if you broke out into song during a regular lunch hour."

"That would be amusing," she agreed. "I work at a call centre, though. People keep to themselves."

"So put customers on hold and sing to them," I offered. "Instead of playing that excruciating elevator music."

LaRose giggled. "That's a good idea."

"We've got to grab every chance we can!" I exclaimed. "The stages are closed. No bookings for live shows of any kind for years, right? People have totally bought into packaged entertainment, pre-paid, mobile, downloadable, reality T.V. smut - it's the same old routine."

"When my friend told me about you guys, it made so much sense to me. This city is so dead. I'm so bored!"

"Do you mind giving me a little sample?"

"What, right here? Now?"

"Why not?"

LaRose's cheeks reddened as she pulled a lock of hair behind her ear. "Ok. Just roll the window up, would you? I don't want to get caught." She started faintly by humming into key, and then sang a quiet verse of a sultry jazz tune she had written herself, beautifully.

"Wow. I think my radio just blushed with envy," I said, applauding.

"It's been a long time since I've done that in front of anyone."

I smiled, knowing full well how freeing it is break the rules and express yourself. No licenses. No laws. We drove in silence for a few blocks, letting the reverberations of LaRose's voice paint the air inside my cab. Taxis have great acoustics, a little known fact. I've always wanted to do a live show in a hall with great acoustics, just to let my voice boom. The silence in this city was deafening.

LaRose leaned over and snuck a glance at the doodle cards I kept lodged between the seats. "Those portraits you've done. People you know?"

"Cab fares. Brief encounters of the transient kind. I give them away as souvenirs."

"They're beautiful." LaRose voice was genuine. "You're really talented."

We stopped at a stoplight. I flicked on the interior light, and looked her straight in the eyes through the rearview mirror. "You know, I never know how to respond to compliments like that. They bother me. It's like commending a tall person on their height."

"Ok, sorry. Don't compliment a jester, got it.'

“I’m being serious. It’s not an ego thing, I know I’m talented. I’ve tried being accepting, humble, dismissive, ambivalent, but none of them feel right. So I figure I should just brag.”

“Wow," she laughed. "Ok then, let me hear you brag.”

“It would be a pleasure.” Clearing my throat, I quickly combed my hair straight up as I drummed up something good. “You know how people say someone is a ‘triple threat?’ That they can act, sing and dance? That’s nothing. I’m a dodecahedron threat! I’m a singing, dancing, acting, multi-instrument playing, improvisational guru who can tell jokes, cartoon, paint and weave stories so crazy they’d blow your head off! No cranium can handle my degree of entertainment stylings. I’m all that and a bag of chips, man!”

LaRose’s smile revealed her amusement. “You’re talented at bragging, too. And yet you’re stuck working a dead end job like the rest of us.”

“That’s a choice. I could get the Green Light tomorrow, but I would never stoop to such uncultured lows.”

LaRose raised her eyebrows at me with suspicion. “Aren’t you ever worried, though?”

“Look. Life is too short to worry about what might happen. Sure, it’s dangerous, but it’s worth it.”

“I mean, aren’t you ever worried people will think you’re a freak?”

“Ha!” The laugh left my mouth in a loud, brazen splash of sound. “‘Freak’ would be a compliment of the highest order! That’s the least of our worries! Who in the world wants to aspire to normal anyway?”

I remembered so clearly when I founded the Jesters. I didn't care what society thought of the idea. We were lifting the mood of that city, and that's all that mattered.

I spun the steering wheel around and u-turned my cab, hitting the gas for the factory district.

LaRose leaned forward to see our direction through the gathering midnight fog. "Where are we going?"

"Your vocal talent tickles my eardrums, LaRose. I know it will impress the others, too. Would you like to meet your fellow freaks?"

"Oh wow! That's amazing, really? When?"

"Does now work for you?"

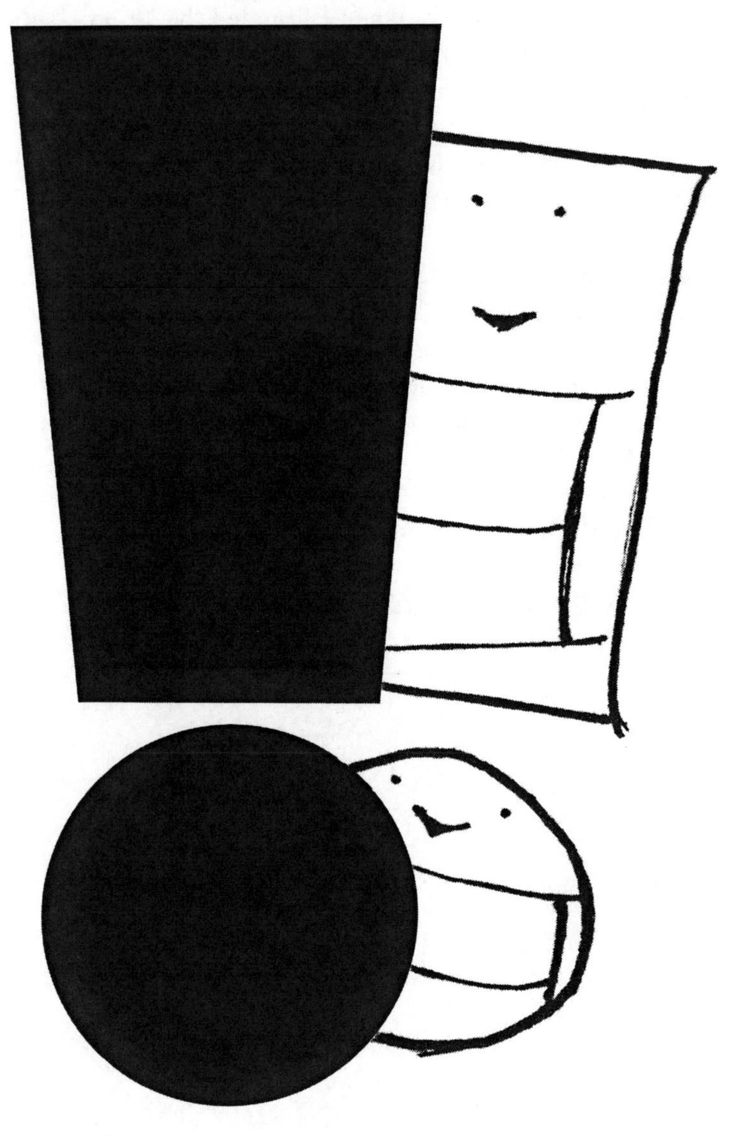

CHAPTER THREE: THE COSMOS DOWN LOW

Cosmos Restaurant is my kind of heaven. It's shaped like a flying saucer, it's dimly lit, the waiters are rude, the coffee is pure molten rocket fuel, the breakfasts are enormous, the booths are rubbery plastic, it's got rats, the milkshakes are so good you want to bathe in them, the table cloths are comics, it is always packed ceiling to drain pipes, and its lovely music is the din of cutlery clanging beneath the line cook's orders and mumblings of its patrons. It was a really real, really greasy, greasy spoon. Oh, and the chocolate mini-muffins are spectacular. If everyone in the world with a case of the Glums, or worse, with a case of the Doldrums, were to have their next breakfast at Cosmos, the simple beauty of the mountainous home fries alone would bring them such peace that their symptoms would simply fade away. Happiness is this simple, they would think. Why weep when you can colour in the place mats? Why worry when you've got a fluffy piece of renegade egg trailing off the corner your mouth?

"This place is disgusting," LaRose said as we stepped inside the restaurant. "I haven't seen a restaurant so low-tech in years."

"We're a crew that flies low on the radar," I said. "Not a lot of Noize out here."

"And that's why you like it? Because it's gross and analogue?"

"It's in my genes to love places like this. I was born with a greasy spoon in my mouth."

"I don't know what that means," LaRose admitted.

“It means I come from a long, zig-zagged line of gypsies.”

The gummed up suction-cup stickiness of our shoes on the checkerboard floors made walking awkward. Squeezing inside my usual booth, I tried waving Nelly the waitress over, but she was too busy racing across the restaurant, balancing orders. They only ever had one waitress on the midnight shift, which was both a grim and groovy situation. Grim because it meant slow service. Groovy because it meant our secret was safe. Nelly was one of us. Our trusty gatekeeper.

My focus drifted out the window and settled upon a boarded up coffee house across the street. Broken glass from its smashed windows confettied the sidewalk outside, and its front was nothing more than a home for wayward graffiti. It used to host poetry readings on the weekends. Ghosts of lost opportunity, now.

Two girls talked in bubbling banter two tables down, and I couldn't help but overhear their desperately sad conversation. "Did you see Jersey Bore last night? Oh my god. I mean, like, I knew what was going to happen ‘cause I totally spoilered it online, so I didn't really care, but can you believe that guy? What a loser. But he’s so hot I would totally marry him!" The absolute tragedy is that they were talking through Vidchat on their power phones whilst sitting right across from one another.

I checked the time on my power phone. 1 am. I had an hour before I needed to get back on shift. Things between me and the boss were already tense, and I knew one too many slip ups at work and I’d be choking on the whimsy snot. And we all know how easy it is to choke on that. Regardless of how much I disliked my boss, I needed my job. You know, to pay for rent and eat. Frivolous stuff. A cabbie’s income barely affords the OuterWeb, let alone food.

“While we’re waiting, let me show you how this all works. Remember, secrecy is paramount.” I pulled the uScroll from my bag, unraveled its flexi-screen across the table, and opened a blueprint of Cosmos.

"Cool! Is that the new meSlate?" a little boy asked, skipping back and forth in the aisles wearing a mini-satellite dish on his hat, and wired on soda.

I laughed and shook my head. "No, and it's not a usPage or a themConsole. It's a uScroll. It does everything. On top of the already 'everything' that's out there already. Digital is getting pretty real these days." The little boy had already lost interest, on to poking around in other booths while downloading a new video game straight from space, through his hat, and into his pocket game console.

"For example?" LaRose asked.

"Well, there's this kitchen app." I tapped a shiny red chef's hat icon and an actual pair of blender blades popped out of the device's metal rods, spinning. "And there's an app that feeds my dog while I'm away." Two more taps and a virtual dog bowl replenished on the screen. "There. Old Smeller is fed!"

"At your house? That's amazing!"

"Well, it would be if I had a dog. My hypothetical dog has been fed."

"Oookaaay…"

"But most spectacular, this is the first device I've been able to over-ride the ETF and PDSs."

"What are they?" LaRose asked.

"Eye-tracking function and personal data streams," I replied, rolling the uScroll back up. "You know, so the king can't follow our every move."

LaRose blinked twice as she took in that last statement. She was oblivious, I could see it in her face.

Nelly finally arrived with two steaming plates of food and my chocolate milkshake, and plunked them down on our table. The blobs of make-up on her face made her look younger, in a sloppy kind of way. Gravity wasn't so forgiving to the rest of her droopy body, though.

"Top of the evening to you, Mr. Meister," she said. Scanning left and right for anyone who might be watching her, she quickly winked and stuck her tongue out at us. Respectfully, I shot her my silly face back. Puffy cheeks and one raised eyebrow. LaRose stared back at us, perplexed.

The silly face was our code. The jester equivalent to a secret handshake. Because our group had already grown to over fifty members, and because we were a secret society, we needed to have a way to greet one another discreetly in public. I realize rolling your eyes and sticking your tongue out at another person is not terribly discreet, but a clever way to know who was one of us, and who wasn't. LaRose had so much to learn that night, and I figured learning by doing was the most effective way.

"LaRose is a recent muster, Nelly," I laughed. "Her face isn't quite rubbery enough to return the favour just yet."

Nelly gave LaRose a motherly smile of encouragement. "You'll do just fine, honey. I recommend stretching in the morning and before bed. It'll loosen all those serious muscles you've got tensed up. Especially your brow and cheek muscles."

LaRose twirled her hair with her finger, blushing. "Thanks for the tip, I think. Um, are you sure this is our food, because I'm pretty sure we haven't ordered yet."

"I'm the only one who knows what you're ordering tonight, sweetie." Nelly slid her Digipad into the pocket of her apron, and put her hand on my shoulder before walking away. "Have a great Moot tonight, Mr. Meister."

"Mr. Meister? That's your name?" LaRose squished her face into a 'you-gotta-be-kidding-me' expression.

I tapped my forehead. "Only to those in the know."

LaRose rolled her eyes. "What kind of organization is this, anyway? What the heck was all that moronic face stuff about?"

"Buffoonery, my dear, in this day and age, is no less threatening than a loaded gun. This is the beginning of a whole new weird for you." I sized LaRose up again. I hoped she would fit into the fray. That she would be a dedicated member.

"Fine. Then tell me, 'Mr. Meister'. Where is this meeting?"

I pushed my plate to the side and leaned in close to speak in a hushed whisper. LaRose bent forward, too.

"Firstly, it's not a meeting, it's a Moot."

"I was not aware of that."

"Secondly, you need to memorize the food on your plate, because it is our password for the night. The meals change every time we have a Moot, and thus, so do the passwords."

"You're crazy."

"Why thank you."

"Who do we say the password to?"

I pulled my uScroll forward to show her a blueprint. "Lastly, you will shout your food order into the toilet so that it is heard through the plumbing systems below. Once received, a door is activated, and you dive through it to land smack dab in the middle of our subterranean celebration."

LaRose blinked twice at me, processing the insanity I had just laid on her, clearly not expecting any of it.

"You're serious about this?"

"Am I laughing?"

"How do you know about the -"

"One of our jesters is a plumber. He discovered that there is a connecting system of chutes across the city, hidden behind handicapped bathroom stalls. For maintenance purposes. All the chutes lead to the same connecting space, where we meet. You'll like what we've done with the place."

The timid vocalist slowly looked at her food. Then back at me.

"Shakespeare said all the world is a stage," I said. "In which case, we believe washrooms are its green rooms. It's how we get around the city undetected."

"Right." LaRose looked like she wanted to run. "So, you want me to put my head in the toilet and just say…"

"There's no time," I said. I rolled up my uScroll and stuffed it in my Omnibag. I picked up my milkshake and grabbed her by the arm. "It's already 1:15, they're all waiting for me. I marched LaRose down the hallway at the back of the restaurant and down the stairs toward the washrooms.

LaRose halted in front of the men's door. "What? You want to go in the men's washroom together?"

“Look, I know we just met, but do you actually think you can creatively express yourself alone?”

The men’s door opened and a man exited, stuffed inside a conservative, tight-fitting business suit. He gave us a look of sincere concern before making his way back up the stairs. I heard him call us ‘sickos’ under his breath.

“You’re right.” LaRose exhaled a huge breath of anxiety. She took out an elastic band and pulled her hair into a pony tail. “This is totally insane, but if I keep on living my brain dead life, I’m going to die of boredom. I’m ready.”

I poked my head in the washroom. It smelled faintly of very re-filtered coffee with aromatic whispers of digested pork. But at least the coast was clear.

“Take a deep breath. I think your LaRose is about to LaWilt.”

We snuck into the handicapped stall together and I closed the door.

“Now, look. Be poetic about the password. We’re not just a boring secret knock kind of foundation. Add some flare with your head down there. Watch.”

Getting down on all fours, I stuck my head into the toilet, just above water level, closed my eyes and shouted theatrically: “Rivers of bright orange egg yolk smothered heavenly pancake clouds next to a train of shimmering sausage links, a dusty mountain of hash browns atop a landscape of lushly buttered rye toast.”

Instantaneously, a large square panel unlocked and slid open along the back wall. A cool gust of air blew out. I watched LaRose’s eyes widen as she leaned in for a closer look down at the chute that dropped drastically into darkness. Ever so faintly, we could hear the beat of a drum and laughter from far below.

Remembering my manners, I motioned to the opening in the wall like a butler would to a guest at the front door. “Ladies first!”

CHAPTER FOUR: FORBID DEN

Jesters, the real 14th through 18th Century ones at least, used to hold meetings called 'Moots'. Early jesters actually formed collectives back then too. There were thousands of them, so smaller troupes met together because they really felt different from the rest of society. We followed in their footsteps, because I know we all felt like outsiders. A lot of artists do.

So I borrowed the idea.

One Moot per week, Saturday nights. They were the real pay off to being a jester. Most of the time our Moots broke out into talent shows or music jams, or games or spontaneous art made on the spot. You never knew what was going to happen when you put a bunch of jesters in the same room. Artists and entertainers of every talent came out of forced retirement and auditioned for us because the idea behind the Jesters was just wacky enough to work.

LaRose and I flew out of the Cosmos bathroom chute like a pair of untrained flying squirrels, caught in midair by our intricate system of tattered fishing nets, and falling ten feet onto a stack of not-so cushiony used mattresses. After she untangled herself and caught her balance, it was delightful to watch her look around in awe. To mentally download our unique, boorish lair beneath the earth.

We called it The Fools' Forbid Den. A massive cavern gaping large with columns of torches reflecting orange firelight upon dented copper walls, and a twenty-foot ceiling riddled with uncountable crooked pipes, all shapes and sizes, churning and gurgling the city's thousands of flushes.

"If you ever feel anything drip on you," I said to LaRose, winking, helping her off the mattresses, "think of it as good luck."

As we left the chutes, I silly-faced fellow jester, Dorkus Lemonius. Always dressed in his signature rubber boots, bathing suit and polka-dotted bow tie, he was the plumber who discovered and manned the Den. He listened intently between all seventeen chutes with his oversized controller in hand at the ready, like a soldier waiting for incoming missiles, and orchestrated each menu-password heard through the pipes with a remote release of the corresponding above-ground doors.

"Raspberry sherbet pastries like rubies in my mouth!" came a holler from the dessert cafe.

"Hamburger clouds floating above French fry fence posts!" bellowed someone from a burger joint.

And the jesters came shooting out like gum balls.

We walked along the central purple carpet, through the crowd of jesters already jostling and jumping around the room. Man the energy was crackling that night! Some jesters came in costume, some wore elaborate hats, and almost everyone brought their instruments. There was a brass quintet jamming out fat saucy notes off in a corner, and a jazz fusion group blowing lyrical lines in another. We passed a trio of giant patchwork puppets dangling from the balconies waving hello, some masked dancers doing cartwheels across the gilded grandstand, and throngs of hands diving into oversized, velvet bags of miscellaneous tricks that floated around the room. It was great to see so many familiar faces.

"What are those things?" LaRose pointed to an extensive shelf of painted objects running along the perimeter of the Den.

“Those are Gourdlies. Every new jester gets a gourd to paint of themselves. There’s a big basket over there whenever you feel so inspired.”

We stopped under a cluster of balloon trees near the grandstand as I pointed out my kindred spirits. “Ok, let’s see how good my memory is:

“See the guy with the long nose and plaid pants? That’s Humdinger, a mathematician/virtuoso hummer. Big ears and buck teeth? That’s Raffleworthy, he owns a casino and sculpts soap statuettes. The guy with the monocle is Woozle, a zookeeper/violinist. Chump is dressed all in black, a professional boxer/mime. Big ears and green hair? That’s Vixtrix, an electrician/keyboard player. Mumfordpie’s the guy wearing pink suspenders, an actor who plays a different person everyday. Blip is the super skinny guy with huge lips, he likes to play the banjo in doctor’s offices. Dr. Demando, in the bowler cap, just runs about town demanding things from strangers. Scalliwag is a secretary/guitar player, the Dingleberry Brothers, I have no idea what they do, Yoink, he steals things and replaces the stuff with cooler things, Slab, a baker/clarinet player, I think that’s Quizzicle with the purple suit and white shoes, um…Glib, Crumb, Pig ’N’ Jig, Smellwagon, Twisty, The Monk, Fuzzy Barenaked, Dozo, Domo, Numbnuts, Slobberhound, Lummox, Apropos…”

LaRose looked thunderstruck. “I…I…don’t know what to say.”

“I know. There’s no other society like the Jesters. We’re like a Fight Club for misfit entertainers.”

Murphy came running from the back of the Den, shouting to me across the crowd. He was wearing another of his million Hawaiian shirts. He said he likes them because their trippy designs hide his skinny, boney frame.

"Murphy is a founding member, LaRose. Stick with him and you'll be looked after. He's a jester who likes to play to a crowd: a storyteller, a comedian, and a master of improvisation. He can tell stories off the top of his head, both awesome and awkward, and gets a kick out of giving very long, boring, unsolicited advice to total strangers. Murphy started a successful moving company a while back called 'The Lucky Movers', whose witty slogan is: 'If your stuff get's there, it's Lucky!'"

"Hm. Always reassuring to know that cheesy advertising will never die," LaRose laughed.

"Hey Mr. Meister! Who's this lovely addition to the team?" Murphy extended his hand to LaRose. "You two make a good looking couple. Hire a few dozen paparazzi to follow you around and boom, you're famous!" He had a unique way of laughing when he was joking around. It sounded like a duck coughing.

Murphy is surf music, with a dash of 50s and 60s rock and roll.

"Nice to meet you, Murphy," LaRose said, shaking his hand.

"Hey Meister, I rode the Ziplinc a couple times this week," said Murphy, already laughing.

"Oh man. I'm surprised the company hasn't handed you over already." I said, rolling my eyes.

"Are you kidding? My costumes are flawless. I've got a grandfather's mask that is impeccable. Had some new thick bottled glasses made too. I look like I'm two hundred years old, and that's what I tell the kids!"

"Do they buy it?"

“Not at all. Until I show them my fake social insurance card. I tell them that I played tennis with Gandhi and read bedtime stories to Moses. I drew a big crowd on Line 27 last week.” Murphy took a step forward and pulled his silver weFling from his pocket, tapping the device with his finger, secretively. “Mr. Meister, there’s something I need to share with the crew tonight. Vital information.”

“Nice, I love surprises!” I glanced at the time on my power phone. I had to be back in the cab in forty minutes, which was barely enough time to bond with my chums. “We should get this Moot started. Would you be a gentleman and make LaRose comfortable, Murph?”

I hopped on the grandstand and took my place at the jester’s podium, a tower of old Magnavox television sets stacked on top of a mess of miscellaneous out-dated electronics. Tucking the explosion of hair on my head inside my jester’s cap, I took my wooden foolstaff in hand and called the Moot to order.

CHAPTER FIVE: MOOT #48

"Friends, fiends and idiot savants! Welcome to the 48th Moot!"

I waited for the murmur to die down before proceeding; getting some of these guys to stop talking is like getting cows to stop farting.

"If you are looking for the local book club, I'm afraid you've crashed the wrong party. If you're hoping to sell insurance tonight, this is definitely the wrong crowd. But if you're looking to welcome a little weird into your world, you're exactly where you need to be! Ladies and gentlemen, I am your host, Mr. Meister, and we are the newfangled Jesters!"

A wave of applause and cheering filled the room. Silly faces abounded, too. I did my best to keep the intros different every time, for this was a breed that abhorred routine.

"If you can find more than one-hundred and eleven non-profane uses for a pickle, you are welcome here! If you devil eggs and wait to see if they do something evil, you may partake. If you can yodel while running a marathon, fire a cracker for not exploding, or convince a child that time doesn't really exist and is merely a convenient concept for managing the misery of adulthood, then you are welcome here! But most of all, if you like surprises, you are welcome here!"

More cheering, laughing and chit chattering peppered each of my bursts of motivation. I drank up the energy in the room, for it was a pure, happy vibe. There was such a momentum to the passion I felt towards being a jester that could have propelled me out of the Den and on to the street, half-dancing, half-running alongside traffic like a mad man. I wanted to tell everyone how amazing it felt to perform! How I longed for a world where live entertainment ruled.

"Make no mistake, fellow jesters and jestettes! We are not purely absurd, no sir! No, a jester's job is serious business. I've been told it's harder to get a CIA agent to break his oath than it is to get a jester to really laugh. All together now, let them hear you outside:

Down with the King, down with the Noize, and down with the Doldrums!"

I raised the uScroll over my head and unraveled it with much dramatic pause. "If you are truly willing to become an authentic jester and join our secret collective, you must be willing to adhere to our six very audacious rules. Shout 'em out if you know them!

1. The Jesters are anonymous! Who you are here is not who you are out there! If anyone asks why you are acting out of the ordinary, just say you're from out of town. Way out of town.

2. The Jesters will accept newcomers, based on recommendation, as long as they are good looking enough to jest in public, that is, not quite ugly enough to be considered for radio.

3. The Jesters must be live and unscripted. Our style is surprise to keep the crowd alive, baby!

4. The Jesters are open to new ideas, but will gladly and openly ridicule any proposed idea that sucks.

5. The Jesters are non-profit, and will neither endorse, sell nor advertise anything or anyone. Why? Because advertising is the lowest form of entertainment."

That last one gets a resounding ‘Here, Here!’ every time. We were about mayhem, not money.

“Now that all the rule reading is out of the way,” I said, slurping my chocolate milkshake, “we’ll take time to open the floor to any present member who would like to share a jest, a tale, a ditty or a blurt with us as they see fit. Are there any jesters with a yarn to spin?”

Fitch, resident pizza delivery guy/bass player, jumped to his feet and ran up the purple carpet swaying his spherical body side to side as he wheeled his double bass in front of him. How he got his bass down a chute, nobody knew. Fitch bounced through the crowd, high-fiving and silly facing as he worked his way to the grandstand. The torchlight reflected off of his shiny bald Asian head, and he was greeted with boisterous fanfare.

“Jester Fitch!” someone yelled above the crowd. “What do you have in your pockets tonight, pray tell!”

“That question would take all night to answer,” Woozle said. “It might be easier to tell us what you don’t have in your pockets!”

“Like, a steady job, you mean?” Murphy jested. Laughter filled the room again.

It doesn’t matter if he’s on a first date or a roller coaster, Fitch is always, always wearing his Pocket Coat. That is, his coat with one hundred and seven pockets. He’s scatterbrained, an understatement, so one of the other jesters designed this coat for him with pockets all over it. It’s made of burlap potato sacks and each pocket is sewn with a different design. It’s rather unsightly, and I think people throw change at him while he’s waiting for the subway or the like, but at least he doesn’t lose things anymore. It just takes him a little longer to figure out which pocket it’s in.

Fitch was polka and ska. Big and bouncy.

"Soyouguysgottahearthiscuzyou'regonnaloveitit'smybestjest yet," Fitch declared, his words undecipherable.

"Fitch," I said, holding the bass players shoulder in concern. "Oxygen is good."

"Right, sorry guys." Fitch took a few big breaths, pulled water bottle from a pocket, and took a swig. "Ok. So, yesterday I was down on Richter St. with my bass and my little amp strapped to my back and I got my first standing ovation, it was so awesome. All I did was lay down some bass lines for people walking up and down the sidewalk. I mean, I walked just behind them playing walking jazz bass lines, you know?"

"That's an awesome idea!" I said.

"Really, you think so?"

"Fitch it's brilliant!" Murphy laughed. "Walking bass lines. Literally. Genius! Then what happened?"

"I just followed people for half a block and if they were walking fast I'd just speed up the tempo, and this one time this businessman I was following was late for the bus so I actually ran behind him and played the fastest bass line I've ever played when he was running. For the bus. He was running for the bus. Did I mention that? Hey, where's my fork?" Fitch patted his Pocket Coat looking for a fork that had nothing to do with his story.

"So where's the standing ovation come in, buddy?" I asked.

"Well I didn't even know it but when I was doing the walking bass lines there was a whole line-up waiting to get into the movies across the street and when they saw me running behind the businessman they gave me this huge applause. It was really cool."

"I don't want to burst your bubble, Fitch," Murphy said. "But wasn't the line-up already standing?"

"Ya."

"So it's not really a standing ovation."

Fitch rubbed his head and took a moment to let the logic soak in. "Oh yeah. Well they could've sat down if they only kind of liked it."

The Den had a good laugh at that one. And that's why we loved Fitch. He was unfiltered creativity, and a good reminder why mainstream entertainment eluded us. We were too outside the box for most conventional styles.

"Gotta give'em something to remember," I said, raising my milkshake to Fitch's efforts. "We only live once, after all!"

Fitch spat out his water. "What did you say?"

"I said we only live once."

"How sure are you about that?"

"Fitch, all evidence seems to be pointing to it."

"Woa. Ok, sorry. Keep talking, I just need to make some phone calls." He patted his pockets in search of his phone and left the grandstand.

"You know, the main reason I stopped watching TV is because Fitch keeps me so entertained," Murphy laughed.

"Attention, scallywags and rascals," I said, getting the meeting back on track. "It's now time to welcome some newbies to the jester fold! We have three new musters tonight!"

The new members were sitting in what we called Zeros, which are inner tubes that are really hard to get in and out of, because we lather them with butter. The first part of their induction into the Jesters happened at the beginning of the night when we pour oil on the floor and whip them in their Zeros across the floor. We odd fellows were not above initiations.

"Keep in mind that your fearless leaders, Breakfast, Murphy, Fitch and myself have already interviewed these individuals, who come highly recommended by many of you to begin with. I'm sure you'll like what you see! So without further yammering, let's give a warm welcome to the new inductees!"

The first to wiggle unceremoniously out of one Zero was a square-jawed muscle man whose arms were so big they couldn't hang by his side. He slipped a few times to our amusement, on account of the butter on his feet, and joined me at the front of the room.

"Hello there! What's your nickname please?"

"Hello Mr. Meister, everyone, nice to finally meet all of you! The name's Underplum."

"Underplum. Well. My expectations just dropped. Do you have a silly face prepared by any chance?"

"I do indeed! I've been practicing all week." Underplum stood back, smiled and then rippled all the muscles in his face. It was a tad creepy, to be honest, like he was about to break out with the mumps.

"Wow! Ok, I won't forget that one! So, tell everyone how you heard about us."

"Scalliwag mentioned it to me, actually. I met her at a bakery I frequent when I'm on shift. She's the one who writes miniature short stories on the backs of people's receipts." The room applauded Scalliwag, who took a fanciful bow. An 'ahhhh' of recognition followed.

"Ah, yes! Scalliwag of the 9th Moot, I believe. Now, Underplum, based on your overall enormity, I'd wager a guess that you are an expert puppeteer…"

"He plays the flute!" Yoink shouted.

"He intimidates tanks!" Pig n' Jig laughed.

"He eats children!" Blip said with a mouthful of sour keys and gummy bears.

"Ok big guy, what's your story?" I asked.

"Well, I'm a police officer by profession, and it'd be faster if I just show you my jest." Underplum asked the jesters to take a few steps back in order to make some space on the floor, and then asked the person nearest to him to stand next to him. It so happened to be LaRose, her cheeks blushing into two plump roses.

"Hey, what do you think of that new band trending right now, Toasterhead?" Underplum asked, politely.

"They're ok," LaRose said, shrugging her shoulders.

"Really? I think they sound pretty burnt out. Ha ha!" Underplum bellowed a mighty laugh and promptly spun into the fastest break-dancing head spin I'd ever seen. With another effortless flip back up to his feet he took a sip of his drink and continued talking to LaRose.

"Wow! That was incredible! I love it!" I said, joining in on the group's applause.

Murphy stood up on a stool, whistling louder than the rest. "That is ground breaking comedy!" he shouted. "A cheesy pun, and then bust out a break-dance move? A kind of, I don't know, physical punch line? It's profound!"

"Give it up for Underplum, fellow jesters! We now have a jester on the police force. Some protection for our social piddling!"

Next was Smallfries, a jester who could not only throw his voice, but also mimic other people's voices and throw them too. He couldn't have been more than seventeen years old, a slight little dude sporting a sideways ball cap.

"Can you give us a sample Smallfries?" I asked.

"Sure, who do you want me to do?"

"Do LaRose," I suggested.

LaRose wore a dubious face, standing in the corner next to the DJ booth. "Why are you picking on me? Ventriloquists give me the creeps!"

Sure enough, Smallfries cupped his hands over his mouth and threw his voice to sound like it was coming from the other side of the Den. "Why are you picking on me? Ventriloquists give me the creeps!"

LaRose's eyes lit up like an arcade. "That kid is good!"

"I bet you could make a guy paranoid, putting voices in his head like that," I said.

"My record is getting people to think they heard somebody's voice from fifty meters away," Smallfries said. "I used to do it all the time as a kid, you know, just imitate my friend's mom calling them for dinner and stuff."

"Reverence and esteem for jester Smallfries!"

Bowls of vibrantly coloured candy salad were being passed between the jesters, sugar boats floating among a sea of madmen. The audible hum of energy seemed to increase with each handful of chocolate almonds and gummy worms consumed. One of these days we'll regret creating candy salad. The amplitude will just be too much.

Turnstylz came aboard that night too; our very first graffiti artist to join! Her flowing blonde hair fell playfully across her face, slightly obscuring her full character. She liked to spray shadows behind objects, or people when they weren't looking. Did them in under a minute. And not just black blobs of paint or anything, either. She worked in colourful designs and patterns.

"Ya, if you want to see some of her stuff, there's an amazing blue tree shadow Turnstylz did near the post office," Murphy said.

"Where did you get the idea?" I asked.

"I don't know," she shrugged shyly. "I just like shadows, I guess. They're impermanent, so I try to capture their awesome shapes before they fade away."

"Well, welcome aboard! Ladies and gentlemen, one more round of applause for our newest members!"

"What about your friend, Mr. Meister?" Slobberhound shouted. "Isn't she going to present her jest tonight, too?"

I looked at LaRose. She wore an expression of complete dread. "If it is acceptable by the collective, we will have LaRose ceremonially inducted next week. I listened to her talent earlier this evening, and I assure you she has plenty of it, but she suffers from a serious case of the Bashfuls."

A shared 'ahhh' of understanding warmed the Den. Courage to perform in such a discouraging world took immeasurable confidence, and everyone of the jesters had felt LaRose's inhibition in the beginning. Apropos offered her a giant blue top hat to wear, to help comfort her.

Mumfordpie heckled from a hammock between the balloon trees. "So are we going to get some music happening tonight or what?"

"Of course!" I said. "Breakfast?"

All heads turned toward the empty DJ booth perched above the floor next to the stage.

"Right, I forgot. Breakfast couldn't be here tonight. Anyone else know how to spin beats?"

Dr. Demando ran up the ladder, tossed some headphones on his noggin and put on an early funk/electronica mash-up. Heads starting bouncing to the rhythm.

"Perfect. Let's do our questions, queries and quacks, and then we can turn this party up a notch, shall we? Are there any pressing issues to bring to the table, oh champions of the absurd?"

Murphy hopped onto the grandstand and silly faced the other jesters, getting their attention. With much dramatic flare, he placed his weFling into his palm flipped the device to projection mode. Northwest Wind Esquire dimmed the lights on cue, and Murphy made a simple, yet exuberant announcement to the crowd. I had no idea what poisonous words would fall out of his mouth.

CHAPTER SIX: YOUBOOB

"Everyone! We're on YouBoob!" Widening the projection coming out of the weFling enough along the wall for all of us to see, Murphy pressed play.

Sure enough there I was in a YouBoob video, sporting a loud leopard print suit and top hat as I drove down the street in my cab, music blaring. It was titled: 'Fly Taxi Guy.'

Was it possible, I thought? Had we actually snuck our way onto YouBoob? At first, excitement popcorned inside me.

"That's not it, folks, there's a whole playlist here!" Murphy continued scrolling down a long thread of videos with oodles of hits and comments already.

There was a shaky video clip of Bumble, his stalky frame dressed entirely in a yellow jumpsuit as she helped old ladies cross the street singing 'Fly Me to the Moon.' That clip was titled: Who is this weirdo?

Next was footage of what looked to be a neighbourhood housewarming party. Mumfordpie kept up an entire conversation by only speaking in limerick, much to the frustration of the woman he was talking with. That clip: Annoying guy.

And then there were the Dingleberry Brothers on the commuter train. They had bags filled with random words scrawled on scraps of paper, asking people to take one out, and then challenging them to an on-the-spot game of word association.

"Can you believe this? We're breaking onto the scene!" Murphy shouted to the crowd.

"I know! It's crazy!" North West Wind, Esquire exclaimed. "And the comments are good, too!"

My jaw was hanging too far open for me to say anything. I couldn't believe what I was watching. After all this time, people got it. And they liked it! They understood what we were trying to do. We had broken through. It was thrilling, but…

"Do you think the Beatles felt this way when their career was starting?" Twisty asked the crowd, jumping up and down. "Did they look around and grin to themselves about who they were becoming before anyone knew who they were? The thrill of starting something big?"

"Less Beatles. More Barney," a Dingleberry laughed.

Murphy hit pause on the uScroll with his eyes fixed on me. "Is that a smile I see, Mr. Meister? You diggin' the attention?"

Apropos banged on his drum, excitedly. "Are you reconsidering the possibility of something bigger, Mr. Meister? Finally, he sees the light!"

The Den broke out in a roar of cheering and hollering, as if our home team had won the championship. I couldn't help but get swept up in the crowd's exhilaration. I imagined all the strangers' eating and drinking above us. People had no idea there was a secret group of entertainers below them, infiltrating their lives. I liked the freedom of being anonymous. I always have. And yet, I loved the fact that people were talking about us, too. I was the embodiment of the central paradox of our times.

“What, me?” I said, coming out of my daze and blinking the stars out of my eyes. “No, I am merely pontificating, inwardly. A mere, fleeting brain undulation.” I took a swig of my milkshake and refocused. “These videos are amazing, I admit. How in the world do you think this happened?”

Quip stepped forward. “Don’t fool yourself, Mr. Meister, there are many backdoors onto the OuterWeb. As mighty as the king’s grip may be, people will always find a way to hack inside for something worthy of their tiny attention spans.”

“Well, need I remind everyone that this is dangerously illegal? Have you forgotten the deadly penalty for live performances? We already lost both Flooby and Nooby to that rooftop accordion stunt they pulled last spring.”

I watched the mood around the room droop from silly to sorrowful with Twisty playing a dying note on her slide trombone. I felt like a nagging mother. I didn’t want to be a killjoy, but how had they forgotten the risk so easily? Why we united in the first place?

“You can’t be serious,” Mumfordpie whined, slapping a pie into his own face. “Just like that? You set us up and then knock us down, is that it? Our first opportunity at breaking in, and you don’t want it?”

“Yeah, Mr. Meister?” Vixtrix teased. “You’re not afraid of a little fame, are you?”

“No, of course not. But if we’re going to be famous, I want it to be on my terms, not the king’s.”

The clammer of mumblings and murmurings rose in the crowd. We all knew that dream would never come true.

“I know it’s enticing, but it’s not the goal of the Jesters. We don’t want that kind of attention, remember? I created the Jesters to bring back live entertainment. Live! That’s the keyword here. To distract from the misery most people live with, addicted to canned shows on their many glowing screens. We've perfected the only way to do that and still satisfy our longing to perform. I don't want to jeopardize that by being yet another disposable blip on TV, or the OuterWeb. Let's stick it in our pockets, shove it under our hats and forget about it."

"Can someone go upstairs and get a waiter?" Vixtrix shouted across the room. "Mr. Meister needs another brain. His head is officially empty."

Murphy shouted above the laughs, scrolling through the long list of jester videos. "Mr. Meister, with all do respect, it is very hard to be original these days, and yet we've done it, and people are into it! I vote we keep jesting, and then when the time is right, boom! We're already half-way famous!"

A heaviness tugged inside me, a lead spider web weaving around my heart. Is that what they really wanted? They were staring at those videos like they were some sort of miracle, as if Jesus and Buddha were back and starring in a buddy comedy. I thought we believed in the same principles. I dreaded the outcome of these persistent discussions of fame and success. It's a trap. Why was I the only one who realized that?

Fitch plopped himself on the edge of the grandstand, returning from his sojourn into whatever reality it is he lives in, and sat down with the rest of us. He pulled some polish and a cloth from his pocket and proceeded to polish his bald head as he addressed the crowd. "Even more than the risk of people talking about these crazy people jesting all over the place, if we get caught up in all of that madness…we might lose our charm."

"Yes!" I said. I jumped off the stage and grabbed him by the ears, giving him a fat kiss on his even fatter forehead. "You got it! It's about our scruples as jesters. We'll turn into those

Flash Mobbing nobs, and we're too cool for that. Where do you think they disappeared to? They fizzled into everyone's distant memory years ago after they actually started flashing their bojangles all over the place before they disappeared. We won't be such a desperate spectacle like that. It's imperative we perform completely offline! Don't let the illusion of mainstream fame distract us so we can continue being creative. Authentically."

Tumbleweed, a sweet 74-year-old jester boasting bushy black eyebrows, a silvery beard, and a penchant for balancing things, raised his hand.

"Mr. Meister, when I joined the Jesters you promised us that we would make money. Do you think I will die before that happens?"

Many murmurings moved through the room. Tumbleweed hit a nerve, and the lead spider web doubled in weight around my heart.

"I agree with Tumbleweed, Mr. Meister," said Noodles. "Money would be nice. Seems like the YouBoob vids could be our ticket."

Many more murmurings now. To be honest, I hadn't realized that anyone cared so much about the cash. But could I blame them? Everybody wants to make a living doing what they love. Tumbleweed couldn't have been more right. Clearly I had misled the bunch in my marketing of the group, after all.

"Fellow Jesters!" I banged my staff on the metal floor of the grandstand. "Believe me, I would love to quit my job tomorrow so I could jest full time. And I'm thinking about ways we could make that happen. I feel like we can do it. But without applying for a license, or risking our lives, I just don't know how."

"So let's audition for a Green Light! What about a TV show?" shouted Ploddington. "Like a candid camera thing?"

"Are you kidding me? We are not a bunch of pranksters! Besides, I detest the paltry excuse for entertainment on TV, and I don't want to be associated with it. We need to stay live."

"Well then we should pitch a different show," said Murphy, rubbing his fingers together. "Let's go back to basics. A variety show for some dough."

"We can't just put on a show!" I pulled off my hat and threw it aside, letting my hair spring into the air like a fresh marshmallow. "How do we replicate the same kind of response we get now on camera? The whole reason jesting works is because we're taking people by surprise. It works because no one knows we're artists and entertainers."

Crumb wheeled his squeaky organ-grinder forward. "Why is that such a big deal? We could get something on the web in no time. That'd be cool, wouldn't it?"

"What about our commitment to spontaneity and surprise?" I countered.

"Click, surprise! Click again, oh a new surprise!" Vixtrix said, laughing. "With all do respect Mr. Meister, the OuterWeb is full of surprises."

"The Web is amazing," I agreed. "But still, when you go on a website you are expecting something to happen."

"Of course you are! Why is that such a big deal?"

I looked across the room at expectant eyes. The responsibility of leadership weighed a little heavier. This Moot had taken an unexpected and disturbing turn, and I worried that our essence might evaporate right then and there.

I couldn't let that happen. The Jesters were the only thing keeping me sane. I cleared my throat in an attempt to speak persuasively.

"Ok, let me give you an example. Say that some people want to laugh, so they go to a comedy club. Seems reasonable, right? But, just by virtue of going to a comedy club there is an expectation of humour that, more often than not, isn't met. The jokes aren't as funny as people want them to be... or think they should be."

"Unless the audience is full of idiots, then I guess surprise is still easy to achieve," Murphy chimed in.

"Right," I continued. "The same can be said for film, musicals, or whatever. People preview and critics spoil the fun long before the art is even enjoyed. The way we consume entertainment is so predictable, that nothing is surprising anymore. Am I wrong?"

"No, you're not wrong," said Fitch again, out of the blue. "And I'd like to support Mr. Meister completely on this. Think about it. If an audience is caught off guard with something, it leaves a lasting impression. The element of surprise is so imperative because it removes the expectation of any kind of experience. So, by literally giving art unexpectedly, both the delivery and reaction to it is true."

"Thanks, Fitch, that was, um, right on point," I said. We collectively stared, dumbfounded at Fitch. You see what I mean? He's not as daft as he seems.

I looked at the time. Over an hour late for my shift already. I needed to wrap this up and get back in the cab before I lost my job for sure. And I needed to say something stirring before I lost the only thing that made me happy in this world.

"Everyone, we all know it's completely ridiculous that we're forced to live on the fringe of society just because the rest of the world is plugged in. But remember, that is our plight as jesters. We have never truly lived to our potential because the king is the one who lays the law. But let me assure everyone that I am ready and willing to lead our group toward a money making venture, as long as I can find a satisfactory…"

"Gimmick," said Murphy. "We need a very sly gimmick to evade the king and still make money."

"Agreed! Let's make a promise right here, right now!" I declared, standing among my friends. "Murphy, can you get this on video? I want to make it official."

The Hawaiian-shirted comedian opened the movie making application on the uScroll, propped the device on the grandstand, and hit record before joining the group.

"We'll keep the Jesters a secret," I said. "We'll keep the Moots exclusive. The buzz on the Internet will stay unmentioned. We're all in agreement that, until we've done all that we can do working the streets, we'll take it to the next level and this city won't know what hit them!"

With cheering and cavorting galore, I felt the tension break in the Den. We pulled our silly faces at the camera, a promise to each other to stay anonymous, for now. I realized it was the best solution, but there wasn't a thread of me that would ever uphold that promise. I'd fold the Jesters before the next level, whatever that may be.

"I need to depart my fellow absurdists!" I proclaimed. "Let's extinguish our real-life woes with a pooh-pooh laugh and sozzled melody, for we carry the tradition of mavericks and eccentrics in our heart! Never forget that! I'll close by saying 'flower pots and feather pillows'!"

"Flower pots and feather pillows!" everyone chanted in return.

The distant warble of a didgeridoo gently enticed the meeting to a close. Fitch picked up his bass and joined in, and circles formed, sharing stories of their last few weeks of jesting. They would party well into the morning. After a few hours of music and merriment, they'll forget this debate even happened, I hoped.

Silly facing my friends farewell, I walked over to the ladders leading up to the exits. Departing the Forbid Den was way worse than arriving, because I could never figure out which ladder led to a manhole, and which one led back to the Cosmos washroom.

"That was an entertaining first meeting." LaRose appeared below, just as I began to climb.

I laughed, pulling my Omnibag over my shoulder. "Wasn't it? You chose a memorable one, at least."

"So, you're just going to leave me here with these freaks?"

"They don't bite. Not all of them at least."

"When I asked you in the taxi if you were a jester, why didn't you tell me you were ***the*** jester?"

"Because I don't like to brag."

"Ha! Where are you going?"

"Back to reality, I'm afraid. I need to think of an excuse I haven't used lately, or I'm out of a job."

"That's boring, Mr. Meister." LaRose contorted her face into one of the silliest I'd ever seen, and shot it at me. A wiggly-nosed and swirly-eyed half-smile expression that really made me laugh.

I contemplated the world above, and then surveyed the fun in the Den.

"Bah! I've got a few minutes to put on a mask or two," I said, hopping off the ladder.

The rest of the night was a blur.

[silly face code]

CHAPTER SEVEN: BENEATH THE SKYBRIDGE

The rising sun peered above the crest of the city line, and I had to shield my eyes from the sudden snap of its glare. A headache began to burn in my temples as I awoke.

Where was I?

Splayed out belly-up like a starfish on the pavement of Fathead's Fish N' Chips parking lot with a man's finger up my nose, that's where I was.

I jerked my head up to see which weirdo would dare do such a thing. It was Fizzlestick, the butcher/costume maker, poking out of a manhole next to me.

"What the? Good god man you don't know where my nose has been!" I shouted, swatting his hand away.

"You mean you don't know where my finger has been," Fizzlestick said wryly.

"Whatever. Honestly, Fizz, what in the world are you doing putting your finger up sleeping men's noses?"

"I wasn't picking your nose, I was measuring it. And you weren't sleeping, you were passed out." Fizzlestick climbed out of the manhole with a measuring tape and notebook in his hands. He wasn't a midget, but he sure didn't play basketball. "Mr. Meister, I want to make you a mask."

I sat up and took a moment to let my brain settle. My eyes blurred in and out of focus, and the buildings rose and fell like the sea. All the music we played the night before rang in a muddled ruckus in my ears, and the smell of rotting fish pouring out of the overflowing bags of garbage made my stomach heave.

I smiled politely to the little man despite my growing headache. "Did you say…a mask?"

"Everyone else has one except you. You never give me enough time to measure your face."

Time. I scrambled for my phone. 6 am. The end of the night shift. The lead spider-web crept heavily inside my chest. So screwed.

Leaping ungracefully to my feet, I snatched my bag and ran. Luckily Fathead's Fish N' Chips rivalled Cosmos in popularity, greasy gunslingers straight across the street from one another.

"What about your mask?" Fizzlestick shouted, throwing his arms up in the air.

"Just start off small. Make a nose hat and take it from there!"

The brisk morning air slapped me awake by the time I got back in the cab. I bolted out from behind Cosmos and into the streets. Much anti-taxi honking followed.

I played the night in rewind to try to figure out how I could have lost track of so much time. What was I saying? I knew very well the effect Moots had on me. They spun me into a feverish trance that became dangerously infectious, causing me to wake up hours late.

I tried to process the evening's craze about our meteoric rise to YouBoobian fame. We needed to be so careful. I swore that if we ever lost another member to the Noize…

Paranoia gripped me. I checked my rearview mirror again for the Noize. Were they on my tail again?

I turned off the main street and on to residential streets. They'd been on me at the train station, which meant my digits were tagged in their system. I needed to stay low.

Plus, there's Shmitty. I had to focus on my above-ground life. A six-hour dinner break was going to get me axed for sure. I couldn't let that happen.

"Open Swype," I ordered my phone. It blinked awake and responded.

"What would you like to Swype?" it asked.

"Swype generics , 'urgent', 'car', 'up arrow'."

"Generics 'car, up arrow', urgent." it repeated. "And the recipient?"

"Send to Breakfast."

"Translating your Swype to Breakfast," the application confirmed.

Swype was my favourite application. *'I need you to pick me up now, it's kind of an emergency'*, is much more efficiently expressed in pictures. Sadly, most people used it as a replacement to texting, which is why it bugged me. Not only were people not talking face to face as much anymore, they couldn't be bothered to send texts with any originality, either. Such are the sacrifices of convenience.

“Swype received. Reply: 'thumbs up'

The application powered down, and my phone went to sleep.

I pulled into Shmitty’s Cabs, a disheveled barracks hidden like a trash infested troll’s nest under the SkyBridge, and wheeled my cab into the furthest most parking lot behind the station. Overflowing decay of last night’s refuse left behind by late night cabbies popped under my tires. Ketchup stained fast-food bags and their crinkly crunched up wrappers. Cellophane evidence of nasty nutrition on the go.

Night was a little longer beneath the Skybridge. Between the fading shadows of night and the murky blue light of morning. Between the final dregs of nightshift cabbies parking their rides, and the dayshift drivers picking up their keys to start their deliveries downtown. It’s a hybrid taxi business. We picked up and dropped off everything from people to packages, flowers to freight. Downtown we rushed hard copy packages to upper management types during the day, but stayed Uptown for picking up rides at night.

I knew if I drove in and got out slowly enough, acting natural, Shmitty wouldn’t recognize me from his office blockhouse above the station. He wouldn’t know if I was parking or picking up a cab. I could see the billows of smoke from another of Shmitty’s million cigarettes leaving his office window, joining the various grey shades of cloud-like emissions gagging and gasping below the Skybridge. I waited until the biggest billow of smoke blocked Shmitty’s line of sight to make my escape...until I heard my name pierce through the silence like an arrow.

“Where’s your buddy Vincent? He stole one of my cabs!”

It was Shmitty’s unmistakable rusty voice, shouting at someone in his office. I jimmied open a cab’s trunk and peeked over top, away from view. Through the window, I could make out the silhouette of Shmitty’s fat head at his desk, and a very tall silhouette of another man. That had to be Breakfast. He was the only seven-foot cabbie in town.

“Get out of town, man. Vincent doesn’t steal sh*t.”

“You’re covering up for him! Do you want to lose your job, mister?”

“Watch your mouth, Shmitty. I don’t take well to accusations. Between the two of us, you know damn well you’re the shady one.”

Shmitty lit a cigarette and exhaled a billow of smoke. The cab owner had no comeback because he knew Breakfast was right. Shmitty is shady, and very familiar with the darker side of the city.

It was about six years ago when Shmitty ran out to the parking lot at the end of Breakfast’s shift. It was four in the morning, and he begged Breakfast to do him a favour. He wanted him to deliver some ‘packages’, except he wouldn’t say what was in the packages. Breakfast only agreed because Shmitty promised him the best cars and extra overtime shifts, and we all needed the cash back then. Long story short, Breakfast had to go into the east end of town and deliver the package, there was gunfire in the shanty house shortly after the delivery (apparently a real shanty house, guard dogs, barred windows, probably even an attic full of dead bodies), and he miraculously got out of there alive with only a temporary case of the heebie jeebies. He drove straight to Shmitty’s house and told him that he owed him, big time. Anything he wanted, or he was going to go to the police and rat him out. Shmitty swore if Breakfast told anyone what happened he'd invite some mobster friends to cut the tongue out of his mouth.

"How else do you explain his cab just disappearing for five hours?" Shmitty asked, lighting another cigarette.

"Maybe he had a long cab fare," Breakfast offered. "Maybe he got wise and starting cabbing for the competition."

The cab owner stood up and stomped on his cigarette butt. "He's on the brink. Tell him not to be surprised if he sees a few more black cars in his rearview mirror."

"Do what you want, Shmitty. Just tell your goons to follow Vincent good and close. He's pretty entertaining."

Like a thief, I hunched over and ran behind the parked cabs, staying as low as I could. Slipping a little on the slope into the gully beneath the SkyBridge, I regained my balance, ran a few more steps and stopped, finally, out of breath by the side of the adjacent road. I walked up the street with a bounce to my step. I had evaded the dreaded Shmitty once more. I just wished Breakfast would steer clear of him, too. The more 'overtime' work he did for our slimy boss, the deeper his association with that illegal life became.

As I neared the end of the Skybridge, on the downtown side, I spotted a shiny new billboard punctuating the skyline. Its letterbox-shaped 3D screen burst with abrasive ads for new movie releases, and I sighed because I simply couldn't avert my eyes.

Robin's Hood: Welcome to the Urban Forest.

Groundhog Night: Same Bad Luck, After Dark.

The Twilight Games: Hunger for Blood

12 Angry Menstruating Women: Run Away. Run Far Away.

“More rip-off sequels,” came a deep, sandpaper voice beside me. It was Murray, another night-shifter, sipping on a cold, burnt cup of java - the free house special at Shmitty’s Cabs. Murray looked so exhausted that his legs were having a hard time holding him up. A poorly stitched rag doll coming undone. Work boots, green-blue bags beneath his eyes, torn sweat pants and a classy, yet understated, stained hooded sweatshirt. Now this was a guy with a serious case of the Doldrums.

Murray was classic rock.

“Yeah, more like ‘don’t bother to see-quels.” And I laughed at my own joke. “So what’s up with you these days? Finally realized life has no meaning and you want to live in a cave?”

“Pretty much," Murray mumbled, his chin tucked so deep into his chest I could barely hear him. "How’s tips tonight?”

It was the same every morning. My tips were fantastic, and his sucked.

“Decent night, dude,” I said. “Better than a kick in the face, I guess.”

“Mine sucked!” Murray said, spilling coffee on himself. “Three drunks puked in my cab tonight. Three!”

Driving taxi isn’t anyone’s first career choice. I certainly don’t remember it ever coming up on the list of options on career day at school. My folks never sat me down and said: ‘We’d like you to aim high, kid. Be a cabby like your granddad’. There’s nothing wrong with being a taxi driver, but there’s a certain, palpable layer of depression that’s cast over the whole profession. Cabs are how wayward dreams wander. Previous plans float astray. So many drivers pilot around the city as if other people's directions will realign their lives. I saw a lot of myself in Murray. That scared me. I had the Doldrums for a long time, too. For years I felt like a smudge of hopeless filth under a better man's shoe.

Shaking off the layer of night-shift slime that coated me, I yawned enormous, and pretzled myself through some improvised yoga stretches before laying it straight on my cabbing colleague.

"Think about it, Murray. If you didn't drive in the same clothes you slept in - you smell like a nuclear waste dump, by the way - and if you stayed out of the bar strips - which are vomit factories, face it - you might actually make some tips. Alternatively, there's always daytime delivery."

"You wouldn't catch me dead on days. That'd suck even worse." Murray chucked his empty cup over the side of the Skybridge, and unceremoniously scratched his ass as he shuffled home with toilet paper trailing off his shoe.

CHAPTER EIGHT: THE LEGENDARY ROXY CITY

A slick black limousine pulled up in front of me.

To my complete amazement, Breakfast stepped of the stretch looking sharp.

Particularly sharp, I might add, because Breakfast usually dressed above and beyond the dress code for a regular cabby. This was more than usual. He was looking red carpet from head to toe. Black shoes with a mirror shine, silver cufflinks on his beige brown suit and white shirt stood out against his black skin. He had it all topped off with his black and silver plated phat headphones that stuck out at least three inches away from his bald head. Breakfast was pushing seven feet, and I'm pretty sure there wasn't anyone, anywhere in the world on any street corner at 6 a.m. so large and in charge.

Breakfast is a few years older than me, and used to headline cabaret shows with Murphy and Fitch. Back when it was legal. They were a musical comedy trio called the Blabbermouths, and three of my best friends.

"Mister Meister, how's the man?" Breakfast took off his headphones and looped them around his neck. Some deep, thick, hip hop oozed out. "You diggin' the new look? Not a bad combo, eh?" he said, admiring himself.

"Ya man, lookin' sharp! Where's your cab, dude?"

Breakfast shone a wide smile. "Your powers of observation are weak, my friend. I got moved up to limo."

The limo's grill smiled wide at us as if proud to be Breakfast's new ride. It definitely suited Breakfast. The man oozed style. And the ladies? They're all over him like maple syrup on French toast. He could easily be a Hollywood type ‘cause he pulls the needle off the record every time he enters a room.

Breakfast is big band jazz. Some shades of reggae, and a smidgen of hip hop.

“That’s nuts! When did all this happen?”

“Starting today. Gonna get me some mad tips with the riches!” He laughed and drummed on my head in synch to the beat. “Limo’s my kind’a ride, no two ways about it. No more hospital runs for old folks’ meds, no more high schools, no headaches on the daytime shift; it’s going to be luxury. This puppy’s got a lush system, too, so I’m gonna mix beats while I drive. How’s that for a funky jest? I’ll be the city’s first personalized, mobilized DJ.”

Music is this man’s life. You never saw him without his headphones on. He slipped into the driver’s seat, closed the door, and stuck his head-phoned head out the window. The coolest looking limo driver I’d ever seen.

“Hey Brekky. Thanks for sticking up for me earlier. I heard Shmitty pulling you into his office.”

“Don’t mention it. Must have been quite a Moot, I’m bummed that I missed it.”

“It rocked, indubitably. We missed your beats. I owe you one.”

“Alright, enough.” Breakfast slapped me on the back, not one for sentimentality. “Can we go now? I’m dying to see how this puppy sounds.”

“Crank it!” I shouted and jumped inside, stretching out on the soft leather seats.

Breakfast turned some early alternative rock tunes up on the sound system; a beautiful soundtrack for the end of my day. Honest to goodness concert hall acoustics. We drove along River Road, and I watched the sun shimmer across the water and onto the teeter totter juxtaposition of our city. Roxy is a city with two faces, you see.

On one side of the Skybridge, where we lived and toiled, Roxy's older neighbourhoods showed a pained grimace of its former, more vibrant self during the day. Midtown, the old market quarter, barely kept itself together with its dilapidated, empty shops and abandoned buildings suffocated by the grass growing around them. Corkville was a shade better; many of its pubs and coffee shops had died, but there were still a few hip locals that tried in vain to keep them afloat. The Plateau had been dismantled, and received reconstructive surgery into its presently cold, cubed landscape of box stores and pseudo-trendy strip malls, a place so packaged people got lost because of its sameness. Driving through Uptown though, the old entertainment district, was the worst. Busted out lights on what were once top-billed marquees and concert halls left as hollow time capsules of great performances now gone. No live music. No originality. Instead, canned dance clubs and franchised eateries let partygoers feel comfortable in knowing they could get the exact same experience regardless of the city they were in. How perfectly mind-numbing.

In its ancient glory, it was gypsies who finally laid down their wagons and gave up their wayward life to settle here in Roxy. They built the city's foundation, its factories and homes, roads, ports and bridges.

But they also built Roxy a legacy.

After each day's tiresome work, when meals digested and candles lit, the citizens used to pick up their instruments and play the most magnificent music ever lifted on the wind. Like-minded groups formed themselves, they say, as grooves interlocked and new styles created. Their music transformed the city from humdrum to historical. The music these nomadic people made attracted every kind of artist imaginable. In fact, the country's very first radio broadcast came out of a Roxy factory studio. Dance, theatre, comedy, painting, storytelling, and sculpting; they all flourished. Gypsies became minstrels, minstrels became jesters, jesters became clowns, clowns became buskers, buskers became headlining acts, jamming led to record deals, street theatre became spots on TV shows, and doodles found their way into art museums. Like a myth, Roxy's reputation as a premiere destination for live music spread across the country, and travellers, like me, came here to catch a part of its history. It's rhapsody.

Breakfast's face appeared on the video screen. "What do you say we cruise by MogulMedia and pretend we're famous?"

"You must be jesting," I said flatly, too exhausted from having already argued the other jesters on this matter already. I was perfectly content reclining in the back of the limo, listening to an old favourite jazz combo track.

The deejay's left eyebrow lifted, egging me on. "You know you want to," he said, with equal parts sincerity and sarcasm. "You are our portal to fame, after all."

On the other side of the Skybride, beyond downtown, stood Roxy's other, more futuristic face: MogulMedia. You could see the MogulMedia Tri-Towers standing like impenetrable swords dominating the horizon from anywhere on either side of the city, a whopper of a complex, and a juggernaut of all things media, technology and entertainment. I'm pretty sure it's bigger than Japan. In contrast to the broken city I drove through every day, it was a shiny vision of a futuristic space kingdom. We, its commoners. It's actually very Vatican-esque, built like a self-contained city in and of itself. A massive wall surrounds the periphery, making it hard to see anything other than the Mogul amphitheatre, its impressive dome behind the glimmering white towers. The amphitheatre is where the annual MogulMedia Expo is held. Every June, thousands of people flock to drool over the latest and greatest innovations MogulMedia has to offer. The newest in tech and entertainment.

Anything a person buys with the 'MM' copyright stamp on it is deemed 'quality' by the powers that be. Apparently.

Craning my neck as we passed by the Ridge, the wealthiest neighbouring area nestled inside the Royal Escarpment, I caught a millisecond glimpse of a movie studio inside the media multiplex. It baffled me how MogulMedia ruined everyone one of their productions, even with their gazillions of dollars. They pumped out more dribble annually than every babbling baby, worldwide. I figured that they must do it on purpose, so that when a good idea comes along, at least that rare, well-made production looks really good by comparison.

Either that or everyone at MogulMedia are all talentless hoopboogers. And we all know how talentless those are.

There is a statue of the late Ludwig Eisenberg, MogulMedia's former CEO in the centre of the company's property. He wears flowing robes made to look like film strips as he held his chin to the sky with determined eyes, stepping forward in a thespian stance. As if that wasn't overdramatic enough, he carries a flatscreen television with the carved words 'Extravaganzas of the Future' in one hand, and a giant thunderbolt in the other.

They say Ludwig Eisenberg rebuilt this city into the majesty it was meant to be. But by the time I blew into the city, Ludwig's son, Cyrus, had already inherited the MogulMedia throne. Unlike his father's vision of an exciting future of entertainment for all, young Cyrus ruled with only greed in mind. He hoarded the MogulMedia empire for himself. He lived secretively, never leaving the towers of his opulent kingdom, sitting on the wealth and power that grew under him. Rumour claims the king drank over 9,000,000 units of

Plazma a day, enough to warp a person beyond repair. It's pointless trying to understand the mind of a madman.

In his entire reign, Cyrus only spoke publicly once, and he did it to decree a new law as king of MogulMedia. And with it, he obliterated creative freedom for all.

The Law of the Green Light:

1. The Green Light is MogulMedia's exclusive licensing rights for any artist or artistic group.

2. The Green Light permits artists to only perform on MogulMedia's recording label, film or television productions, or appear in any digital medium available for download or streaming on YouBoob, Critter, Buttbook, and all other social networking sites.

3. It is a crime to perform without a Green Light, or upload performances on the OuterWeb.

4. Any digital encryptions on materials, devices or software other than MogulMedia's trademarked Green Light, is illegal.

5. MogulMedia has the right to utilize any unlicensed art for its own production.

If the king gave you the Green Light, you belonged to MogulMedia, and could perform for them, exclusively. On canned TV shows with fake studio audiences, or fabricated film sets in sterile studios. Bravo.

Rumours also claim if the king didn't give you the Green Light, or you were caught performing without one, the penalty was severe. You were dragged before the king to audition; if he liked your talent you were offered the Green Light. If he didn't, or you refused to join the MogulMedia mega-corporation, it meant torture and/or death, depending on the whim of King Cyrus. Lovely.

MogulMedia is to the law as helicopters armed with triple-barrel flame throwers are to children with sling shots.

The Green Light was not a license one kept in a wallet, or saved in a power phone. It was an actual green light about the size of a radish, pulsating with a robotic drone illumination. Designed to look like fashionable necklaces, performers wore it around their necks so they could be identified.

The Noize, knights of MogulMedia kingdom, ruthlessly enforced valid Green Lights. Kicking down people's doors, tackling mimes who dared perform on the street, or even ambushing campfire sing-a-longs out in the woods. All live performances were outlawed because the king couldn't profit without regulation. So many people recorded without permission, and it drove Cyrus mad that he couldn't control it. What's more, the Noize arrested anyone making excessive, unlicensed noise with the twisted logic that it was disturbing individuals' consumption of entertainment on their personal devices.

Cyrus had taken up old Ludwig's lightening bolt shot down from the future, and blasted our lives away. Could he not have thought of something a little more reasonable? What about an entertainment tax? Or, wait, what am I saying? What happened to the days of sharing for free? For the fun of it? Heck, take a few steps back from that even. What happened to the live entertainment the city was built upon?

It was either fight for a Green Light and sell out for the media mainstream, or watch your dreams float down the stream. MogulMedia sucked all the talent out of the city, all but shut it down. The independent scene disintegrated. The vibrant, mythological Roxy became a tired, melancholic memory. Performers everywhere were in the same boat. We were forced to get jobs we didn't want to do. And audiences were forced to consume only the entertainment MogulMedia provided. I hated the king, plain and simple. With every ounce of my being, every follicle on my noggin.

The limo ride rounded out with one of Breakfast's tasty Afrobeat mixes. Alas, a pleasure trip ending too soon.

"You sure I can't accompany you, Brekky? Just hang out with people in the back of the limo for the day?" I asked, stepping out with a clearer understanding why they call limos 'stretches'. "This thing is better than my apartment."

"No chance, dude, you ain't stealing this thunder," Breakfast laughed as he pulled his leather driving glove off his right hand. "And you don't need to tell me about your pathetic excuse for a home. Your place is so nasty it's ashamed of itself."

I turned to see the front door to my basement apartment without a hinge, sagging like the building's one loose tooth. Soon the million cigarette butts would seed a cancer tree on the receding hairline of the front lawn. Freshly sprayed graffiti spread wide over the top floor read: LIFE IS A JOKE. YOU IS THE PUNCHLINE.

"There's a pleasant reassurance," I said. "Depressing and grammatically incorrect. This world is doomed."

"Vince, I never showed you the Soundbomber I was telling you about." Breakfast produced a sleek silver pen from his breast pocket, and tapped it twice on one end. A mini speaker dish fanned out from its top, and while still leaning out his window, Breakfast angled the dish towards a series of condos down the street. "See that guy taking groceries out of the trunk of his car?"

"I see him."

“That sucker’s about to be sound bombed!” Breakfast smiled like a ten-year-old and pressed the play button. I could see a slight kick back from the speaker dish as it lobbed its invisible orb of sound at the grocery man. A five second blast of marching band music hit him, causing him to trip over himself and spill his groceries across the parking lot. “Woops. That wasn’t supposed to happen.”

“What is supposed to happen?” I held the Soundbomber and checked it out for myself. “I assume the point is not to give people heart attacks, am I right?”

“No, man. It makes ‘em dance! Like I used to when I deejayed!” Breakfast tucked the device back into his silk shirt pocket. “The coolest part is that you can aim it at anyone, and only they hear it.”

Like an unexpected flash of lightening, a black and red striped cruiser decloaked around the corner and came hurtling through the air toward us with deafening silence.

“It’s the Noize!” Breakfast shouted. The deejay hit the gas so hard it caused the limo’s tires to screech, billowing smoke behind it. I stumbled backwards off the road and fell into the bushes. The two vehicles blasted over the hill’s crest, and the taser canon attached to the top of the Noize’s cruiser hummed electric with its buzzing blue sparks.

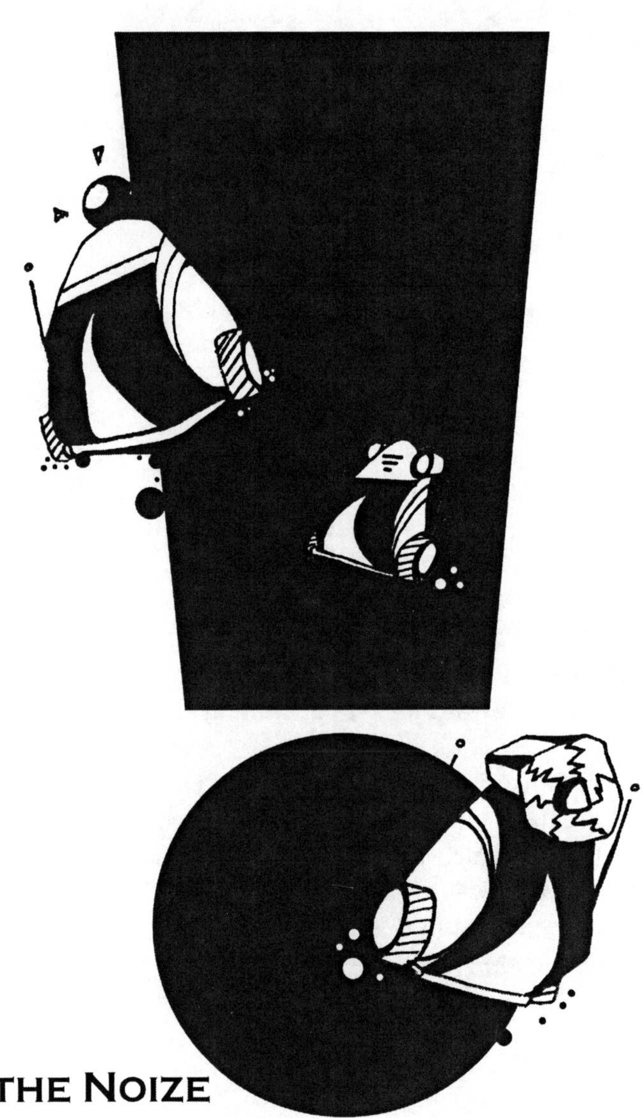

THE NOIZE

CHAPTER NINE: MEANWHILE

I scrambled into my apartment and slammed the door behind me; beads of sweat trailed off my brow out of pure fright. I'd never seen the Noize get that close before.

Tripping over one of the seven books I had strewn across the living room floor, I fell backwards and knocked over a dusty stack of sketchbooks holding up my drawing table, which was propped up on the other side with cardboard boxes, string and the glowing fibre optic Christmas tree that I got at the local swap store. Loose sketches flew up into every corner of the room (including my portraits of the lesser-known superheroes, Captain Obvious and Ambivalent Boy), and the falling drawing table overturned my trumpet case off the shelf, which happened to be filled with half-eaten cheese sandwiches and a month old chocolate milkshake.

I subscribe to the philosophy that if you don't stress about organizing, and just put things down in your house without touching them for a long time, it's way easier to retrace your steps when you lose something. It makes MogulMedia's newest search tool for houses: ANYBODY SEEN THAT THINGAMAJIG?, make living like a slob acceptable. And tripping, more attainable.

Still panicked for Breakfast, I picked myself up and onto the sofa, unrolled my uScroll, and pressed my shaking finger on the app, MEANWHILE. Apropos, our resident computer hacker stumbled upon the idea one day as he established a secure server for the Jesters. I waited impatiently as the satellite linked me to his current position, synching up with Breakfast's power phone. The live feed connected, and I could see his limo doing everything he could to escape the

Noize. The video screen blurred as he swerved up one-way alleyways and straight through hectic intersections. He knew just as well as any of us his life was at risk. The picture came into focus again. Breakfast snaked the limo through a few blocks in Corksville only cabbies would know, and popped out right in front of the Fandango Ballroom. It looked like hundreds of people were celebrating a wedding inside the hall, with at least three dozen identical limousines parked out front. What a genius! With over a minute of breathing room, Breakfast hopped out, slipped on his emergency license plates, and joined the other drivers drinking a coffee. The Noize scanned the scene, found nothing, and moved on.

It doesn't get much luckier than that. My phone vibrated seconds later. It was Breakfast.

> Remind me to get my Soundbomber fixed.

My body sunk into the sofa with a giant exhale, but my heart still raced. Pumping as hard as it could past the weighty tension of the lead web around it. The thought of losing another close friend caused my breathing to quicken, my head dizzy. I felt trapped.

"I can't take much more of this," I said to myself. "Maybe it's time to terminate the Jesters while we're still ahead."

I looked at my buddy Chester. Chester the Jester.

Chester is a stuffed jester doll that sat on my piano. That's right. I'm a grown man with a doll. And you know what else? I talk to him. I won't deny it.

"You wouldn't be upset if I shut down the Den, would you pal?"

I met Chester for the first time when I was just a 10-year old daydreamer. He wore a triangular purple jester's cap to match his purple motley, his face was paper white, and his make-up had strong black and reds. My mother brought Chester home one day from a craft fair, and placed him on top of the piano.

There he sat while I practiced my scales and the piano would shake – as would Chester – wiggling as though he were alive.

Chester kept me company for a good chunk of my youth. I learned the cello and the trumpet and practiced all three instruments in that very same room where he resided; draped on top of the piano like a pompous fool overlooking his empire. That was the same room where I started drawing, too, where I let my imagination run wild. So, I started talking to him, just for fun. I found him amusing. Well, I made him amusing. I would think, and he would retort. Simple as that. You know when you talk back to yourself, and you can literally hear your own thoughts? I imagined that was Chester's voice. It's a reasonable thing to do. Depending on my mood, Chester's retorts were sarcastic, or witty. Sometimes we enjoyed insightful discussions together, and other days we were disgusting, absurd, or down right mocking of one another. Chester the Jester had become a self-made personification by my own invention. And he made practicing the piano much more tolerable.

I took him with me when I came to Roxy. Stuffed him in a box and promptly forgot about him. I was seventeen then and keeping a large, purple jester doll in your apartment didn't leave the clearest impression on women. More than this though, when my dreams of becoming an artist had been squashed, Chester was hardly relevant to a defeated cab driver.

Not so funnily enough, I came to Roxy to 'make it' as a performer. I hoped it would be where I could fit in, where I could carry on the tradition my gypsy forefathers began, and actually make a living at what I love to do. My parents gave up on their talents a long time ago, and I wished for fame, even, to avoid their same soul-squashing fate. I promised to never give up my artistic freedom to a maniacal king. But

Cyrus' Green Light killed dream, too. As soon as I started driving taxi, the Doldrums overcame me, and I forgot that promise.

When you leave what you love to do it's almost impossible to find the spark again.

It was a miserably uninspired life living behind the wheel. I called my cab's windshield my 'Life TV', and I didn't much like the programming. I sunk deeper into the Doldrums as I watched society's rushing around, its anger, its apathy, the pushing, the competition, the attitude, the complaints, the unfriendliness, the lying, the arguing, the deceit, the greed and worse. Roxy became cold and predictable. A monotonous container for depressed, plugged in, over-worked people and I didn't see any time being made for fun or good old fashioned, face to face connections. People would jump into my cab and bark out an address with their face buried in their power phones for the whole trip. They'd throw money at me and continue on, oblivious to everything they passed by during their ride.

Life warped; expression became irrelevant.

Then I'd wake up the next day and watch it all over again. Sadly, Life TV didn't have PVR. No pausing, and no fast forwarding. Society seemed to look worse everyday, and I got deeper and deeper into the Doldrums because of it. My heart almost stopped beating for lack of inspiration.

Three years later, after a particularly bad night behind the wheel, I downloaded a new self-help app called 'GetALifeDipshit'. I was desperate. Down and out in the worst way. The app sent daily quotations and inspirations that helped more than I could have imagined. As I sat amongst the piles of my chronic messiness, and my brain addicted to TV, that app delivered this simple message:

Change your mind, and you'll change your mood.

Find something you like to do, or used to do, and do it.
It's up to us to choose how we look at life.
Do it for no reason, dip shit!

It was all I needed to remember.

I pulled Chester out of hiding that fateful night, stuffed among the scattered papers and pieces of my life at the bottom of the biggest box in my hall closet, and shook the dust off my old friend. He was folded up and still smiling despite the mildew, a smile just as sly as I remembered. His marble eyes danced with laughter. They seemed to say, 'What took you so long?'

He planted the seed in my mind. Why not do what street jesters used to do? They didn't need permission to perform. They entertained when and wherever they pleased and, if memory serves, they all seemed pretty happy doing it, too! So why don't I do that? Why don't I become a jester?

I felt renewed spirit welling up in my heart. Like the anticipation you feel before you're about hit the stage. Like breathing in when a gust of wind rushes past, the idea filled me up with hope again. There Chester had sat, patiently waiting to steer me toward the beautiful absurdity of life all that time.

The decision was mine. Did I want to be miserable, or did I want to be happy? Did I want to be ruled by the king, or did I want the freedom of being a jester? The choice was clear. If happiness meant making other people happy, then bring it on! Do something I like to do, and do it for no reason. I wanted to perform. Like a jester.

I never looked back.

A year of illegal performing passed. Such a rush to find so many artists wanting release from the same prison. I still felt proud to be the leader of such a spirited sub-society, but I couldn't shake the familiar feeling of the Doldrums creeping back into my chest. Why did it feel like the thrill ride was coming to an end?

Someone suddenly banged on the front door; a loud steady banging causing me to pee a little bit in my pants.

A pause.

And then again, more banging. Heavier this time.

Holy muffingtons, they found me, I thought, and the sweat started pouring again. The Noize must have seen me enter my apartment.

I considered the exits. One little window I'd barely fit through. And a back door into the rear parking lot. Both too exposed. If only there was a chute to the Forbid Den in my washroom…

The banging stopped. A piece of paper slid beneath the door. It read:

EVICTION NOTICE.
THREE MONTHS RENTS IN BACK PAYMENT DUE AT THE END OF THE MONTH, OR YOU MUST EVACUATE THE APARTMENT.

I looked back at my jester doll again, whose grin proclaimed total amusement at the irritating notice. "That better be it, Chester. I can't handle any more stress."

And then, as though the uScroll understood how to deliver an impeccably timed punch line, I received a message. It was Shmitty, who blared in all caps: GET YOUR ASS INTO THE STATION, NOW!

CHAPTER TEN: SHMITTY

"Where you been, Mr. Singer?"

"It's Meistersinger, Shmitty. I've been working for you three years now, and you still don't know my name?"

My crusty boss stared me down as he combed the few strands of hair he had left on his head, rocked back and forth on his heels and jingled the loose change in his pocket. He looked like turtle road kill; his strained swollen face bore a pale green colour, and his bulbous eyes rolled around independently of one another. He carried all of that ugliness around with his hunched over, oblong body. His shape was so geometrically impossible it seemed a marvel the man could even stand up. Shmitty is guaranteed negativity, and a reliable dose of disappointment. I can't remember once coming into work and seeing a smile on his face. If Breakfast and I had worked the whole weekend without sleep he'd be just as suspicious and miserable.

I hadn't seen him that agitated since the time I pulled into the station dressed as a surgeon.

Shmitty was heavy metal.

"We got a lot of calls about you the other night buck-o, and I'm sick of it!" The words fired from his mouth in a shower of spittle, and he marched over to my cab and ripped the figurines I had forgotten to take off my dash. "Do you know how much those cabs cost Measleyslipper? More than your life! And your mother's life, and your mother's mother's life! Nobody wants a ride around in a junk shop!"

"I like to think of it as mobile creativity." I said, walking over to the canteen to pour myself a cup of stale coffee.

Shmitty grabbed me by the ear and stuck his face in mine. The stench from his garbled smoker's breath was so bad it made my nose hairs wilt. I swear I saw a bug skitter behind his ear. "Can you say that again Misterstripper? I didn't hear you."

It was no use. Shmitty was destined to be a miserable idiot. Happiness was not in his lexicon, so the best defense, I have found in a case like this, is absurdity. A blindside of pure 'randomness' is the only way to deflect an unsavoury situation. Yet another jester-skill I impart to you.

"I said you have wonderful shoes. I wish I had such shrewd taste in footwear, and aren't the flowers just delightful this time of year, shmoo, shmoo."

He let go of my ear and backed a few steps away. "You've gone all macaroni on me, haven't you?" he shouted, more spittle raining about the floor. He stormed upstairs into his office and stopped to point at me from his steel landing. "No more nights for you. You're working delivery from now on. Starting today! I'm on to you pal!" His sentence got chopped off as he slammed his door.

The day shift? The Doldrums wove heavier cobwebs then, weighing down my arms and legs. Did Shmitty just say I was driving the day shift?

It was futile to defend myself at that point. Whatever words came out of my mouth, my desperate pleas to keep me on the night shift, were already drowned out by the drilling and loud clanking of metal from the docking bay. There were at least a dozen men, some kind of technicians judging by the utility belts they wore, working on the inside of the cabs, pulling large sections of their insides apart.

Murray shuffled by, that unshaven man-creature, unknowingly carrying the same trail of toilet paper from his heal. He didn't seem phased at all by the tearing apart of our cabs.

"Murray! What's all the hubbub about?" I shouted above the noise.

"Who cares," he muttered, indifferently. "Shmitty just said we've got a new sponsor, so we're getting upgrades or something."

I watched the installation guy move into the back seat and begin drilling a new plastic divider between the front and back seats. Great, I thought. There goes my audience.

"I think it's like a touch screen something or other, satellite TV, SPG. The whole package."

"GPS? Seriously?"

"Right, whatever, GPS, LMNOP, whatever the hell it is."

"What a waste of money. We know the city like the back of our hand."

"That's not why I'm doing it, moron!" Shmitty appeared between us suddenly, as if he teleported himself back. "I'm sick of not knowing where you jokers go all the time! This thing will let me who to keep my eye on. I wanna know who's scooping rides, who's taking extra long breaks..."

I poked my head inside the cab. A large glossy black screen replaced the stereo in the center of the console, and the silver GPS unit was clipped above it. "Well, it definitely looks pretty flash," I said. "Where's the stereo been moved to?"

"You're being paid to drive, buddy, not listen to the stereo."

My heart sank. Radio has always been a favourite medium of mine. Unlike so many others, it doesn't deny its audience of their imagination. My heart sank further into as I watched the installation guy lift the 'monitor' into the back seat.

That was no monitor.

"You're kidding me. You're putting a 4DTV in the cab?" I said, flabbergasted.

Shmitty lit another cigarette, sucking hard enough on it to inhale its filter. "It's what the public wants, pal, get your head out of your sphincter. Our sponsors' commercials are gonna run all the time, between the weather and news and that junk. And if people want to surf the Web, we got that too now. Extra cash never hurt anyone."

"Our sponsor?"

Shmitty gave me an unfortunate wink and a nod over his shoulder motioning to the sky. To MogulMedia, the castle of commercialism that loomed over everyone's shoulder. Of course. I could feel a sharp sting behind my eye. A headache unearthed.

"You're running late," Shmitty said, stepping on his butt and blowing the smoke in my face. "Radio in as soon as that monitor is hooked up."

Burying my face in my hands, I took pause from all that had just been said to me, breathed deeply, exhaled, and then opened my hands again to see, traumatically, that it wasn't a dream after all. My cab was being desecrated! Surely there was something I could do. I leaned into the cab again and had a word with the installation guy.

"Hey, man. This is pretty cool gear," I lied, speaking the best tech lingo I knew. I watched, in pain, as the installation guy remodeled my taxi into a mobile media machine. "How do I turn this stuff off?"

"You don't."

"I can't override it?

"Nope. That's one of the reason's we're upgrading it. Sick of you drivers turning the systems off."

"What about in case of an emergency?"

"It's smart technology. If there's an emergency it'll help you more than you can help it. You don't want to turn anything off."

My headache worsened as my blood pressure rose. "Well let's say there's a couple guys in the back of the cab who are really hyper, like out of control maniacs, and they start hitting stuff and fooling around. Where should I tell them not to do that exactly?"

"Nice try, buddy. Listen to your boss. Just drive the car."

With a heavy heart, I gassed up my cab, logged on to the new system, and did my best not to let this sudden development derail me. But it couldn't get much worse, I thought. Maybe Shmitty would let me live in the cab if I don't make rent. Wait, what was I thinking? In this entertainment trap? What a nightmare.

A bright yellow button appeared next to the GPS map on the new screen, flashing. It read 'Incoming Shmitty'. That's a frightening combination of words, I thought. I pressed the button and a video screen enlarged to fill the screen with a close up of Shmitty's nose. The moron had no idea how to use electronics himself. Better than having his entire face in my cab, I guess.

"Mastersappy! Is there a reason why you aren't heading to the post office? I want your packages out by noon! This is your last chance!"

Shmitty.

Sunshine personified.

CHAPTER ELEVEN: DOWNTOWN ROXY

I immediately popped my headphones in to block out the cacophony in my cab. Rachmaninoff Prelude in G minor op. 23 #5. The piano soothed and calmed my soul, placing me in the soft, serene bubble I needed to venture over the SkyBridge and into downtown Roxy. Maybe day shift wasn't going to be that bad, I hoped. It could be cool to be a part of the buzz about town during working hours for a change.

And then my power phone battery died. So much for the solace of music.

Twelve hours trapped in the cab with televised drivel running on loop would guarantee me a one-way ticket on the express train to depression again. Even in the short distance from the station and over the bridge into downtown, I heard the miracles of a ridiculous game show called 'Psychic Trivia', where the contestants, who were all undoubtedly actors pretending to be psychics, competed to see who could predict the questions the fastest. Quirky, yes. But only the first time! By the third time I needed to roll the window down and get some air.

It's amazing how persuasive sponsors can be. MogulMedia. Pffft.

Whatever. Shmitty said the public wanted a souped-up idiot-box on wheels, but not me. He hadn't driven cab in over forty years. I had always taken comfort in the fact that my apartment and the cab were the two places I could, without fail, escape the trappings of media. To think. Sketch. Create. Be ridiculous. To Dream. It's not that I don't like media, please! And I adore the tech world, too. I was born and raised on both, very happy to live in an age with plenty of distance from the gout-ridden, hard workin' 'olden days' of clunky video game consoles and manually activated television sets.

It's just.

It's just that it had all become such overkill.

As I approached the heart of downtown, the streets rolled out into an unending digital landscape before me. MogulMedia wired downtown from the ground up; a pulsating 'media-opolis' with 3-D video billboards that blocked out most of the sky, and a thousand more rectangular screens patching the rest of the city, like a digital chessboard for we pedestrian pawns to live upon. Roxy had a clean downtown in comparison to the rusty uptown quarters mind you, and the electronics that permeated it actually added to its 'next century' charm. Sleek. Metallic. It looked cool, at least.

I ran a few packages to a law office and passed a few school kids, late for school, who were mesmerized by the movie trailers blaring in a storefront window. I saw a gaggle of retired folks stop every ten steps to catch the talk-show airing on the screens along their morning walk in the malls. Carrying a couple bags of dog food to the 23rd floor of an apartment building, I played around with the select-a-muzak screen in the elevator, and then watched from above as a business man stared down at the newscast screens embedded inside the sidewalk square beneath his feet. My bathroom break got me caught up on some fashion tips conveniently delivered to me on the inside of bathroom stalls.

Critter updates feeding down office buildings on their tall digital walls; an extended bug-like assembly of words spelling out the hottest buzz of every trending topic. High-definition restaurant menus with eye-popping animations, and OuterWeb table tops at coffee shops boasting interactive screens at the pop of a power phone. Ziplinc commuters whisked their way across the top of the city while tuning into weather reports in the privacy of their silver pods. Subway windows blocked out by animated ads dissolving in three-second successions. Some of the government offices I delivered to had video screen doors. And as I stopped my cab at intersections, I saw mini music videos playing beside the stoplights dangling above, barely audible by the other electronic street noise.

I'm sure people went to and from work with no recollection of having travelled at all, their brains hijacked by the addictive glow of monitors along the way. If a person wanted to, they could watch their favourite shows while going about in the city, and never miss a scene!

Our city's addiction to pre-programmed living bugged me worse than a thousand mothers' non-stop nagging. No performer should have to compete with this madness! These omni-present entertainment machines, quietly reprogramming our minds. But what bothered me so much is whether people noticed the spontaneous delights around them any more. Would they see the design the fallen paperclips had made when they were spilt? Or would they stop to appreciate the wicked graffiti splashed against their car park walls? Would they bother retelling a short but interesting anecdote about their lives? Do they even have any interesting anecdotes to tell? And that's just the tech in the city I saw in a few hours! Fathom the many more millions of screens glowing in people's pockets. Echoing in their homes and cars.

I hit the gas hard. My mood worsened with every delivery I made. The chaos inside the cab began to penetrate my skull. I struggled to keep the nauseating Doldrums away with the incessant dog food commercials subliminally guaranteeing stay-at-home moms that their dog will jump higher, and that if they used the new eye-ball whitener other people in the neighbourhood will be jealous of their gleaming sclera. And the canned laugh tracks on sitcom clips playing over and over had me writhing in my seat as though the devil's own fiery laughs scorched my very life essence. Sports commentaries with hosts pretending to sound like they knew what the words on the cue cards meant. Cartoons so offensive they'd make the Pope weep. And the one-minute news bulletins reminding us that terrible things are still happening, so be sure to tune into the makeover show coming up next in order to numb any effect the bad news may have.

I finished my deliveries, desperately needing to escape the mobile torture. My tires squealed as I pulled off the road and parked my cab at a slapdash angle outside a convenience store, radioed into the station for a much needed sanity break, and stumbled out of the cab literally gasping for air. Usually on a fifteen-minute break I'd listen to music, or sketch a little, but there was too much noise in my head that afternoon. With the sizzle off the hot noon sun, I decided to seek refuge in the convenience store and grab myself a bite to eat.

A cold gust of air blew over me as I stepped inside; two high school girls stood with the fridge door open deciding which drink to choose whilst taking pictures of the event to post on Buttbook. An older gentleman swiped through the videos of new issue of AutoZone on the Vidzine rack. A teenager, wearing a pair of Googles and grooving to some music he was plugged into, waited in line behind a dusty construction worker responding in grunts on his YellowFang at the front counter. The raft of TV screens running along the ceiling trim provided the store with the requisite amount of canned entertainment, and the latest radio hit played too, which comprised of nothing more than a single, sustained, high-pitched note with an angry drumbeat that machine-gunned behind it.

No one spoke. Not even the cashier to the customers, who clearly had his wireless headphones connected to the video game he was playing. I once gave a ride to a guy who told me about a bizarre phenomenon called 'cyber-mutes': people who stopped speaking because it was no longer a relevant form of communication. Instead, they emailed and Crittered and Buttbooked and YouBoobed and trended and blogged and dated and photo shared and webinared and banked and shopped and read and studied and published their lives online without ever having to utter a word.

And here I thought my mood would improve by being in the company of other humans.

A rotund woman entered the store in a huff, and marched right past me to stand in line behind the teenager. She carried a strange, oblong box under her arm. The word 'Cradler' was written in bold letters across one side. Since she was the only one not plugged in, I grabbed a tuna sandwich and the opportunity to chat with her. I felt punchy, and needed to jest.

"What is a Cradler?" I asked. She wore a breezy summer dress showing just how much she had fattened up over the winter. Every winter of her life.

"Oh, it's an addition to a bed," she said. "It makes it easier for the gently obese to rock themselves on and off the mattress with more ease. It's an adult cradle. But I'm returning it because it doesn't work."

"How, um, innovative," I said. "I've never heard of such a thing. The term 'gently obese' seems kind of harsh though, don't you think?"

"What do you mean?"

"That's just social labeling, that's what that is. I think you might want to grab a thesaurus and look up some more appropriate words to describe the heavier populace. Replace 'gently' with 'softly', and 'obese' with 'mysterious', maybe. Softly mysterious sounds about right. Before you know it, they're going to be calling these poor people 'hopelessly screwed', or 'pathetically handicapped', and that isn't right at all!"

The woman looked skeptically at me as she processed the words that had just left my mouth. When the sarcasm finally hit, her face turned to 'totally disgruntled'. "I think you're an asshole," she spat. "Obesity is a serious problem."

"See, there's more social labelling! Why are people always running around calling each other assholes? Not only does it evoke a rather unsavoury image, but it's a way overused insult. Why not call me a knee? Or a femur. I'd even be moderately offended if you called me an earlobe."

The woman turned her back to my angrily, hitting me in the shoulder with the Cradler. I admit, my first one-on-one jest of the day came out a little biting, but after enduring five hours bottled up, my amped-up energy would have short-circuited every device in that store if I didn't let some out.

Behind me, I heard the encouraging sound of snickering. The older gentleman and the two girls stood behind me in line, and had heard my little jest. I shrugged my shoulders at them as if the comments had come out of me like an innocent burp. Happy to have a tiny audience, I kept going.

"Ah! I see you've selected the Vidzine, huh old timer? A smart choice, it's easy on the eyes. Of course there's gotta be a place around here that can get you a new pair of eyes, no?"

The teenager laughed. He had lifted his Googles off his face to make his purchase, and the construction worker smiled at me as he left the store.

"Girls, what do you have there?" Giggling, one of the girls lifted the toy she had in her hand called the 'AutoPeep.' A palm-sized robot with a single camera lens for an eye rested inside.

"Okay, I'm going to take a guess at what that is," I said. "Don't tell me! Um, I bet you it's a robot that hangs out with your friends so you don't have to. And it 'creeps' and 'posts' and all that good stuff for you."

"Pretty much," she said. "And it flies."

"Of course!" I exclaimed, slapping myself in the face. "If they make anything, and I mean anything else, from here on in that doesn't fly, I'm going to quit life. Forever. I want flying tuna sandwiches!"

"Hey, that thing in your pocket is vibrating," the cashier noticed.

"Huh? That's weird," I said, taking out and looking at a small, rectangular package again. "I don't remember even putting in my pocket." It continued to vibrate, and could see no button to turn it off.

"What is it?" he asked.

"I have no idea. I guess it's another package I have to deliver today."

"Let's open it!" the girls blurted.

"That'd put me in jail. It's government property."

"Is it set on a timer or something?" the teenager asked.

"Beats me." The package let out a dull humming sound as it buzzed in my hands. "It's stressing me out a little."

"It's probably just a toy," the cashier offered. "You must of triggered it by mistake."

I scanned the package with my phone and had a glance at the mapping system. "Wow, that's way out of town. Northwest in the middle of nowhere." I popped the vibrating package back in my breast pocket, paid for my sandwich, and headed for the door. "Thanks for the group effort everyone! Next week? Same time, same store?"

CHAPTER TWELVE: EMITEMOTIMETER

Was it a bomb? The thing wouldn't stop vibrating! Was it some sort of tracking device Shmitty planted? I flipped on the radio to drown out the incessant buzzing of that damn package - that's right. No radio. Even above the unabating clamour coming from the TV, the package's buzzing rattle were all I could hear. I stuffed it way back in the glove compartment. With sweat beading down my brow I gripped the wheel tighter; my anxiety churned with frustration as I drove farther away from the city.

Still, that buzzing. Where the hell was this place? I had already been driving for almost an hour. Making matters more stressful, Shmitty's handy GPS couldn't register an exact destination, and I had never heard of the place either. A farm address: #75, Concession 36.

I wanted to throw it out the window. Next to the worry of blowing up, I wasn't going to win any more brownie points with the boss by driving outside of the city centre to an address that may or may not exist because it was sure to put me behind schedule even more. If I could find the place quick enough and hustle back to the city, I'd be an hour late at best. I'll blame it on an accident, or construction, or the fact that the Jesters were on YouBoob, I thought. Shmitty would be sympathetic to that last one.

My cab blew back billows of dust the farther away from the city I drove. A flatter horizon laid before me, where buildings were replaced by thousands of giant silver steel cone receivers in the Signal Fields. The satellite radars perched on top of the pointed tips swivelled back and forth; synchronized dishes catching data on invisible airwaves. They stretched out forever, seemingly. I remembered seeing the Signal Fields for the first time when I came to Roxy. It blew my mind to learn that MogulMedia intercepts billions of incoming signals per second. I had no idea such technology existed, like cryptosystems and authentication radars. But how else could the Noize intercept and track voice, text and hyperdata on the OuterWeb?

I turned onto Regional Road 37, the quickest artery running the exterior perimeter of the Signal Fields, and sped toward the narrow countryside roads of cornfields and fruit farms. Dusty gravel roads came next, and eventually I found myself driving toward a dense forest with no sign of farms, or homes at all. I made another turn onto a road barely wide enough for the cab and awkwardly angled, zigzagging back and forth. I drove along the forest's edge, shadowed and awfully quiet. I half expected to see an 'End of the World' sign as I inched forward. This guy better not be on my regular route, I mumbled to myself.

And then, a sudden swift sound, like the snap of a whip, ran right through the cab. It rocked the vehicle back and forth once and succeeded in scaring the wits out of me. All of my wits. Gone. That was all of them, no more wits.

I slammed on the brakes and white-knuckled the steering wheel. I thought it was that cursed package. Nothing was burning. The GPS went dead. My power phone, too. The sun was sitting peacefully in a clear early-afternoon sky, so unless someone had gone and invented a new kind of invisible 'no storm included' lightening, there was no explanation. The cab was still running though, which was a very good thing, except the zigzag road made it impossible to back up without going into the ditch, so I was forced to drive straight on.

Thank you package, I thought. I was officially fired.

I made a deal with myself that if I saw the house before I saw a place to turn around safely, I'd deliver the package. If it was the other way around, I would just chuck the thing into the forest, sign the pad myself, and never speak of it again. Roger, whoever he was, should really buy more realistic real estate.

Lo and behold, a farmhouse did appear over the cusp of a little hill up the road. Roger, or who I assumed to be Roger, was standing in the doorway holding a spiral flask and jumper cables for a car battery. He wore mismatched tube-socks and ankle-high army boots (later telling me that its rubber soles were imperative for grounding electric currents), and a lab coat. It was his letterbox black sunglasses, one side black, one side white, that told me he was some rich city dink who decided to get back to nature in his later years. To read all the books he missed earlier in life, write his autobiography, eat vegetarian from his own garden and practice silent meditation to clear the mind. Urban Granolas, I call them. Figured. I was probably delivering his new organically fed, biodegradable, inflatable sandals.

"You must be Roger," I said, slamming my door.

"Indeed. I must," he replied softly, confirming my sharp prediction.

"Well, I don't even want to know. I don't do business with other people's business. Spare me your bizarre hermit in the forest routine, and sign for your delivery? The tiniest package ever in the history of packages is yours, I hope?"

Roger dropped his jumper cables when he saw me the package. "It's fluctuating?" he stammered.

In one complete motion he lunged grabbed the parcel out of my hands and ripped off the packaging. He uncovered a thin white rod with three tiny satellite-looking spheres on one side. As he turned it over to examine it I could see a length word written on its side, but couldn't make it out.

“980,000 Hertz!” Roger shouted. “That is…” He shifted his glasses down a notch on his nose to look over them at me. “Was it on you when it started vibrating?”

“Yeah. Why?”

“What were you doing when it started?”

“Talking. Buying a tuna sandwich.”

“So you were interacting with someone. Interesting…wait a second,” Roger said with his hand on his chin in the thinking position. “Of course!” he said and then disappeared in the farmhouse.

“You still need to sign the Digipad,” I shouted after him. I looked down at the Digipad. It was dead too.

“Hey, by the way,” I shouted again. “Can you explain what happened back there? Something zapped my electronics dead. What is that all about?”

“This farm is a Zero Broadcast Zone.” He spoke slowly and purposefully, annunciating his words with precision. “No reception of any kind gets in or out. The anti-signal dome blocks out incoming signals.”

“I didn’t see a dome,” I said.

“It’s invisible.”

“Ah. Of course it is.”

I took a few steps around the side of the house and saw a gigantic antenna looming directly behind the farmhouse. It was a massive metal tripod with an eclectic mess of vines and bark and overgrown moss growing from its base to its tip. It pierced the sky just slightly above the towering treetops around it, and an old red barn sat lonely at the feet of the giant antennae foundations, making it look like a miniature model in comparison. A few cars were parked outside of the barn, some of them looking to have been there before salt was invented. A Studebaker. An Alfa Romeo. A Beetle. Ford Thunderbolt.

My curiosity was peaked. Roger was an anomaly well worth the drive out there, I quickly realized.

"So, you live off the grid, as they say?" I shouted to him.

"Yes, that's right. But not in the conventional way that they say it."

Further back on the property was a dense, untouched forest with a long stretch of overgrown fields leading up to it. I couldn't remember when I had seen open space like that.

"It's just you out here, man?"

"We're never alone! Energy is everywhere!"

I rolled my eyes. This guy was off his rocker. "What do you do with all this land?"

"Not much. I do all my work underground."

Huh. Me too, I thought.

"Can you come down here for a moment?" Roger asked, still inside. "I need to run some experiments on you immediately."

I hesitated. Roger seemed sane enough to have a casual conversation with, but insane enough to decline an offer of spontaneous experimentation. Especially in the middle of nowhere on communication lockdown. Call me weird, but I like to know my strangers before I let them experiment on me.

“Look pal, thanks very much for the offer, and don’t worry about signing the Digi-Pad or anything, ok? Can you just turn off your invisible fence please? I’m going to be on my way.”

Roger appeared in the doorway again, this time wearing deep blue coloured goggles that shone like headlights. He had changed out of his mud boots into tight green rubber shoes, and carried a glass globe in one hand.

“It is imperative you join me in the basement so I can run some tests. I’ve never registered energy at such a formidable level.”

“Sorry captain, I’m a little weary of wayward time travellers.”

Roger lifted his goggles to rest on his forehead. “My friend, if your reading on the Emitemotimeter is in line with my predictions, and my experiments produce tangible results, time travel will be a discovery of secondary, or tertiary importance, at best.”

“What’s an E-m-i-t-e-m-o-t-i-m-e-t-e-r…?”

“Emit-emoti-meter: a meter that reads emitted emotions. The apparatus you delivered.”

“Emitemotimeter. Emitemotimeter. Rolls of the tongue. Who gave it that ridiculous name?”

“I did.”

“Ah, sorry about that.”

“I didn’t get your name.”

“Vincent.”

"Vincent, in all earnestness, please reconsider helping me. This research could be very, very, very big."

"That big eh?" I asked.

"Noble Peace Prize big."

"Be straight with me, Roger. Are you a psychopath that lives alone in the woods?"

"No modicum of me is psychotic, I assure you. I'm a quantum physicist."

"And that means…?"

"I study human energy on an atomic and subatomic level. My personal research is directed in finding out the mathematical possibility of human energy being measurable through the quantum field theory, or by measurement of the wave function. I attempt to isolate human energy and harness it as actual sound waves by means of the Terahertz Exitron."

My brain hurt. "Enlighten me. What's that?"

"The Terahertz Exitron is an advanced piece of machinery designed to excite atoms in order to release the energy inside them. It is constructed to harness energy at high revolutionary speeds."

I had a hard time concentrating on what Roger was saying because his idiosyncrasies were peculiar to the point of uncomfortable. You know when you are talking to somebody and they feign eye contact? You presume they are looking at you in the eye, but in truth they are looking just off to the side, maybe at your ear, your nose or your temple. Roger does that and wow is it distracting. Oh, and he moves as slowly and as purposefully as he speaks. He told me later that he does this to make sure that each one of his movements are placed succinctly, with intention, so that they are secure in the fabric of space, time and history.

Roger is Electronica.

"So you want me to go into this, uh, Exihertz with you?"

"I would be very grateful. And we wouldn't be in together. I need to isolate your energy, not mine."

"Painful?"

"Not in the least."

"How long?"

"Approximately one hour. It will feel like much longer."

I looked back at my cab. My lengthy disappearance was sure to be giving Shmitty an ulcer. I smiled. Serves him right for putting me on day shift.

"Ok, I'll do it. And I'll do it for two reasons, which may or may not interest you. First, I'll do it out of spite for my boss. He is a rancid waste of flesh who pollutes my soul. Second, I'll do it out of curiosity. My personal research is good stories, so if it'll make a good one, I'll go for it. Stories are what make the world go round, don't ya know."

CHAPTER THIRTEEN: EVENTUALLY, ROGER

Roger's dilapidated farmhouse stands atop an extensive, spotless stainless steel basement laboratory. Moving between the two levels was like stepping between two centuries. The one room wooden structure above was what one might imagine the inside of a farmhouse to look like; a fireplace, a rocking chair, and a bookshelf with requisite dusty books. I half expected to see a grandmother sewing and/or a man in overalls spitting into a can. Through a door slightly left ajar on the far side of the living room, I spotted an impressive collection of old radios lining shelves along a wall. Curious.

"For a guy who insists on having a 'no signal zone', you must get pretty frustrated not being able to listen to any of your radios," I said.

"It's a hobby," Roger replied. "Sound fascinates me."

"Sound is profound, I suppose." I pulled my sketchpad out of my jeans pocket and whipped up a sketch of my new found friend as we walked. "So, is Roger your first name?"

"Last name, actually."

"And your first?"

"Eventually."

"What's wrong with telling me now?"

"Eventually is my first name."

"Your name is Eventually Roger?"

“That is correct.”

“Wow. Weird. Why would your parents do that to you?”

“They didn’t choose it, it’s a nickname. I accidentally sent myself 33 minutes into the past in a failed time travelling experiment, and as a result, I’m always late. When a colleague asked when I would arrive at an important meeting, another replied, 'Eventually.' The name stuck. Please, follow me.”

Leading me into the kitchen, he opened the basement door and proceeded down below.

The laboratory was as deep as his house was tall. It housed his smaller equipment, he said, all handmade and polished with care. A bank of eleven computer monitors were fastened to the wall in the far corner of the lab, L-shaped, above a well-decorated console of equal length. Customized hard-drive towers blinked their lights underneath the console in an array of buttons, dials and switches on top.

“Please, have a seat,” Roger said. He turned two dials on the side of an armchair that sat in the middle of the room. A faint humming sound came from the chair after he turned it on, and when I walked around to the front of it I saw a multitude of dinner plate-sized metal discs embedded into the fabric.

“This thing looks like it’s could suck the marrow out of my bones.”

“The Magnachair is completely safe. It emits a repetitive, low frequency transcranial magnetic stimulation. That is, it will polarize your energy, which will give me an accurate reading. You won’t feel a thing.”

The humming got a little louder as I settled in. "Magnachair? I'm going to be ok in the *Magnachair*? I'm putting a lot of faith in you, Eventually."

"I do appreciate your help, Vincent. Now, I want you to sit back and focus on the 'Optitron' on the far wall. Its visualizations will hold your focus and help you to relax. I'll get the Tellmet."

"The Optitron?" I laughed. "The Tellmet? Who comes up with these names?"

"I do," Roger said plainly.

"Right, sorry. I forgot."

The Optitron was a round monitor with a mirror finish at least a meter wide. It produced animated rain that slowly trickled down as if it were a windowpane, a soothing cascade of multi-coloured droplets leaving lime green, yellow and blue streaks as they fell. My breathing steadied as I relaxed my weight into the chair.

Roger interrupted my growing trance. He carried a translucent bike helmet with a short, stout antennae popping out of a tiny black box fastened at the back. It was his 'tour de force' creation, the 'Tellmet'.

"The Tellmet is equipped with neuron sensors, which display patterns of thought, and show the location of neurons when they're firing in the brain." Roger said, fastening the helmet with a tight yank of the chinstrap.

Roger walked over to the back wall and dimmed the lights. From the corner of my eye I could see the blue beam of his goggles stride over to the computer console.

“Keep staring at the Optitron, Vincent. The Terahertz Exitron is designed so that you won’t feel the 53km per hour rotations.”

“You’ve built the suspension up enough, Roger. Where is this Terahertz whatchimabob?”

“We are inside it. The whole room is the machine. The outer wall revolves in order to generate the necessary spin for quantum isolation, and extraction. Your chair will rotate in the opposite direction.”

“Great. So, while I’m puking all over myself, I’ll keep the Noble Peace Prize in mind.”

And the room began to spin.

CHAPTER FOURTEEN: SEE THE VISION FOR THE TREES

What's the difference between a lucid dream and a vision? I always get the two of them mixed up. Both of them look and feel real, but I think a lucid dream is when you know you are dreaming, and you can interact and change stuff as it goes. And a vision is also really vivid, but it's different because it you don't have to be sleeping when it happens, and people say visions are mystical experiences that tell you about your future.

I don't know which one I had while I sat in Roger's Exihertz, but I'm telling you, it was vivid. I'll call it a lucid vision dream, how about that?

First I imagined myself walking behind Roger's property. Its clean air and beautiful, fragile sounds soothed my nerves: the creaking of tree limbs up high, the waking birds' songs, and the crunch of my footsteps through dew speckled grass. I headed straight back into the woods, away from everything. The sun streamed through the leaves casting warm, golden spots of light on the forest floor, and the deeper I walked through the forest I felt at peace.

Then I dreamt of the path I took to my Sunday morning piano lessons. It rolled out across a schoolyard, through a gully forest, over the red bridge, and then popped out on the other side into a nearby neighbourhood. I saw myself as a small boy standing on the red bridge before my lesson, a comfortable little spot to stop and imagine. I remember staring into the glassy reflection of the stream running beneath the tiny red bridge, with its world of minnows and frogs and insects galore. I acted out characters in my head and sang silly songs. The forests' leaves clapped for me.

Then I found myself back in Roger's forest again, as an adult. I stopped and sat on a stump to listen to the silence.

Just hidden behind a tree, I spotted the side of an old stone well in a modest clearing just ahead of me. I walked over to take a look at it. As I came around the side of the tree I saw, low and behold, there was a jester sitting on the stone well. It was a real life jester, no joke.

Maybe because I was so relaxed I barely registered it at first. He was dressed in a red-velvet motley and smiling to himself. He grinned feverishly and looked out into the forest, completely enthralled. It was like he was watching something I couldn't see. He held a bag of popcorn and hummed blissfully to himself as he popped kernels into his mouth. I watched him, unnoticed for quite a while with my jaw dropped at its full extension, but a moment later he sensed something behind him, and jumped up from the well when he noticed me.

"Well helllloooooo!" he shouted, popcorn scattering all over the forest floor. "So nice for you to join me finally!"

I tripped and fell backwards out of total fright. It was Chester the Jester. My doll, for crying out loud! Except it was alive and talking…to me!

"It is you, isn't it? Yes, yes it is!" he laughed as he danced about the woods. "You found me!"

Chester sang a little bit and danced some more, then he pulled the rope on the well and up came another basket of popcorn for us to share. Sauntering toward me he had a regal expression of pride on his face. He shoved the popcorn bag into my chest, cleared his throat, leaned his head back dramatically and filled the forest with a resounding laugh.

Despite the fact that nothing around was obviously funny to me, I laughed too. It was as if Chester knew the punch line to a joke that hadn't happened yet.

“Spectacular to see you again Vincent! You don’t look a day older than yesterday!” Chester’s boisterous voice sent birds fluttering from their trees.

“What…what the hell is this?” I asked, flabbergasted. I thought it might have been one of the other Jester members playing a joke on me somehow.

“This is me and you, shooting the breeze! We’re chewing the fat! Sit down and rap with me, brother!”

“What…? My brain is playing tricks on me. I’m hallucinating. Roger! He drugged me somehow!” I shouted in my dream, but Chester just ignored it.

“You like being entertained, don’t you buddy?” Chester shoved a handful of popcorn in his mouth, ignoring me. “Of course you do!” He scanned the forest floor and then motioned me to come over and look at a tiny mushroom growing out of a stump. “Check that out! I mean really look at it! Isn’t that the most amazing programming you’ve ever seen?”

Chester was wired. Next he shimmied up a tree and pulled a leaf off it. “This leaf is 100% live and unplugged, my friend. As are you!” He jumped down, curled into a ball and cartwheeled right next to me. “The forest would not be complete without us! We add to the symphony already arranged!”

He sounded like me. He had the same delivery as I do. He was creeping me out. In one motion he set his popcorn down and swept his arms around him, turning and pointing slowly around the forest, mimicking a film director’s panoramic gestures, and in the same swoosh movement, he zoomed in and got right in my face. He even sported the same quarter note on his cheek as the doll did.

"Enjoy your popcorn and take a look around Vincent. Guaranteed it's the best entertainment you've ever seen...or heard!"

Chester suddenly wasn't there. I was left in the forest alone with my popcorn. I remember looking around, still shell shocked, and feeling like time had slowed down. I ate one kernel at a time, and when I did there was a blip, like when a record skips, and when I looked down at my hands holding the popcorn, I saw that I was wearing the jester's costume!

I jumped back and dropped the popcorn, startled. In the same instant, Chester reappeared there again by my side.

"What the hell is going on?" I asked. "You're…just…" I couldn't spit the words out.

"A figment of your imagination?" he asked.

Chester paced around the well twice and stopped to pull an egg out of his hat. It was hardboiled, and he cracked it on the edge of the well and let the broken shell drop inside it. Then, for no reason, he threw the unshelled egg in, too.

"You are on to something, Vincent. You really are. Remember when you came up with the idea for LifeTV in your cab? That was a good one. Funny. Edgy. And the Jesters? A genius idea!"

Chester sat on the well again, with his legs crossed looking pensive. At his feet I saw three mini flying robots appear out of the grass. They carried tiny laser guns and had satellite dishes on their helmets. Had I officially gone crazy?

"But, be honest with yourself. You've got this great idea, so why aren't you willing to live your dream full time? Is it fear of failure? Of fame?"

With his finger, Chester drew a square in the air beside him and a video of me in my cab appeared. It showed me driving in the city dressed as a chicken; some of my feathers stuck out of the door.

"Are you happy living a life of mediocrity? You keep that up you're going to die a 'nobody cabbie' who was quirky and wore funny hats. That's all. People might remember you, but probably not. Most likely you'll be a forgotten footnote in someone else's biography."

That hit a nerve strong enough to snap me out of my confused state.

"I am doing what I love to do," I fired back, glaring at him, "and I'd be a proud footnote in anyone's biography. It would mean I made a difference in someone else's life."

"Perfect. Aim high." Chester pulled a pair of spoons from his pocket and began playing them on his knee, mocking me. "I sure love playing music for people on the street. That's 'cuz I get all the happiness I need from the sunshine beaming off of people's faces when they walk by!"

"It's not like that at all."

"Bumstuckers! Yes it is! The Jesters are just glorified buskers. Except you guys don't even get paid! And what's worse, you have to sneak up on your audience!" Chester looked up to the sky and laughed again, sent ringing ripples throughout the forest.

"So? At least we're doing something with our creativity, which is more than a lot of people can say. And it's not about sneaking around. The surprise is the …"

"Surprise is the key ingredient to entertainment. I know, I know, you write about it all the time in your sketchbook." One of the tiny flying robots buzzed by his ear and Chester swatted it away. “Your problem is clear. The Jesters don’t fit into any marketing, do they? You’re looking for the next step, right?”

“I can’t market unpredictability.”

“A-ha! I know how,” Chester said with a grin. He replaced his spoons with a mini synthesizer. He pulled it out of his hat and held a few chords for atmospheric suspense. “The next step might be the one right behind you.”

“Very dramatic,” I said. “How can I do it then, smart guy?”

“You need to find out what channel LifeTV is on,” he said.

“What channel?”

“If you can tune into that, you’re laughing!”

“What do you mean?”

“What do you mean what do I mean?” He laughed and climbed into the bucket hanging from the well’s crossbar. “Don’t be a fool! It’s YOUR time to unleash the entertainment, Vincent, once and for all!”

I remember seeing the forest spin in front of me like an amusement park ride. I gripped the side of the stone well to balance myself. Chester’s riddles weren’t helping my nausea. “What are you talking about? How in the world do I package surprise entertainment?”

A box fell from the trees after the words left my mouth. It dropped right by my feet and squished one of the floating robots. It was indistinguishable from all the boxes I had delivered earlier that day, save for the faded design on its side. An exclamation mark.

“There you go! Strike while the iron’s hot, old friend! And don’t be afraid of success, it happens to the best of us!”

Chester pointed to the crank. “Can you be a good alter ego and lower me down?”

My surreal doll made animate faded away slowly, giving me the double thumbs up. I had barely turned the crank three times before he vanished. The tiny floating robots, the popcorn, the eggshells, the spoons, the keyboard and the package all followed, bursting into the air as a bubble pops.

I sat on the edge of the well myself and looked back towards the way I came.

A gust of wind started the applause of a billion leaves.

CHAPTER FIFTEEN: QUANTUM LEAPS

I was fried. It felt as though all twenty of my digits had been plugged into wall sockets when I woke up that night. Wincing from the pain of my gigantic headache, it took me a moment to realize that I wasn't in the Magnachair, or in Roger's basement lab either. I woke up reclined in a La-Z-Boy in the room with all the radios, upstairs. Along the wall in front of me were the dozens of Roger's radios lined up on the shelves. And I had slept the rest of the day with that bloody Tellmet strapped to my head.

I panicked. What was that dream I had? Did I dream it, or was this part of Roger's twisted experiment? Convinced that Roger was putting thoughts in my head, I struggled to take the Tellmet off, but it was locked tightly under my chin. Its metal straps made it impossible to cut. I had no idea how long I had been out for. Dread suddenly filled my boots. This scenario had horror movie written all over it. I was alone in the middle of nowhere with a brain-sucking device locked to my head. This was the Twilight Zone.

"Roger?" I called out. No answer.

I hopped up from the chair and ran into the kitchen, or at least tried to run, as the weight of the Tellmet made movement difficult, causing me to teeter and totter backwards and forward to maintain my balance as I moved forward. I tried to yank the basement door open. It was locked, but a note was stuck to the door, which read:

Vincent,
Compelling data. Your quantum energy is vivid. Want to review notes with you. Please have patience.
Roger

p.s. Tellmet is still downloading. Do not remove or leave house. Will lose connectivity.

My quantum energy is vivid. Classic. If I do lose my job after all this, that will have to go on my new resume: Vincent Meistersinger, additional qualifications: vivid quantum energy.

With careful steps, I turned around and walked up the few stairs into the living room, steadying my wobbly balance against the piece of goofy machinery on my head.

Dust particles played weightlessly through the day's fading beams of sunlight, somehow piercing through the thick layer of grime on the windows, and the floorboards creaked in protest of my steps. The whole house was curiously sparse. In addition to the requisite farmhouse decor, I spotted a tattered patched sofa sitting in the corner that I hadn't seen when I first came in. The sofa was facing a peculiar oversized glass orb with thick copper cables attached to its back that ran up the wall and out the window. It looked like a squat, retro lava lamp...?

I decided to investigate the radio room to see if I could learn something about him. It was an impressive collection that must have taken years. The one that caught my eye above the rest was old, squat, yellow and brown with the name 'Fisher 500 hi-fi' branded along the side. It truly looked to have a face. Five dials ran along its front, its teeth, and above them were three smaller displays, its eyes and nose. One display indicated the AM/FM band, the other two 'hertz' and 'modulation'.

Picking up the Fisher 500 hi-fi, I blew the dust off of it and noticed a yellowed piece of paper taped underneath as I gingerly turned it over. The handwriting on the paper read: 'DIN 45500' 'Advanced Frequency Response' 'Marconi's Law'. The paper also bore the stamp 'F.F.' in black lettering. I lifted a few others off of their shelves, each with different faces and personalities to their build. The Diora RS-Z 50, the Corsair, the Philco Cathedral, the Talisman 308. Each with a piece of paper attached to its underside, and each with the F.F. stamp.

What the hell did that mean, I wondered. F.F.? And what about all that other stuff he had in the lab? The Emitimotimeter, the Tellmet, the Magnachair, the Optitron; this guy had inventions I'm pretty sure no one had ever heard of before. Why was that?

I spotted a notebook on the coffee table next to the La-Z-Boy's armrest. Looks important, I thought. Looks personal. I picked it up and thumbed through it pages, a series of pencil drawings, each of them precise and instantly spellbinding. More machinery, by the looks of it. One caught my eye above the rest, a sketch of a headband in the middle of the page with tiny discs around it. I also caught a glimpse of the same 'FF' stamp on the inside cover of the book just before the basement door creaked open, causing my heart to nearly burst out of my chest. I dropped the book, tripped over my own feet, backwards onto the La-Z-Boy.

Roger appeared from behind the door. He walked toward me to help me up, but I sprang out of the chair and backed away from him. I wanted the gizmo off my head, I wanted answers, and then I wanted the hell out of here.

"There's a lot of weird things around here," I said, struggling to get the helmet off my head. "I'd like to know what it is you do *exactly*, Roger."

"I'll do my best to answer your questions," Roger said. "Please keep the helmet on, Vincent, it is not yet done downloading."

"Downloading what, exactly? Warped dreams? This helmet burned a doozy onto my hard-drive, Roger. It felt disturbingly real."

“Ah. You experienced a hyper pyschological state called a ‘Vizmo’. A temporal visualization modification of the metaphoric data stored in your cerebellum. Don’t worry, the effect is only temporary.”

“Right. Well. Thanks very much for that. How about this thing?” I shook the notebook in his face. “Who sits and draws space headgear alone on a creepy farm?”

Roger walked over and took the notepad from my hand. “This is my next venture. I call it the Telexcelerator. A rough sketch at the moment, but it will be a teleportation device.”

“Of course,” I said. “How silly of me to even ask! Teleportation! It’s such a logical step for you, from farmer, to failed time traveler, to quantum physicist, to whatever the hell...”

“Indeed. The dynamic properties of quantum energy will be able to be used as fuel for the Telexcelerator. Any device could theoretically be fuelled by quantum energy. My colleagues are a little skeptical, but time will tell.”

“Your colleagues, huh? Would they be able to tell me about this ‘FF’ stamp I keep seeing all over the place, too?”

Roger looked noticeably unsettled at my question. He walked over to the window and paused, standing with his hands clasped behind his back. Taking a deep breath in he said, “I’d need a lot more time to tell you everything I know, Vincent. Why don’t we start with the exciting results from last night’s experiment?”

I wasn’t satisfied with his answer at all, and I was no more at ease as a result. In truth I was sufficiently weirded out.

“You know Roger, thanks for the mind-bending experience, but I should be getting back to the station. How’s about taking the Tellmet off my head and I'll be on my way."

Too focused on his work, the quantum physicist ignored me completely and headed downstairs. "Follow me," he said. "You can only believe this if you see it. Or hear it, more accurately."

I had no other choice. The man had me by the cerebellum.

Back in the basement, the Terahertz Exitron, Roger flipped a switch on his console. With a mighty heave and scraping of metal on metal, a large, thick, metal door opened on the rear wall of the laboratory, revealing a dark tunnel. I could feel the cool tunnel's wind on my skin, silently enticing, and I leaned in to see what lay within. The tunnel looked to be made from the same stainless steel material as the basement. Roger turned another dial to softly illuminate the tunnel in a murky grey light, and started walking down it, oblivious to my hesitation in following him.

All previous suspicion on Roger was laid to rest at that moment. The court was adjourned, Roger was definitely a scientist, and a serious one at that.

"Curiosity will take you places in life," Roger said, his voice shrinking the further down the tunnel he walked. "Opportunities are not something to pass up. Something tells me that you know that just as well as I do, Vincent. I want to show you what I've been working on. You'll find it rather awe-inspiring."

I listened to his footsteps echo through the metal tunnel; fading slowly the deeper he walked. I sighed to myself and knew that I'd regret not following him. The surreal Chester dream and Tellmet aside, my deeper instincts told me he could, in fact, be trusted after all. His mysteriousness outweighed my concerns, so with reluctance, I followed him into the tunnel.

“Humans have energy trapped inside their atoms, and that energy is as strong as lightning,” he said, walking slowly a few steps ahead. The florescent lighting along the upper left side of the tunnel flickered, casting quick shadows of us on the walls. “Little tiny microscopic storms are active inside of all of us, all the time. Scientists know this already, so that is no mystery.” Roger stopped at the first bend in the tunnel and looked over his shoulder at me. “But thanks to you Vincent, I have discovered energy is measurable outside the body!”

“I’ve heard of auras,” I offered. I had to lean over a little to keep the Tellmet from hitting the top of the tunnel. “Some people say they can see colour floating over people’s bodies. Is that what you’re talking about?”

“That’s the right idea, yes. But I have discovered that human energy is emitted not only as a visible color, but, more amazingly, as an audible frequency!” Roger banged his fist up against the wall of the steel tunnel and the sound reverberated around us. “The Exihertz excites the atoms, which releases the energy and then, at an increased velocity sends it through this tunnel. Can you imagine billions of sub-atomic particles hurtling through here? Spectacular, raw, spiraling energy!”

Roger was getting me riled up, too. “So, I’m pretty amped with energy then, am I?”

“Vincent, you are a human radio tower! You sent out a stronger signal than I have ever before read. Your energy is the first to show me which channel, or radio wave, on which human energy can be harnessed.”

We climbed a submarine-like ladder that Roger released remotely from above, and I could see that the tunnel ended a little further on. That end of the tunnel was made of thick, black rubber layers in interlocking, triangular sections.

“So where does the energy go?” I asked.

"You'll see," Roger said. He heaved the vault door open with his shoulder and we climbed above.

The room we entered was pitch black. It was the single crack in the roof letting in the moonlight that told me we were in the red barn at the other side of Roger's property.

"Please stay along the walls, Vincent. Touch nothing."

I stood and waited in the dark. I had no clue what to expect. Roger would make a good host to a haunted farm tour, I thought; he had mastered suspense.

Roger's voice had moved to the other side of the barn. "Are you ready to witness a discovery never before fathomed by man?"

"I'm not sure, but I'm glad I kept the helmet on."

Bust out
the beats inside
your sub-atomic
selves!

CHAPTER SIXTEEN: FREQUENCIFIER

Two blasts of white light shot the darkness away, illuminating the barn and revealing an incredible surprise within.

Roger called it the Frequencifier. A massive, cylindrical metal vault, wider than it is tall, sat in the back of the barn, filling it with its otherworldly, robotic mass. It had two industrial iron sections on top and bottom, and a glass window in the middle. I watched, spellbound, as a phosphorescent purple cloud with trailing sparks of magenta drifted and swirled inside the Frequencifier. Tiny flashes of light flickering about the cloud at random, like fireflies. And as if the sight of a swirling cloud wasn't enough stimuli, I heard a distinct funk bass line, with a slight hint of disco backing up a classical melody that floated on top of the rhythm.

I closed my eyes to let the sound embrace me. It was the best music I had ever heard! So familiar to me, and yet I hadn't heard it before.

"Man, this giant machine is pumping out a dead funky groove!" I said, bouncing my head back and forth to the music. "I love it!"

"That's because it is 100% Vincent," Roger walked around the vault, waving his hands in the air excitedly. "The Frequencifier is a storage vault for live frequencies. We're listening to your energy!"

"You mean, we're actually listening to my vibe?"

"Indeed! If that's what you prefer to call it."

You know how people say, like, that guy's got a good vibe? Or, I get a good vibe from this place. Or a bad vibe even?

Well, if you ever hear the sound of your own vibe, it will spin you into another state. It gives you a thrill like riding a roller coaster; it drops you down and spins you around. I was at its every command, excited and nervous at the same time.

Roger turned a dial on the remote he held, and the volume increased. "When listened to, human energy is discernable, audible music. Can you believe it? Beautiful melodies can actually be heard from the energy inside our bodies! As you can hear, the rich tones and melodies, they have a unique reverberation to them. I've worked for a very long time to prove my theory, and I…" Roger choked up for a moment as he described his achievement. "The key to finding this came from your reading on the Emitemotimeter, Vincent! I would never have thought my machinery could withstand such high amplitude. Do you understand how revolutionary this is? We give off a 'musical' signal on a sub-atomic frequency that we can finally hear! It is our essence! Music is our essence!"

"I'm freaking out over here," I laughed with a wide grin across my face. It was the first time I'd felt a genuine smile in a long time. "Our vibe…er, energy...is actually...man, I sound good!"

"Yes! And the baffling part is that there's only a little bit of your quantum wave frequency inside the storage unit at the moment, and yet it emits so much music!"

Roger turned a dial on his remote up incrementally, savouring each sound as the volume increased. I felt shivers and goose bumps skitter across my skin. Had anyone told me I would have been standing in a barn with a hermit genius listening to the sound of my own vibe by the end of my day shift, I would have called them an exaggerating numbrocket. And we all know how they like to exaggerate.

"At this stage, I only know some core fundamentals," Roger shouted above the super cool bass line pouring out around us. "The frequency can be recorded and stored as transferrable energy. Transferrable, in that it can also be outputted as music. We can hear it and see it, and if the reception is good we can even feel vibes. But the only way to do that is to make sure we're tuned into the same channel."

"The quantum channel?" I joked. "Right after the Disney Channel, before the channel with all those people making cakes?"

"Channel One," Roger answered, matter-of-factly. "Human frequencies, or vibes, to use your vernacular, are receivable on a channel never before available on any radio band: Channel One. You might think of it at the station that carries life. Literally."

Roger's words caught me off guard and I became weak at the knees, barely strong enough to stop myself from falling. The physicist ran over to help me get back on my feet. "Sorry about that, Roger. It's all a little overwhelming. Let's remove this unnecessarily heavy helmet off my head, shall we?"

"Yes, of course! I completely forgot." Roger disappeared behind the vault to retrieve the Tellmet key.

It hit me like a wave. Channel One! That's what Chester the Jester told me to find. With all his shouting and dancing around, he was trying to tell me that 'real-life' was all on Channel One! Reality, or nature…or life…has it's own frequency? It seemed so absurd to me. And yet, how else could such a coincidence be explained? And why would my childhood doll want me to know that anyway?

Roger returned with the key, talking as he walked. "It makes sense, right? Have you ever tried to tune into a Channel One on the radio or TV? Nothing, right? Channel One wasn't audible before this because scientists didn't have the right calibrations! Perhaps it was so difficult because it's so simple!"

"You've left me speechless, Roger." I marveled at the Frequencifier again, with my purple splash of energy darting about inside it like a trapped shooting star. "How many vibes can this vault hold?"

"Billions, I hope! But capacity is only one part of my research. I want to verify that the Channel One frequency carries all human vibes, and that each person's vibe is measurable, containable and transferrable. More than this, I want to research how vibes interact."

Roger handed me the Emitemotimeter and asked for a base-line reading on his energy. It registered 675,430 mega-hertz, more than 300,000 units lower than my energy reading. A befuddled expression overcame Roger.

"Once I can devise a way to trap energy at 980,000 vibrations, I can research the way in which people communicate nonverbally: our wants, our needs and feelings on a truer, deeper level than emotions. A sixth sense is what I am proposing. And last but not least I want to know if a person's vibe changes over time. The music we all have is as unique to us as our fingerprints or our DNA. But I can only be sure of that until I hear it."

The two of us stopped and swung our heads around to the barn doors at the same time. Roger turned the volume on my vibe down. "Did you hear that noise?"

CHAPTER SEVENTEEN: MOOD GLOBES

Four jesters and a quantum physicist walk into a barn. Stop me if you've heard that one.

Roger and I swung the barn doors wide open and saw the Blabbermouths huddled outside like a trio of villains conspiring their next dupe. Before we had a chance to react, Breakfast ran inside and pointed to the vault.

"You've got the vibe!" Breakfast could barely contain himself from what he was witnessing, jumping up and down like a teenage girl at a Justin Squealer concert. "Holy crap! This is insane!"

Murphy and Fitch walked toward the vault like two ants staring at the immensity of a great galaxy, hallucinated by the swirling designs dancing to the music that filled the barn.

I'm not sure who was more surprised. Me seeing my fellow jesters appear like that, seemingly out of thin air, or Roger standing frozen with his jaw hanging open, stupefied by the unannounced intrusion. He simply stared in dread as the three strangers sauntered inside, closer to the immense Frequencifier. The physicist snapped out of his bewilderment and ran between them and the vault, waving his arms.

"Be careful, you idiots! Don't touch a thing! Vincent, were these people with you all along?"

"No, no!" I said defensively. "These are my friends. I had no idea I was going to be followed."

"This is highly confidential research! What are they doing here?" Roger ripped off his goggles and threw them to the ground, enraged.

"Honestly. I know them better than their mothers. You can trust them. Well, maybe not Fitch, but the other two are dependable. It's a good question though. What are you guys doing here?"

"Shmitty is on the hunt for you Vince," Breakfast said, ignoring the scientist completely, but keeping half an eye on me and the other eye and a half on the Frequencifier. "He's hired the Noize to start following you. He's pissed. Thought you should know."

"Gee, thanks." I wished I could have thrown my cab keys in the forest right then and there. Then I remembered the eviction notice from earlier. My life was perpetually foiled by reality.

"We followed you through your data trail on Critter," Murphy said. "You should creep more often man, it's impossible to creep a guy who doesn't creep."

"I'm not taking any chances," Roger said. He spun a dial on his remote that dimmed the magnificent light in the Frequencifier. A second spin of another dial lowered the music. The barn sank to near-pitch black save for the single, purple swirl of the colour still quietly illuminated in the storage tank. A tiny, playful, quantum glow fish.

"With all due respect to you and your friends, I will not have today's breakthrough ruined by a breach of secrecy. My experiments have taken me too long, and too much is at stake."

"We won't say a thing, will we boys?" I said.

"Believe us, sir, we can keep a secret," Fitch said. "We've got our own secret society."

"Nice one, Fitch," Breakfast said.

We saw the seriousness in Roger's eyes, and his hand holding the remote quivered. "Please, you must swear to me that you will tell no one of my work. It is of paramount importance."

"Sorry to ask the obvious," Murphy quipped. "But how can we tell anyone about what this is until we know what it is?"

After some convincing, some thorough explaining, and some stale restaurant mints from one of Fitch's pockets, Roger decided to believe our story. Once the physicist felt satisfied with our sworn oaths of silence, he explained the complexities of the quantum energy as he did for me, and then proceeded in blowing our minds away by the scope of his research project in conjunction to the Frequencifier. The four of us sat on a few cobwebbed milk crates we found laying around and gathered like school children at Roger's very impressive show and tell. We may not have understood the technicality behind Roger's discovery, but we certainly appreciated its brilliance. A unique blend of surrealism and surprise thrills a jester.

Behind a stack of dusty milk crates in the corner were a few other, bigger boxes, one of which Roger rummaged around in, and pulled out three glass globes. He placed them on the floor in front of us.

"You see, vibes can only be harnessed if the subject's energy is open. If the subject's energy isn't open, I believe it needs to be aligned by another magnetic force." Roger turned a few dials on his remote. "I'm synchronizing the globes to Channel One now."

The three globes quivered slightly as he did so, as if coming alive. They were slightly refurbished snow globes, you know, those groovy Christmas decorations that have miniature winter scenes. The ones you can shake the confetti inside to make it snow. They were empty though, about the size of a grapefruit, and stood on a basic black stand. Two thick wires ran from the bottom of the glass globes along one side, where they thinned and merged into a short, curly antenna that stood vertical to one side of the globe.

"So those are mini vaults?" Murphy asked.

"Yes, precisely. In order to get tuned into a frequency, the subjects have to make sure they're near a receiver. These gadgets here are mini-receivers, designed to receive the vibe frequency at short distances. Allow me to demonstrate. Vincent could you come and stand beside this globe, please?"

"You don't have to strap me into a chair or anything?" I asked as I stepped next to the tiny glass device.

Instantaneously, a purple spark ignited inside the globe next to me. It had successfully caught my vibe, floating in unison to the other energy deposit in the Frequencifier.

"Just as I predicted," Roger said. "This is what I mean by some people having 'open' energy. Before Vincent appeared on my doorstep today with a reading of 980,000 mega-hertz, I couldn't harness human energy. Now I know vibes are transmittable on Channel One."

"I can't take the suspense!" Breakfast grabbed one of the other globes from the box. In an instant, a neon green cyclone spun inside it. We all crowded around to listen as he shook it. His vibe was Sinatra jazz and reggae with dollops of acid-jazz, hip-hop and even a whisper of anarchist punk. "Whoa. Punk. I didn't see that coming," he said.

Fitch and Murphy grabbed one each, and the globes instantly buzzed with color; aqua blue and blood orange respectively. Fitch shook his globe, and a subtle Ska and

Polka vibe poured out. 50s and 60s rock n' roll melodies were backed up surf rhythms from Murphy's globe.

Roger pulled the Emitemotimeter out of his pocket and scanned each one of us, one by one. Each time Roger's face showed more disbelief. "How in the world are all four of your frequencies at 980,000 mega-hertz? It's impossible! Do you have any idea how rare that is?"

"I know," Murphy laughed. "And none of us have Vincent's afro. That thing picks up transmissions from planet Zagulon."

"Why? What's yours at Roger?" Fitch asked.

"Believe me, I've tried a million times and my energy doesn't vibrate nearly as high as 980,000! To have four people with open energy is highly irregular."

"Didn't you say you'd be able to harness anyone's vibe, though?" Murphy asked.

"I did, yes." Roger suddenly went quiet and paced a few steps. "I need a magnetic stimulant. Gentlemen, please excuse me for a minute. I need to run some variable calculations."

We barely noticed Roger leaving the barn as we each held our globes in silence and stared, in awe, at our personalized vibes. Knowing that the colourful wisps and music inside were literally sample of our life energy was almost too much to comprehend.

"Is this happening right now?" Murphy asked. "Like, are we in a barn holding our own energy? For real?"

"It's for 'surreal'," I said. We laughed a little and our vibes bounced in unison with the jump in our energy. My purple colour cloud grew slightly larger and showed a few streaks of white. Our music got louder, too.

Fitch piped up amidst the buzz of music. "Mood Globes."

The three of us turned to him in unison and asked: "What?"

"That's what we'll call them," Fitch fished into a few different pockets pulling out cheese burger, some water wings, a wireless printer, and finally a plastic ring with a fake rubber jewel on top. "These globes look like those mood rings kids get at summer festivals and stuff, remember?" He slid the ring on his finger and we saw it turn from black to light blue.

"I remember those," Murphy said. "And wasn't there a little booklet that came with them explaining what the colour of each mood meant?"

"Good moods and bad moods," I said. "Yeah, I remember those."

Our globes vibrated a little again, and as our vibes enlarged, our music got louder.

"He said the music was recordable, didn't he?" Breakfast asked.

"I think so," Murphy said. "Why? What are you thinking?"

"I'm thinking DJ Breakfast spinning some live vibes, that's what I'm thinking! 100% original music. Stick some of these globe thingies around a club and download the vibes right from the dance floor to a line straight into my decks! Are you with me on this?"

Roger returned from his laboratory, picked out a globe for himself and set it by his feet, just as we had done.

"There's nothing in your Mood Globe yet," Fitch said.

"My what?"

“That’s Fitch’s new name for your globe doohickeys,” Murphy said.

“Indeed,” Roger gave Fitch a look of true concern. “Well, you gentlemen have heard people tell you that you have a ‘magnetic personality’, haven’t you?”

“I can’t tell a lie,” Breakfast said.

“And most people think it’s just an expression. It’s not. I believe I won’t need an artificial magnetic stimulant anymore! Subjects with energy already at 980,000 mega-hertz *are* the magnetic source!”

“So you mean we can amp up your energy?” Breakfast asked.

“I guarantee it! Your energy is already open, so I’m willing to wager that if I spent enough time with you, my energy would jump to 980,000 mega-hertz! With the globes open to receive my energy on the Channel One frequency, we’d hear my quantum energy in no time.”

A light went on in my head. Vibes were the equivalent to emotions. And what were the Jesters all about? We got a rise out of people! We elicited an emotional response.

“That makes so much sense!” I shouted. “Think about it guys! All we do is get a reaction out of people. He’s just talking about it in ‘science speak.’ We need to amp Roger up with some jests! Murphy did you save our YouBoob videos by any chance?”

“Damn right I did!” Murphy pulled out his weFling from his pocket and turned it on, its projected light cast large against the barn’s dusty wooden far wall. “Take a look at some of these clips. It should get your sub-atomic energy vibrating.”

All it took was one clip. Our only 350-pound jester, Cousin Weakbelly, jested a crowd at a movie theatre. Before the film started, Weakbelly stood up and asked the audience for movies for him to reenact in thirty seconds or less. He brought down the house with a brilliant reenactment of Transboremers, and a hilarious impression of every single bad guy in the James Conned movies. Security chased him out of the building, but the crowd loved every minute of him.

Just as soon as the laughter left Roger's mouth and his demeanor warmed up a little, we saw a tiny spark ignite in the globe. A bright, splash of electric red buzzed inside the glass.

"Wonderful!" He brought his globe over to us and shook it. Very faintly at first, we heard an R&B baseline emanating from the globe. Roger shook it some more and the music got louder, now with a hint of electronica music, and some salsa. It was baffling. The globe didn't have a speaker, and nor did Roger do anything to physically transfer the signal. The little antennae on the globe was pretty powerful.

"I so wouldn't have called you as a Blues man, man," Breakfast said, sizing Roger up. "And salsa? Damn buddy, you're spicy inside!"

Roger walked back to the Frequencifier and turned a giant-sized dial at the very left of the storage unit that was labeled INPUT on the left, and OUTPUT on the right. He turned the dial all the way to the left. Pausing, he looked at us with a earnest seriousness in his eyes. "Please, never, touch my equipment," he said flatly. "Especially this dial. We only want signals coming into the Frequencifier. Outputting the energy could be catastrophic."

The vault now housed all five of our glowing vibes inside. The spectacle of energy that had danced in the little globe moments before was duplicated in the quantum storage unit. It harnessed our sound, 100% original, and the result was magnificent. You might think that the music would clash and be hard on the ears, but somehow our vibes blended. The salsa rhythms gave way to some gentle folk melodies, and the blues played with funky orchestration. It sounded as if our vibes were conversing. We watched in amazement as the vibes floated in the container together, at times brushing up with one another like fish in an aquarium.

"Gentlemen, as a scientist I don't believe in the concept of fate, but I do feel strongly that our meeting today is serendipitous. What I did not anticipate is that you could be an essential component to the next step of my research."

"Which is what?" I asked.

"I need to distribute these globes to perform my city-wide research project. In order to first validate the quantum frequency Channel One as concrete and measurable, I need data to back it up. Are there many other, um, in your jester team?"

I looked at my friends and knew immediately we were on the same wavelength. Breakfast's idea of using the vibes for our own jesting purposes was precisely the next step we had been looking for. My imaginary friend Chester even told me so.

"Indubitably, my new quantum friend. And I guarantee all of us have magnetic personalities buzzing at 980,000 mega-hertz," I said. "I'm pretty sure we can get you more energy than you'll be able to handle. All we need to figure out is what's in it for us."

mood globes

CHAPTER EIGHTEEN: THE LUCKY VAN PLAN

We left Roger's farm at the first sliver of dawn's light. None of us wanted to leave - it was all too fantastic - but Breakfast reminded me that Shmitty had the Noize on my tail, and that no amount of quantum energy was worth risking my life over.

As souvenirs of our auspicious evening together, Roger let us keep our Mood Globes. "Keep them away from clutter," he said, as we got in our cars. "Near a window, on a balcony, a high shelf, you get the idea. The farther away from other devices receiving signals and closer to open space, the clearer the music will be."

I shook hands with Roger. "We'll return at week's end with a solid plan. I'm not sure exactly how to make it work, but we'll figure something out. We have a knack for thinking outside the box."

"Something discreet, I hope," Roger said. "Unsanctioned science experiments with unsuspecting subjects are not usually welcome practice." He slipped me a tiny LensFlare that he had cupped in his palm as we shook hands.

"What's this?" I asked.

"The data from your Tellmet," he said. "A small token of my appreciation."

The drive back to the city felt like I was returning from another planet. My vibe swirled inside the Mood Globe, which sat on the dash like an otherworldly talisman, a very hip addition to my many other earthly trinkets. I flipped the LensFlare between my fingers as I followed the Lucky van back into the city, and listened to the funk music coming from the globe. My music! It was impossible to know what to consider first - the whole night was just so overwhelming!

I pulled up to the cab station with Murphy's Lucky moving van in tow. Lucky for me, the place was empty save for a couple of drivers coming in late from their night shift. I parked my cab, tore a piece of paper out of my sketchbook and drew a quick caricature of Shmitty: a turtle with tire tread through its middle, smoking a cigarette. I chuckled to myself as I slipped it under the windshield wiper. That will piss him off, I thought.

I hopped in the back of the Lucky van where Breakfast was curled up, asleep among the undelivered furniture. He snapped awake as the van jolted forward. "That was out of this world!" Breakfast exclaimed. "Did any of it even happen?"

We shared a moment of collective contemplation, all of us too baffled to answer. Each of us had our personalized Mood Globes on our laps as we listened to the pleasant mixture of tones and rhythms above the heavy banging of the moving van.

"How many of those globes do you think he has?" Breakfast asked.

"Crates and crates of them," Murphy said. "He said he salvaged them before they reached the dump."

"So ok, let me see if I understand this," Breakfast said with his ear pressed up against the glass of his Mood Globe. "All we have to do is jest a person a little bit to snag their vibe, and then Roger can receive and keep the signal in that big storage vault thing?"

"That's my understanding," I said. "Their energy has to reach 980,000 mega-hertz for their vibe to be harnessed."

“When the globe goes ping, the vibe starts to sing!” Fitch added as he rummaged through his pockets. “Oh, hey, I’ve got a donut in here.”

“But we have to continue jesting in order to do that. We’re the magnetic charge, right?” Breakfast pulled the donut from Fitch’s fingers and gobbled it in a single bite.

“It’d be mighty strange to just hand a person a swirling globe of quantum energy after we jest them though,” Murphy added. “It’s a groovy souvenir, but it’s an awkward one.”

“Can Roger actually know where the signal is in the city, and exactly what kind of music each one has?” Breakfast asked.

Fitch pulled out a submarine sandwich from his inside pocket and stuck his tongue out at Breakfast before taking a bite. “I think Roger said it’s like a homing device,” he said with a mouthful of assorted meat. "Not only do they tell us ***where*** people are, but they also tell us what ***kind*** of people they are! They literally show us their vibes, ***and*** the kind of music they like!"

Breakfast smiled wide. “Unbelievable. We can use these doohickeys to market the Jesters. The people we jest remember us from the street, they keep their Mood Globes, and we’ll use those somehow so people can…”

“Can what?” Murphy asked.

“I don’t know what. Yet.” Breakfast said.

“The best part is that Channel One is undetectable," I said, tucking my globe into my Omnibag. "Roger said none of the signal systems MogulMedia uses pick up Channel One. They don’t know the frequency even exists! We’re laughing! We've happened upon a foolproof anti-Noize device! Now all we need is a gimmick to make it work.”

CHAPTER NINETEEN: MYCEREBELLUM.COM

I woke up thinking I was late for work. Yes, basement apartments are great for sleeping, but they're confusing as hell to wake up in. I jumped in my jeans, put my head under a blast of cold shower and slapped my shoes and shirt on as I ran up the stairs to the street. Oddly enough, it was Sally the prostitute who made me realize it was still nighttime, not the darkness.

"Evenin' sailor," Sally said, swinging her purse. Her lipstick was halfway up the side of her face. "Think you can squeeze me into your busy schedule tonight?"

"Thanks, Sally, but my calendar's full. Until forever." I went back inside and the wonky door teetered closed behind me as I entered my pad, collapsed, relieved, on the couch. Shmitty would have killed me if I had missed another shift.

I swiped off random remnants from the stereo, the plastic cups, cold pizza slices, and the random heaps of candy. I turned on a bluegrass track I liked, and then slapped together a bologna sandwich. No mayo, so I used marshmallow spread. From the kitchen I could see my Mood Globe poking out of my bag that had toppled onto its side on to the floor, looking like a mythic relic peering out at a modern world.

Munching on my sandwich, I walked into my living room and moved the globe on top of the stereo, but immediately heard static coming out of the speakers.

Oh right, I thought. Globe + electronics = bad.

Reaching up to the windowsill, I perched the globe firmly on the ledge where I could see my swirling vibe swim. I stood for a few moments considering its compelling composition again, when I felt another's eyes considering me. My doll Chester was sitting on his stool near the window, on the piano, smiling up at me.

The weirdest part of the whole Roger experience was seeing Chester the Jester in my vision. It felt so real interacting with him that it bordered on 'clown' creepy. I really should put a poll up on Buttbook. Which is creepier: clowns or jesters? And he seemed to know me so well, and said so many things I felt like I needed to hear. It was as if he could read my mind.

I changed the music to Mahler's 2nd Symphony, amazing music to listen to in the middle of the night, and watched my vibe pop a few darker shades of purple inside the globe as the music descended into a minor key. Sitting down to the piano, I played some of the chords along with the music. Ascending fifths, descending minor thirds. A lift, some tremolo, a bass recitative, and back to the major theme…

I looked at the doll again and tried to remember all he had said to me. *"What's taking you so long?"* I imagined him asking me with his silly grin.

The LensFlare! Reaching my hand into my pants pocket I pulled out Roger's tiny digital gift and inspected it. It was metallic green, weighed a little heavier than a contact lens, and had the same symbol etched into its center: 'FF'. All of the Tellmet's data, he'd said.

Roger's a spy, I thought. Or an alien disguised as a spy. Disguised as a quantum physicist. Whatever he was, I couldn't wait to get another piece to his puzzle!

I laid the LensFlare onto the flexi-monitor of my uScroll and watched it dissolve onto the screen, uploading its information in a few green blinks of its activation light. The uScroll screen rippled as if suddenly stuffed with a job it couldn't possibly do, and its micro fans kicked into a higher speed. I backed my chair away from the machine, ready for it to explode.

Almost anticlimactically, my web browser opened up. The tiny text in its top left corner read: remote secure server. In the next second a password appeared in the middle of the screen, with a ten second counter counting down. I copied the password, just before the screen transitioned to a web page no one ever knew existed until that moment.

mycerebellum.com

The welcome screen was white with black silhouettes of five tall figures along its bottom. Above the silhouettes was a pulsating brain, within which a spot to insert my password. I quickly pasted my password, and braced myself before hitting 'enter'.

My mouth hung open in a half-shock, half-smile.

I had gained access to my account in the mycerebellum site, which showed a hallway of white doors numbered 1-19. I could scroll through the hallway right and left, like a flow of folders, and that's all it was: door, after door, after door. I randomly chose door #10 and double clicked it open.

Inside were a series of nodes, scattered across the screen like a game of marbles. I selected one. A window opened and a video began playing. To my amazement, I saw my childhood friends and me fishing at the creek behind my parents' house. When I was ten years old! The colours were vivid, as if I were there again. As if I had my memory taken in and Photoshopped! My friends and I called each other stupid names and bragged about a fish I never even caught; I was watching one of my very own memories! From my very own brain! The Tellmet had sucked it out of my head for crying out loud!! I fast-forwarded through and saw my father checking if I had brushed my teeth standing at the bathroom mirror, and my brother and sister teasing me by pulling my pyjama pants down as I walked up the stairs to my bedroom.

Each door represented a year of my life. Each node represented one day.

"Who is this guy, Roger?" I asked Chester. "And why is he sharing this with *me*?"

A small dialogue box appeared when I closed the node, prompting me to name that memory. I called it 'Fishing with Friends' and saved it. It made sense to have to sort through our own memories.

I opened another node. It showed a video of disjointed images strung together; crazy faces morphed and twisted in close-up to the camera, and then a mountain range, and then a few blips of conversations with farm animals, and then me drinking cartons of chocolate milk falling from the sky. I stopped that video pretty fast. 'Crazy face mountain dream', I labeled it.

"If this day gets any more surreal, Chester, I'm going to have to make another appointment with my shrink," I said to my stuffed friend on the piano.

Can you imagine all the memories we have forgotten, but would die to see again? Imagine how different life would be if everyone had instant access to their memories. Their dreams? I don't think society would ever be ready for the seriously sci-fi stuff that'd start happening. Of course Roger kept this site secure.

Leaning closer to the screen, five hours of my life whipped by in the time it takes to clean your ears. The payoff was the load of memories I got back in return. After a few tangential excursions into a few choice memories, including the time I drank tea with an East-Indian family at their gourmet hotdog restaurant, and when I won the first ever blonde afro award at an international hairstylist competition, I scrolled all the way to the end of the hallway of doors until I reached #19, and double-clicked it. I eventually found the vision of myself walking into the forest and meeting my old friend Chester just hours earlier. I listened to each and every word intently. I knew he was trying to tell me something.

I paused the dream when he said: 'the next step is the one right behind me.'

"What do you mean by that?" I crumpled up the eviction notice and threw it at my doll's head, his grin unaltered. "The step behind me will let me have my next step? What?"

"Are you of nimble enough mind to consider an idea you had a long time ago, but forgot about?" I imagined him saying in reply.

"You mean I can go further because of something I did in the past? Is that it?"

"If you consider thinking, doing."

"An idea I had, you mean?"

"Bravo young jester, we can postpone the lobotomy after all." I heard him say.

My eyes moved to the base of the well in the Chester dream, where tiny floating robots hovered about the grass and flowers. There was also a tiny little road inlaid on the forest's floor with a couple miniature people waiting for a bus. Further along in the dream, the box with the exclamation dropped from above.

Those dreamy hallucinations weren't random, I finally realized. Those were some of my drawings!

My thoughts turned to the dozens of sketchbooks littered across the floor, inside of which were a million forgotten drawings. Dormant ideas locked away in those pages, another, more analog memory time capsule. Grabbing a few, I began rifling through their pages. Some sketchbooks were duct taped at the spine, others were pocket-sized, the perfect size for occupying myself at boring dinner parties. There were key chains from cities I had visited and concert ticket stubs and photos, and scrap paper thoughts littering every page.

And at last, the answer came to me. Letting the sketchbook fall from my lap I sat back in awe. In the corner of one page I discovered a very detailed drawing of those very same laser-bearing robots that appeared in my vision! I had even drawn musical notes as though they were bubbles floating up to the sky. On the very next page there was a quick sketch of the very same exclamation box drawn in purple and blue pencil crayon. Grade 11 Math class, I think it was. The subconscious is a powerful thing!

I turned the page and saw about twenty more exclamation marks in a variety of shapes and sizes fill the page. One of the exclamation mark was circled a few times, and I had drawn a smiling face in its bottom ball. Beside it I wrote, 'logo?'

Chester was looking down at me sitting on the floor of the apartment, covered in paper memories. *"Don't you love little surprises like that?"* I could hear him say. *"They're like messages from the former you."*

“Yeah,” I replied. "I was going to work on that logo idea…”

"No time like the present!" Chester's voice almost sounded like it was in the room.

CHAPTER TWENTY: THE EXCLAMATION BOX

To my dismay, Shmitty was on my case when I got to the station the next morning. He stood like a bouncer outside the docking bays. If I didn't need the money so bad, if cabbing hadn't become part of me, I wouldn't have any time for his unwelcoming mug.

"I'm on to you, Meisterzippy. You see that black cruiser over there?"

Across the street from the station and down a ways, a Noize cruiser hovered, watching me. I could see cigarette smoke billowing out of the driver-side window.

"Ya, I see it. Is that a friend of yours?" I asked.

"What do you think?"

"I don't think you have any friends. And judging by how much he smokes he's racing you to win the cancer race, too."

"Dying of unnatural causes isn't uncommon in this town, pal," Shmitty sneered.

"If you need to hire the Noize because you want to find out what makes one of your drivers so entertaining, Shmitty, you must be living one very, very boring life."

I could see my words had stung him a little, the way he blinked and stepped back from me. "Just watch your step, kid," he said, walking away.

I finished my morning parcel deliveries, radioed out and stopped for lunch at Fountain Park on the lower West side of town. I bought a box of greasy French fries from a fry wagon parked up the street, because grease compliments fake sandwich meat so well, don't you know.

Pulling out my sketchbook, I reclined into brainstorming mode with some German techno-punk playing on my power phone.

"Nothing like the present," I said to myself, sketching another version of the box with an exclamation on it. It could be a kind of present, I thought. The best part of presents is not knowing what's inside, the surprise is the key. Fitting with our jester motto. My mind wandered back to Murphy's comment about handing unsuspecting audiences souvenirs after street jests. He was right, it would be weird if we just handed strangers Mood Globes. But what if we packaged them differently? For fun. It could be a little souvenir from the jesters. Who doesn't like a free gift once in a while? We wouldn't be breaking the rules with innocent gift giving…

My phone vibrated. A text from DJ Breakfast.

>Dude.

<Salulations.

>Jester down.

<Down where? Down south? Columbia?

>Down like dead.

<No! Who?

>LaSpaz. He was finishing the ends of other people's sentences up in Hyde Park. With a mega-phone. People complained.

<You can't be serious.

>Sorry bro. The Noize killed another one of ours.

My hands shook, too emotional to focus. LaSpaz had a great life. A girlfriend. He was a hard worker at the Fibre Optic plant, a true contributor to society. He was our only bilingual jester, with us from the beginning. A tear splotched the dot on my exclamation mark, running its ink down the page.

Looking up, I saw the same cruiser that was parked outside of Shmitty's station that morning in my rearview mirror, still watching me. At that moment I felt a surge of immense anger overcome me, so strong that if I were a fighting man I would have beat that Noize agent dead. I imagined myself marching over to his cruiser and smashing his head against the pavement over and over again.

But I wasn't a fighter.

I was a lanky cabbie.

And even though I swore I'd shut down the Jesters if we lost another member, the fury firing through my veins told me it was time to break that oath.

Tossing the French fry box out the window, I watched each fry hit the pavement. Like the jesters who lost their lives doing what they loved. Deep fried fallen soldiers, delicious no more. I reached into my Omnibag and sifted through the mess inside it. I pulled out a stick of gum, sketches of random cartoons, a LensFlare with some indie rock I didn't much mind parting with, an already scratched lottery ticket, and a toy elephant some kid dropped in my cab a while back. I stuffed my random assortment into the empty fry box, and drew an exclamation mark in black marker on each side of the box, closed the lid, and got out of the car. My body shook with anger.

I was officially through living in fear of the king's stupid Green Light law. A new dawn for dunderheads and dipsticks was long over ripe.

I marched right up to the window of the Noize cruiser. The window was open, and the agent was sleeping. A lucky break. His loud snoring made my sneak attack easier. I'd never actually been up close to one before, nor seen an agent in person. The agent must have been quadruple my size in pure hulking muscle, goateed with a black wrap-around visor and silver armoured suit. What morons, I thought. When will they realize that enforcement only looks cool in comic books. In practice, their costumes were more farcical than any jesters'.

Holding my breath, I leaned into the window and carefully spied into the cruiser. A console of silver switches ran straight up the centre of the cockpit above his head, and a wall of stereo cones behind. The direct feed from the 360 degree bubble cam stretched on a monitor the length of the dash, displaying both a street and satellite view of the city, and the pulsing sound of the sonar tracking system gave a reading of the surrounding area's current noise level. The agent slept with one arm on the Sidestick controller, ready to take off at any moment. The other rested on his long range taser heater on his lap, ready to take a head off at any moment.

Knowing there was only way to combat this degree of suppression, I slid the exclamation box onto his dash, satisfying my rage.

The note I attached read: ***The best revenge? Surprise!***

CHAPTER TWENTY-ONE: MOOT #49

For anyone who has had an idea, and a good one at that, they'll know that sleep is a common sacrifice for the cause. Scars are to boxers as black bags under the eyes are to artists. In fact, it took the Blabbermouths and me the rest of the week, twenty-three pots of coffee (nine of which Fitch drank), and four epic pillow fights for us to agree on how we were to carry out our ideas. But we did it! Thinking about it now, I'm pretty impressed at how we managed to make it all work out in the end. Fashioning a quantum physics research experiment into a marketing tool for a ragtag group of jesters is no small feat. As long as all voted in favour of our idea, we'd be in business.

The Den was full that night of the 49th Moot. Fitch planned a candlelight vigil for LaSpaz to rally the troops before the meeting. Turnstylz spray painted a shadow of our fallen jester long against one wall in his remembrance, and Breakfast smashed his Gourdly after a eulogy he wrote to a killer backbeat. LaRose sang an original of hers, 'Champions of the Absurd'. A fitting tribute, and an elegant way for the jesters to witness LaRose's talent, finally.

Then, Madame Feathertip lightened the mood with a story about her most recent successful jest.

"Good evening everyone. I'd like to tell you about a new suit I made," she said as she put her arms through the sleeves of a regular looking tweed coat. "I call it ThreadFX. It's wired to pick up on every movement I make, and produce a sound effect for it." Feathertip sat on a chair and the suit played a sound, like a bomb dropping, and the jesters burst out with laughter and applause. "The effects are played out of its microscopic speakers in the fibers, so it's impossible to know where the sound is coming from." She took some steps toward Fitch, and cows mooed, and then shook his hand and, the suit played the tinkling of coins falling on the ground. Again, we cheered for her amazing creation. “I’ve sampled thousands of sounds, and the ThreadFX just randomizes the effects so you almost never hear one repeated. Just yesterday I walked through the city library, and you should have seen the faces!”

Feathertip took a bow, which sounded like a haunted house door creaking, and Murphy moved the meeting along by turning on the projector and dimming the lights. I waited for the crowd to settle down before unveiling our big news.

“Fellow Jesters! Welcome to our 49th Moot. Let me begin by saying you are all hooligans, and the only reason I continue to hang out with any of you is because you do wonders for my ego.”

“And you smell a lot better than you look, Mr. Meister!” shouted a jester from the back of the room.

“Good one, whoever that was. I should write that down. Anyway, it is both a glum and great evening my friends. We say goodbye to a worthy friend, and at the same time we unveil a new chapter for the Jesters. I can think of no better time to recognize LaSpaz’s lost future than by carving a new one of our own! Tonight we become entertainment company! Behold!”

A round of applause accompanied the first slide that had a drawing of my exclamation mark, and our slogan:

Live like a King, Hire a Jester
www.jestersincognito.com

“Pretty catchy, no? Every company needs a decent slogan. A fetching logo. And every company needs a gimmick, too. So, hang on to your hootenannies kids, we have found a solution to our woes. We can finally steer our chaotic club in a profitable direction as an organized entertainment company. And we'll call ourselves…wait for it…the Jesters Incognito!"

Dead air. So quiet I could hear the drips from the pipes above splattering on the Den's floor. Dozo and Domo wheeled up on their tandem bike. "Where the hell is cognito? And why are we in it?"

"No, no. Incognito. It means in disguise. In our ongoing mission of bringing art to the people, the Jesters Incognito will host parties in disguise - a surprise party planning business! Tell me that idea doesn't rock the proverbial Kasbah!"

"So what's the idea Mr. Meister?" Noodles heckled. "You're booking us into kids' birthday parties and retirement homes?"

"You got me. I thought we'd all enjoy a slow death together dressing up as clowns."

Boos and hisses rippled across the room. Too Tall Ted, a jester who worked a lot with props, even threw some macaroni salad that hit me in the face. Our collective hate for clowns ran deep.

"Don't get the wrong idea," I reassured, scraping the goopy pasta off. "These will be parties that still offer the spontaneity of our day-to-day jesting, but with paying audiences. The king hasn't made it illegal to throw parties, yet. Let us illuminate the idea for you."

Lowering the lights, Murphy showed a YouBoob clip of Warthog and Moog, our resident graffiti jesters, who were caught on tape painting a car to look like a jellybean with a crowd of people cheering them on.

Another YouBoob video simply showed a twenty-second clip of a woman at a park bench laughing her head off with one of our crew, Sonar, another comedian forced into retirement.

“As you know already, we have a growing number of hits on YouBoob. This means people know about us, which we can use to our advantage. But they need to know who we are, how they can hire us, and what we can do!”

“Imagine if the people watching these jesters walked away with a souvenir after seeing them work.” Murphy said. “Some person-to-person marketing. You know, just a little something to remind them of what they saw, and to introduce them to the Jesters Incognito.”

“That’s where these gift boxes come in!” Fitch said, joining Murphy and I on the grandstand. “We call these Exclamation Boxes.” He held the prototype box up in the air, a very accurate recreation from my sketches. “Think of them like loot bags. Except they’re loot boxes!”

“It’s our calling card” Murphy said. “We thought it would catch people’s attention because they are designed with Mr. Meister’s cool, stylized exclamation mark, our new Jester logo! There’ll be a surprise inside each one: a toy and some candy, maybe a novelty pin, some random fridge magnets, some pottery, a fortune cookie, you name it!”

“We’d be doing the party backwards – the loot before the party!” I added. “These Exclamation Boxes are the best marketing tools on the planet!”

“And it’s not all cheap toys and trinkets, boys and girls,” Breakfast said as he stepped up on the grandstand carrying his own Exclamation Box. He reached inside and pulled out a Mood Globe. A collective ‘ooooh’ spread through the crowd. “This is called a Mood Globe. There will be one in every box. Each one is different, which is perfect as a jester signature souvenir.”

“What is it?” Twisty asked.

“It’s space gumball!” Raffleworthy blurted.

“It’s a dragon’s eye!” Scalliway’s voice came.

“It’s a very groovy decoration,” Breakfast said. “Each one plays different music, when you shake it, and it displays different colours. It shows a person’s mood, hence the name. We met a person recently who makes them, and he’s willing to supply us with as many Mood Globes as we need.”

Breakfast and Fitch passed their Mood Globes around the room. It was an exciting moment, watching the Jesters witness the colour and music coming from the globes for the very first time. In the darkened Den, the effect was exceptionally magical, as their faces were illuminated by the reflection of colourful vibes. Of course, we never disclosed the true purpose of the Mood Globes. It is actually kind of illegal to conduct experiments without people’s consent, so we just made it look like a novelty gift and stayed true to our promise to Roger.

“It’s classy. It’s cryptic. And it’s different,” Murphy said, changing the slide to the homepage of our new website. “As long as our unsuspecting audience take the globes back home with them, and want to know what the hell a jester is and what we do, and as long as they are open-minded enough to take a chance, they’ll visit the website and try us out.”

“We’ve got a website?” Humperdink asked.

“How do people know about the website?” Fizzlestick added. “And what’s does any of this have to do with surprise parties?”

“Ok, ok, one question at a time,” Murphy said. “As you can see, we’ve stamped our website and slogan onto the bottom of each Mood Globe. It’s a simple website with nothing more than our exclamation mark logo on it. We want to maintain the element of surprise, and stay off radar, of course."

"So, people email us via our secure server and we do a show for them," Breakfast said. "There's a comment box on our website where people can contact us. But we're not going to do a regular show. We want to make it different."

The slide changed again to a picture of a crowd of people at a cocktail party, standing around in a generic living room and socializing. The camera zoomed in on a trio in the corner of the room, two of whom were laughing, and the third had Fitch's face pasted crudely to its body. The jesters roared with laughter.

"What?" Fitch asked, laughing a little, too. "I'm always the life of the party!"

"As you can see from the picture," Breakfast explained, "the people with Fitch are being jested. But the best thing about it is that they have no idea he's a jester! They have no idea he's not a regular guest. He's been hired to entertain guests in disguise."

"Let's keep our flair!" I exclaimed, standing tall on my television podium. "We entertain at a party, except in disguise. The only people who know we're there are the people who hire us. They let us plan the party and give us complete artistic license to do whatever we want. Now, if we can do that…that's original!"

"Oh, I see. More like a hired jester," Twisty said, juggling the Mood Globes. "Like in a king's court."

"Exactly! We can jest old school, like we do on the streets. We'll loosely improvise each party and show up as different characters!"

Murphy flipped to slides of a holiday celebration, a community barbecue, a bachelor party, each one with Fitch's bald melon pasted onto a random person in the crowd. “It’ll be like working the audience, except the people won’t know they even are an audience at all! We’ll never throw the same party twice.”

“We can guarantee great music, that’s for sure!” Breakfast added, winking to me.

“And we perform with more freedom. We still don’t need the king’s precious Green Light, and we can make money at it! It’s the answer we’ve been looking for!” I cartwheeled across the stage, silly facing as I spun.

The room erupted into applause, laughter and cheering. There wasn’t a jester in the Den who didn’t love the idea. It felt so great to bring the spirit of my fellow jesters up again; it was a new renaissance for us. Once we had the surprise party premise, there was no end to what we could create. We had never considered entertainment like this before…and the great thing for us was that nobody else had either.

“Space bats and plaid lollipops,” I bellowed.

“Space bats and plaid lollipops,” the Den echoed.

CHAPTER TWENTY-TWO: SURPRISE!

Breakfast and I returned to Roger's barn to pick up our first supply of Mood Globes after the Moot's revelry. Roger was 33 minutes late in meeting us, but just as ecstatic as the jesters when we described our plan to him.

"These parties could kill two proverbial birds with two theoretical stones!" Roger said, looking off the side of my face, at maybe my ear, or a mole. "If your jesters are filling globes at a party, I could get a reading on a variety of vibes, and then…" Roger stopped and stared off into space, deep in thought.

Breakfast got in Roger's face and snapped his fingers to bring him back to Earth. "Listen, Roger, I'm dying to DJ again. You gotta tell me, can we stream the vibes from the Frequencifier through to my mixer? Do you think we can do that? Is human energy streamable?"

"Yes, of course, if you wanted to transfer those vibes into a portable storage unit in order to mix some new music, I'm sure I could put something together. A larger mood globe with greater amplification perhaps, I would need some time, however." He ran over to a computer behind the Frequencifier and started typing away.

"Yes!" Breakfast high-fived me. "There's no question in my mind that we're going to be the hottest party planners to ever hit this town!"

"A guaranteed audience, Brekky! Can you picture it?" I said as I loaded boxes of Mood Globes into the limo. "We can tailor every party based on the vibes, so we guarantee a great time."

Roger came back around the vault and slipped his blue-lit goggles off of his eyes. "Analytics complete. Channel One reception is wide open on my antennae, straight across the city. We're going to be gathering some serious data, indeed!"

In a week we handed out a hundred and eleven boxes. Not bad for a first week. Truth be told, the beginning of the Jester's surprise party marketing scheme fell short of our expectations. The reception was cold.

After working a guy's energy up with a quirky story and a few jokes during a delivery, I offered him the Exclamation Box as a 'special bonus', and he promptly punched me in the face. I think he got the wrong idea. And a mother slapped me in the face for offering the box to their kids with a cartoon I had drawn. People aren't used to unsolicited entertainment followed by free merchandise. It just doesn't compute.

Mashed Potatoes, our only jester poet, was actually chased by the cops for disturbing the peace. It was to be expected in his case. Mashed Potatoes used our secret plumbing routes and popped out of handicapped washroom stalls across the city, reciting poetry to people while they were on the can. He then slipped the Exclamation Boxes under the stalls. It doesn't matter what city you're in, if a random person appears out of the blue, in a public washroom, and then hands you a box as a gift…well, that's just disturbing, worldwide.

Surprisingly, Breakfast was met with a cold reception when he offered his Exclamation Box to an attractive young lady in a retro record store. He told me they were getting along real well at first. He was telling jokes and doing impressions of some of the bands she was looking at buying. Then when it came time to exchange numbers, she got weirded out when he pulled the box out of his bag. Apparently a petrified look came over her face, and she yelled, “You walk around with presents for every girl you meet?” for the whole store to hear, and then ran out.

We knew it would be hard at first. But at least in each of those failed attempts we still managed to get vibes in Mood Globes. That trusty ‘PING' sound meant Roger had another subject in the Frequencifier. In the weeks following, we had a lot more luck. We figured out that jesters could get a jest and deliver the Exclamation Boxes by just being themselves at their regular jobs.

Big Dawg is a rather large, intimidating jester, as his name suggests, so his shenanigans aren't often questioned. Whispering is his jest. That’s it. He whispers silly, nonsensical stuff while keeping a serious expression. It’s a hilarious sight coming from such a large man. It was the middle of the afternoon during a big executive meeting, and Big Dawg whispered little one-liners or observations to the clients. Before he knew it they started giggling and the boss got upset. Dawg got a vibe out those guys really easily. Once the meeting ended, and the last person to leave paused to scan the room before closing the door and turning off the light, he noticed it. The eye-catching purple and black Exclamation Box under the conference desk. PING! Mission accomplished.

Fiddle, a talented wordsmith, had the idea to build oversized crossword puzzles and leave them inside Ziplinc platforms. She hid her Exclamation Boxes behind the huge piece of paper in the hopes that the person willing to complete a crossword would see the box as a reward and take it home with them. Every night when she did her nightly janitor rounds, she was happy to see the boxes were gone. PING!

The Man Whose Scarf is Too Long works as a security guard at a mall. His method was simply genius. Using his authority to accuse a person of some made up crime, shoplifting, say, he would then bring the accused back to his office and entertain them with shadow puppets. PING!

By the end of the month, we got our first email. Murphy and me were having breakfast at Cosmos when he noticed the comment on our website. The comedian shouted excitedly with scrambled eggs dribbling out of his mouth.

"Someone wants to hire us for a party! Listen to this:"

Thank you for my Mood Globe.
A nice gesture from a jester. What do you guys do?
Curious, Naomi

"Our very first bite!" I shouted.

"What do we do?" Murphy looked as if he'd been asked out on his first date.

"We write her back! Something engaging. Profound. We don't want to lose our only potential customer."

Murphy and I took turns passing the uScroll back and forth, crafting a message. This is what we finally sent back to Naomi.

Want to host the party of a lifetime? The Jesters Incognito is an out-of-the-box entertainment group who make sure that the events you want are nothing like you expect. We guarantee parties that will surprise and delight every time. Great music included! (No, this is not a joke.)

Two days later Naomi wrote back. She was interested! But she wanted to meet one of us face to face to make sure she wasn't being scammed. Understandable, I think, especially in a world where strangers rarely strike up conversation anymore. We sent Breakfast as our 'host liaison' to find out more about her and pitch our idea. A couple of hours after their meeting, I got a text from Breakfast.

>Naomi wants us 2 throw a bday bash.

<When?

>Next week.

<Wicked!

>She can't $ much.

<But she gets the idea?

>She's coolz with da rulz. Digz it.

<How many jesters do we need?

>Not many. 10 I think.

<K. Very doable.

>Believe it baby! We're goin' live!

Roger, the genius of all geniuses, designed the Frequencifier to keep a record of where and when frequencies were received on Channel One. So in order to listen to Naomi's vibe, we needed to know exactly when and where she received her Exclamation Box. Thus, Breakfast asked her (for marketing purposes, as if we were already that popular!), for the coordinates of where and when she was jested. Murphy drove the four of us back to Roger's, eager to have a listen.

"I am able to isolate every single frequency," Roger said, turning another dial on his remote control. He had set up two speaker towers on either side of the Frequencifer, taller than most rock concert systems. "I can amplify its signal loud enough to hear every nuance in dynamics, every subtlety in tempo and cadence and variation in rhythmic pattern. Did you know vibes are in different keys, even?"

"Roger, we're dying over here," Breakfast said impatiently. "Which one is hers?"

"Give me a moment," he said, his tongue sticking out in concentration. "Reception on singular quantum frequencies can be elusive."

The energy pulsating in the giant vault had already spawned into a radiant cluster of clouds. Bursts of microscopic lighting flashed inside the denser areas where different colours collided, and wisps of variant hues spun inside leaving effervescent undulations in its wake.

"She better not be opera," Murphy said. "Anything but opera. It's musical barf."

"Why?" Fitch asked. "A room full of opera lovers would be a hilarious party! We could drink white wine and talk about the best place to get our poodles shaved."

"There! I've isolated it!" Roger locked the Frequencifier and stepped back to see her energy enter the vault.

Naomi's vibe poured out of the speakers, a cool mix of bluegrass, African drumming, and flamenco guitar.

"This chick is world music! Cool! South American with a whisper of gypsy rolled into one. I can't believe how perfect all those styles blend," Breakfast said. "No DJ can mix beats like that!"

"Should be a cool party," I said. "And birds of a feather flock together, right? Which, in other words, friends of a groove bust out the same move!"

"She mentioned she had spent some time in Spain during university," Breakfast said. "Judging by her accent, her roots are in Texas maybe?"

"That explains the flamenco guitar and bluegrass," Roger said. "I wonder where the drumming comes from?"

"Maybe her mom is a Zulu Warrior," Fitch said.

"Don't be ridiculous," Murphy laughed. "Zulu warriors only listen to Death Metal!"

I brushed my hair up into a veritable poof of grandeur, thinking over the schematics of our first party venture. "Guys, we must not let our excitement take our attention away to one very important detail I only now realized. That is, Breakfast, in agreeing to be the deejay, and thus the veritable face of the performance, are you willing to be our 'fall guy'?"

Breakfast stopped grooving to Naomi's beats and pulled his headphones off. "Come again?"

"Think about it. The rest of us are posing as guests, so we'll be fine. And it's no crime to throw a party, so the guests will be ok. But if the Noize storm the party, you'll clearly be the only one performing. Are you willing to take that risk, my friend?"

Roger poked his head into the conversation. "This is of no concern. The Channel One frequency cannot be detected by regular means. Once activated, it creates a protective no-signal zone of its own. The Noize won't hear a microscopic peep."

Murphy shook his head. "But we're still not foolproof. The Noize dress as civilians all the time. They could be at the party already, and they'll see Breakfast performing without a Green Light."

The deejay stood tall and brought the rest of us in for a huddle. "I'm putting my money on Roger with this one, boys. Let them crash our party. Once the Noize gets a taste of my beats they'll forget why they even showed up in the first place. They'll put their tasers away and cut a rug with the rest of us."

Like an army of tight rope walkers over a yawning canyon, the Jesters had a slim shot over certain death. But we stood on the shoulders of our seven-foot jester who showed no fear in our mission to bring live entertainment back to Roxy. I looked into my friends' eyes as we bent over in our huddle, relieved to see Breakfast's courage had also set them at ease. We knew what we were getting into, and the danger wouldn't keep us down.

Murphy told a joke about renaming our group 'The Noize' because we'd be the ones making a lot of it. Breakfast did an impression of a Noize agent trying to beat box. Fitch kindly offered us all a lick of his watermelon-flavoured sunglasses.

The only way to break the live entertainment law was with a sneak attack of ridiculousness.

CHAPTER TWENTY-THREE: BADDA BING BADDA BOOM

Naomi chose the Badda Bing Badda Boom Bar for her birthday party. Rich in black leather furniture and red velvet carpeting, it's a very smooth, svelte restaurant. And Naomi wanted us to keep the party classy too. She advertised it as semi-formal dress, with cocktails, dinner and dancing on the bill.

You know how it is just before the guests show up to a party. It's thrillingly chaotic. The caterers set up, jesters who happen to be professional chefs, bringing crates of food and beverages, and rolling in the dishes, tablecloths, and napkins to put each place at the tables. Our resident magician/florist carefully carried the many floral arrangements around the room and Breakfast got ready, too, with his deejay cases strewn about and electrical cords attached. I soaked up the adrenaline rush of preparations, the worry of not being done on time, because things were a bit of a mess, with crumpled to-do lists and bubble wrap strewn over the floor. I loved the tension so much because it was the closest thing to a performance we had ever had.

Breakfast and I positioned about two-dozen mood globes around the room. Some we stuck to the bottom of tables and chairs, others we tucked behind plants or lamps. All of them strategically placed as close to the guests as possible while still out of sight.

"Vincent, check out the new source of my happiness," Breakfast said, pulling me over to his DJ booth. "I'm calling them Sonic Sticks."

He lifted a hinged door below the decks to reveal two long, thin metallic contraptions, the same shape as florescent tubing. The ends of each were connected to Breakfast' turntables with slightly longer Mood Globe antennas.

"Roger came through for us, bro," he said, turning the Sonic Sticks on. A warm orange hue glowed mutely inside their metal casing. "I can spin the vibes produced at the party, no sweat! Now there's some fresh beats!"

"I can't believe we're scooping peoples vibes," I said, zoning out a bit. "It's a strange concept, don't you think?"

"Yeah, it's a little surreal. Just think of it more like 'sampling' their vibes. And the sticks don't store the vibes; we're streaming it on a parallel broadcast signal. It goes to the vault on the farm right back to the Sonic Sticks."

"You're right," I said, still deep in thought. "It's like we're going to show them what their vibes are capable of. I bet you some of them don't even know they have one."

With the Mood Globes in place, the jesters were set to concentrate on what we set out to do – jest! Fitch was the bartender, I was the waiter, and Murphy was the Maitre'd. Breakfast was legitimately himself, DJ Breakfast. Twisty, LaRose, the Dingleberry Brothers, Yoink, and SmallFries came to the party as guests. With over forty people invited, no one ever suspected they weren't friends of Naomi. We passed Twisty and SmallFries off as high-school friends, and LaRose was the mailroom clerk at Naomi's office. The Dinglberry Brothers met Naomi on a plane one time, and we decided it would be funny if Yoink was a neighbour with the hots for Naomi.

Yoink came up to me at the bar minutes before the real guests arrived. He was a yodeler with a stutter.

"So how d-d-do you want m-m-m-e to play it, Mr. Meist-t-t-er?" I could see beads of sweat tickling down his brow. "Should I c-c-come on strong at the end, you know, like build it up-p-p over the night? And what a-b-b-bout my st-t-t-utter? Should I keep it?"

"You can turn it on and off?" I asked.

"Sure. But if I want to stop stuttering then I have to clench my butt cheeks."

"Huh. That's a stumper. I don't know which is funnier. Do what you want, Yoink, just think of tonight like a party you've actually been invited to. It's not a performance, really. You're just here to have a good time and jest a little."

That was the key for me. All I wanted was to be remembered as 'that quirky guy that told those funny stories', and that's it. Seeing as this was our first step into the party-planning world, we needed to play it low key and stay as believable guests. It was ok to be eccentric, flamboyant at times even, but we weren't there to dominate the party.

As Naomi's guests arrived and I made my rounds serving cocktails and appetizers, it was clear that the jesters had slipped into the evening completely unnoticed. Between the ten of us working the crowd, we sparked some decent conversation, and I could quickly feel the energy of the room bump up a notch or two. Fitch threw in some foolish impressions here or there for a couple of laughs; LaRose told a story about a senile aunt of hers who is convinced she saw Santa Clause buying condoms at the supermarket. We had the guests in the palms of our hands, and the great thing is that they were the most important part of our jests. More often than not they were the entertaining ones!

Throughout the night I passed by a plant, or a table where we had stashed a Mood Globe just in time to hear a 'PING!' The vibes were flowing!

Breakfast kept the music at a good energy level. He played popular licensed artists first, like Hazard Rat, Walk on the

Moon, and Shipwrecked 5. As the evening progressed, Breakfast turned up the volume and got the energy bouncing around the room more and more. It was just after dessert when I took a rest from waiting tables, and joined in on a few conversations myself.

"How do you like being a waiter?" one of the guests asked me, a twenty-something guy wearing a frumpy sweater and glasses.

"Love it!" I said, smiling ear to ear. "It's a strange name for the job though. If anything, you people are the waiters. You wait, right? They should rename the job and call it the 'walk really fast and bring me what I wanters'." PING!

I overheard the Dingleberry Brothers talking to a group of girls while playing cards and drinking espresso.

"And that was when I decided that…" Dingleberry #1 stopped and lowered his eyes shyly.

"You decided what?" a girl asked.

"No, it's going to sound stupid, forget about it."

Dingleberry #2 encouraged him to explain himself with a hand on his shoulder. "It's nothing to be ashamed of," he said.

"Ok," Dingleberry #1 said. He lifted his head and took a big breath. The girls' eyes were wide in anticipation. "It's just that I travel so much, you know, and I miss my family a lot. So, I made finger puppets of all five of them. Now I can speak to them wherever I go." He took his hand out of his vest pocket and showed the girls his family of finger puppets. Some were too polite to laugh, but a few of the girls just howled as he proceeded to introduce his finger puppet mother, finger puppet father… PING!

The key was to get the guest's vibes individually at first, and then, after Roger had each signal locked in and set for analysis, Breakfast activated the Sonic Sticks. The direct feed from the blended frequencies created the most blow-the-head-off-your-shoulders music I had ever heard. By midnight Breakfast was pumping out beats that had everyone up and dancing. I mean, who could possibly spin classical, bluegrass, hip hop, alternative rock and African jazz into a set? Seamlessly and simultaneously! By 1 a.m., the party unhooked! People from the other side of the restaurant joined us and the room was charged with great music.

Breakfast, drenched in sweat, shouted to Fitch and me over at the bar. "These vibes are too intense, boys! I can barely keep up!" He looked as if he might pass out from sheer exhaustion.

At the end of the night the jesters left along with the rest of the guests, no one the wiser that we were there. Naomi handed out the Exclamation Boxes to everyone and simply said she knew a company that made loot boxes.

Her friends later told her that they had never had a better night out.

Quite frankly, neither had we.

which is why
i'll never hitchhike,
or eat perogies
ever again.
You dig banjo?
!

CHAPTER TWENTY-FOUR: CREEPING THE OUTERWEB

In no time, old school word of mouth hurtled us forward, and we found ourselves performing shows twice a week, with another two hundred Exclamation Boxes handed out by the end of the second month. We scored a number of smaller gigs from that first party which gave us a stage so to speak, to practice what was slowly evolving into a whole new art form: Surprise Entertainment.

We could barely keep up. Assembly lines became a staple item on the agenda of our Forbid Den Moots. We saw so many new jesters attending every week, I quickly lost count of how many we were. It was all happening so fast!

Murphy, Tiddlywinks and Dribble hosted a party uptown, a book launch at the central library. Murphy went as the Dean of Literature of a university that doesn't exist (it satisfied his penchant for playing older bearded characters), Tiddlywinks was the MC with a severe drinking problem, and Dribble set up an elaborate window cleaner prop at the library, behind the book signing area for good old fashioned slapstick laughs. I heard later that Murphy inspired the crowd to sing a four-part round of an old Irish folksong. The newspaper reported it to be the liveliest book-signing ever. Fifty Mood Globes got filled at that gig with vibes raging from disco to punk to grunge. We never knew what we were going to get.

We sent Sonar to a pool party as a master BBQ chef, where he stuffed fortunes into random sausage buns.

Slobberhound refereed a regional ping-pong competition and narrated over the mic what the players might have been thinking as they played.

Vixtrix, Scalliwag and Numbnuts showed up to a summer solstice camp out as a trio of biologists, and proceeded to marvel the party goers with false origin stories for everything natural.

I remember that we once juggled three parties in a single day. The first was a doctor's retirement party at noon, complete with a string quartet that posed as caterers, and LaRose as the host. The jester working that party asked the doctor a few stories from his career beforehand, and then lavishly embellished them for the crowd. That party's vibe pumped out some baroque piano melodies over ragtime rhythms. A curious mix.

The second was the grand opening of a furniture store. Fitch and Feathertip wore the ThreadFX coats and posed as customers who followed the salesmen around asking if *they* needed any help, much to the manager's entertainment. The vibe at that event was largely soul music, surprisingly.

That same night we jested a high school football championship party, where Smallfries and myself posed as science nerds. We decided, foolishly, to create a drinking game challenge to the team, whereby two challengers at a time would face off to answer questions from either a muscle or mind category. Last man standing won. Lucky for us Smallfries threw those guys off by throwing his voice. They thought they were hallucinating! The vibe that night was death metal and ballroom big bands. Football isn't what they used to be, I guess.

What a rush! We were in on 'shows' that only we knew was happening. Shows that distracted people from their pre-recorded entertainment, and engaged them again in the spontaneity of life! And we had complete creative license too! What kind of Green Light performer has that much freedom? With the help of all the chatter zipping across the Outerweb, social media helped us make our first real splash in the city's exclusive entertainment pool. A small splash, yes, but people were talking about us. The creeps popped up on Critter faster than we could pop out of bathrooms and manholes across the city.

Humphrey&Associates
A stuttering yodeler sang to me on the streetcar this morning. And then handed me a present. Anyone know something I don't?

Jumpsuit
@humphry&associates Funny, a tiny little man in a hat made of bread followed me out of a bakery and told me how bad my sense of fashion was. Then he gave me a present too. #jesters

Stylist
Jesters, jesters, jesters! Come out, come out where ever you are! Went to a great party last night…hmmm. #jesters

Just Noodles
It's my birthday on Friday night. You'd be a fool not to come! [wink] #jesters

Hancock
Who 'dem freaks running around town. R crazy. 'Nuff said. #jesters

SammyPants
I met a charming man at cafe yesterday. Played a diddy on his thumb piano for me. Then he gave me a gift, went to the washrooms and never came back. What's up with that? #jesters

Beatdrop
Cruised a sick DJ show on the weekend. One dude flyest of 'em all. Crazy beats! #jesters

Black black
@Stylist I like not knowing! #jesters

Ferrell
Some nerds on the subway decided to have a drumming jam during rush hour. Your stupid gifts didn't make up for the headache, losers! #jesters

Stylist
@ Black black Me too. But the curiosity is going to be the death of me. #jesters

Grudge
My kid is telling me that the mailman who leaves poorly drawn cartoons in our mailbox every day, is really a jester in disguise. What does that even mean? I just can't communicate with my kids anymore. #jesters

Just Noodles
@ Hancock I can see why you would think that. But crazy is relative. Crazy can be creative. Creative can be insightful. Crazy is perfectly normal for some people you know? #jesters

Smithwicks
@humphry&associate @jumpsuit Jesters are amazing. They throw surprise parties. Best entertainment in town. #jesters

I HEART JESTERS
@humphry&associate @jumpsuit @smithwicks You're lucky to get an Exclamation Box! The Jesters Rock! Follow my thread! #jesters

Humphry&Associates
@jumpsuit Look under the globe in the box. You'll see a website link. www.jestersincognito.com #jesters

Bamboohotdog
Hello I'm Japan! What you wanna jester ok? What that is? Yay!! #jesters

CHAPTER TWENTY-FIVE: UPGRADES

About six months into our underground entertainment mission, I hitched a ride with Fitch in his pizza delivery jalopy to Roger's farm on a brisk, Spring midnight. Fitch happily shared the pizza he was supposed to be delivering as we sped past the Signal Fields.

“I think that we should figure out a new system to supersede race as a way to determine commonalities between humans as a species.” Fitch said, wiping some tomato sauce from his chin.

I almost choked on my slice. “Did you just say supersede? And did you just use it in a sentence properly?”

“How about fashion? People who wear tube socks, that could be a race.”

“That’s too hard to keep track of." I pulled a fresh slice from the box. "Fashion changes. What about facial characteristics? Think about it. Black, White, Asian, Caucasian, we’re all unique in culture, but facial features are similar across cultures, too. We could categorize people by their faces.”

“Like people with no lips; that could be a race," Fitch offered, dipping his pizza into an open pocket with *I don't know what* inside it. "I’ve actually noticed that no-lippers are typically shy, but very well read.”

“The no-lippers? Really.”

“People with droopy cheeks," he continued, "they’re extroverted and usually nosey. People with under-bites are confused.”

“Ok, I'm with ya. Long earlobes are wise, bushy eyebrows are conceded, and missing teeth are daydreamers. Sounds good to me.”

“But that’s still categorizing people, which isn’t any different than race, right? The under-biters might not like the long-earlobers, and then riots will happen because of that instead.”

“Oh man, you are nuts, Fitch. I never know what’s going to come out of your mouth.”

“That’s because I have a big nose, and you have dimples. You don’t know my people,” the bass player laughed as we pulled up the zigzagged driveway.

We parked and walked across Roger's farm, silly-facing Murphy as he emptied out his Lucky van in preparation for our next big gig. Murphy decided that the van would make a great mobile changing room, so we needed to outfit it with coat hangers for costumes, with space for props and mirrors along the walls. We were transforming into an extraordinarily undercover, mobile enterprise.

Breakfast popped his head out between the giant barn doors and called me over. “Hang on to your brain, Mr. Meister! We’re kicking this company up a notch!”

Inside the barn, Breakfast’s limo was up on a makeshift hoist, and Roger’s legs stuck out from underneath it. “You are going to love this!” Breakfast said giving me his signature slap on the back. “We’re not driving cab no more bro! We’re driving Mood Mobiles!”

“Indeed,” Roger said. He turned and cranked and adjusted things under the limo as he spoke. “I’m installing Sonic Sticks for your vehicles. I figured out that if I shorten the tubing to fit in the middle console of the cab, between the driver’s and passenger's seat, and hardwire it to the audio system, you could have your customer's vibes pumping instantaneously."

"When we get our customers in the groove to their own frequencies, our tip jar is going to be pouring over!" Breakfast said, dancing out his excitement.

"A mobile music machine," I said. "That's brilliant!"

Roger came out from underneath the limo and tossed his wrench into a toolbox. Wiping the grease off his hands and onto his pants, he proceeded to blow our minds even further. "It is best for all of us if our vehicles are Channel One ready. We have so many Mood Globes in place across the city gentlemen, and we need to do everything we can to keep track of them."

I looked up at the mammoth Frequencifier. It stood like a monumental kaleidoscope above our busy work, its vibrant colours rolling into one another like the building up of electric storm clouds. I could have lost myself staring into the hundreds of harlequin vibes.

"I have engineered a Channel One 'VPS': Vibration Positioning System. It works along the same principle as GPS, wherein vibe signals can be located. It will help us to see what areas of the city we haven't covered yet. Likewise, your tomfoolery mission will be better informed as well, as you won't always need to reference me to locate and isolate one of your client's vibes."

Murphy and Fitch joined and all four of us crowded around the small, rectangular gadget Roger held in his hands. The VPS displayed the city as a grid, with dots indicating the location of mood globes. Tiny dots pulsated across the city, some in clusters, others in pairs or other random configurations. Roger explained the pattern he saw emerging.

"Instinctively, humans seem to live near complementary frequencies," he said, scrolling through the touch screen on different areas of the city. "There are pockets of reggae in the city, and pockets of heavy metal, and so on. I don't mean to say that is the exclusive music being produced, but it is the dominant vibe we're receiving."

Breakfast piped up. "You mean we could actually have the VPS in our cabs and give each other directions based on music? Like, 'Yo Vincent, turn left at the funk and go straight on that for a while. Make a quick right at Latin jazz and park it around the corner from disco!'"

We had a good laugh at how perfectly absurd that sounded. And yet, it made sense.

"That's correct," Roger replied. "You are able to set your Sonic Sticks to wide reception and you'll literally hear where you are going in conjunction to the VPS."

Not so absurd, I guess.

Roger pinched the screen and then released to zoom in on an area. "Now, let me show you something peculiar. Notice that some of the dots are silver, and some of the dots are red. After analyzing the vibes, I've come to the current supposition that some vibes are lighter, freer, and more energetic, so I've coded those vibes silver. The vibes I've received that have a notably heavier, darker and choppier sound I've coded as red."

Murphy chuckled to himself. "Good vibes and bad vibes? Is that what you're saying?"

"I don't like to categorize in terms of good and bad, but I can understand why you see it in those terms. All the vibes we've received can be placed into those two distinct categories, and if you listen to the differences you would agree that one has a good sound, and the other has an unarguably less good sound."

It was easy to see the distribution. The silver dots far out numbered the red in one area. The ratio looked to be about 10:1.

"So, for the approximate six out of the ten districts of the city you've covered, positive frequencies dominate."

"Which means the good vibes outnumber the bad vibes in most of the city," Murphy concluded with a wink at Roger.

"It would seem as such, but look at this." Roger zoomed out as far as he could on the VGS and gave us a complete bird's eye view of the city.

The pattern was unmistakable. The silver dots outnumbered the red in most areas, but the opposite was true for the rest of the city. Red dots dominated downtown, and large clusters were in the northeast, south, and, interestingly enough, in the financial district. It was amazing how those areas were almost solid red.

Fitch pointed to the northwest area of the city. "How come that area is totally dark? Hasn't anybody got globes up there yet?"

Breakfast slapped Fitch upside his bald head. "That's MogulMedia you idiot! You think Cyrus himself would just open his gates for us? Of course nobody has gone in there!"

Roger switched the screen to graph mode, which laid our a series of stats and peaked lines. "What I want to show you, aside from the distribution of the two vibes, is in some areas I've observed silver vibes overtaking red vibes. In a matter of just a few days, frequencies that were red actually changed their characteristics and emitted a different frequency, lightening up the sound."

"Of course they do! This city has had the Doldrums for years," I said. "I've seen it a million times in my cab. People get in depressed, and after a little light jesting magic, they leave with a smile on their faces. It's what we're here to do."

"Looks like the Beach Boys knew about this techno-babble all along," Murphy laughed. "Good vibrations, guys!"

The physicist looked at Murphy as if the comedian had spoken an alien language. "Yes, well, remember we can't make the frequencies, they exist in their own right. All we do is reveal them, release them. I suppose over time a person's frequency could shift from dark to light. Unfortunately however, my research is indicating that this phenomenon is only true in some areas. In the majority of the city, your so called 'bad vibes' dominate."

"Well then let's prove physics wrong and change some frequencies in this town!" I bellowed with my arms open to the quantum vault and its swirling music. "Fellow erratics, do tell, what's the next gig? Something big I hope!"

Murphy pulled his weFling from his pocket and shone an image of the Fandango Ballroom up against the barn wall. "It's big alright. A wedding reception. Four hundred guests plus. They want something 'over the top'."

"Hmm. How perfectly enticing." Turning to a fresh page in my sketchbook, I perched myself of the limo's hood and started brainstorming. "I do believe we can accommodate that request!"

CHAPTER TWENTY-SIX: QUANTUM CAB

I HEART JESTERS
The jesters are filling a void. They are igniting a forgotten spark in our city again. #partyincognito

HISTORYBUFF
For the first time since the age of ancient England, jesters are back among us! Now bring on the jousting! #partyincognito

HENLEY
A great summer solstice party that will go down in history. I've never seen masks like that before. Not offline at least. #partyincognito

BOMBAYSALAD:
Live like a King! Hire a Jester! Do it, really, you won't be disappointed! They threw the best party for my aunt's birthday. #partyincognito

BETTYSTRIPES
@I HEART JESTERS The funeral I attended this afternoon ended in an art exhibit. Unplanned. Not so sure how I feel about this. #partyincognito

BIGUP
It was supposed to be a bachelor party. Just me, the boys, and some video games. But then an orchestra showed up. I still got hammered, so it's cool. #partyincognito

A&E
The Jesters are agents of change, bringers of authentic entertainment. Their vehicle is surprise and their destination

is everywhere! #partyincognito

STREET BEAT
The Jesters Incognito are the coolest entertainment you never knew existed, and you'll never see the same jest twice. Tune in, people. The surprise is alive! #partyincognito

HISTORYBUFF
@BETTYSTRIPES What was the exhibit on? #partyincognito

EDGAR
New treats incognito tonight @8 people. You know I'm tunin' in! #partyincognito

LEMONTWIST
Ever gone bowling with a comedian? Whole. New. Game. #partyincognito

LARRYYORICK
The acting, the music, the timing, the staging. The jesters don't just sizzle, they crackle! #partyincognito

STARS&MOON
@LarryYorick It goes to show you don't need to win @TALENTTONIGHT to become famous! If you've got what it takes they'll want you! #partyincognito

BETTYSTRIPES
@HISTORYBUFF It was called 'Afterlives We'd Like to See.' #partyincognito

HELL BENT
Jesters = renegade social misfits. They are the peaceful anarchy this planet needs. Bring it. Thanks for the lovely music globe too! #partyincognito

SPATRAT

Just got back from a family reunion, with seven family members I had never heard of before. They were more entertaining than anyone I'm related to. Still not convinced tho. #partyincognito

MIDDLE EARTH
Tolkein wrote in The Silmarillion that the world was created by music. Based on the music I heard last night, I believe this now to be true. #partyincognito

ELOVE
The new boss says music makes us happier people. I agree. He lets us make playlists and play it at work. It gives us something to talk about other than the weather and how crappy TV is. #partyincognito

BEATDROP
Jesters got skillz. They improv in life. Make it look easy, 2. Gots to get me hooked up cuz them music dope yo! #partyincognito

ELOVE
He also lets us take naps and have poetry breaks instead of smoke breaks. He is a jester through gesture. #partyincognito

MUSTANG ED
The two head chefs at our restaurant love to sing. They get the customers singing. Singing makes you feel alive. They haven't said whether they're jesters, but they should be. #partyincognito

We started making money. The ideas, and the vibes, were flowing. And while we were surprising people across the city, it was us who were probably most surprised. I can't even describe how much I loved what our group was doing, and how far we had come in such a short amount of time. It felt amazing to give people something to talk about. An authentic performance, an experience they'd have for the rest of their lives. That is irreplaceable. What I loved the most is that I didn't have to worry about putting on any fake persona. The fame we received, live and anonymously, suited me just fine.

That being said, surprise entertainment is exhausting work. So, about six months after launching our business, I took a break. Laid low to recharge my batteries. I sat out on the gigs one Friday night and switched my day schedule with Murray without telling Shmitty; I was tired of the boring old day shift anyway. The tranquility in my cab had returned, thanks to Roger's wizardry. He was able to disconnect the backseat TV, eliminating all of its incessant, blathering noise. This was much needed medicine for me. But more than this, it was my first trip in my upgraded cab!

I opened the glove compartment and ran my hand along its inside seam until I found the button Roger installed. I felt a tingle of excitement when I pressed it that first time - every kid's dream to have a car with secret buttons, right? The button released a tiny jet of air between the two front seats removing its middle column, and a set of sonic sticks rested underneath, glowing a mystical purple light in the cab, powered by a series of tiny Mood Globes, installed out of view along the underside of the cab's dash, along the roof, and behind the passenger's seats.

I didn't drive a cab anymore. I drove a quantum cab.

With my arm out my cab's window, I cruised along with a long, satisfied smile painted across my face. My vibe was playing a light rhumba that night, dancing along with the early wisps of autumn air spinning short respites through the August heat.

The view from my taxi's windshield looked better than ever before, and driving through the up-market dining district, I let real life entertain me for a change. I saw line-ups in front of many restaurants with people talking and laughing with one another. Women in tight fitting fashion on power phones showing their girlfriends groovy stuff online, and the smells wandering out of the eateries spun merriment throughout the collective vibe of the whole strip.

I noticed the simple beauty in a orange candle flame flickering in a restaurant window as I drove by. I thought about how elegant a woman's hands were when she handed me a tip that night. I heard a cheesy radio commercial advertising a new brand of cereal, and instead of ragging on commercialism, I found myself humming the jingle later on that night and thinking it was kind of catchy. Programming on 'Life TV' wasn't all doom and gloom after all. Roger worried that society's bad vibes couldn't be changed? Nonsense! The Jesters were having an awesome impact on the city. We were the cure to the urban Doldrums!

Tuning into my favourite college radio station up the road I caught a greasy sounding DJ on the microphone muttering some news over the airwaves.

"Ok, like, this just in everybody. The press has reported intermittent communication breakdowns throughout the city over the last few days. They, like, don't really know what's causing it, maybe just weather problems. Nothing serious enough to worry about; it's just a blip of static here and there. But, ya, they say cell phones have been breaking up, wireless signals too, and people have reported GPS devices going all crazy and stuff. I guess the worst of all though was TV. It blacked out for an hour or more yesterday in some areas. I think that's a good thing though, because more people should be listening to my radio show more. We'll see what's going to happen when all of a sudden you can't get your precious soap operas, people! Alright, so, in the spirit of that I think we should play some Gil Scott Heron for everyone out there tonight. The Revolution Will Not Be Televised. Dig it!"

That's odd, I thought. Every time I drove by the Signal Fields on my way out to the farm, nothing looked to have changed. Probably just an irregular weather pattern. Or aliens contacting us. One of the two.

Turning a corner, my thoughts got redirected by a black SUV I spotted driving slowly, about a half a block behind me. Its polished rims reflected a snap of bright light off a reflective high rise at the bottom of the street, catching my attention.

The SUV drove slowly and kept its distance, purposely. Tinted windows. Rather sinister. My stomach dropped a bit as I tried to keep my cool.

Is this guy tailing me? The Noize undercover? Did Shmitty find out I was on night shift?

Two corners later, it was still following. I gained speed with my foot a little heavier on the pedal now, subconsciously. The SUV stepped up its clip and shortened its distance. A few quick turns and I was out of downtown and into the entertainment district. I looked back. Blaring marquee lights splattered bright colour on its polished black, still in determined pursuit of me.

There's a direct correlation between being freaked out and the speed at which you drive a car. There's also a link between fear, speed, and bowel movements. Luckily I wasn't there yet.

Whatever. I knew I had nothing to be afraid of. I was a cabbie, looking for rides. I hadn't done anything wrong. I had nothing to hide, and Shmitty could accuse me of nothing as long as I concentrated on my job. I eased up on the gas, took a few deep breaths, and ignored my pursuer.

The SUV pulled up next to me at the next red light. My bowel movement trigger almost tripped. I didn't turn my head. I pretended I didn't know the car was even there, but I felt whoever it was watching me. My heart beat loud and deep. It felt like the longest light of my life. It stayed red for an eternity, I swear. I could have sat down at one of the restaurants on the strip and enjoyed a leisurely eight course meal, used the washroom, slid down to the Den, dressed up as a maid and popped out at the Ritz Hotel and challenged the guests to a game of insults, zoomed down the chute and back up again still to see my cab parked at that light. No exaggeration whatsoever.

The car pulled up so its back passenger window was aligned with mine. Its tinted window lowered slowly. Discreetly glancing back, I saw a fat man's face shadowed in the backseat. I could barely make out his profile, as only a sliver of light illuminated one side of his sunglasses and the sagging end of his fleshy jowl. The smell of cologne and cigar caught the wind and wafted into my cab. It smelled the stench of a filthy rich man.

After a long unbroken silence, the window rose and the fat man's SUV slowly drove off into the labyrinth of city streets.

I had the feeling that whoever he was, he knew who I was.

What was I saying about anonymity?

CHAPTER TWENTY-SEVEN: LITTLE FLOATING LIGHTBULBS

No sooner had the SUV pulled out of view, I heard a familiar voice beside me in the empty cab out of the blue. "Nice ride old pal!" he exclaimed, slapping the dash.

Looking over at the passenger side, I saw Chester the Jester grinning at me wildly, his eyes alive and laughing. I shrieked and hit the gas, totally spooked. I blitzed right through the intersection and hopped up on to the sidewalk, whipping the steering wheel around, barely missing screaming pedestrians. The Sonic Sticks blared a cacophony of music.

It was a real, life-sized vision of my childhood doll sitting there, right next to me! From the rearview mirror I saw a bunch of mini, multicoloured light bulbs floating in the back seat.

Chester bopped his head to the music and looked at me, a crafty look in his eye. He casually crossed his legs and leaned up against the passenger door to look directly at me, his one arm draped over the back of the seat, and his other hanging out of the window. I heard a few of the floating light bulbs burst like balloons, doing nothing for my already compromised nerves.

"So, Mr. Meister, you're driving, right?" his voice was unnervingly familiar to me.

I swerved in my lane and took a sudden left turn to get off the main drag before I killed someone. I tried to convince myself that Chester was a hallucination. Had Roger unlocked some mysterious ability of mine to visualize my thoughts? That Vizmo Roger talked about, had he -

“No, he didn’t.” Chester said. “That’s ridiculous.”

“What the…you can hear my thoughts, too?” I asked incredulously.

“Vincent I am your thoughts!” Chester said, laughing loudly. “You’re not crazy. Officially, that is. I heard you talking to yourself and thought I might join in. Whaddya say we get some real music happening here?” Chester exclaimed, rattling my nerves again.

The Sonic Sticks picked up on my shift in vibrations. Classical piano with a faint swing rhythm section behind it. A handful of floating lightbulbs drifted into the front seat.

“I’ll ask you again, old buddy. You’re driving, right?” Chester’s voice had a fine thread of insult running through it.

“Of course I’m driving!” I shouted and let my foot off the gas finally. “What does it look like?”

“Now, now, let’s not get defensive,” Chester balked. “Perhaps the real question is not whether you are driving, but whether you know where you are driving?”

“I don’t know what you mean. I’m just driving.”

“Exactly! And therein lies your problem, Vincent! Surely you don’t think this new business of yours is going to last if you just drive in circles. Time to ‘man up’ and get some direction Mr. Jester! You're getting some attention, right? So where are you going with it?”

I couldn’t think straight, I couldn’t drive straight. I swatted a few more of the light bulb balloon away from my face like flies. This was not the time to be having a mental breakdown,

I thought, with everything going so well.

“Remember when I told you to find out what channel LifeTV was on?” Chester asked.

“Channel One.” I said, not looking at him.

“Right, and you’ve got it - I’m so proud of you!” The sarcasm dripped from his words. “But now you’re just driving around with it. Round and round. Cute little parties, blah blah blah. You need to get off autopilot if you want to do something truly amazing.”

“All I want is to be an artist full time,” I said to Chester. “I’ll never be a Green Light sell out.”

“Ah-ha! Ha, ha, ha, ha, ha!” He laughed good and hard with his head out of the window, dog-like. “Do you have any idea how stupid that sounds? Isn’t that like saying you’d prefer to write a book and not get it published?”

“Yes, exactly! Why is that so funny? A meaningful book unpublished is better than one pumped out to make money!”

“No artist’s goal is obscurity, Vincent.”

I stopped the cab at a set of lights and rolled down the windows to release the glowing light bulb balloons into the night air. Chester was right. Annoyingly right. I started this troupe with the promise to my friends it would take us somewhere; that we could be recognized artists. I told them the Jesters would be our ticket to something bigger. I knew the surprise party gimmick could only last so long.

“The hard part about being a real jester, my old friend, is that they’re smarter than most. The world is filled to the brim with idiots, but it’s impossible for you to be one, too. Instead, idiocy is a jester’s tool. Use it, you slappy happy farce of man!”

"You think that should be my goal?" I motioned to the TV in the back seat.

"Kid, I'm saying you are destined for something a little more legendary than that! Aim higher! Higher than the spittle off an eagle's beak!"

"The public already loves us, which is pretty cool I suppose. We're the biggest thing on social media, you know."

"Precise-a-mundo! If social networking existed in the 14th Century, every fool in every country would be elected king, and the kings would be at their sides playing penny whistles with their noses. You've got a lot more power than you think you do, Vincent. So, I'll ask you again. Where are you driving?"

A single blue light bulb burst just above my head. "Wherever I want," I said, my hands firmly on the wheel.

The Sonic Sticks transitioned back to funk music, and Chester vanished.

I pulled my cab over and took a deep breath. I hoped no one saw any of that. Watching people talk to themselves in cars is one thing…

Not wanting to forget what had just happened, I pulled my sketchbook out of my Omnibag and wrote down as much as I could remember. Next to my scribblings I sketched a light bulb floating out of my cab and into the air.

My doll was trying to tell me something, I realized.

I also realized how disturbing that sounded.

Brushing my hair into a twirled coif, I spun the car around and headed out of Roxy. I needed to have a word with Roger about this not-so-temporary experimental after-effect.

CHAPTER TWENTY-EIGHT: BUTTBOOK EXCERPTS I

John Tuntington via Buttbook I saw a guard outside the art museum who would suddenly start dancing to really wicked beats, and then go back to being stoic guard guy. The closer I got, I couldn't hear where the music was coming from. After I passed him though he busted a groove again, all goofy-like ~ I'm pretty sure he had a system inside his hat. Then he gave everyone these nifty boxes with exclamation marks on them. Sweet!

Pierce Analton via Buttbook: The jesters are all on drugs. I've been to one of the jester parties and the music was very unsettling. My therapist bills have gone up since being subjected to their absurdity. Not knowing when these lunatics are going to jump out from next does nothing for my chronic paranoia. No thank you, don't mind if I don't.

Schneider Wiener via ButtBook: Best movie night ever. My buddies and me went to check out a flick a couple months ago and then, like, some guys jumped up from their seats and ran the aisles giving out clickers with a b c d on them. Do you know what it was? A choose your own adventure flick man! Like the movie stopped and we voted what we wanted the characters to do next…majority vote won and it was totally awesome. They spliced some whack flicks together and made a whole new plot. It was jokes! You guys should make your own! And we got these cool gift boxes for going too but I lost mine and it's gone now boo.

CHAPTER TWENTY-NINE: ON THE SUBJECT OF SOUND

Roger was sitting in the main room of his farmhouse, relaxing on his sofa and watching a short-circuit broadcast of the Frequencifier on his glass orb when I swung by for a visit after the wedding party. I wasn't far off in my guessing that the device looked like a lava lamp after all.

"Let's hear the new mix, Roger!" I said, joining the scientist on the sofa.

We music aficionados watched and listened to the vibes together; neither of us saying a word. Majestic colours burned energy brighter and more vivacious now, with spiraling greens dancing with lightning bolt gold, as if brewing in the eye of a storm. Bursts of blue energy intermittently exploded deep inside the energy cloud, and a pulsating brass thread darted like a meteor in space between it all. Roger turned up the volume on the remote, and the Frequencifier illuminated a little. He turned another dial to isolate one frequency that glowed in response to his tweaking, a brown bubble that floated a little brighter than the rest, and then it's vibe played out over the speaker system. A string quartet was faintly audible; playful arpeggios and simple repeated melodies.

"That's my vibe," Roger said, leaning forward, as if examining a specimen. "At least that's my vibe today. It was calypso about a month ago. Incredible, isn't it?"

"Calypso? You gotta be kidding me! You?"

"Indeed. I spent a year in the Caribbean. I guess it rubbed off on my sub-atomic particles. I now believe our vibes change with our experiences, our moods, and the other vibes from people around us. Our frequencies could very well morph from one month to the next."

"That's what thought. A situation of vibration transformation." I smiled at my rhyming nonsensicality.

We enjoyed more moments of musical meditation together; the sounds washing over us were total bliss.

"Every time I come here, all I think about is how new musical styles are born," I said, my eyes closed deep in thought. "And everything you just said makes a lot of sense. Musicians jam and their unique vibes blend until they find a sound that sticks. Then they listen to each other's energies, which meld and morph and then who knows what crazy style comes out of it. Like calypso. That is one cool beat! One night in Trinidad some groovy players just let their vibes connect to make a whole new sound."

Again, we sat without speaking. Syncopated rhythms dotted melodies that branched out in different directions, distant woodwinds played long legato lines and the sound of a didgeridoo made the room feel like it was breathing in its earthy tones.

"My thoughts are less mystical," Roger said. "I like to think of the individual sound waves, which are similar to water currents. Ripples in the water, wherein water is air. Sound moves like that, and the airwaves, or sound vibrations, push against receptors we've all got built in."

"Ears are microphones for the brain," I said. "Easy enough."

"Indeed. And then I think about what's happening when two people or more hear the same sound. When you hit a key on a piano, its string vibrates, but it also creates a sympathetic vibration to the strings around it too. So, if two people are hearing the same music, it is a synchronistic neurological connection that is unique to those people, at that moment, and the energy they're feeling through the music is also resonating through their bodies back and forth to one another; and then, all of a sudden there's another level of unspoken connection. Like a closed electric circuit, really, and that's the same thing that's happening in our bodies. In essence, vibes are the closest things humans have to a sixth sense."

I stared at Roger incredulously. "Yes. In essence. Anyway. Roger, I came to talk to you about the experiment you did on me. You said that visual hallucination I had would go away, right?"

"Indeed I did."

"Well it didn't. In fact, I just had another one, while wide awake for crying out loud. And driving!"

"Yes, well, that's nothing to worry about. The Vizmo side-effects are only temporary." Roger stood up and attached his blue goggles to his face while walking toward the door.

"That's what you said last time! I gotta tell you, having one while driving across the city is not a good time. My pants were soaked afterwards!"

Roger paused in the doorway. "Curious. Well, wait until I tell you about what else is happening across the city. The distortion that's been on the news is more widespread than I thought, and it seems to be pointing back to my research. Perhaps we should all carry an extra pair of trousers around with us."

CHAPTER THIRTY: A WEDDING SINKER

"Friends and family of the newlyweds," I announced in my cheesiest radio voice behind the MC podium at the front of the ballroom. "It has been decreed by the king and queen of the evening, your precious bride and charming groom, that the first at any table to spill or drop food must join me at the front of the hall to be subject to some on-the-spot roasting by yours truly!"

My cover at the Fandango Ballroom wedding reception was as the groom's cousin. I very much enjoyed sporting a handlebar moustache for the role, as well as the blonde ponytail LaRose managed to sculpt my hair into. I don't care what you think, but dressing in disguise in public is the best fun going. Try it sometime. You'll like it.

The four hundred guests were digging into appetizers, drinks and schmoozing conversations at the top of wedding reception, and I kept the mood mellow and intimate, as if everyone were a customer in the back of my cab. No small feat for our biggest party yet! The Mood Globes were positioned under the long fabric of every chair, and DJ Breakfast had the music under control like a pro, spinning vibes already streaming from the vault: a tasty combo of East Indian Tabla rhythms and indie rock melodies.

"We've got one!" one of the guests stood up at his table and shouted to me. "This woman just dropped an escargot down her cleavage!"

"Bring the lucky lady up here!" I shouted back and got the crowd to cheer her on.

"What's your name, ma'am?" I asked. She was a cute blonde woman in her early thirties.

"Veronica," she said. Her face blushed brighter than a red rose.

"I understand you dropped an escargot down your top, is that right?" She nodded and covered her cheeks. "Well, I say it's a good thing he's a snail, 'cuz at least he's got an excuse for taking his sweet time getting out of there!" PING!

There, with the laughter and applause, the music changed slightly; now with a hint of reggae. The brilliance of human energy will never cease to amaze me.

"You wouldn't mind if I drew your portrait while we talked a bit, would you Veronica?" I pulled out an easel and drawing paper from behind my podium and placed it on the other side from where she stood. "Tell me about yourself. Where do you live, what do you do for a living, what do you like?"

"Well, I live…"

I interrupted. "A life of sin? To party? For your Thursday night reality TV show fix?" PING!

"In a house," she said, rolling her eyes at me. "But yeah, I like reality TV, too."

"Tell me you're joking," I said. I started drawing a caricature of Veronica in front of a wide screen television. "How boring is your life? Do you know how much cheaper it is to buy a cup of coffee and just make up plots about the people you see? I bet you have a 4-D TV, too. Am I right?"

"Oh my god, how did you know?" She played it up. I think she liked the limelight.

"You got sucked into that gimmick too? Yeah, that's right, because petty, rumoring, fake television reality trash actors are so much *more* convincing in 4-D. I would rather be a dead snail in your cleavage than have to be subjected to that crap!" PING!

I finished the picture with a few more strokes and lifted it up for her and the guests to see. It was a picture of Veronica at home, watching her TV and both her and the snail peeking out of her blouse were wearing the 4-D glasses. PING! PING! PING! PING! PING! PING! PING! PING! PING!

Breakfast walked over from his decks and whispered in my ear. "Dude, you're killing tonight! Keep it up, the vibes are pumping!"

"Agreed! Spectacular energy in here!" I fixed my bow-tie and noticed Breakfast's hands shook a little as he racked up his next musical selection.

"What's up Brekky? Everything cool?"

He wiped a few lines of sweat from his brow. "Yeah…just…a little nervous about tonight. Are you sure we should do this?"

I looked my friend straight in his eyes. "It's happening, Mr. Deejay. We came up with the idea together, remember? Everyone voted on it at the last Moot."

"I know, I know. I'm just second-guessing it now. This is a way bigger step than just having a deejay on stage."

Our first full on performance. No more hiding behind personas and fake moustaches. The jesters all agreed that if we were going to really break the Green Light law together, we were going to do it in style. After much debate and many exhilarating hours, we rehearsed an extravaganza for end of the evening that would take the partygoers by storm.

"Look Brekky, I have my own trepidation, I admit." I smiled at the bride and groom, who gave me the thumbs up. "But think of the rush a live performance will give us. You know the jesters want more than just invisible entertaining. We want to perform! To ignite! To surprise! And so do you. Nobody else in the city is doing anything even remotely as cool as we are. If we want to stay on top, we need to bump it up a notch. Now's the time!"

Breakfast put his headphones back on and powered up the Sonic Sticks under his Digidecks. "Alright Mr. Meister, I'm with you. I just hope those masks Fizzlestick made stay on good and tight, and there ain't no Noize out tonight."

I knew my friend would be ok. Shaky nerves didn't always mean uncertainty. They reminded us we were breaking past the ordinary, being true to our principles as jesters. Which meant dressing up in ridiculous costumes and acting like idiots. Bah!

Getting back into character, I sat at the head table to enjoy the main course with the wedding party. We had plenty of time until our culminating performance, so I could afford a little break. I panned across the room. What a thrilling sight! Members of our crew sat at every table, sparking mood globes with ease, and warming up the crowd. I had lost count of how many of us were working the wedding.

There was FlipFlop and The-Man-Whose-Scarf-Was-Too-Long, posing as Swedish immigrant cousins of the bride. Their schtick was to ask people for the meanings of common words, while nosing through their Swedish to English dictionary and perpetually getting the translation wrong. Classic translation humour. Such an easy way to insult someone and get away with it. Across from them was Humdinger, challenging people to guess the popular melody he hummed.

At table nine was Humperdink, a jester who thrived on holding conversation by only speaking in questions, and managed to do so every time one of the guests at his table was about to take a drink. At the same table sat Crumb, who kept a photo journal of everything he owned and loved sharing it with whoever happened to be nearby, and Harrington, a master impressionist of people no one had ever heard of before.

There was Schmoozle at the best friend table, regaling them about her most recent trip to Europe. She bluntly told them all how terribly bad their tastes in fashion were, and the reactions were priceless. She then went around the table and predicted how successful everyone was based on how ugly they were. Some people laughed, some people didn't, but Schmoozle was a jester who didn't care. She got people's energy up to 980,000 mega-hertz with ease.

The many other jesters working the floor that night looked to be in fine form. One of our jesters at a table in the far corner of the ballroom stood out above many of the others on account of his flamboyant gesturing whilst talking at a guest. At least I thought he was one of our jesters. I squinted a little harder. There were so many of us now, it could have been that I just hadn't met him. I joined Breakfast at his decks to see if he knew his name.

"Which one?" he asked, flipping one headphone off his ear.

"The guy with the red shirt and the silver tie," I said. "I don't think I know him."

"Ya, I saw Murphy jesting that guy earlier."

"Really? He's not one of ours?"

"I don't think so. Man, look at him! You can smell his cheesiness from here. The guy looks like he was torn right out of a fashion Vidzine."

Breakfast called it. Slightly unshaven, gold necklace, greased back hair. He talked with over exaggerated gestures and waved his hands around like a car salesman trying make a deal.

“He’s not jesting her,” I said. “He’s playing her.”

“Yeah, dude. And she’s eating up everything he’s serving. Look. Nodding her head and laughing at every cue. He’s definitely not one of ours."

“He could be a guest. I’ll check with the groom. Remember where’s he’s at, Breakfast, I want to hear the Mood Globe under his seat at the end of the night.”

The music changed again to an upbeat roots rock reggae blend sporting a horn line with attitude. I took up the microphone for another roasting.

CHAPTER THIRTY-ONE: OF MASKS AND MEN

Fitch and Fizzlestick waited outside in the Lucky van parked around the back of the building. Much more than just a moving van now, it had become a mobile green room with a make up area and changing rooms, and costume trunks replete with various outfits, wigs, masks and props. From the street, no one was the wiser; it was still a simple moving van. Little did passersby realize that there were a ragtag group of entertainers inside on a simple mission of spreading spontaneous absurdity across the city.

I swung the van doors open and hopped inside. The Dingleberry Brothers and LaRose were right behind me.

"No time to waste boys and girls," I said, grabbing my motley off a hanger. "They're slopping up their chocolate mousses, it's time to lay on the show-stopper!"

Fizzlestick rummaged though a trunk of his handmade masks, each adorned with colourful features and unique to the face of its jester. "Do we have enough bells on each of the hats? They'll be coming in to change any minute!" The little jester moved about the van in a flurry of preparations.

"There are six bells on each hat," Fitch replied. He stashed a particularly shiny one into a pocket as he worked. "And I've tested them all, every single bell lights up in the same colour as the costume."

"Jesters don't wear costumes," Fizzlestick said with condescension in his voice. "They wear motleys."

"Really? They have a special name?" Fitch hung one of the motleys up and admired the work Fizzlestick had put into making it. Gold and black diamonds patterned the arms and legs, with a velvet green torso and matching hat. All sixty motleys hanging in the van were different.

"Motley means mixture," Fizzlestick said. "Like a mixture of stuff that doesn't belong together. You've never heard the expression 'motley crew?'"

"No, but I've heard the band."

"Speaking of which, where is the jazz band? Shouldn't they tuning up or something?" LaRose asked as she slipped into the changing room.

"In the kitchen," Fizzlestick said. "There isn't enough space in here for all their instruments. Luckily waiters and musicians dress pretty much the same. Fitch, your double bass is in the kitchen, isn't it?"

Fitch froze. He frantically padded his coat as if he would find his bass in one of his pockets. He smiled sheepishly at us and then ran out the van doors to join the other musicians. Twisty, Tumbleweed, Sonar and a few other jesters hopped in the van as Fitch was leaving, and a steady stream of jesters arrived in tow.

"There's not a lot of time to get changed, everybody," I said. Fizzlestick was on his stool fixing my hat while I spoke. He connected the wires running through the seams to activate the blinking lights. "Get in your motley, put on your masks, and then get into the bathroom and wait for Murphy's cue. The others will be coming up from the Den by now, too."

"If we wait too long to start," Fizzlestick added, "the guests might notice that we've all suspiciously excused ourselves to the washroom at the same time. Which would be odd."

LaRose stepped out of the changing room wearing a motley 'dress' cut just above the knee, easily the sexiest jester in any century. Her tarnish brass mask matched her hair with elegance. “You look like one of your drawings,” she said to me with a smile.

She was right. It was as if one of my doodles had been pulled out of my sketchbooks and shaken to life, standing there in the mirror in front of me. An honest to goodness jester was there staring back at me. Fizzlestick had fashioned a bright red mask with an extra long nose, and arched eyebrows, which gave it a mysterious expression; half jovial, half devious. The costume felt amazing, invigorating, like superheroes must feel when donning disguises for the very first time, or how Zeus felt when he first lifted the weight of his thunderbolt. I slowly let the realization wash over me that I was ready, finally, to unveil myself, my brainchild, to the public. Not only that, but we were bringing the group to the next level, too. I needed to have faith in Chester’s words.

“I think this is the persona I’m born to play,” I said to LaRose, smugly. “Funny that it’s taken me this long to do it.”

CHAPTER THIRTY-TWO: MAXIMUM HYPE

Twenty minutes later, the waiters cleared the dessert plates. Murphy, positioned in the AV room on the second floor, killed the lights and shone a spotlight on Breakfast who had some funky backbeats playing. Fitch wheeled his bass into the spotlight next to Breakfast, plugged in, and the two of them started jamming. While the guests had their eyes on them, the waiters grabbed their instruments and quietly took their places along the walls of the ballroom. A trumpet player, an oboist, some guitars and a marimba...

As they started the opening few bars of Fitch's original tune, 'The Pocket Rocket', Murphy put the spotlight on the our musicians who joined in, backed by drums and a tuba. And just as the introduction gave way to the main melody, Murphy turned on all the house lights. Like a blast of energy, the Jesters' took their cue and entered the ballroom running!

"Ladies and gentlemen, the Jesters Incognito!" I hollered, running in with the group. The guests had no idea what hit them!

We launched into our choreographed musical dance number, with over forty jesters filling the ballroom in full motley splendour. The jesters with expertise in dance and acrobatics took centre stage and busted out their best moves to the music. At the start of the next tune, Breakfast and the band brought the music down a little and steadied the energy. This was Murphy's cue to start the bride and groom's slideshow. At the same time, a group of jesters assembled at the front of the ballroom and acted out the photos that were projected, mimicking and mocking as they saw fit. We had the crowd enthralled; those who weren't clapping cheered and laughed and soaked up every detail of our performance.

Roger had plenty of his research, and we had plenty of ours. Surprise entertainment gets the best results, every time.

"We are honoured to entertain you this evening, folks! As long as no one has had a heart attack, and everyone goes home smiling, then we have done our job! Please give your hosts this evening a round of applause as they take centre stage for their first dance as a married couple."

The lights dimmed again and LaRose brought the party back down into a more intimate setting and sang a groovy, slower R&B number. Beautiful. Our illuminated jester caps glowed exquisitely for their moment.

Our biggest show to date was a complete success! Following the applause, DJ Breakfast packed the dance floor within seconds. He gave me the thumbs up from across the room, and could see the relief on his face. We knew that people would be grooving to his fresh beats well into the night. We even prepared an Exclamation Box for each and every mesmerized guest, matching the Mood Globes to the names on the seats, so their very own vibe was packaged and ready for them on their way out.

Murphy met me at the back of the ballroom as I headed back out to the van to get changed. "Congratulations, Mr. Meister, what a spectacular party! We're going to have more gigs than we can handle after this whopper!"

I couldn't stop myself from smiling. When we turned the corner and headed down the hallway toward the exit doors, we saw the suspicious red shirt and silver tie guy talking to another guest outside of the washrooms.

"You see this guy, Vince?" Murphy whispered as we walked toward him. "He's the kind of guy you do everything you can to avoid at a party. He is *annoying*. He kept butting into people's conversations about some new watch he bought or something."

"He's not on the guest list, and he's not one of ours. Did you give him a good jest?"

"I don't think he needs one. I bet that guy's energy is pushing a million mega-hertz, easily. At one point, though, I did manage to derail him with a story about a grandfather's clock in our family that actually had a real yellow cuckoo bird that came out on every hour, and…"

"Great, great, I'm sure it was hilarious. I need to know who this guy is."

With his Exclamation Box in hand, the mystery man gyrated his body around in order to describe something that was obviously very exciting. He looked slimier than a car salesman. I couldn't have been more right in fact. When he spotted Murphy and me he immediately excused himself from his conversation and was on us in a flash.

"Great job out there guys," he said, shaking our hands aggressively. "Really, awesome party. The name's Max. Max Hype."

"Thanks very much," I said. He lifted his eyebrows up and down, and winked at us as he spoke, all the while chewing on a wad of gum. I could hear a faint music coming from inside Max Hype's Exclamation Box.

He was pop music.

"Look, I don't want to bother you guys for too long, you should be out there celebrating a great show, but I just wanted to know what the catch is. Where's the payoff here?"

"What do you mean, exactly, by 'the catch'? I don't follow."

"Sales. The payoff. What are you selling here?"

“We’re not selling anything,” I said, offended by the question. "We're transmitting human expression, old school styles."

“Yeah. We're retro new mod hipster types. Why? What are you selling?” Murphy asked.

“What? Are you kidding? You are way too good not to be milking these people for something. This crowd loved you jester guys! I’d love to get you working for us. We could make a lot of money together!” Max pressed a button on his power phone and flashed us his digital business card. It read:

Media Men: We Tell You What You Need.

Murphy and I stared at the guy for a second, looked at each other and proceeded to walk away. “We’re tired, Max. Thanks, but no thanks. Email us your sales pitch and we’ll be sure to delete it.”

He stepped in front of us, blocking us from leaving. “Hang on a second, you don’t even know what we do. We’re not that different, you know.” I heard his pop vibe shift into a minor chord. Max gyrated around so much as he spoke, his collar opened just wide enough to reveal a Green Light hanging around his gold chain. It’s hypnotic emerald glimmer unmistakable. Such a coveted passport, like king’s gold. The key to fame and infinite opportunity. It hung from a simple black band with a single, royal green ruby. And I’m afraid to say it stole my breath away.

“I’m a live advertiser,” Max continued, tucking the Green Light inside his shirt. “There’s a lot of us, actually. We’re called Media Men. I’m a real-life, walking, talking billboard that brings the product to the people. Doesn’t that sound, like, awesome?”

“So you crash other people’s parties to…sell things?” I asked, dubiously.

“Yeah, you got it! Everything I’ve got on me right now is top quality merchandise; my Gucci belt, my Armani shirt, the earrings, my aftershave, my watch…I get paid to make this stuff look good! And it’s all cutting edge stuff too! Like, take my new phone, for example.” Max waved his phone in our faces.

“Looks dead to me,” Murphy quipped. “Not a convincing pitch yet.”

The Media Man’s expression dropped. “Weird. I’m not getting any reception.” Tucking it back in his back pocket, Max returned to cheesy mode without missing a beat. “Anyway, this model hasn’t even been released in stores yet, so it’s going to catch people’s eyes. You got me? They see it on the street before they see it on television or the Web, and when they do ~ boom! They got to have it! That chick you saw back there? Do you know where’s she’s going in the morning? To the mall baby! She likes what Daddy’s wearing!” He pointed to his gaudy gold watch and flashed me a well-rehearsed smile.

I was utterly disgusted. “You think we’re similar? You are no jester, Max. You are the anti-jester.”

“Ha! Anti-jester! That’s awesome. You guys are quick!” Murphy and I shot each other another skeptical glance. “And guys, with talent like you got? Think about it. The great thing is after you do this Media Man marketing gig for a while, you get some time on television shows, or music videos or whatever. It’s the key to hitting the MogulMedia mainstream!”

An earthquake of anger erupted inside me. Max Hype represented everything I hated about MogulMedia. Human advertisers making their way up the entertainment ladder by selling their soul to unsuspecting people? Selling people stuff without them knowing is called brainwashing, not art! If I could have puked into a bag and handed it to him right there, I would have.

"I don't know how you managed to get onto this guest list pal, but if you ever show your face at another one of our shows, the only thing you'll be famous for is your picture on the Web with all your fancy merchandise shoved up at least four of your major orifices. You are a talentless slug, and will never understand what it means to truly entertain."

I stormed outside, enraged.

Max's final words killed my vibe completely.

"It's a very dangerous game you and your friends are playing! You may have blocked out the Noize, but you can't block out the king. We found you once, and we'll find you again!"

CHAPTER THIRTY-THREE: POP GOES THE CHASE

The door slammed against the outside wall of the Fandango Ballroom as I stormed out of the building, echoing a thud through the shadowed alleyway. Murphy was a few steps behind me.

"Is he gone?" I asked.

"Yeah. How hilarious was that doofus, eh?"

"Hilarious?" I shouted. "How did this creep know to crash our party? How long do you think he's been crashing our parties? Who does he think he is using the jesters as a platform for selling his crap?"

"Whoa, Vincent, easy buddy. I agree the guy's got a bad vibe, but…"

"Look, Murphy. There's some cheesy Green Light schmuck creeping our scene! He knows where our parties are going to be."

"So? I don't see that as such a bad thing. We could sell some stuff and make even more money! Bling bling!"

"What? It's a very bad thing! It's Jester Code #5. We do not advertise, it's the lowest form of entertainment. This is our brainchild right? *We* are the live entertainment for this city, no one else."

It started to rain. Big, thick drops fell from the sky with seconds between them, running the paint on my face. An idea percolated.

“I’m going to try to follow this guy,” I said. “I can’t believe he works for MogulMedia. I won’t believe it.”

“How are you going to do that?”

“I’ll follow his vibe!” I shouted. “Catch up with you guys at Cosmos later.”

I left Murphy in the alleyway and ran back towards my cab in the rain, now heavier. I didn’t bother changing out of my costume, even though the make-up ran down my face with each falling droplet. It would make for a more dramatic chase, I thought.

The VPS in my cab illuminated with the turn of my ignition and the Sonic Sticks gave off a purple glow as I reversed out of my parking spot and headed on to the main street. I headed straight in an alternative rock neighbourhood.

All I needed to do is catch his vibe on the VPS and then follow him. Sadly, I wasn’t the fastest quantum energy isolator in the galaxy. I set the VPS to bird’s satellite-view and flipped the setting to sonar tracking. Red dots, bad, silver dots, good, I thought. On sonar mode, green dots appeared on the screen. What were they? I pressed a green dot nearby and heard a kind of harmonica duet transmission, and the time 9:28 popped up. 9:31, an acoustic guitar signal came through, 9:37 a saxophone ballad and some dance music. *Roger, you’re a genius,* I whispered. Green dots are new vibes!

The Sonic Sticks blasted some heavy metal and then quickly switched to a deep soul area of the city as I left the lower Eastside. Every stoplight emitted its own unique music. Delta blues, Italian opera, Franco-country, Indie folk, Motown…I needed to isolate a cheesy pop signal. Particularly cheesy. It should be pretty fresh in the tank, I thought, and not far from the Fandango Ballroom. I kept my eye on the VPS for more little green dots; it was amazing to see the city’s vibes illuminated in denser clusters than they had been even a week prior.

The green dot appeared on the VPS screen moments later, heading north along the Ridge. It's area was dense in Rock Opera, oddly enough. The vibe blinked slowly as it made its way north. I was only a few blocks away. Past Rumba, past Neo-classical metal, and in no time I turned the corner to put me right behind Mr. Media Man and his cheesy music.

Wrong. Wrong car, wrong vibe. I was following a Jeep with two college-aged girls whooping it up to House Music, not Pop at all. One of the girls caught a glimpse of me out of the corner of her eye and belted out screams at the top of her lungs. Understandably; the sight of a jester driving a cab with a mask and melted make up would look downright disturbing in the middle of the night.

"Come on!" I shouted at the VPS as I pulled into an empty parking lot. "I don't have time for a music lesson. Think Lady Gag Gag, or that kid, Pluto Saturn." Not all pop music is bad of course, but most of it makes me want to bury myself alive. It's as mainstream as music can get, the fast food of audio art.

Then, the welcome glow of a green dot registered Pop at 9:55. In the west end, near Borges Park. I spotted the new target on the VPS and took off after it. Straight up Barbershop Quartets for three blocks, left and through Jazz drumming under the steal turnpike as fast as a wimplecherry. And we all know how fast they are. I gripped the steering wheel, hoping I'd run right into Pop.

Our musical guidance system worked like a charm. Just less than five minutes later I picked up the worst kind of Top 40 bottled music on the Sonic Sticks. I stood corrected. This guy's vibe was another whole level of cheese. I was tailing a black SUV. It's vanity license plate read MEDIAKING gave it away. It was the same SUV that had tailed me before. There was only one possible place where the SUV was headed. This time it was my turn to tail.

The SUV drove a quick clip toward the heart of downtown, passed through China Town, a string quartet, and over the midtown bridge. We drove beyond the Financial District, a cold, haunting choir of soprano voices, and over to the opposite side of the city.

I parked the cab and killed the lights about two blocks back from the Ridge, the elevated crest upon which MogulMedia dynasty stood. The SUV looked ant-sized in comparison, and gained easy entry into the entertainment Mecca's property; through the heavily guarded, locked gates, and up the mile-long driveway toward the central tower.

"Holy crap," I said out loud, freaking out as I took off back through the city streets. "MogulMedia *was* actually following *me*? How the hell did they know how to find us?"

CHAPTER THIRTY-FOUR: A RED HERRING

"I bet they want in on your business," a voice came to me.

It wasn't my voice, but Chester the Jester's again.

I spun my head around, but couldn't see him anywhere. The shock of his voice, however, forced my hands to freeze on the wheel, and without registering the snowflakes falling on my windshield, I let my cab hop up onto the grass of a park directly ahead of me, running smack into the side of an igloo.

It was not winter. There should not have been snow in that neighbourhood park.

Chester appeared in the distance, ice-fishing on a frozen river, and wearing a flamboyantly designed purple fur coat. He stood with his arms wide open to greet me, clearly ready for another jest.

"It would seem by the freckle on your cherry chin wart my good man, you've caught the king's attention!"

"Yeah," I said. I turned off the cab and watched the colours drain out of the Sonic Sticks before I stepped outside. "Him and his advertising minions."

Chester whipped his fishing rod up and a slippery red herring landed onto the snow, flopping about. "So the bait's a little cold. Who cares? It means you've got something he wants! MogulMedia is following you! And I don't mean on Critter!"

"Are you kidding? I'd never stoop to subversive advertising like that. It would kill my vibe completely. Isn't MogulMedia bigger than that?"

"That's a stupid question," the doll guffawed, blowing into his cupped hands to keep warm. Walking closer I saw an open guitar case leaned up against the igloo with a candle burning inside. "You've created a perfect market for advertising. Eisenberg wants in on the buzz you've got online. He probably feels threatened. Next question please, a little harder if you don't mind, I'm already bored."

"Wow, I forgot how much of a jerk you can be."

"If you can't take a jest, get out of the cab! Whose line is that again?"

"Look, Chester. If Media Men have to brainwash people into buying the latest junk to score careers in industry, I want nothing to do with MogulMedia. I'm willing to do some bigger shows, but I don't want to sell out my ideas. It'll sacrifice the quality of our work. Unlike a lot of the idiots in the industry, I'm more interested in expression over money and fame."

Chester was curled up in a ball on the snow, pretending to sleep. One eye opened just a crack to see if I was done talking, then he stretched his legs and put his hands behind his head to look up at me, upside down. "Whose to say a person needs to use every rung of a ladder to get to the top? I'd give anything to be one of those idiots if I were you."

We looked at each other. The irony of that statement was not lost on either one of us.

"You think I should sell stuff for Cyrus Eisenberg?"

Chester tossed his fishing rod into the hole in the ice, then cartwheeled over to the igloo. "I think you're at a crossroads old buddy, parked at the junction of Fame and Integrity Avenue. A long time ago you decided to just stayed parked, but now you've got a second chance to choose. So dream big! Go play the fame game!" My imaginary friend took the candle and climbed into the igloo, the shadow of his three-pronged shadow dancing black against the snow's soft white. He then carved a quick window in the side of the structure and offered me the red herring, now barbecued. I accepted.

"We're talking life at the press of a button," he continued. "Jet planes instead of walking. Respect just because of the face you've got stretched across your skull. And money, buddy. M-o-n-e-y. Remember. An intelligent idiot has more power than his king."

Chester and his arctic environment melted away, sinking into the grass like water into a drainpipe. Leaving me in the park with a stick in my hands, not a baked fish at all. These hallucinations had to stop happening, I thought. In public, at least.

I mulled over Chester's advice back in the cab, driving block after block without the Sonic Sticks on. I felt bigger somehow, like the cab wasn't quite my size anymore. I cruised by my apartment building and saw my Mood Globe still swirling brightly in the window. The original vibe. The energy that started it all, one might say. Maybe Chester was right. Didn't it deserve to get some more attention than the rest?

At a red light, I took my hat off and shook my hair out into a bedraggled mop, and quickly jotted down all that Chester had said in my sketchbook. A large red fish adorned the centre of the page.

The Sonic Sticks activated suddenly, and transitioned into a yellow hue that sent out punk music in the night as some guy I didn't see hopped in the back of my cab. He sported a faux-hawk hair do and smelled of cigarettes. "Hey pal, hook me up with a lift to the…" He stopped mid sentence when he looked up and saw me in my jester get-up, melted make-up, mask and all. "Woa. Ok, two things. I want to know where you download that sick music, and where you party!"

Then, with a mighty, guttural heave, he puked all over the backseat.

CHAPTER THIRTY-FIVE: DISTORTION

Another busy Saturday midnight at Cosmos. A few booths down from our regular spot, Nelly waited on a group of high school students zoned out on their tablets, and the construction crew fixing the nebular dishes across town just walked in to pick up coffees for the rest of their site. The other tables were peppered with the usual crowd looking to gobble some grease during the graveyard shift. Quiet ghosts of Roxy's nightlife. It felt good to stream some ordinary life with the Blabbermouths after such an unbelievable turn of events.

"I feel like I don't have any pants on," Murphy whined.

Fitch looked under the table. "You're totally wearing pants." He then pulled out two cans of whipping cream from his pockets and filled his mouth. He offered Breakfast and me a shot, we politely declined.

"I mean I feel naked," Murphy said, fidgeting with the salt and pepper. "I'm speaking metaphorically. I'm dying without my weFling! It's like I lost my best friend. Or a limb, even."

"No technology to call your own?" Breakfast faked sympathy. "You mustn't feel human. When did that happen?"

"Last week, probably; while I was working the crowd as a voodoo medicine man on the bus. No joke, I've lost a part of my digital DNA."

Breakfast waved Nelly over to their booth, feigning interest in Murphy's problem with a half nod. The Trip Hop music he was listening to on his headphones was loud enough for everyone in Cosmos to hear.

Nelly strolled over, making her silly face at us with a heaping plates of food on her tray. “There it is boys. Two baskets of mini-muffins on the house, a chocolate milkshake for Mr. Meister, and the Moot midnight special breakfast. Enjoy.”

“Oh, and get my friend here a weFling, would ya, Nelly?” Breakfast said, looking over at Murphy to see if he succeeded in razzing him. “Or anything digital. The poor guy needs a fix.”

Finishing up my drawing of the red fish and igloo experience, my gaze was slowly pulled over to the newscast on the corner TV. The screen was fuzzy, unclear with intermittent static, but it cleared long enough to show footage of a person shooting a gun at a laptop from short range.

“Hey Nelly, turn that up would ya?” I shouted after her. The newscaster's voice sounded believably worried.

The disturbances in our communication services are worsening with each day, it seems. All kinds of signals across the city are jamming more frequently. Officials say this is an unexplainable turn of events.

“Yeah man, my phone keeps cutting out on me!” one of the high school kids shouted from the booth behind us. “It’s pissing me off!”

“I think it’s a conspiracy myself,” Nelly suggested. “Every afternoon this week when I went to watch my soaps, it was static. But my boyfriend didn’t have no problem watching his stupid crime shows. What are the chances?”

Along with the growing phone calls of complaints, the press has joined in and started blaming poor service from MogulMedia, the nation’s media provider. Any press is good press? Not in this case! The owner of MogulMedia, Cyrus Eisenberg, allegedly lost his cool completely when

people started breaking contracts with his company and looking for other providers. He was not available for comment, but his PR team assures us that MogulMedia is not to blame. City engineers hope to have the problem resolved as soon as possible.

"Uh-oh." I closed my sketchbook and stared at my friends. "Roger gave me the low down on the whole distortion thing."

"And?" Murphy asked.

"It's the Mood Globes. They're interfering with other frequencies. Some gobble-d-gook about human energy, no Channel One ever used before or something, dynamics of sound waves, it's over my head."

"And your hair." Fitch said with a mouthful of mini-muffins.

"I thought the distortion was nothing serious," Breakfast said. "Just a blip of static here and there."

"Technically this isn't really our fault," I said. "People aren't reading the directions that are clearly written. No globes too close to electronics. We even drew them a picture."

"But I feel these people's pain," Murphy said, holding his chest dramatically. "I've gone without my weFling for a day and I'm telling you, I'm really messed up, guys. I've got serious digital withdraw!"

"Screw sympathy," I said, popping a handful of mini-muffins in my mouth and munching away. "I don't feel the least bit bad about it. Why should I? MogulMedia can afford to take a hit for once. Besides, people obsess over their gadgets. No offence, Murph."

Fitch spat out his muffins and knocked the maple syrup onto Breakfast's lap, pointing at the TV. "It's our logo!"

Smack dab in the middle of the screen was our exclamation mark logo. For the first time since our inception, heck, for the first time in our careers, we had made the news on a mainstream network.

And just before we sign off tonight, here's some news on the lighter side of life. It seems like you don't have to buy a ticket to England, or a time machine even, to meet a jester these days. That's right, the Jesters Incognito are for hire. They host parties for every occasion, and people are just raving about their music. Their signature style is surprise entertainment, which means the best show in town could be anywhere, at anytime! Social networking sites, the press, radio stations, you name it; it seems that the Jesters Incognito are on everyone's lips lately. Expect a jester to pop out whenever you least expect him to, and brighten your life in a way you never knew you needed. And I have to say, what with our recent issues with unreliable reception on TVs and wireless devices, perhaps good old-fashioned live entertainment is a decent solution!

"Here here! We made the news!" Fitch said, taking out his whipping cream cans again and topping our coffees off.

"Fitch! Keep your voice down you fool!" Breakfast said, mopping up the syrup from his lap. "I swear I'm gonna murder your ass and bury you in a giant pocket."

"Well, that's pretty cool," Murphy laughed. "We made the news and we didn't have to get naked or shoot anybody or nothing."

Looking outside the window of the rain-streaked window pane, I saw a much different picture than I normally did. In the foreground sat dark, empty, broken storefronts at street level, and in the background stood the magnificent image of corporate perfection, MogulMedia. Before, the MogulMedia Tri-Towers looked like a smear on the city skyline, an impenetrable juggernaut of power. But looking at the towers that night, after my conversation with Chester, they looked like a beacon of opportunity. I found myself considering MogulMedia as an actual leverage point for the jesters, and remarkably, the idea didn't make me feel sick.

"I choose to embrace this very fortuitous turn of events, my friends, because we can use it to our advantage."

"For what, Vince?" Breakfast said, turning up the volume on his Acid Jazz/Hip Hop mix. "Think it's time to audition for a Green Light?"

"What? Never! Only someone your height would make such a Sasquatch-sized insult!"

"Then spit it out, frizz-head. What are you talking about?"

"Well, I've got wicked news and crappy news of my own," I said as we got up and headed for the washroom together. "The crappy news is that our operation has been infiltrated."

"It's the clowns, isn't it?" Breakfast threw his loose change on the table in disgust. "One of our members is recruiting for clown school? I'm telling you, those clowns are plotting to take us down!"

"Breakfast, relax," Murphy said. "Vincent's talking about that guy at the reception tonight. The guy in the red shirt? I met him, too. Guy didn't walk. He slithered."

"His name is Max Hype. What a name. Max works for MogulMedia and calls himself a Media Man. He 'advertises' stuff, and he's been using our shows to get at our audiences. Can you believe that?"

Fitch pocketed some sugar packets as we made our way downstairs. "Did we actually initiate him into the foolhood?"

"No, that's the weird thing. He just slips into our shows and poses as a jester. He knows, somehow, where we're going to be."

"Are you telling me that *the* Cyrus Eisenberg needs to sell stuff?" Breakfast asked. "Like what stuff? The man is CEO of the biggest media company in the country."

The four us stood in the men's washroom in a huddle. Murphy checked under the stalls to make sure no one else was inside.

"If I had the Web right now, I could show you that MogulMedia is not just a media provider. Far from it. It's the brand behind the brand. Cyrus Eisenberg directly and indirectly owns a lot of things in the market. MogulMedia makes fruit cups and cigarettes, cereal and baby wipes – they are a commercial superpower, and not that many people know that. The frozen pizza you buy at the supermarket is called Easy Rise, but if you read the fine print, which is impossible to do, you'll see the MM logo. Look closely. The tissue paper has the MM, the toothpaste has the MM, the furniture, the vehicles, the real estate; you name it! Everyone knows the man has to have it all, no matter what."

"I heard it's a whole other city inside," Fitch said. "Some of the other pizza drivers call it the Fatican. Like the Vatican, but for fat cats."

"Ok. Enough of the bad vibes. What's the wicked news, Vince?" Breakfast asked.

"We have the king's attention," I said. "And it's pissing him off. We're trashing his frequencies, the Mood Globes are screwing up his business, and we're more popular with the people than he is right now."

Breakfast gave me 'the look.' The one that could put out fires. It could melt ice, and bring women to their knees. If he did it for long enough, he could probably get you to admit to committing a crime you didn't do. "Look man, I happen to know that Eisenberg is a serious mafia boss, Vincent. The other guys working favours for Shmitty tell me Cyrus is crazy dangerous, too. I don't see how that fits into the 'wicked news' category."

"Cyrus Eisenberg is an idiot," I snarked. "Have we all forgotten how he forced us into getting crappy jobs because he made it impossible for us to make a living at what we love to do? And how he sucked all the spirit out of this city and farmed it and packaged it and killed the very notion of pure creativity? Hell, he killed our fellow jesters! That man is the biggest boolittle to ever soil the earth! And we all know how big that is."

"I agree with Vincent," Murphy said. "We have MogulMedia's audience, and we're in control for once. It's a good thing; we should use it to our advantage."

I opened the handicapped stall and we all stepped inside. "Right, and the less people are glued to any one of their many rectangular screens, the more people will come to our shows."

"Let's fry the signals!" Murphy laughed as he pulled the receipt from his pants pocket, ready to shout the password into the toilet. "Word of mouth worked once, and it'll work again!"

"So what do we do now?" Breakfast asked.

"We do exactly the thing that annoys the king!" I proclaimed. "We take the attention away from him!"

CHAPTER THIRTY-SIX: BUTTBOOK EXCERPTS II

Wilma Tarotown via Buttbook
Why is everyone all hot on jesters? You aren't good enough for mainstream and that's why you just force your art on people. If you didn't shove it in our faces we certainly wouldn't choose to give any of you idiots the time of day. Screw you from all of us who are Green Light artists and play by the rules.

Watercolour Dood via Buttbook What's up jesters? I don't know if you are even on here, but I had to write to let you know that you guys have brought colour to my life. Thank you for giving us this space. It's important for you to hear because, you know, a bunch of us were talking and we're not sure you even realize how much of an impact it's had on us. And other people too.

You know I used to get up for work everyday and my chest was heavy; I was a lifeless mass punching the clock. And now that I've allowed myself to pick up the water colours and start painting again, knowing that the customers at work dig my stuff, the sky is bluer, food is tastier, and I can breathe again! So simple: I paint between five to ten postcard-sized illos everyday. After a customer makes a purchase, I just staple the painting to the receipt and wish them a good day. Sure it was awkward at first, and some customers (often the rushed types) take a look at my art, shoot me glance, and then just slap it back to me on the counter in refusal and walk off. That's cool. The good thing is that the majority of people like the drawings, they get the 'kind gesture' idea, thank me and leave with a smile on their face. Some of the regulars actually give me new ideas, and then the my stuff becomes a spontaneous collaborative art piece between two people and in my opinion that's more profound than any conversation I've ever had. You know? Well. Of course you do.

Dick Farthington via Buttbook I don't know. The Jesters are kind of too surreal for me. I can't decide if I like them or not. I was at a Stag and Doe and they hired the Jester's DJ. The music was good. It so bang on though, song after song, and like, the weird thing was that the tunes all sounded so familiar. But they weren't famous or popular; I hadn't heard them before. And then half way through the party an art show slowly set up and we were all checking out this woman's art…and then we were given frames to attach to our heads and being told that we were all works of art. Ya. Right. I just wanted to get drunk. But. I guess some people are into that.

Aurthur Wilhemson via Buttbook During a recent psychology lecture at York University I decided to spice things up a little bit and hire two jesters to lecture along side with me. The notion of lecturing to the students (with three-heads as one I should add) to convey multiple personality disorder worked rather effectively, if I don't say so myself. Or, myselfs ~ ha! The jesters were magnificent; they finished my sentences in character and for the first time in 23 years I felt my students were alive and captivated with the lesson. There is more potential in your merry band of morons than you think!

Oliver Young via Buttbook So, check this out. I'm using the washroom at the bus station downtown, just standing at the urinals like whatever, when all of a sudden three dudes come out of the handicapped stall. Dressed up like nut jobs with crazy hats and loud pants. What the *%$^ is going on?

BOO.

CHAPTER THIRTY-SEVEN: THE UGLY DUCKSEDOS

The best part of Halloween, if it's even possible to choose just one thing, is the glorious cold, slimy feeling when scooping out the pulp from the inside of a pumpkin. Scaring people and losing yourself in costumed personas is great too, and we, the illustrious Jesters Incognito, clearly don't need Halloween to enjoy that. But I really love how pumpkin brains will squeeze between your fists and flop onto the floor, how they will sit in a vomit-like pile of lobotomy surrender, the guts of a carver's willingness to create art out of something as common place as a gourd. That's a beautiful thing. Carving a pumpkin kicks off the fun to follow; it's a rite of passage that slows time down and gears up the imagination for the rest of the night. Halloween, in truth, is the one night a year when everyone gets in touch with his or her inner jester.

With so many good vibes flowing through the city, there were a lot of people up for just that.

Word spread that we were hosting our Halloween party at the Skyrocket, the city's most high-profile club in the heart of Chinatown. This would explain why the guests were so willing to go along with our gimmick. For the first time in history, as far as we knew, we threw a costume party that did not require a costume. That's right, the nightclub owners advertised it as the world's first plain-clothes costume party; instead, we provided the costumes for the guests! People received a number at the door and were ushered into the costume shop we had set up in the basement. Face paint, masks, hats, fake teeth, wigs, believable blood, full body costumes and silly props – we had it all. The guests were up for whatever costume we gave them, and we were even savvy enough to put their clothes in their exclamation 'loot' boxes to take home when they left.

The jesters working the basement costume shop worked amazingly well under pressure, and yet still created a few of my favorite Halloween costumes of all time. Along with the excellent robots, wizards, and giant pieces of fruit, we also produced a Gorilla Accountant, Russian Gymnast (sporting an exaggerated endowment), The Work of Art (a guy with a frame around his head, his face pushed through a cheap oil painting), Shitler (a quick Hitler wig, the Nazi uniform, and a fake piece of poo attached as a moustache), and Thorilla (Thor on the top, Godzilla at the back). It amazed me how well each partygoer got into the character of their costume too; proof yet again that society wants to be creative, and they want to be part of the show, but they just need a little bit of collective oddity to get them going!

Roger outdid himself. He created novelty exclamation mark necklaces that we gave to every guest that night. Fitch named them Vibe Vials, miniature Mood Globes that glowed the colour of people's vibes, just like the Frequencifier itself. Tiny little frequencies were emitted by the Vibe Vials, amplified by the Sonic Sticks decorating the ceilings and the floors of the club, and then zapped through Breakfast' quantum deck. That way people didn't have to be near a Mood Globe for us to get their energy. I loved them because they were our very own Green Lights, giving us permission to perform however we liked. Roger really outdid himself.

The Blabbermouths and myself dressed as ducks in tuxedos, or, Ducksedoes, and served as the hosts to each of the nightclub's five floors. Our bright yellow duck masks and crisp bowties were very stylish, and our sleek black headsets gave us that extra dollop of coolness. We kept in contact via headset, and for the first hour or two everything was fine.

The Skyrocket was a five-venue show under one roof. From the fifth floor, the very top of the club, Breakfast spun vibes straight from the excitement of the people standing in line to get in, and those frequencies alone were broadcasting some serious beats. Boom! Right off the bat we had some crazy hip-hop, funk, Latin mixes pumping out of the speakers and the place was grooving in no time.

Each floor showcased our jesterly performance art, to keep the party spicy. One floor was decked out with large, white cloth canvasses for some of the graffiti artist jesters in our group. Break-dancers brought down the house on another floor, where I saw a polka-dotted Dracula type-dude going head-to-head with a crocodile. Back-flips and the worm and everything! The third floor had a green screen set up for people to film improvised scenes off the cuff. The fourth floor was particularly cool, because every Jester brought in instruments and we set up a soundproof jam studio. Hand drums, cellos, nose flutes, penny whistles, synthesizers, we had it all.

Around 11 p.m., when the club was really pumping, we noticed a significant change in the vibe of the whole party. It was like the music shifted slightly minor. There was a new, subtle tension on the airwaves, slightly ominous, with a hint of suspense.

"Did anybody else hear that?" Breakfast radioed to us.

"Affirmative. I feel it, too," Murphy said.

"The Sonic Sticks are really dark," Fitch said. "Good though, like blood red for Halloween!"

I felt nothing good. Although slightly muffled through the fabric of my duck mask, I could hear a distant, high-pitched static buzzing my ear. It sounded like the feedback you hear when a guitar is plugged in too close to its amp.

A gargoyle bumped into me with a smile, its teeth yellowy-white against its stone-grey make-up. "My girlfriend and I are totally eavesdropping on you, I hope that's cool." A Pez dispenser waved politely next to him.

"I appreciate the heads up," I laughed. "I'm totally ambivalent towards your eavesdropping on me."

"We heard you talking about the music tonight and we are, like, such huge Jesters fans. We've seen almost sixty of their shows. Wasn't tonight totally sick?"

"Fully and completely sick," I agreed. *Sixty shows?* I thought to myself. *Have we done that many already?*

"We drove from out West for this show. Never seen a five venue gig before though!"

"Out West, like, Corkville?"

"No, man! I'm talking way out West! Where they're building the new fibre optic pipeline. Took us five days to get here, and that's straight driving!"

The noise rose a few decibels and distortion pierced my ears again. The metal clammer made it impossible for me to know if they heard the man correctly.

"But you said you've been to sixty shows!" I shouted above the noise. "How is that possible?"

The gargoyle laughed, helping the Pez up again. "Believe me, we're not those lame-os who watch them on the Web, that's for sure. Nope, after tonight we'll have seen every show in every city across the country."

"Different chapters across the country…" my voice trailed off in disbelief.

"You bet! Can you believe this is our first time to Roxy? It's a huge rush to be in the birthplace of it all, I tell ya!" The gargoyle gave his Pez girlfriend a huge hug and lifted her off the ground. “Five venue gig, sweetie! Can you believe it? Five venue gig!”

Tumbleweed, our oldest jester, dressed as a bowl of cherries that night, shuffled over to me. “Do you think a guy as old as me gives a damn about cologne?” he shouted over the music.

“I don’t know. But if someone is hitting on you, Tumbleweed, you should go for it!”

“There’s two women over there that just talked my ear off about some cologne I should try,” he said. I could see the confusion on his face. “Check’em out. Their costumes are totally popping all my cherries.”

Sure enough, two cute girls at the bar were waving flirtatiously at Tumbleweed from across the room. One was dressed as Little Bo Peep, and the other as Little Red Riding Hood. I spotted right away that both of them had dark Vibe Vials hanging around their necks along with their glowing Green Lights. Another sting of static pierced my ears, causing me to wince.

My radar went off. Pushing cologne at a party?

Max had come to crash our party again.

CHAPTER THIRTY-EIGHT: CLOWNS VERSUS JESTERS

I scanned the room and connected more Green Lights. A she-devil talking another guest up about the skirt she was wearing. A Martian playing the latest video game device with another couple college aged kids. There were six or seven Media Men on the first floor alone.

Almost on cue I spotted Max Hype standing right among a group of suckers too stupid not to see through his shtick. It was his fake laugh that gave him away. That, and he had dressed as an evil clown. He came with a posse of evil clowns by his side, and the crowd couldn't get enough of him. There were at least twenty people crowded around them, taking pictures and ooohing and ahhhing, undoubtedly thinking he was a legit jester. I knew something like this was bound to happen eventually.

My blood pressure launched. Who did these chumps think they were? This was not their turf, and I wasn't about to let them get away with advertising their junk at our guests again.

Max walked up to the bar, threw down some cash and sauntered right up to me like he owned the party. I have to give it to him though; his clown costume was pretty cool. His blindingly white face paint in the black lighting was mesmerizing, his eyebrows in pointed arches and his smile a deep purple grin off to one side of his face. The designer label silver and black hat, and the actual silver and purple costume he wore looked to have tiny diamonds sewn directly into the fabric. Looking closer, I could see the Vibe Vials around his neck was darker than the rest ~ black and grey, lifeless almost.

"Oh, hey, you ***are*** here!" he said, peeking inside my bill, shining his whitened teeth in my face. "Vincent, right?

Vincent Meistersinger? I didn't catch your name the last time we met." He put out his hand. I did not shake it. I collected myself and motioned him to speak to me in the corner to avoid a scene.

"I want you the hell out of here!" I demanded, poking his chest.

"Whoa, chill out Vince. I'm not here to kill your vibe or anything. But I am glad to bump into you again. First of all, props on the jester schtick pal! People love it!" Max winked, as though he 'got' what the jesters were all about.

"You're dressed like a clown, not a jester. And you are killing the vibe here, and you're pushing the limit of my patience."

Max turned his red rubber nose on tightly. "Mr. Eisenberg is very familiar with you, Vincent. He sent me to come and pick you up tonight. He's a little disappointed to hear you declined our earlier offer of employment."

"What?" I thought I misheard him as the distortion grew louder in my ears.

"He doesn't just want to meet you pal, he wants to hire you. How crazy is that, right? Cyrus doesn't do that for just anybody. So here's what's going to happen. We'll work your party for a bit, and then I'll get the limos pulled around for us."

Max barely looked at me as he was saying all of this. He spotted someone he was talking to earlier and waved his power phone in the air. "Here's a tip: it's all about making a solid first impression as a 'Media Man', Vince. You'll see." Max started to text, but stopped with a puzzled look on his face. "Weird, there's no reception in this place." He then looked up at me with suspicion in his eyes, "You wouldn't know anything about that, would you pal?"

The distortion. They had made the connection. The evil clowns around Max were bodybuilder big, I noticed then, leading me to believe his 'offer' to take me to Cyrus wasn't negotiable. Breakfast was right, the king was dangerous and most likely not too pleased about our Mood Globes. I needed to be quick, and blunt.

"Max, let Mr. Eisenberg know I'm not for hire, but thank him for considering me anyway. I mean, I've barely had time to polish up the resume, you know?"

Max laughed and gave me the thumbs up. Condescending putz. "Vincent, that's great! Just great! That's exactly the energy Eisenberg likes!" Max emphasized the word 'energy' and winked at me again. How much had they found out?

I felt a formidable shift in the very core of my kind-hearted, pacifist self. Normally in confrontation, I could deflect the tension with a quick impression, or a serve some sarcasm to cool my jets. But not with this Max moron. Who was he to come to one of my parties and boss me around like this? And had he no idea how much more intelligent jesters are than clowns?

"Don't let the duck mask fool you, pal, I'm not joking here." I stepped closer into the clowns face. "You can tell Eisenberg I think MogulMedia manufactures stupidity, that he hasn't produced an ounce of worthwhile art in decades. So I want you, your disposable friends, and your 'best-before' merchandise out of here. If you aren't out by midnight, I'll call the police on disturbance of the peace."

"Sure, sure, Vince, whatever you say! Oh hey, good news by the way. All my Media Man hard work paid off! I'm going to be in a new movie with that guy…you know, what's his face…well, whatever, it doesn't matter. But I'm on my way up buddy ~ you could be too! Look, don't make a mistake here Vince. When Cyrus wants to talk, I'd take him up on his offer."

The only reason I didn't spit in his face was because I knew I wouldn't be able to aim out of the tiny slit on my duck mask. Instead, my body reacted on its own before I was actually able to control it. I jumped up on the bar stool and started beating Max's face like a pound of ground beef.

It's all a blur now, but I must have done a decent number on Max rather quickly, because I remember laying down five or six final punches and making it halfway up the stairs before I looked back over my shoulder to see him drop to the floor, unconscious.

The music was deafening. A warped mixture of heavy metal and grunge slowed the party into a sinister state. The Sonic Sticks carried dense browns and dark red energy, thick but far from vibrant.

Breakfast took his headphones off when I ran up and shouted in his ear. I could barely hear my own voice.

"Media Men! Eisenberg sent them!" I said, breathing heavily from climbing the five flights. "They know about the distortion!"

Breakfast shot me a look of honest to goodness fear. "That's heavy mafia, dude!" he screamed back. "We need to get the hell out of here!"

He was right. Many stories have been told about companies who didn't want to 'collaborate' with MogulMedia. Artists whose careers were squashed because of lack of compliance with Eisenberg's terms. You suddenly didn't hear much from them anymore.

We left his decks and hopped off the stage, through the door leading down the back stairwell of the club. The growing distortion grew louder, buzzing the pumping music, now a muffled vibration through the concrete walls. Scrambling down the steps, I tried my best to keep up to Breakfasts long legs, skipping four or five stairs at a time. He had had a taste of sketchy encounters with Shmitty, and knew to be more scared than me because of it.

"I punched one of them," I admitted as we ran.

Breakfast stopped and turned to stare at me with his eyes bugging out. "Tell me you are joking."

"I just snapped. Involuntarily. I don't think he's dead or anything, but I don't think he'll be on the big screen anytime soon."

We spotted an evil clown two flights beneath us, running up the staircase and stopping on each floor to scan the rooms for me. Breakfast motioned for us to slip through the door nearest to us. We raced across the cinematic floor in fast forward, hiding behind a video screen playing old black and white horrors. This proved to be a very stupid idea. Our shadows appeared, big, black, and bold - a obvious giveaway to the two evil clowns who spotted us on the other side of the screen.

We lunged back behind the screen and then did our best to merge with the dancing partygoers in the next room. Ripping his duck mask off, Breakfast pulled a cowboy hat off of one person and a beard off of someone else, much to their displeasure. "Take yours off!" he shouted to me. I tried to yank it off, but it was stuck. I was a sitting duck.

Through two more rooms the long way around the rest of the floor, we made our way down the last three flights of the club, and party whirred into a frantic, dizzying blur around me.

"Mr. Meister, come in," Murphy radioed came through now very heavy static.

"What is it? I can barely hear you!"

"The Noize just showed up," he shouted.

"Are you kidding me?"

"Negative! This is not a joke. There's about twenty cruisers outside!"

"VincenttheNoizearehere whatshouldIdo?Theygotshieldsand gunsandeverything!" Fitch's voice blared in our ears.

I couldn't process the information, it was just too much to take in. And the distortion had reached its loudest level, forcing me to hold my ears as we ran down the stairs, a sharp crescendo of ear-shattering dissonance. When we reached ground floor, I heard about five or six sharp bursts of exploding glass, popping like overheated light bulbs.

Breakfast and I dashed out the back kitchen doors and toward the Lucky van parked down the adjacent alleyway. Low and behold, there was Max, leaning on the now infamous black SUV with his posse. It looked like a warped dream I'd describe to my therapist. Six more clowns burst through the door and joined Max, who stepped forward, ripping his Vibe Vial off his neck.

"It's a good thing I see my plastic surgeon every Monday, otherwise I'd be really angry about this. What it'll be, Vincent? Are you coming peacefully, or does this have to hurt?"

"What, right now? Little late, don't you think? I didn't pack my pyjamas. Maybe one of you guys can sell me a pair?"

The back door flew open and a gaggle more of our jester crew poured out. Tumbleweed as a bowl of cherries, Woozle as a living room lamp, Chump as a boxing mime, Glib as the

Vampire State Building, Humdinger looking pretty pale as a zombie with a noose around his neck, five knives in his back and a bucket of acid on his foot, the Dingleberry Brothers as a hamburger and fries, Pig'N'Jig as a shark, followed by Turnstylz as some kind of troll wearing a bakers hat…I was glad they showed up. A fight was brewing. We needed the backup.

Allow me a moment to pause and explain the historical significance of this impending clash.

You see, clowns will tell you they came first, but jesters existed two centuries earlier. Without us, clowns would have never existed. In 1651, a travelling salesman by the name of Jakobius Klown happened upon a Moot in the woods one night, where he befriended a band of court jesters and town fools. They had been exiled from the kingdom after King Charles was overthrown in the Civil War. His country was a mess, and his council then decided jesters didn't serve a purpose in the court any longer. Jakobius, the trickiest of bootlicking salesmen, sold the sad crew his new product, imported straight from Japan, called 'permanent make-up'. He told them it would give them a new face. Lift their spirits. The jesters took great delight in Mr. Klown's make up that night, painting their faces and acting crazier, goofier than ever. They acted sad with giant frowns, and moronic with apple red noses. That Moot began the legendary divide. Klown saw opportunity, became their manager, promising them great fame and reward. Soon, those buffoons wore over-sized shoes and pants, entertaining kids with the stupidest shows. Falling down and pulling handkerchiefs out of their pockets. It took no intelligence to paint a face white and pretend to cry. And yet the public loved them. Thus, by shooting for cheap laughs and parlour tricks, the clowns ruined the jester tradition forevermore. And we'll never forgive them.

This long-awaited showdown was worthy of a photo, actually. A full moon with a sound track of muted, twisted reggae music pulsating through the walls of the club and a hundred jack o' lanterns glowing orange spotlight on two ancient enemies ready to scrap. The tension in the alleyway rose higher. Breakfast, all seven feet of the music man, stood tall to cast a lofty shadow across the alleyway. He bellowed with his fist in the air: "Jesters versus clowns! Fiiiiiight!"

Absurdity and buffoonery rushed in.

In a blur I saw a polka-dotted clown cock his fist and wallop our living room lamp; Woozle's light bulbs shattered on the pavement as his face got beaten in. A baggy pantsed red-noser threw his weight at Glib, toppling the Vampire State Building. Glib tried to bite his neck, but the clown's collar was just too puffy.

Turnstylz had a brazen fighting spirit. He hurled a giant, troll sized loaf of bread at his attackers, slamming a sneering white-face to the ground. Marbles flew out from the clown's pockets, scattering everywhere. Two more, a hobo and a slapsticker, tripped over the marbles, giving me a chance to pull two floppy shoes off of their feet and slap them both across the face repeatedly.

While a midget clown clawed at Breakfast's legs, the deejay pulled out his Soundbomber and aimed the speaker dish directly in the middle of the clown battalion, and pressed play. Bright blaring Glam rock loudly showered the back alley way, hurling the clowns onto their asses. Breakfast effortlessly pulled the midget off his leg and whipped him against the wall.

I'll never forget the nightmarish expressions on the clown faces, half-smiling, half-psychotic in delight of a good old fashioned bang up. We were sunk. A lanky, psychotic-looking clown stabbed Pin'N'Jig with a knife while the french-fry Dingleberry brother received the pile driver into a dumpster by a tubby striped bozo. The sounds of the mayhem inside the Skyrocket club rose above our clash. Megaphone orders blasted past the swinging saxophone as a weightlifter clown sporting a joke cigar and tiny top hat broke both of Humdinger's legs in a figure-four leg lock. Tumbleweed lost consciousness before any clown could get to him, it turns out that Chump is a terrible boxer, and without a chance to react, I received three lightening swift upper cuts from Max himself, knocking me out.

The clowns threw me in the trunk of their SUV.

"Just leave the rest," I heard Max say before I passed out. "He's the only one Cyrus wants."

CHAPTER THIRTY-NINE: MOGULMEDIA

My head was spinning when I came to. My brain was thunderstorm jello.

I pulled myself up to look out of the rear window of the SUV to orient myself, and my hand throbbed as I supported the weight of my body. A painful reminder of the pummeling I made on Max's stupid clown's face. I couldn't have been out for very long, because we were just passing The Ridge and pulling into the gates of MogulMedia. Into the grip of the king's fist. The blaring distortion in my ears had subsided, thankfully, but I feared I was headed for some different kind of feedback.

We pulled into the lower level parking, lit up in Hollywood spot lighting that sent daggers into my eyes, magnifying my headache. A clown pulled me out of the back, dragged me up a red carpet where two attractive women waited. The women wore slinky, shimmering dresses and introduced themselves as Cinnamon and Butterscotch. I introduced myself as plain vanilla ice cream. They giggled as they each took one of my arms and lead me into the elevator. If only all kidnappings were so sexy.

A third woman waited inside the elevator, her back to us while she spoke in hushed tones on her power phone. She was tall red liquorices: long red hair and even longer, alluring legs. Looking over her shoulder at me, she ended her call and introduced herself.

"Mr. Meistersinger, it is a sincere pleasure to meet you. My name is Samantha Devlin." She spoke with an over-affected drama in her voice, as though she was a woman of the theatre and had rehearsed her lines beforehand. "I am Mr.

Eisenberg's Vice-President and Executive Promoter; both Mr. Eisenberg and I have been dying to meet you. Welcome to MogulMedia."

"Thanks very much, Samantha," I said, shaking her hand. "It's a pleasure to have been beaten up, dragged here, and forced to make your acquaintance."

"Max told us about your charming sense of humour. It's good. Cyrus likes to be entertained. You can take your duck mask off now. Mr. Eisenberg might find it a bit disrespectful."

"Right, thanks," I said. I had totally forgotten I still had it on. "I may need some help though." Much tugging and grunting followed, and finally the disguise popped off my head. "I never thought I'd find myself in an elevator trying to tug a duck mask off my head. I'm a poor man's Batman, what can I say?'

Ms. Devlin took a slow, sexy step forward and caressed my cheek with the back of her hand. "What a pleasant surprise to see the mystery man is handsome. This is a face we can work with, isn't it girls?" She snapped a quick picture of me with her phone and sized me up in pixels. "But we'll need to do something about that hair."

I should have been more scared in retrospect. Cyrus Eisenberg 'sent' for me after all. Surprisingly, I wasn't. The rumours of his ruthlessness didn't concern me, somehow - I felt prepared for this surprise. Chester told me Eisenberg could be a key player in furthering my plot, which I believed, all I needed to find out was if he meant ending it.

Ms. Devlin's transparent show biz personality aside, it was a breathtaking ride up to the top of world. The stupendous view of the city through the elevator's glass walls made me feel like I was being lifted up above reality, up into space, beyond the trivialities of regular life. That's why the rich like to live up high, right? They want to separate themselves from the squalor below? My little life was so trivial suddenly, so small. It didn't even seem possible that my tiny dump of a basement apartment even existed as I watched the sparkling city shrink beneath me. Life below zoomed way out, and I could barely make out the spotlights from the Skyrocket nightclub. Thoughts turned to my friends left in the mess below…hope they got back into the Den safely, I thought.

The elevator doors opened at the penthouse floor. Up on every wall, in pure gold lettering was the MogulMedia logo against the gleaming silver and black decorated foyer. The walls shimmered silver and black, and a dozen or so AutoPeeps stood along a shelf at the top of the wall, as if soldiers on guard. Butterscotch and Cinnamon stayed in the elevator and Ms. Devlin escorted me across the foyer and down a short hallway where we stopped in front of the two biggest, most grandiose doors I had ever seen. Replete with jewels and rubies the size of my head embedded in its intricate wooden carvings, the doors were at least fifteen-feet tall and screamed majesty.

"Impressive, isn't it?" Ms. Devlin said. "It's a gift from the Sultan of Egypt."

"Yeah, it's incredible. No need to keep the receipt on that one. What was the gift for?"

"The Sultan wanted to thank Mr. Eisenberg for buying his country."

That was about the point when I got a little scared. Just a touch. I was dangerously out of my league.

king cyrus

CHAPTER FORTY: INTO AN ILLUSION

The doors swung wide revealing a palatial penthouse, decorated entirely stark white. The marble floors, the leather furniture, and solid ivory columns reaching thirty feet to the ceiling. All of it, white like the empty pages of a sketchbook. Only one immense, pitch-black wall above a slate fireplace shimmered a subtle metallic as Ms. Devlin and I stepped inside. The fire burned white flames rather than red, yet the air was frigid like a meat locker. Not one item looked out of place. The sterling silver place settings just so, the satin white pillows on the horseshoe couch well fluffed. Impeccably clean with a mirror shine.

What disoriented me most was the vacuum of utter silence enshrouding the penthouse. It felt like I had entered an illusion.

And there, across the room, was the most powerful man in media. King Cyrus Eisenberg sat in a very quintessential 'mogul' stance atop a tall throne that hovered noiselessly about a foot off the floor. He was fatter than I expected. Stuffed into a charcoal grey and black pinstriped suit, complete with white suspenders and matching, oversized cufflinks. His jowls sagged below his chin, and his eyes looked as if they'd been awake for nights on end. Matching the rest of the room, his white hair rested in a perfect poof atop his head.

He took a long look at me in my beaten up tuxedo, his expression neutral, unreadable. After a pregnant silence, he finally motioned with a slow nod for me to come and join him by the window. Another dismissive wave ushered Ms. Devlin out of the room.

I stood beside the king. He said nothing, still scrutinizing me from head to toe. Slowly, the king turned his hover throne to face the window, looking across Roxy City as if surveying his kingdom. He made no eye contact as he spoke.

"So you're the jester, are you?" His voice had a rather thick dollop of German in it.

"That's right," I said simply.

Cyrus leaned over the side of his throne and put his arm around me. His fat arm, thick sausage fingers and musky smelling cologne would surely become etched in my sensory memory forever.

"I want you to look down below at my city, little jester man. The city is mine. The people below are mine. They are nothing more than mice in a very lucrative science experiment."

An interesting introduction, I'll give him that. I guess that made me a lab rat being released from its labyrinth. Did this mean the experiment was over? Was I going to be enlightened, to have a glimpse how the maze-makers live?

"And you are no different. You dance and joke and sing for these people because when you were a little boy, you watched the famous celebrities dancing and singing and joking on the TV, you wanted to be just like them, didn't you?"

"I like to think of it as genetics myself, but…"

"Bite your tongue!" The king's voice boomed across his sterile penthouse like a cannon. "Media creates everybody, there are no exceptions! You are a product of the collective consciousness, brought to you by yours truly, MogulMedia. Suggesting otherwise makes me very displeased."

The ‘s’ on his ‘displeased’ slipped snake-like between his teeth. How dare I contradict the king! I could see his hand trembling atop his armrest. The silence following my having corrected the king was deafening. This was it, I thought. He was going to torture me. Any moment he’d order some giant bodyguard to ‘show me the balcony.’

He turned away from the window, and hovered his throne toward the bar. Cyrus pressed a button on a bracelet he wore to remotely access one of the hundred flasks from a towering glass vending machine embedded in the wall. The flasks ranged from white on the bottom rack, all the way up through subtle shades of grey to the black flasks on the top rack. With a barely audible ‘woosh’, one popped out of the machine, a mid-grey selection, and Cyrus poured himself a stiff something-or-other into a clear, slim vial. The liquid gave off a gaseous smoke, as though the drink was on fire.

The king ordered me to have a seat on the enormous leather horseshoe sofa in the middle of the penthouse, in front of the fireplace.

“Cinnamon! Butterscotch! Enter!” he shouted suddenly, and immediately the giant doors opened with Cinnamon carrying a Mood Globe, and Butterscotch carrying an Exclamation Box. They placed the two on the table in front of us.

“Start the Jacuzzi for us, ladies. And fix Mr. Meistersinger a drink, would you? What do you drink?”

I tried to ignore the single, trembling bead of sweat running down my back. “I could go for a milkshake, if that’s no too much to ask?”

Eisenberg’s raised eyebrow toward me. “Put some Plazma in it,” he ordered, and the models left the room as quickly as they had come in.

Of course, the Plazma! The rumours were true. The only person I knew who ever got hooked on Plazma was Tiddlywinks. He ended up developing speech patterns out of gibberish, while constantly trying to find glasses to improve his hindsight.

Cyrus picked up the Mood Globe and turned it over in his hands. I could hear a dark muffled tremolo from where I sat, but that was it; black with spots of red and without any motion to it at all. His eyebrows arched at a wrinkled point above his bulbous nose as he held the globe in front of me, and tapped the glass aggressively. "The way I see it, you are responsible for all my problems."

With a flick of the metal band on his wrist, the metallic wall uncloaked itself to be the biggest monitor I had ever seen. Two more flicks of the king's fat arm, and the wall flipped to one of MogulMedia's million television channels. A dog wearing a ballet skirt and a laser beam on its head showed on screen, dancing and shooting cats with each spin. Quality entertainment. Cyrus then lifted the globe closer to it with an outstretched arm. Sure enough the image went static. Any doubt I had before of him not knowing the effect the globes were having on the city's reception immediately extinguished.

"I'm not as angry as I was." Eisenberg looked over at me and grinned. "The week before though, I was so angry I actually killed two of my staff."

"Are you kidding?" I asked, that tiny bubble of fear in my stomach again.

"Perhaps," he said. The king chuckled to himself. This guy was extremely unstable, as his reputation foretold. I've always steered away from death jokes, myself. Especially when they could be true.

Cyrus set the globe down and took another gulp of his smoldering Plazma. "Now that we know your little toys are causing the disturbance, we can fix the glitch. The bad press upset me more than the technical issue itself. People are saying mainstream media is dead. They say the Jesters are better than any entertainment available today. It upsets me to think that a bunch of amateurs can get this kind of press."

Thankfully Butterscotch brought me my chocolate milkshake and broke the tension in the room. It was as tall as my arm is long, and I took a slow sip to help cool me down. Eisenberg shot more Plazma down his throat and slammed the vial down on the bar in one very well practiced motion; he turned toward me a brighter expression on his face. He wasn't smiling, but the shot had visibly improved his mood.

"My Parropotamus is trying to say hello to you."

There was no way of guessing that that was going to come of his mouth next. There was also no way of knowing what he meant by 'Parropotamus' either. How strong was that drink? A tad paranoid as to what to expect, I cautiously looked around the suite. I didn't see a thing.

"Right there," Eisenberg pointed. "On the armrest beside you! It's Parropo!"

I jumped up and let out a high-pitched yelp, falling off the couch like an idiot. A lime green, animal/alien thing was sitting on the armrest, right beside me, staring at me with its slimy amphibian eyes. A flourish of aqua blue, orange tipped wings complemented its tropical snout. Eisenberg laughed loud and hard, nearly falling over himself.

"I heard you like surprises, boy! So do I! Surprise!" Eisenberg stood up and maneuvered his bloated gut around his belt. He wiped the tears of laughter from his eyes and pulled out a long cigar from another pocket, bit off the end and spat it into the fireplace.

I scrambled to my feet and backed up a safe distance from the freakish creature. “What the hell is it? Or, actually, I don’t care what it is! Why the hell do you have it?”

“It’s part parrot, part hippopotamus. I had the wizard downstairs in the lab create him. I like to have an animal around, they are good company. Don’t you like animals?”

“I like animals, yes, I don’t like aliens, though. That thing is definitely not of this world.”

“Don’t be a wimp! Pick him up and say hello! You’ll like him.”

There was no avoiding it. The man wanted me to pick up his genetic science experiment pet. It was like trying to refuse pasta in an Italian family’s house. Whatever, I thought. I’ve done weirder things in my life. The little green thing hopped toward me onto one of the cushions of the sofa. I held out my hands and scooped Parropo up, but it passed between my fingers!

“It’s a…”

“Hologram.” Eisenberg smirked, pleased with himself. “I can’t be bothered to feed animals and clean up their shit. Plus, holograms give me any kind of companion I want.”

I swiped my hand through the apparition twice more. “Woa...that is the coolest thing…”

“Don’t patronize me. It’s a toy. Just another toy.” The media king had switched back into angry mode, it seemed. “I've got enough toys. I’m looking for ideas.”

Patronize him? Was he serious? His sudden shift in moods unsettled me. I had heard he was eccentric, not multi-personality disordered. I just kept my mouth shut and watched Cyrus spark up his cigar and fire some more Plazma down his throat as he hovered toward me on his throne.

"I'm willing to ignore all the trouble you've caused me. As long as you play my game. We drink and talk and eat like savages tonight, and if I decide you are not a complete idiot, if I like your ideas by the night's end, you're hired."

I took a breath of relief. Nice to know he wasn't going to kill me. Not yet at least. "Hired to do what?"

"To be my jester, of course! That is your business, is it not?"

Hearing this caused the little bubble of fear I had before to disappear. I could see right through Eisenberg's game. He was nothing more than another classic, power-hungry superiority complex that just wanted to be in vogue. And this year, jesters happened to be the latest craze. Chester was right. I had more power than I realized, and I could jest with him, no problem.

"Yes sir, that's exactly what I do," I said, and I kicked my feet up on the couch. "But what's in it for me, Cyrus? Surely the king of mainstream entertainment has something worthwhile to offer the king of underground entertainment?"

"I've done my research on jesters," he said, his German accent sounding sly. "I know you are a cunning species. Shrewd. That's what intrigues me about you." He flipped open the lid of the Exclamation Box and reached inside of it. "I also learned a thing or two about that which jester's like. Perhaps you'll consider this foolstaff worthwhile?"

Cyrus pulled out a short golden staff that looked like a simple section of plumbing pipe, small enough to fit in my pocket. The trillion-dollar king would have to do better than that, I thought - my old wooden foolstaff in the Den was leagues better. Unimpressive, to be sure, until the king triggered a hidden button flush along its golden surface. The staff expanded like a telescope more than five times its length, and at the top, it branched out in the shape of the three curled points of a jester's cap. I stared, enthralled, as the metal clicked and clacked in gnarled bends until three Green Lights appeared as the baubles at the end of each point of the foolstaff's cap.

At that point, I became mesmerized. Hypnotized, even, by their mystical glow. The king, the penthouse, my body seemed to dissolve around me, and I fixated upon the foolstaff's not one Green Light, but three. A spellbound cat captivated by its master's charm. A worthwhile offer, indeed.

The king handed me the foolstaff and pushed its hidden button again, collapsing it. I blinked as if awaken by a trance.

His two lovely toppings reappeared at the door, Cinnamon and Butterscotch, wearing bikinis revealing.

Cyrus smiled at me. "Fancy a Jacuzzi?"

CHAPTER FORTY-ONE: THE KING'S BLATHERINGS

Ancient court jesters carried a foolstaff with them, too, called a marotte. It indicated their authority as royal advisors to the king. And rather than a jester's cap that rested on top of mine, marottes carried miniature jester heads dressed in the same motley as the jester who carried it. Some jesters, the really eccentric ones, would talk to their marottes like a best friend, whispering wild ideas and royal secrets when no one was near.

I quickly discovered that my futuristic foolstaff had many surprises programmed into its machinery. Pressing the hidden button twice activated a jukebox menu on the foolstaff, and an infinite playlist of music seeped out of its microspeakers. The fool's cap turned as the music played, and my eyes remained fixated on the precious Green Lights dangling. Pressing the button three times opened a monitor offering an array of options; access to the OuterWeb, projector system, and more apps than any power phone. This little toy would baffle the cleverest of old school jesters. What's more, the two speakers, button and monitor looked like a laughing face.

Under regular circumstances, not even the most amazing of foolstaffs would get me to work for the king. Cyrus had many of my best friends killed. You already know I despised the man more than a jabberwocky does detest a bandersnatch. And we all know how much that is.

But their glow. There was something about those Green Lights that convinced me to wait and see how the night would play out.

King Cyrus' mouth slapped open and close that night like a slobbering bulldog chowing down on a wet bowl of slop, and he waved his hand around like a drunken philosopher as the four of us soaked in the Jacuzzi.

“You wanna be in entertainment kid-o? Well learn this now: money makes the world go round! And it makes me a little round too! Ha!” He drank more Plazma than your average raging alcoholic does in a lifetime. His lame jokes made the girls giggle, which I’m sure they were paid to do, but it made me want to puke.

Eisenberg pointed his bloated sausage fingers in my face to expound his ‘virtuous’ ideals. “And you know what? Every celebrity in this country today has paid their dues at MogulMedia. They owe me for their fame. They are my merchandise, too!” The king shifted his girth about the water and belched once or twice as he reached for whatever his hand landed on; in this case, it was a saucy rack of ribs.

“You have to look at the entertainment industry like this,” he said, slopping sauce into the water. “It’s all just medication for the masses. All of it! My technology, my TV programs, my food and even my ‘puppets’ dancing on TV networks and movie studios. It’s nothing more than social pacification.”

The shameful words oozed out of him like spewing sewage, and the more he drank, the worse he sounded. Such moronic blatherings would normally have offended me to my very core, yet I listened unfazed whilst staring at my hypnotic gift. The light jazz it played spun me into a delightful, mindless state.

“Pay attention while I’m talking to you, boy,” his words slurring more and more. The king reached over and pressed the button, collapsing the foolstaff. “Consumers are mindless fools. Surely you know that by now. They buy whatever the media tells them is the ‘latest craze.’ So I’m not the bad guy here. The fact of the matter is that consumers have the power to choose.”

He stopped blathering for a moment and looked suddenly nauseous. “I need some air. Let’s go on the roof,” he said.

Butterscotch, Cinnamon and I helped the bloated king stumble out of the Jacuzzi. The girls showered and changed him into his evening robes. Black, like his soul. I changed back into my tuxedo, still reeking from Hallowe'en brouhaha. Leaving the ladies behind, Eisenberg grabbed two flasks, darker grey this time, and I followed him into the glass elevator with my foolstaff and milkshake in hand, all the way up to the 100th floor.

"This is my favourite place in the world," he said, and the elevator door opened onto the roof. A spectacular view. The spire we stood on towered above the moon below us. Miniscule streetlights punctured the darkness below, a sequenced pattern across the city's mainframe. I took out my foolstaff and expanded it again. Slow electronica, and the glow illuminated my face aqua green. I looked down on the city, half-listening to Eisenberg spout more of his tired philosophies.

"I'm not stupid, boy. And I think you have figured it out on your own. People, in the end, have the choice to tune in or tune out. All forms of media are only popular because people keep buying them."

Not to point out the obvious, but old Cyrus and I are polar opposites. Our ideals stand like gunslingers, or jousters, or geez I don't know, wildebeests circling each other to lock horns and fight to the death.

"Take video games, for example," he said, sauntering around the roof as if master of the universe. "All kids want nowadays are video games. They choose them! And thank God they do, because they're the ultimate merchandise! Video games are bigger than the movie industry! Even better, they distract kids from their pathetic insignificance in the world! Those games are doing them a favour! Kids are better off not knowing how useless they are! What do you think of that?"

The king snatched the foolstaff from my hand again and shrunk it down to size. It took a moment for my foggy mind to catch up to all that he had said, and then a light went on. The king knew I would disagree with everything he said. He was pushing my buttons on purpose, I realized. All he craved was a good old-fashioned jest! The old man was bored! He had said he wanted ideas. This was my chance to speak my mind to the king, an opportunity I wouldn't miss in the world.

"You might consider designing a new game," I jested. "Actually call it 'Pathetic Insignificance'. Make it about loser kids who have no life or future because they play too many video games. See if they catch on to the fact they're playing themselves!"

"Yes! I like that!" the king bellowed, pleasantly surprised at my response. "I bet we could get away with it, too! Very edgy."

"Replace the kids with robots from the future and no one would know the difference."

Eisenberg stumbled back a few steps drunkenly. He squinted his eyes and pointed his finger again, challenging me. "Do you know what the highest grossing movie genre is these days?"

"Zombie vampire teen action drama? That's a genre, right?"

"Wrong! Romantic comedy! And they're the cheapest to make, too!"

I rolled my eyes. "Rom-com is the biggest drug since cocaine. People like them at first; it's innocent enough with plenty of cute, innocent jokes and puke-inducing cuddles. But by the time they realize it's actually some of the worst story lines and acting ever, or if they ever do, it's too late. They're hooked, and end up spending all of their money trying to find a rom-com that was as good as the first. You should really consider opening up rom-com rehab centres. That's where the real money is."

Slowly, I started to make the fat man laugh. A breakthrough! His eyes glimmered fiendishly beneath his bushy brows, and he leaned forward in my face the more excited and intoxicated, he became. The king's stagnant vibe began to churn.

"What do you think of the band Ticklejack?" He raised his right eyebrow, eager to get an earful.

"I can't say I have much of an opinion on the musicians themselves ~ they seem like nice enough guys. But their music is the equivalent to being stabbed in the ears with glass. Followed by nails and then knives. Then sprinkled with salt. They've pumped out some of the worst formulaic crap I've ever heard! They should invent a time machine for the sole purpose of making sure Ticklejack never existed. Either launch them into space or create a new genre of rock called: Good Music to Kill Yourself To."

He laughed again, his jowls jostling about his face. "Is this how it is with you, jester? Either love it or launch it?"

"That's about the extent of it. There's so much unfiltered junk out there that those are the only two options. And space is considerably less cruel than actually blowing things up."

Oh yeah I said it, and it felt SO good. My lofty ideals of the garbage that passed off as entertainment had been bottled up for so long, and finally this was my chance to let it all out. In front of the man who makes it all happen, no less! In fact, the more drunk he got, the more control I had.

"Do you have a piano?" I asked, wanting to spice things up.

Eisenberg held his belly and laughed. "Boy, you see that dome over there?" he said, pointing aimlessly in the distance. "The enormous one? That's my *amphitheatre*. I'm pretty sure we rustle you up a piano in there."

He threw his arm over my shoulders and I carried his bulking mass over to the elevator down to the first floor where he pulled up his hover throne via remote with another flick of his magical wristband. Another remote control ejected a large white pillow on a brass box spring from the lower right side of the throne. It was a hover throne with a sidecar, like those old school motorbikes, except no helmet, sadly.

The king assumed his royal seat, his weight causing the throne to lean, and I hopped on my plush pillow once the ride was secure. We floated around the outside of MogulMedia in his pimped out throne, which sported a mini bar, and, of course, retractable TV screens.

"What about Singing Stars?" he asked, turning the channel to the show with a flick of his wrist.

"The singing TV show competition? Those shows make me puke. Competing to be an artist totally goes against the whole point of being an artist! Launch it!"

Eisenberg belted out another massive laugh. "Yes, I like your fire! How about the new video pop up ads we have on the Web?"

"Ads can be creative. But the only people who like them are corporations and advertisers. Most of them are drivel, and annoying. Launch it."

We drove by the MogulMedia TV and movie studios, a line of long rectangular buildings housing multitudes of sets and production equipment. My heart jumped. I had never been in a studio before. It was always a dream of mine to be in the movies.

“Sitcoms?” Eisenberg asked, filling my glass again.

I began to feel heavy headed myself. The Plazma milkshake and the surrealism were catching up with me. “That’s tough. Most of them you can launch, but some of them I love. The problem is that you guys make them for a million seasons and the jokes get tired and everything goes limp, like a wet noodle on a wet poodle.”

“Yes, but that’s how it works, like it or not. We produce it, and if people like it, we give them as much of it as possible until the idea is completely milked.”

“That’s the problem. Good ideas die because they’re all pumped out just for money. It’s empty, repetitive - I've seen more soulful creativity in booger-faced kindergartener's finger painting.”

Eisenberg exhaled a billow of cigar smoke into the air. His energy was shifting again, I could feel it. “Don’t fool yourself. You perform for the money, too.”

A low blow. I can’t believe he had the audacity to compare the Jesters Incognito to the junk produced at MogulMedia. He didn’t want to hear that the whole reason people dig the Jesters is because our ‘programming’ is one time only. It works because it’s live and unpredictable! If I had told him that I had found a way to have creative freedom and a pure feeling of joy every time I connected with someone, it would have been like speaking gibberish to him.

The hover throne arrived at the rear doors of MogulMedia amphitheatre, and again I helped Eisenberg stumble his way forward through the backstage hallways, and into the most marvelous building I had ever set foot in.

I’m betting that my sub-atomic atoms were buzzing at 400,000 mega-hertz as my excitement jumped another level.

With only the stage illuminated I couldn't see out into the darkness, but I sure felt small walking out into the vacuous space I knew was just beyond the stage's edge. Small, but so alive! A grand piano sat majestically at stage left, and I walked over and ran my hand over the keys. The sound popped out of the piano in round, rich tones, and lifted vibrantly into the hall.

"Amazing acoustics!" I shouted to Cyrus, now sitting with his legs dangling at the edge of the stage. He nodded his head and waved dismissively at me, too drunk to speak.

"Well, I'd like to play a number for you, sir, if you'll amuse me. I had no idea I'd end up here tonight, but this song has been on my mind since I got here. You seem to have a passion for money, and you've succeed at making me feel inferior my whole life for not being famous, or rich, or on a screen of some kind. So how about a rendition of an old tune my friends and I wrote called "Me Filming You Filming Us Filming Them." It' a catchy little ditty that about sums up your little kingdom here."

I launched right into the catchy (and heavily ironic) song, enjoying every sound I produced. It was a dream come true to play on a massive stage like that; my skin was literally tingling with energy! And it only took one round of the chorus before Eisenberg was on his feet dancing to my singing and playing. He looked like a fat marionette and the music pulled *his* strings. He hooted and hollered and drank more Plazma and eventually stumbled over next to me. Leaning up against the piano as I came to the song's big finish, he blurted, "What's your name again?" and then smiled like a debauched fool himself.

"It's Vincent Meistersinger, sir."

"That's a stupid name," he blurted. Cyrus pulled my foolstaff from his pocket and activated it. The Green Lights comforted me again; I felt hazy as I watched the piano, the stage and the auditorium blur out of focus. The king turned to the darkness beyond the stage, raised both of his arms theatrically to the invisible audience and bellowed: “You will work for me, and your name will be Jester!”

And there it was. From street jester to court jester, based on a night of debauchery and total honesty, I was deemed funny and creatively savvy enough to score a job with the most powerful man in media.

He offered me $5 million a month.

We shook on it. I passed out. The last thing I remember thinking, my head swimming nonsensical as I lay on the floor of the stage with my precious foolstaff on my chest, was that the way Eisenberg slurred his words, it almost sounded like he called me Chester.

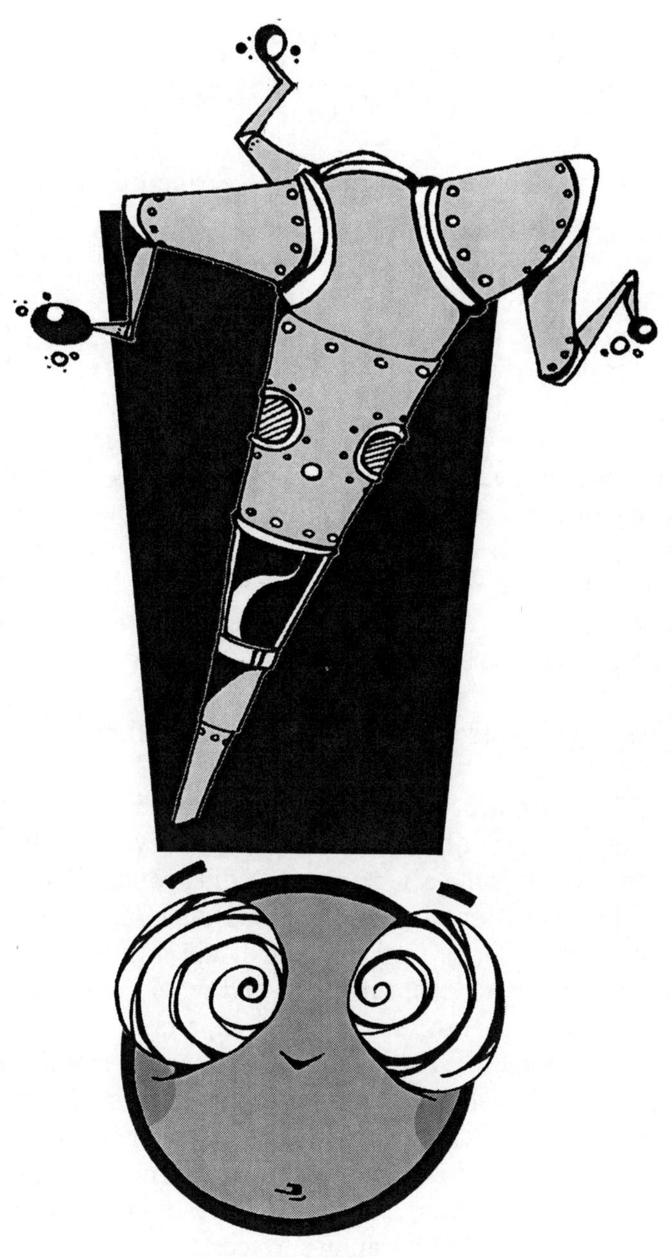

CHAPTER FORTY-TWO: BEHIND THE THRONE

When you wake up because the smell of your own breath is too much to handle, you know it was a wild night. It was more than my mouth that reeked; I looked like tuxedo road kill, too. The film reel in my mind fast-forwarded to the present moment, verifying my Cyrus experience had not been a dream.

The suite I woke up in was not one we had seen the night before. I was in a large bed with chic satin sheets and a huge mirror against one wall, magnifying how terrible I looked. Luckily the room's black and grey interior was easy on my headache. Kicking my feet over the side of the bed I took a moment to check my balance, to stop the room from spinning, and then walked into an adjacent bathroom with delicate steps.

Much splashing and scrubbing and flushing followed.

The bathroom mirror activated when I stepped in front of it, displaying an array of windows floating above its surface. There were video game selections, including Mildly Perturbed Birds, Monkey Assassin, and Insects vs Vampires. A revolving, virtual globe in the center of the mirror displayed international news videos, fun facts, and movie releases; and beside that, a Web browser showed an array of the latest trending social networking apps: InstaOunce, iCan'tThinkForMyself, and Groupoff. As soon as the steam cleared from the glass, I watched a blue laser grid appear at the top of the mirror and move slowly down its length. I couldn't figure out what its function was, until my name appeared in the centre of its shiny surface:

Vincent Meistersinger, installed onto the MogulMedia mainframe.

Face recognition software, I should have known. The logo at the bottom corner said it all: *MagicMirror*.

Feeling better after the clean up, I toured the suite with little-boy-waking-up-on-Christmas-morning awe. It was huge! A large sitting area with three cathedral style windows stood in the middle of the suite, looking over a brilliant view of the city. Next to that, the suite had an open concept kitchen with modern black barstools and a blue phone on the counter with 'chef' as its one and only contact on speed-dial. And then past the kitchen there was another door that led into a study where a leather armchair with massage remote beckoned weary bones, and a wall-sized screen waited silent and black along the far wall.

Sitting on a side table by the study's door was a stack of digital business cards. They read in crisp, multi-coloured 3-D font:

The Jester^MM

It was all completely real. It had happened. I had become Eisenberg's jester! What a fantastically brilliant turn of events! If the 'big time' felt this good hung over, I couldn't imagine…

The foolstaff caught my gaze, leaned over in the corner next to the bed; my new modern mascot. It was official. The king had given me the coveted Green Light!

A knock on my door interrupted my dumbfoundedness. A long-legged redhead popped her head into my room, and asked if she could enter. It was Ms. Samantha Devlin from the elevator. Utter nonsense came out of my mouth in reply, still too spaced out to fathom everything that was happening around me.

She stepped into my quarters balancing a heavy bundle of vibrantly coloured clothing in one hand, and a tablet in the other. She walked directly into the bedroom to lay the clothes on my bed, and then sat down on its corner to catch her breath. Her piercing green eyes, I remember, intensified her stunning beauty.

"Welcome to MogulMedia, Mr. Meistersinger. I trust you had a restful sleep in your new suite."

I skootched beside her on the bed. "Please. Call me Jester."

Ms. Devlin fixed her glasses and smirked. "We need you to sign the contract, Vincent. Mr. Eisenberg has asked me to lay out the responsibilities to your offer of employment as, um, yes, the company jester. We've never had a position like this before, and I've never had to draw up a contract like this before, so you'll see the roles and responsibilities are rather broad. Each day you are to report to Mr. Eisenberg at breakfast, lunch and dinner unless otherwise instructed, and are required to join him on engagements of his choice. As his creative advisor, ergo jester, you are his brain trust, which means any and all ideas you have are property of the MogulMedia Corporation. They are confidential and we trust you to uphold that."

"That's it? He's paying me to hang out and dine with him. You sure he doesn't want to change my title to 'date'?"

She smiled and gave me the stylus to sign her tablet. I liked the way she smirked with one corner of her mouth. It softened the cold chip she had on her shoulder. Spellbound, I began to sign my name without hesitation, but then stopped short.

"What about the rest of the Jesters?" I asked.

"The contract is yours only. Cyrus did say, however, that if your friends would like to host some more high-profile parties, he has an impressive contact list at your disposal. On the condition there are no more globes. The distortion drove him crazy. And you don't want to see him crazy."

Two more strokes completed my signature just as she finished her sentence. It was all I needed to hear, and it was all too good to be true!

"I have to tell you Mr. Meistersinger, I'm very excited that Mr. Eisenberg brought you on board. I have been working with Cyrus for years. I've promoted a myriad of shows and products for MogulMedia, not to mention the countless ratings I've rescued for flailing actors and actresses. Yours is the only story I've covered in recent memory that I can say I've actually enjoyed tracking. I've even been to one of your shows."

"How very pleased I am to hear that, Samantha. You have good taste. Do you remember which one?"

She came alive, taking off her glasses and flicking her hair back over her shoulder. "It was at the aquarium! You guys sang some blues tunes to lament all the fish you'd loved, and then eaten before. We thought you were all tourists until you put on those hats."

"Oh ya, that was a good one, if I do say so myself. Spontaneous songs and giant fish hats is a great way to hijack an audience. I wore the coral reef hat. But without the hat."

"You do realize how big of an underground celebrity you are?"

Ms. Devlin had stars in her eyes, there was no question about it. We shared what the Romantics call 'a moment.' She was as excited to be sitting next to me as I was about sitting next to her, I could feel it. I might go so far to say she was my first fan-flirt.

“Anyway,” she adjusted her glasses and pulled the bundle of clothes over to resume focus. “You’re about to get popular above ground very soon, Mr. Meistersinger. Mr. Eisenberg is committed to this whole idea of court jester, and he insists on the aesthetics be just right. He was rather picky about the authenticity of your motley, and had a closet full of jester outfits tailored for you. He wants you to try these samples on first to see if you like them.”

There were at least ten full-body motleys, all ready to go, with hats and bells and stylish poufy cuffs and all. All major labels: Dolce and Cantabile, Hugo Chief, Timbersea…I liked the Joe Fighter brand myself because they looked like the most fun pyjamas ever invented.

“So, Cyrus wants me to wear these all the time?” I asked, hoping the answer was yes.

“Yes. He's rather obsessed with the retro-chic look of it all."

"Retro. Yeah, 18th century is pretty retro all right."

"Keep in mind he’s looking to you for inspiration now.” Devlin gave me another grin before she stood up to leave the room. “You can do whatever you want. Just be ready to meet with the king in an hour.”

Do whatever you want. Music to my ears.

Ms. Devlin was very, very smooth jazz.

I had to call the Blabbermouths to tell them my good news. They were probably at Cosmos, I thought. It felt so bizarre to have the bacon and eggs routine juxtaposed with this new escargot existence.

Checking the entire suite, I couldn’t find my uScroll anywhere.

I picked up my foolstaff, wondering if my foolstaff had a communication device built in. As soon as I expanded it, my vision zoomed into its enchanting glow again; the room melted away.

My intentions vanished just as soon as I picked it up.

Whatever, I thought. I'll catch up with those clowns later.

CHAPTER FORTY-THREE: COMPANY JESTER

First official meeting as the company jester. Noon brunch with the king.

Wearing a flashy purple and white striped motley with my hair stuffed into a matching hat, I dined in Cyrus Eisenberg's suite overlooking a distant downtown at a table as long as my cab. The hum of a conveyor belt system slowly whirred above the table, carrying a sumptuous exhibition of delectables for me to choose from. Sweet-smelling apple and cherry pies hung from plates with baskets of fresh bread, fruit, and steaming meat platters that would make most starving countries weep.

"My doctor says it's not good for my health to have the robots feed me anymore," the king said, begrudgingly stabbing his fork into a hunk of beef. "So they hooked this contraption up for me. At least this way I'm getting some exercise when I reach for the food."

"Your noon sippy sip, sir," Cinnamon said, approaching the table from an adjacent room. She poured another dark grey flask into his orange juice. As he chugged the concoction, his complexion changed from gaunt to a light peach shade, and he spun his eyes behind his eyelids to get them into focus. Another dose of the king's elixir. The grease to his proverbial gears. Cinnamon kissed him on the cheek, and cleared his soiled plates before leaving.

Sippy sip? If Plazma that strong is called something as babyish as that, I'd like to know what they call the Plazma from the black flasks. Just as Cyrus finished his drink, I spotted the king's holographic companion of the day; a tiny blue cartoon balloon man with an umbrella as a hat sitting on the rim of his glass.

"It's not polite to stare, Jester. Go ahead and introduce yourself. I call him 'Quip'."

"Hello Quip," I said, amused with the little dude. "Nice to meet you. Aren't you hungry?"

"I'm between hungers, thank you. Please enjoy." Quip looked quite content with his quip.

"That thing is amazing. I totally want one! Can you project anything?"

"We can scan and animate almost any image to project. A few weeks ago we scanned a hologram pickle and hid it in Ms. Devlin's hamburger. Priceless. The hamburger ended up on the ceiling."

"Ha! All people need to do now is scan themselves and we could all stop going to work."

I plucked a bunch of grapes that swung by and munched on a hot cinnamon bun. I didn't realize how hungry I was until I tucked in. They even had a chocolate milkshake for me on the conveyor belt. The taste of such luxury would take no getting used to.

Cyrus leaned over and squeezed out a long, butt cheek-on-chair fart.

The *smell* of such luxury, would.

"I want to introduce you to everyone tomorrow, but there won't be time. Between my massage, private screenings and taste testing of the new head chef's dinner menu, we're booked solid. There are almost 8,000 people working at MogulMedia, so…" he paused and looked me squarely in the eye. "Do you have any ideas for a suitable introduction, Jester?"

"Well sure. Ideas are as plentiful to me as nanopixels on a grandmother board. I often wish I had a bigger mouth just so I could get all the ideas piled up in my head..."

Eisenberg pounded his fist on the table. "Don't babble Jester! God dammit just say it! I don't have patience for wordiness this early in the morning!" Little Quip dropped into the orange juice, scared out of his holographic mind.

Just like my first night, there was that switch again: from jovial to stern on a dime.

"Understood, your Excellency. My ideas will henceforth be delivered as brazenly as your flatulence."

"Spit it out, Jester."

"I'd like to simply introduce myself unexpectedly. To surprise your staff."

"I'm listening," Eisenberg said, sucking the smoking froth of the top of his vial.

"I'll ride the elevators tomorrow so I can jest the staff in person. It will give me some time to make an impression on people, small numbers at a time. "

"An excellent idea! It's weird, but I like it. You'll come with me to my meetings after that. Ms. Devlin will see that you have everything you need."

Polishing off his drink, the king punched a quick code into his bracelet and the kitchen help appeared to clean off the table, followed instantly by the massage therapy staff who, with a few quick clicks, turns and folds, transformed it into a massage bed for the king. The fat man had his clothes off and was on his stomach getting his flesh worked out before you could say lumlum. And we all know how fast that is.

“Tell me a story, Jester, to pass the time,” he said. “There’s really nothing entertaining on TV these days anyway.” From where I was seated, I had a lovely view of his tiny towel barely covering his bits and bobs.

“Have you heard the tale of Rumpleforeskin?” I asked.

“Yes, yes, the one about the little man and his collection of…”

“That’s the one, sir.”

“No, I want to hear something about the outside, Jester. Tell me what it’s like out there these days?”

This seemed a tad bizarre to me. The man owned the collective consciousness of the country, and yet he had no idea of what it’s like outside his kingdom?

I picked up my foolstaff, selected some polka music off the menu screen, and settled on the first best thing that came to mind.

“This story’s about a colourful pizza delivery guy, called ‘Fitch of Many Pockets’.”

“Delightful!” The king’s word came out in a fragrant burp.

CHAPTER FORTY-FOUR: VERTICAL VIBES

The next day, Monday.

Very early, well before the kingdom of MogulMedia began work, Ms. Devlin had the props guys set up a chaise lounge and reading lamp for me in elevator eight. Oh, I have no shame. With my foolstaff, my bag of tricks, a sketchbook and a pen, I was off to work. Butterflies fluttered about in my belly. I was so excited to jest a new audience!

“There’s twenty elevators between the two towers,” Ms. Devlin said. “And you’re telling me you’re going to ‘make an appearance’ in all of them?”

“You bet! I’m looking forward to it.” I brushed a few speckles of dirt off my aqua blue motley. “In fact, I’ve often fantasized about being trapped in an elevator.”

“You don’t say.”

“They’re like tiny apartments. Nice and cozy. No rent.”

“You’re nuts.”

"And you, Samantha, are 'raisin' my heartbeat!"

"Wow." Ms. Devlin adjusted her glasses and raised her eyebrows, worryingly. "Go easy on my staff today, will you? They have no idea what's in store."

3rd FLOOR: DESIGN

“Good morning!” I boomed enthusiastically to a peacock looking woman with her face in an eBook. She just about laid an egg.

“Huh, huh, hiii…” she stammered, sizing me up in my modern motley. I looked ridiculously hip, emphasis on the ridiculous.

“My name’s Jester, I’m a new addition to the Mogul mega-corporation. I’m hoping you’d like to play a game with me.

“Oh…kay…”

“Great! It’s called “Say a word backwards and guess what it is! Does that sound annoying enough to be fun this early in the morning? Sure it does!”

14th FLOOR: MARKETING

Three rectangular-shaped-glasses people were chattering away, and I shouted to them as soon as the doors closed. “Don’t make a move!”

They froze. One woman dropped her coffee.

“No need for panic. I’ve got the situation under control. I’m Eisenberg’s new Jester.” I walked around the trio and pretended to stare deeply at them. Then I pulled out three thumb-sized pieces of paper, a pen, and proceeded to scribble little thoughts on them.

“Listen pal, we’ve got a meeting to get to,” one guy said, pressing his floor’s button a few more times.

“No problem. Nothing worse than bad breath and a serious attitude before a meeting!”

It was an old school jest from the early cabbing days I liked to call Misfortune Gum. I slipped the pieces of paper with ridiculous ideas written on them. Stream of consciousness stuff and offered them the three sticks. With reluctance, they accepted and got off the elevator, quickly shoving the gum in their pockets dismissively.

Didn't matter, because the longer they wait to open their misfortunes, the quirkier they'll be. Good gags gotta marinate!

'When your feet start seeing other shoes, your toes gossip.'
'Your bed is a time machine. You get in and wake up the next day.'
'Never smile. People might think you're actually happy.'

24th FLOOR: CONFERENCE ROOMS

"The only gift I have for you today sir is music," I expanded my foolstaff and got the Green Lights spinning. "Would you like to select your elevator soundtrack today? Are we feeling up, or are we feeling down? Sorry, I know, bad pun."

47th FLOOR: FILM PRODUCTION

"Can I speak frankly, buddy?" I asked the tall, pony-tailed man entering the elevator. He wore all black and carried a black tablet close to his chest.

"I'm not sure how Frank speaks, but sure, go ahead," he replied with a smirk.

"Ha! I like that! Ok, I'll speak Bobly."

"Touche."

"I think you guys should give up on sequels. For crying out loud, they're worse than bathing your eyes in onions."

“That bad, are they?” he said. “What novel idea do you propose?”

I hopped up from my chaise lounge and did a little dance of excitement at his feet. “Movie Mash-Ups! Very simple. Start with a main character in an action movie, for example. Then kill off that character halfway through and follow a secondary character's plot. Turn it into a comedy. Two totally different stories! People will never see it coming!”

The pony-tailed man didn’t react much, standing rather unfazed by the idea.

“That is a wacky idea,” the man said to himself. “I like speaking Bobly with you, Mr…?”

“Jester. Just Jester," I said.

And so on, and so forth. Some people were so thoroughly surprised they missed their floors; other times conversations weren’t prompted at all, so we just enjoyed the music while I requested tag lines for the silly cartoons I drew on the chaise lounge.

It didn’t take long before word was out that Eisenberg had hired himself a jester. Which in turn meant that for the first time in my life, I felt like I was kind of a big deal. I didn’t have to hide. I had the Green Light. And that felt good.

At least twenty elevators ran up and down each of the two towers, so when I wanted to mix it up and move to another one for fun, the props guys were at my disposal. They were a delightful duo named Keith and Kevin, very flamboyant partners who wore matching jumpsuits each day, kind enough to show me around the buildings during my early days at the media kingdom. At the end of my day elevating moods, I got the inside scoop on every single detail of every single floor, and more.

Together, Keith and Kevin were Salsa dance hall, all the way.

"Now this is interesting," Keith said as we walked through the main rotunda. "MogulMedia has almost 8,000 full time staff, but there's only one washroom on each floor. How is that even possible, right?"

Kevin rolled his eyes. "Keith, there's 80 floors between the two towers. There's plenty of washrooms to go around. Furthermore, why is that relevant to Jesty?"

"Well, I still don't understand where all the pee and poo really goes anyway," Keith said. "8,000 people peeing and pooing all the time and it just magically disappears? You expect me to believe that?"

Between the three of us, I was definitely not the jester.

"What's up with these walls," I asked as we walked around another floor. Every section of wall carried a slight shimmer to them. "Doesn't Eisenberg believe in windows?"

Kevin let out a little laugh. "You obviously didn't attend the Expo last year. These are WonderWalls!" From the unsuspecting eye, the walls looked to be concrete, but Kevin proved otherwise. We stopped in front of one towering section of wall, and Kevin reached out to touch its surface. The spot he touched rippled like a rock dropped in water.

"They're enormous monitors, basically. Super cool, like a tablet on steroids." Kevin used both of his hands to gesture across the WonderWall in a whirl, opening windows, resizing them and moving them around as he spoke. "They've got a touch screen interface so you can access the net, your MogulMedia accounts, watch any of our TV networks, teleconferencing, music players, the mapping system…it's endless."

"Wow. Windows to a fabricated a world. What a dream come true," I said, chuckling. It was impressive, actually, except for the preprogrammed TV channels. Plugged in, 24-7. I guess that's why they call it 'programming.'

"You can open up a weather channel window if you want, or there's a virtual window application, too," Kevin said, sweeping his hand over the virtual console and opening a new image of rolling hills beneath a pastel blue sky.

"Yeah, that's as good as a breath of fresh air!"

"Ok, Mr. My-Hair-Looks-Like-A-Million-Naked-Albino-Sea Monkeys. If that doesn't turn your crank, take a look at this."

Keith nudged his partner to the side and clicked on a film reel icon. The WonderWall transitioned to the newest release in theatres, an acclaimed comic book revenge movie called B for Bruschetta. The resolution on the wall was unreal! The image crisp, the graphics so clean!

"And that's only 4-D, Jesty," Keith said. "Check out 7-D!"

With a swift flick of the wrist, the three of us were suddenly standing inside the movie itself! That is, the film came out of the wall, and projected itself onto the space we were standing. We weren't on Floor 16 anymore, we were standing in a virtual park behind the actors.

"So, we're extras all of a sudden?"

"Yeah, isn't it cool? We can hang out and see the movie from a bunch of different angles. It's how I like to take my coffee breaks!"

"It won't be long before film makers will program multiple scenarios for their actors," Kevin added. "Anyone could be in a movie, then, and wander around as they liked."

Keith turned off the 7-D application and I took a moment to rub my eyes. "I've never seen such technological sorcery in my life," I said, looking around the regular hallway as if returning from a dream. "But, it's still just a novelty though, right? We're interacting with actors everyday, aren't we? Changing each other's plots?"

"Maybe you are Jesty," Kevin said. "Most people are working everyday, changing their dirty undies!"

I tapped an icon that brought a detailed floor-by-floor map of the entire complex on screen. Thousands of coloured avatars moved around the mega-complex, each distinguishable by a unique icon. It was like staring at a digital beehive.

"So every one of those avatars is a MM employee?" I asked them.

"You got it! Ooooh! Look, yours is a star! That's about as high as you can get!"

"How does it know I'm even here?"

Keith and Kevin looked at each other.

"They didn't tell you that, did they?" Keith said. "God, they're so secretive sometimes it drives me crazy. They inserted it on the back of your neck while you were sleeping; under your skin, like a dog."

"What?" I dropped my foolstaff and frantically started feeling around on the back of my neck.

They held nothing back laughing at my expense. "Just kidding Jesty! It's probably in your fancy staff! Got ya!" Kevin and Keith doubled over with laughter.

"Hilarious. I hope you guys die laughing."

"Well, how could you not know that? All MogulMedia employees have chips. Haven't you noticed all the Bling the staff are wearing?" Kevin pointed to the bracelet around his right wrist. It looked similar to the one Cyrus wore, but thinner, less intricate. "They give us access to all double-clickable surfaces, the AutoPeeps, and of course they let the king know where everyone is, all the time."

"Yeah, that's a comforting thought." I pointed to a solid grey block underneath the towers on the map. "Doesn't look like anyone's down there."

"That's the basement. It's Mr. Eisenberg's secret manufacturing zone. No one is allowed down there. Well, not technically."

"Keith. Don't. You. Dare!" Kevin had almost no drama in his voice. "You can't say a word!"

"What? The man's a jester. What does he care about basements anyway? It's no big deal. The props offices are on the first basement level see?" Kevin pointed with his finger. MogulMedia looked to go at least fifteen levels deep! "Then there's facilities and maintenance, and the third level down where they develop the new products for MogulMedia Expo. But you didn't hear it from me, ok?"

I laughed at the pair. They were two I'd never trust a secret with. "My lips are like the navy, boys. They're sealed."

Goin' up? Or gettin' down?!
(trick question, my friends, 'cuz we're gonna do both!)

CHAPTER FORTY-FIVE: AUDITION AQUARIUM

They say getting lost is how you find out where you are, or something equally prophetically meaningless. My philosophy on getting lost is that it's only tolerable as long as you stumble upon a beautiful woman. Because at that point it doesn't matter where you are.

MogulMedia bustled with the same frantic fullness of a mega-tropolis subway system. Employees plugged into ear buds and heads down at tablets flooded the corridors from every which way, bustling, elbows out, and above them flew a steady flow of AutoPeeps, programmed to fetch their owners a coffee, or deliver a hard copy document to a co-worker on another floor. The stream of people was relentless, and I always seemed to be walking against current. Even with the incredible WonderWall mapping system at my fingertips and bright yellow star avatar to guide me, I still managed to get lost on my way back to my suite. The two major towers are identical, as are the series of glass tunnels connecting them, and Eisenberg's central spire is only accessible by three entrances that change regularly because his spire rotates.

After almost an hour, I realized why I was getting paid to jest, not lead the blind.

I stepped into a hallway somewhere inside the 21st Floor, away from the chaos, and toward a steady beat I heard thumping from the far end. Some drumming. And electric bass. Following the sound, I soon found myself in front of a series of recording studios. Not a bad thing to stumble upon, I thought. There were at least a dozen studios down one corridor, and every one of them was packed with musicians jamming their hearts out. The recording equipment looked to be of the highest quality. Man, I wished the Jesters could afford gear like that.

Ms. Devlin strutted past the music studios wing, yapping on her power phone. I waved and jogged up to her, thankful to see a familiar face. A gorgeous, familiar face.

She cupped her hand over her phone. “Give me a minute, I’m in the middle of a huge record deal.”

I watched one group play, but still couldn’t hear much above a faint rhythm from inside the studios. I could tell from the looks on all of their faces that the bands were giving it their all, and then some. Waterfalls of sweat poured off the drummers’ brow and the lead singer contorted his body in a desperate attempt to nail down a signature style. Watching through the windows, it was like visiting an audition aquarium.

Samantha joined me after a few minutes, tucking her phone with a grin of satisfaction on her face.

“And?” I asked.

“The deal’s done.”

“Great! Which one?”

“All of them.”

“Whoa! You’re signing all of these kids?”

“We’re squeezing every note that comes out of them,” she said.

“I see.” I looked again at the musicians, at their eager young faces belting out the next canned tracked of sardine music for the masses. I even spotted a faint reflection of myself in the glass. “Well, you have to harvest while the fruit is ripe, I guess. You know Samantha, I know some amazing talent that would make these bands shrivel up with envy. I could make a phone call."

"Thanks, but we've got our hands full here," she said, texting as we walked toward the elevators together.

"Ok, but what about live entertainment? This place could use some live music in a big way. What about a band on every floor?"

"That's a cute idea. I'll make a note of it."

"Cool! And even in the city. How cool would it be if MogulMedia paid live bands to play around town? Costmo', Sprawlmart? Like, why is every store playing the same packaged noise when there's spectacular musicians at home collecting welfare checks?"

The elevator doors opened in front of us, and some dudes from Marketing got out. One of them recognized me, and gave me the high-five.

"Yo! Meistersinger! What's up buddy? This is the dude I was telling you about!" he said to his buddies. "Good news ~ that illustration you did for us got the Green Light! It's the product's new logo!"

Samantha chuckled to herself, pretending her phone had most of her attention while I twirled my foolstaff in the air and did a spin before catching it. "A new logo? That's loco! I'll catch up with you lads in the cafeteria. We'll have fries and like, totally gossip."

Ms. Devlin stopped abruptly and stood tall on her stilettos so she could look down her nose at me. "You've got a lot of ideas, don't you?"

"Genius is a terrible curse, but I've learned to cope."

She flicked her hair over her shoulder and pursed her lips a little before she spoke. “I love your enthusiasm, Vincent, honestly, it’s so endearing. Where are you going, anyway?”

“I’m going to a restaurant to have dinner with you,” I said with a bow and a turn.

“Is that so?” Samantha turned slowly to face me and smiled. Her eyes softened. “I can’t do dinner, but how about dessert sometime?”

“Oh my god,” I said, clapping my hands together. “Milkshakes?”

I finally got a laugh out of her, and a roll of the eyes. She was much more beautiful when she let down her guard. “Vincent. Honestly? Grow up, ok?”

“I can’t grow up. It’s too late. But I’m halfway through a self-help program on how to act in public!”

Samantha stepped into an elevator back to the top of the world, and left me alone again, wondering why I didn’t go with her.

I still had no idea where in the kingdom I was.

CHAPTER FORTY-SIX: INKWELL, INC.

On Tuesday, I accompanied the king during his various meetings and appointments across MogulMedia. Cyrus and I floated on his throne through the Quartz Quadrangle, a stunning courtyard with waterfalls pouring over yellow stone cliffs, as he introduced me to some key players in the behind-the-scenes corporate world of entertainment. My job, he decreed, was to sit in the corner, in costume, observe and entertain as I saw fit.

That's it. Pretty wild gig, huh?

He brought me to a meeting he had scheduled with the owners of Inkwell industries, who had flown in from Japan just a few hours before so that they could finalize the arrangements on the components for a new device.

"I hate working with this company," he said, unceremoniously picking his nose. "It's like talking to robots. There's more emotion in their product."

"Which is what, exactly?" I asked, waving to many of my new fans as we sped through the boardroom corridor.

"Inkwell is a machine that stores and synthesizes all the data on the OuterWeb. It analyzes and assembles all of the ideas generated by the public into novels, scripts, apps, and any other idea their algorithms."

"A machine that writes books?"

"There's a lot of nifty ideas floating out there, unclaimed. Best part is that the public don't have the faintest clue. And they don't need to."

He stepped off of the hover throne to tuck in his shirt, shifting his belt around his belly a few times before stepping back on. "Now add a little spice to this meeting to keep me awake, would you Jester?"

The idea of a machine creating art struck a minor chord with me. I knew they monitored the OuterWeb, which is why the jesters developed our own sub-server, but I had no idea MogulMedia was scanning and collecting people's emails and personal websites just to reassemble the ideas and sell it right back to us. I'd love to see this Inkwell, I thought, just so I could destroy it.

Cyrus stopped before we entered the room. "Oh, and Jester. Don't forget your foolstaff."

Of course! I couldn't make a proper entrance without my eye-catching scepter. I expanded the golden rod, and the Green Lights began to spin as we floated inside.

Six Japanese men in well-pressed suits sat stoic around the table, except for one overly polite Japanese woman who greeted us and served us tea as soon as we finished our bowing and took our seats. Cyrus introduced me as his jester, and nothing else was said on the matter of his new, eccentrically dressed companion.

"Good morning, Mr. Eisenberg," said Mr. Kurokawa, standing up at the front of the room. "On behalf of Inkwell, Inc., we would like to sank you for the opportunity to be meeting us this day. As you know, our patent has finished final testing." Dimming the lights, he proceeded to talk us through a series of pictures of tiny computer parts. Cyrus' eyes glazed over as the meeting proceeded, and ten minutes in I could see what he meant. This crowd was dry and needed some serious greasing.

I thought back to some of the Japanese fares in my cab and remembered having a great time with most of them.

Awesome sense of humour. I recalled dancing to some Taeko drumming with a Japanese businessman outside of a burger joint one night. I could tap into the playful vibes of the Inkwell guys, too. A good dose of absurdity began to brew in my noggin.

I reached into my bag and pulled out a sack of rubber animal noses. I had Kevin and Keith whip me up a few ‘nose hats’: a toucan’s beak and an elephant’s trunk and a koala bear’s nose, to name a few. Fizzlestick would be proud our idea was in effect. I strapped on a pig’s snout and raised my hand as if in grade school.

“Let’s play a game!” I blurted.

Mr. Kurokawa froze in mid-presentation. It was easy to see he wasn’t prepared for interruptions. Especially from a pig. The other six men turned and stared at me with a mixture of perplexed and perturbed expressions. Eisenberg perked up a little in his chair.

“Yes? Do you have a question?” Kurokawa asked, his voice quivering.

“Not a question, no. But I would like to play a game! Or, ‘pray a game-u’, if that’s easier for you to understand.”

Kurokawa fixed his glasses squarely on his nose and swallowed nervously as he watched me stand up and walk to the front of the room, beside him.

“It’s pretty simple, even for you linear, technological types! I want you to continue with your presentation where you left off. Except this time you’re going to do it wearing a funny animal nose!”

“Why for you want do me that?”

“Well, because. It’s a wacky fun time happy presentation style we’re trying out here these days!” I reached into my sack and pulled out a donkey’s nose and strapped it over Kurokawa’s. “So I’m going to pick a word, and whisper it to everyone else. A secret word. So if you say it, I’m going to shout out and then you’re have to act like your animal. Got it?”

“Who the hell are you? This is serious meeting!” One of the men barked, completely insulted by the idea.

“He is my Jester, that’s who!” Cyrus erupted, his fat jowls quivering.

I put my hand on the king’s shoulder, assuredly. “I’m a pig, what does it look like?” I tromped around doing my best pig impression. “Now, don’t fret, you’re not the only one who’s going to wear one. We all are! If any of you laugh at Mr. Kurokawa, even a snicker, you’ll have to act out your animal too, and then continue the presentation. Wacky? Most definitely.”

The Inkwell men looked at each other with trepidation in their eyes. They must have thought I was mad, not that I blame them. They came to make a deal, but were instead following my crazy instructions and putting on rubber noses.

Reluctantly, they played along, and the meeting proceeded. Kurokawa picked up where he left off and did well at keeping his composure for another slide or two until the first snicker came four-minutes after from the female hostess. She had the elephant trunk and her laugh came out like bizarre guffaw on impulse. She was a good sport and followed through with the rules, giggling between her trumpeting impressions of an elephant. Three more people laughed out loud: a squirrel, a dragon, and a hyena. Well, I thought it was a hyena, there was some debate, but you get the idea. Over the course of the hour our impressions got a little less inhibited, the laughter became more robust and eventually that boardroom was so relaxed that the deal sealed itself.

Cyrus doubled over laughing the whole time, thoroughly entertained. "See?" he said, shaking everyone's hands at the end, "What is a meeting without laughter?"

"This was the most of funny," said Mr. Kurokawa. "Maybe we find a crazy clown for Inkwell, too!"

"Easy, pal," I said. "Don't let the rubber noses fool you. I'm no clown."

Later that afternoon I met with the producer of a TV series that was going into its 14th season, and he didn't want to admit the story line had died 13 seasons ago. Ratings were down. Actors were burnt out. They had gone through a myriad of writers. So, after his tired, forty-five minute spiel as to why the series should continue, I cut in.

"I'd like to get your opinion on something I'm dealing with. My grandfather has been on life support for, oh, I dunno, fourteen years or so, and he's never going to recover. We don't even visit anymore because we're sick of how depressing it all is. So, assisted suicide? Euthanasia? Should we just unplug the old man or what? Can we get a quick group vote on the issue?"

I was trying my hand at dark, ironic subtext humour, but no one responded; there was a mixed silent tension of unease and a whisper of anger at my crassness. Some people flat out didn't get it. It's not a jester's job to be obvious, you know. Or nice, for that matter.

"Ok, well, if we don't unplug him then, can I ask a favour? Could you pay him a visit sometime? I just can't take it any more. Visiting times are from 7-8 on Thursday nights ~ oh, oh wait, that's the same time as your show, sir. Well, I guess none of us can turn off the pain!"

Laughter. Frustration. Clearer discussion. More laughter.

The show was axed and we went for drinks.

Cyrus stood on his chair in front of the crowd that night and raised his Plazma glass to my milkshake. He was twelve shades to the wind with most of the menu in his belly. "Jester, tell everyone what you think of the new tablet we're rolling out for Expo!"

"Love the tablet. Hate the name. If I see another product with 'i' in front of it *I'll* puke."

"And tell everyone here: what did you think of the movie trailer we saw today, Jester?"

"Repulsive. Trailers that show the whole story line, excessive explosions, extreme close ups, or trite love scenes succeed in lowering the collective I.Q. of society. They are the direct reason why the world is so stupid."

I thoroughly enjoyed jesting the king and listening to his booming laughs filling the suite. I felt in total control. I was living famous in the coolest way possible. The king wrapped his fat arm around me as though I were his son. "This jester is the most talented genius I have ever owned! I don't know what we've done without him all these years!"

"Hey, take it easy! I never claimed to be a genius. But if that's what people are saying, I can work with it!"

Who was he kidding? A genius? No, just an extremely lucky cab driver. That's it. But I have to say I didn't get tired of the accolades. Being praised by the biggest player in the business fed into my ego like the money he was feeding into my account. It didn't take long before the fame started distorting my perspective, I soon found out.

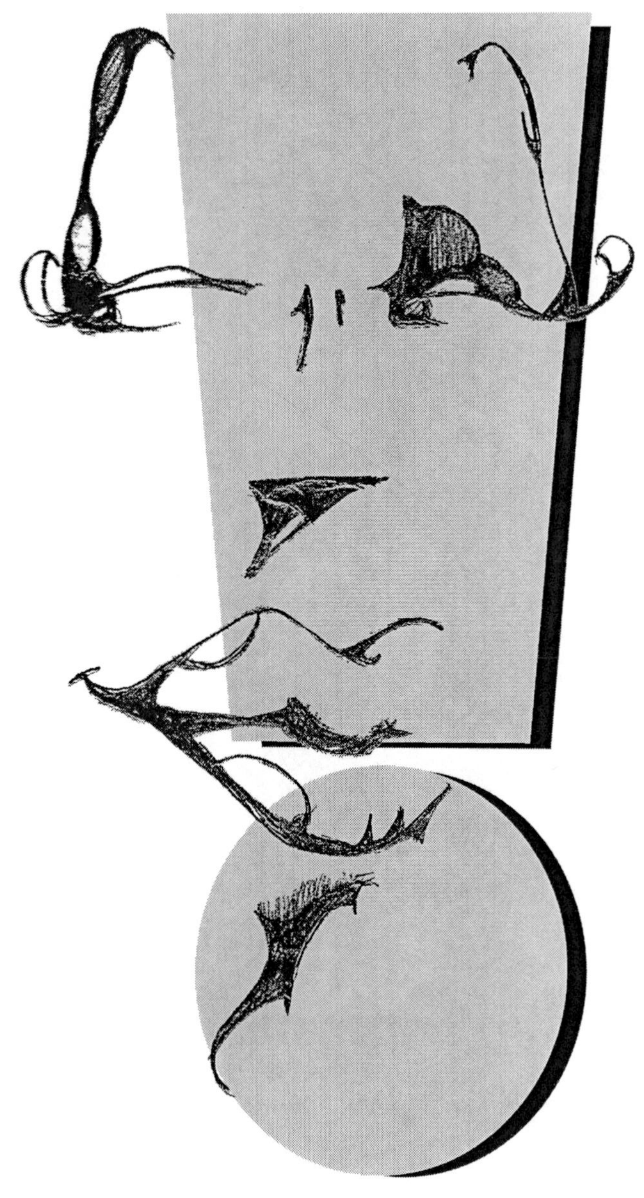

CHAPTER FORTY-SEVEN: A DATE WITH THE DEVIL

"Vincent, please come in. I just had the milkshakes brought up." Ms. Devlin opened the doors to her palatial suite wearing a long, green velvet dress with a foxy cut up the right side, and a string of sparkling red jewels around her neck. The suite's lighting dimmed perfectly when I stepped inside, and her seductive aroma craftily interwove with the sultry jazz playing on her WonderWall.

I also looked sexy. From the ankles up, at least. Having become used to living entirely indoors, I often forgot to take off my slippers when I walked around at night. Hopefully my all black silk motley made up for it.

"Sorry, I'm late, Samantha. When you said your place was 'strategically stationed' one floor above Eisenberg's, I thought you were speaking in metaphor."

Her trademark smirk appeared in the corner of her mouth. "Mr. Eisenberg would never admit I live one floor up from him. If you ask him about it, he'll just dismiss the issue and claim that my suite is smaller."

"Well, I've been sitting on the roof for the last twenty minutes waiting for his tower to rotate, trying to figure it out. Butterscotch had to show me the hidden elevator button, too. Very sly, very stylish, madame."

She offered me a seat on her aqua-massage love seats, set the Shiatsu setting to 'high', and walked over to the kitchen. Her dress caught a shimmer of light, accenting her forest eyes. "What do you take in your milkshake, Vincent?"

"Chocolate. Straight up." My voice sounded machine gun robotic off of the chair's vibrations. "Actually, I brought chips for us to share, but I kind of ate the entire bag up on the roof."

Although great comedic relief at first, and it's always smart to get your date laughing right away I've heard, the slipperiness of my silk suit in combination with the aqua love seat and milkshake resulted in us having to find more stable seating arrangements. I had never had a serious date in my life, let alone with a drop-dead woman. And even though Devlin and I had a chance to flirt, I felt it a little bold for her to suggest her bedroom as a suitable place to finish our drinks. There were no seats in there, after all. As inconspicuously as possible, I breathed deeply to calm the army of boxers making a punching bag of my heart.

Her WonderWall displayed mesmerizing visualizations, and the music sounded smoother than in the other room, all of a sudden. Still jazz, just more French or something.

"So where did you come up with this whole crazy 'jester' idea, anyway?"
"An app, actually, called 'Get A Life, Dipshit'.

She laughed. "The one that ends all of its advice with 'dip shit'? Funny, I gave that app the Green Light. Good to know it works."

I slurped the chocolate dregs from the bottom of my glass. "Yeah, I found its balance between sincere and insulting exactly what I needed to hear at that particular point in my life. That point being when my life had no point."

Samantha rolled over on her side to face me. She flirtatiously played with a lock of my springy hair, making my heart jump. "I think I'm attracted to your mysteriousness, Mr. Meistersinger."

“Freak is the new geek,” I said, stretching out on the bed with one hand behind my head, trying my best to play it cool. The music shifted again. A jazz ballad, full orchestra. The lights dimmed lower, and a few Digi-flames ignited on candles around the room. The change in the room’s mood seemed to match mine perfectly.

“Certainly your brainchild began before a measly app?”

“Most certainly! You can’t install genius, Samantha. Not on this hard-drive.” I wasn’t about to tell her about Chester. She’d think I had lost my mind for sure.

“So, what where do you get your ideas? Who are you? It drives me nuts that I couldn’t find any information on Infinoogle about you!”

“Hard to know where inspiration comes from. Perhaps it is a childhood gift. A snipit of conversation at a cafe, the sound of a forest, the fanciful idea of a movie extra’s unwritten plot. All I can tell you is creative inspiration is in my blood. And the reason you can’t find any info on me is because us Meistersingers haven’t had a fixed address since the 14th Century. We’ve been entertaining offline, gypsy styles, ever since.”

“I see. So that’s where your mythological charm comes from, young Jester.” Samantha bit her lower lip, then smiled sensually.

I almost choked on the romance escalating in the room. “How about you, Samantha? How did you become the queen of the mega-corporation of the century?”

“Queen, I like the sound of that.” Devlin set her glass on the bedside table and rolled over on her stomach. “Vincent, be a doll and unbutton the top few buttons on my dress for me? It's getting hot in here."

I hadn't noticed the temperature before she suggested a provocative unbuttoning, but the eruption of sweat beading down my back as a result of touching her dress could most definitely attest to the heat. Luckily, the air conditioning kicked in by the time I reached the fourth button, cooling us both off.

"Well, my story is pretty simple. There have been many more before Butterscotch and Cinnamon. Caramel. Double Fudge."

"Oh, no! Spoiler alert! Spoiler alert! You're one of Eisenberg's toppings?"

"The original. Strawberry."

We shared a laugh at how funny that came out, although the mental image of any part of her being on top of Cyrus revolted me. I couldn't help but notice the music turning slightly again once our laughs died down. This time with a percentage or two more funk. "Man, I love the music you've got on tonight, Samantha."

"You should," she said, pulling out her power phone, texting away. "You chose it."

"I don't know what you mean by that."

"No," she looked up from her phone and flashed me a condescending smile. "I wouldn't expect you would."

The woman switched at that moment, from sultry date to cold queen as she rolled off of the bed and buttoned herself back up handily.

"Ok, Mr. Popular," she sighed. "What do you need me for this week?"

I had no idea what provoked the odd change in her character, but decided it best to simply play along. Somehow I had made it to the bed portion of the date, so I didn't want to screw anything else up. "Ok. Let's see. I've got business meetings back to back all day tomorrow, so it might be fun to have some stilts for those. Oh! Do you guys have any better masks? The old ones you gave me a rash. It'd be great to have some new ones for the low self-esteem charity event on Wednesday."

"Your wish is my command, Jester."

"Samantha, what's up with you? I kind of feel like we've grown apart. Over the last twenty-seven seconds."

"Save it for your audience, Vincent, we're working associates, nothing more."

"Ok, no pressure. I just hoped we'd have had a better rapport by now is all. I hope it's nothing you've said!"

"Don't be ridiculous." She made no eye contact as she marched across her suite and opened the front door, ushering me out. "You've surpassed our expectations. It seems you can do no wrong. Cyrus is certainly content, and that's all that matters."

"What a crazy turn," I said, walking defeated toward the door. "Do you want to at least try to unbutton something of mine?"

"Just continue the Jester routine, keep Eisenberg happy, and everything will be ok." Queen Devlin's words turned wicked as she slammed the door in my face where I abruptly found myself walking down the colder, more harshly lit, and far less acoustically pleasing hallway.

Stepping into the elevator, I expanded my foolstaff and downloaded the 'GetALife,Dipshit!' app. I was looking for some reassurance, some explanation to the night's ill events:

"When you realize how perfect everything is, you will tilt your head back and laugh at the sky, dip shit!"

It's true. The only thing missing from that date was a laugh track.

CHAPTER FORTY-EIGHT: COUCH TREASURES

On Thursday morning, I noticed a photo sticking out of an ornate wooden chest, which sat with a hidden resolve beneath the king's horseshoe sofa. It looked like a tongue coming out of a thirsty beast's mouth. It had been opened earlier obviously, what with the picture and the chest angled slightly toward the edge of the sofa.

Odd that I hadn't noticed the chest before. I'd been in the king's penthouse many times.

Of course, I'd never been on the floor trying to sober him up before, either.

That's just how I found him when I showed up. He had scheduled me to draw a caricature of him on the throne after brunch, and I skipped in with easel in hand, only to find him barely breathing. Which was a relief, actually, as I had no interest in trying to move the fat fleshy beast. I spent a long time examining the king as he lied there, a pool of Plazma creeping across the floor toward him. His balloon nose was replete with moon craters and dead skin. His flushed cheeks matched the red suspenders he wore that day. A bizarre specimen, he was. Almost a parody of himself. Maybe I could do a caricature of him like that, I mused.

His new holographic buddy hovering above the table was also intriguing: a banana playing the blues on a banjo. Eisenberg's holographic friends usually carried meaning. Expressed something he couldn't...

My eyes were drawn back to the secret chest. If a king wanted something hidden, wouldn't a stronghold safe be a tad more secure than beneath a couch, like a commoner? That was the first time I'd been in his suite alone, essentially, and even though I've never let my curiosity lead me to snoop, he was basically begging for someone to take a peek. Right?

Besides. The king loved me. I could do no wrong…

Taking long, quiet steps, I reached underneath the sofa and silently slid the chest toward me, my left eye on the drooling king. I pinched the corner of the picture and slipped it out of the chest's mouth. At first I didn't understand what I was looking at. A troop of actors and a pit band orchestra were in the photo, on a modest sized stage. But after a few seconds, looking back and forth between the bloated, booze slain king splayed out on the floor and the dashing movie-star model standing on stage left, it was shockingly clear - they were one in the same! It must have been forty years ago, at least! The king was unrecognizable. Healthy. Happy. Old Eisenberg used to wax a life dramatic? An actor?!

Down on my knees now, I was useless against the temptation to snoop deeper inside the chest. I pulled out a stack of pictures and quickly thumbed through them.

A young Eisenberg played clarinet in a community band in front of a huge audience!

He worked in a costume shop and made props for children's television programs!

He even played the part of King Lear for crying out loud! I couldn't believe my eyes! Audition DVDs and keep sakes filled the chest, and suddenly the king gained another, more human dimension in my eyes. Creativity flowed in his veins, along with the rivers of Plazma.

Like the abrupt and halting horn off a Mack truck, Eisenberg's belch rattled me so hard I nearly flung the pictures across the room. Luckily he took his time waking up, so I had enough time to stuff the contents back into the chest, fix it firmly in its place, and scamper back to my seat.

Just as the king pulled his carcass up into standing position, I opened my drawing materials, began drawing, and pretended as if I was simply telling another of my stories.

"So, without a care in the world, the three intrepid travellers said farewell to their lovers and headed back to the convent to sell some cheese...Ah! Eisenberg! Feeling better after your post-meal nap?"

As if it were an exhausted sitcom punch line, Eisenberg wiped his mouth as he slumped into his throne and said, "Yes, I did. It was a nice little snack."

"So, have you any jesting for me to do today? You know I'm ready for it!"

He lifted a brow with a look of disgruntlement. "Why don't you take the day off? You deserve a rest."

"Come, on. There must be some meeting I can crash? A movie I can screen? Ridicule a paparazzi maybe?"

"I'm not in the mood for it today, Jester. Don't push it."

"The last thing I want to do is bug you, sir. But it's still in my job description! Ha!" No reaction. Not even a guffaw. Clearly something big bothered the king. Something big, and stuffed away in a secret chest.

"You don't mind if I ask why you seem down, today sir? Usually your nine-eggs-and-half-a-pig breakfast puts a smile on your face. Is everything ok?"

The king leaned back and adjusted himself. He stared out the window and simply said: "I get the Doldrums from time to time."

The man owns entire pharmaceutical companies; surely he could get some decent medicine to help him out. Heck, he's to blame for the city's collective misery, so why should I even care? "I see, that's tragic, your Excellency. What are your Doldrums about?"

"Everything. Nothing. I'm bored. It happens once in a while. Let's not dwell on it."

At last, I had a complete picture of my king. Surrounded by lavish opulence in his castle of luxury, I realized then that he was trapped by his success. It made him lonely, and depressed, and moody to boot. He was worse than I had been all those years watching LifeTV from my cab. Looking at life from the outside in. Success brainwashed him into thinking money was life's goal. And now I knew how many dreams he flushed down the toilet to crawl to the top. And how many dreams of others.

"Well, sir," I said. "Don't forget how great all the money you have is! I mean, money can't buy happiness, but it sure makes misery easier to live with."

"Yes, wise words, Jester." Eisenberg's eyes softened, and he squirmed in his chair a bit. "You know what? I think it's time you were rewarded for a job well done. I was going to give you this later, but what the hell!"

He shouted for Butterscotch and Cinnamon to 'fetch the Jester's gift'.

"Eisenberg, please, you don't need to get me anything," I said as I felt a cobweb of guilt descend upon me. I wish I hadn't looked in that chest.

"Nonsense! You've brought a lot to the company, Jester. It's a token of my appreciation for my trusted advisor!"

The man liked me so much because I reminded him of how he was, once upon a time. His creative dreams were wiped out, too. Now that I understood, it seemed such twisted irony that the king utterly repulsed me when I first met him, but was growing on me the longer I stayed. I wondered if I was the closest person the man had as a friend.

Butterscotch and Cinnamon appeared each carrying a small Exclamation Box resting on a royal purple pillow. My eyes bulged out of their sockets. These boxes weren't made of used cardboard. They were stunning, sterling silver!

"Go on and open them, Jester! I can't take the suspense, and I know what's in them!"

I lifted the lid off Butterscotch's box and saw hundreds of tiny mesh circles, each no bigger than a shirt button.

"Eisenberg, I haven't the faintest clue what these are."

"Those are just accessories, nothing special. Magnetic dots, that's all. We call them Magnodots. Go on, open the other one!"

Lifting the lid from Cinnamon's box, I saw a small, flat, black device on a short tripod. I still had no idea what it was. It was pretty heavy for its size. I turned it over in my hands and checked it out from all angles, and then felt a tiny switch tucked under and behind one of its legs. The thing turned on with a warm clear blue light beneath the top section, and gave off a soft hum. Standing it on the table I just waited to see what it did.

"Any guesses, Jester?"

"No serious ones, no. I'm kind of waiting for it to come alive and crawl around."

“There’s only two in the world – mine and yours, and they won’t be on the market years. It’s a Holographix.”

“Cyrus this is amazing! I don’t know what to say!” I hopped up and gave the fat man a hug.

“I saw how much you liked mine, so I had the new wizard downstairs whip one up for you.”

Ms. Devlin entered the room behind the king like an apparition, and glared at the two us getting along so well. She marched up to the table and stood beside Eisenberg. I noticed a faint look of guilt appear on Eisenberg’s face as she stood there. She raised her voice and spat pure bitterness.

“You know, I don’t know why people stopped hiring jesters, Eisenberg!” she said. “They are such jolly idiots, aren’t they? No, they’re not idiots, they are more like dogs. Funny, crazy dogs that everyone likes having around the house! Just one quirky escapade after another!” And she laughed at her own joke.

I admit her words stung a bit. Nobody takes very well to being called a dog. I can’t say she got a lot of laughs from that analogy, so, in true dog faithfulness, I played along. I licked up my plate, sniffed Devlin up and down, and climbed up on the table and pretended to defecate in the centerpiece.

“What were you saying about being an idiot, Ms. Devlin? Works for me!”

She grabbed a champagne glass and smashed it against the wall, her fiery red headed character unleashed.

“Don’t let Samantha get under your skin, Vincent,” the king said in a hushed tone as she left the room. “She’s the jealous type, you know.”

Devlin envied my relationship with Eisenberg? Absurd.

Eisenberg reclined his chair and got comfortable. His Doldrums lifted quite quickly; he probably mistook them for the Glums. “How about another tale of the outside world, Jester? Something funny to lighten the mood. Let’s do that portrait while we’re at it.”

“Sure thing, boss,” I picked up my pen and turned a clean white page on my easel. “How about a tale about a guy who rides public transportation in his free time as different characters. It's called: ‘Murphy’s Many Masks’.”

CHAPTER FOURTY-NINE: CHANNEL ONE

By Friday night, my energy had drained from my body like laptop batteries after a marathon online gaming battle.

Too exhausted to take off my motley and crawl into bed, I only made it to my study before I collapsed into a worn out heap on the carpet.

Rolling over on to my back, I pulled my jester's cap over my eyes, and used my foolstaff as a the world's most uncomfortable pillow. It was my first night off since arriving, so any sleep I got, wherever I got it, was gold. As a heavy slumber began to take my body hostage, I found myself replaying the week's events in my mind.

My foolstaff and I played the fool across the kingdom, greasing up the biggest big wigs I met. And there was nothing anyone could say about my antics, because I was under direct order from the king! Thrilling dream job? Yes sir. I performed poetry for advertising executives, and sang show tunes for the employees in the cafeteria. I jested in disguise like the early days, which never got tired, and I shook some vibes alive for guests at cocktail parties for King Cyrus. Now and again I popped up during casting auditions to throw actors off as they read their lines. I lived on pure adrenaline, feeling funnier, faster and more 'on' than ever before.

But something kept me awake. Something nagging.

I couldn't shake the feeling that I had forgotten to do something important.

I snapped awake, suddenly remembering.

The jesters! I was going to phone them, but got sidetracked somehow.

I had it in the back of my mind all week to tell them about the a-list luncheons and dinner parties, the screenings and film shoots, the grand openings and the charity events where I met with stars and producers from every branch of the industry. I felt a pang of guilt, because I had the contacts to get the Jesters mind blowing gigs.

But life was moving so fast I must have kept forgetting to call.

Picking myself up with as much grace as zombie road kill, I was about to search my suite for my uScroll until I remembered doing the same thing my very first morning in the suite. I was going to check to see if my foolstaff made calls, but then the swirling vortex of corporate jesting took over. Perhaps the king's Plazma had given my brain holes, I thought.

I reached for my prized possession and was about to open it, but a knock on my front door stole my attention. It was Cinnamon on the other side, summoning me into the king's penthouse for a private meeting. The phone call would have to wait a little longer, I shrugged.

Cyrus welcomed me with open arms as I shuffled inside. To my surprise and delight, his holographic companion that night was an animated exclamation mark. It hovered above his shoulder and changed colours as I followed him into his suite. How cute! And coincidental, I thought.

Unfortunately, my mood took a sudden dip when I saw my two least favourite people at MogulMedia, Max, sipping a glass of champagne on the couch, and Devlin, looking out the windows on her phone. Max shouted a fake schmoozy hello and jumped up with his arm outstretched for a greeting. He looked like he was hosting a game show. It was painful to have to shake his hand.

"Long time no see 'Mr. Man!' Sorry to dip into the bubbly before you came buddy, but we're pretty excited! It's a big day for us!"

I feigned a grin and nodded politely. I hadn't the faintest idea what he was talking about. "A little bubbly wubbly is never a bad thing," I chimed in, helping myself to a glass. "It'll make tolerating you a little easier."

Ms. Devlin started waving her arms back and forth at something outside and shouted into her phone. "Higher, higher. A little to the left! Yes, stop! Stop! That's perfect!"

The three of us joined her at the window, and the sight was utterly shocking. For a guy who likes surprises, that's saying a lot.

A helicopter hovered above a large condominium a few blocks away from MogulMedia where a few men had just finished unhooking a giant banner. To my disbelief, fastened to the sidewall of that condominium was the Jester Incognito logo: the exclamation mark! It stood tall and superb; a blend of reds and purple, and it even carried the quizzical face in the ball of the mark, just as I had drawn in my sketchbooks for years. It was huge! And…it was mine! They ripped me off!

My mood plummeted as low as it could go. I needed to sit down before my knees gave out.

"Overwhelmed, eh buddy?" Max said, laughing and giving me the thumbs up. "It's got to be quite a rush to see your brainchild larger than life!"

Ms. Devlin was in top form that morning, too. She spoke to me as condescendingly as a mother to her child. "Mr. Meistersinger, your vision is finally realized! Judging by the look on your face, you have no idea that you've created one of the biggest entertainment movements of the millennium, and the beauty of it is that you didn't have to sell anyone anything. Well, not consciously, that is."

I glared at the woman, too psychologically thwacked to respond.

"It has taken many months of hard work, but we are ready for the unveiling. The Jesters have paved a way for truly meaningful, authentic entertainment…tailored for each individual. It has been such an honour to assemble this promo."

Cyrus dimmed the lights and turned on the WonderWall with a flick of his wrist. "Jester, prepare to be amazed! This is the product we've been working on. It's a simple demo we used to sell the product to our manufacturers, but of course I know you will market this with much more creativity."

Market a product? Dread landed like a rock in the pit of my stomach.

Max put his arm around me and messed up my hair, playfully. "I can't wait to show it to you Vince, I think you're going to love it!"

The commercial they screened for me will be burned onto my cerebellum forevermore. Worse, it was an infomercial - the cheesiest of cheese on TV.

It began with a black and white image of an antenna on a grey background, and as a symphony built up in the background, a voice over came on with accompanying text: WELCOME TO A WORLD THAT KNOWS HOW YOU FEEL. At that moment the antenna started sending out vibrant colours in its signals, and the camera followed those signals through the city streets, swiftly darting along the roads and in between buildings…

The camera followed the signals up and into the condominium where a bunch of friends were sitting down to watch television together. At first they looked bored flipping around the channels, and then a friend of theirs popped by for a visit. That friend was no other than plastic Max.

Max: Hello Jack! Hello Wilma! I present to you the cutting edge of MogulMedia's smartest technologies. [He holds up an array of tiny, circular gizmos in his hand. Each is a different size and color.]

Wilma: Wow! Very sleek design, very colourful and eye-catching too.

Max: Would you guys mind if I used you as guinea pigs for a moment?

Together: Why not?! [laughter]

Max: Let me turn the television on first. Now, Jack, all I want you to do is walk up to that television set and watch T.V. Can you handle that?

Jack: Not sure. Can you repeat the instructions again? [laughter]

Max: But before you do, could you just tell us some of your interests. Be honest now!

Jack: Ok, like any interest?

Max: Any interest at all. What makes Jack, Jack?

Jack: Well, I like comedy. I'm into old Western movies. I enjoy nature, uh, meat, muscle cars…

Max: Great, super, more than enough. I just want to make it clear that I asked Jack to make his interests known to you at home before he sits down to watch TV. I guarantee you, you have my absolute word, there is no behind-the-scenes trickery happening here tonight. Jack, if you would please have a seat.

[Jack sits down. Max walks over the television and attaches the palm-sized gizmo to the upper right hand corner of the front of the TV. Immediately, the TV flips to a nature documentary. A few seconds later it switches to a how-to show on car maintenance, then to some stand up comedy… [canned applause]

Max: My friends! The world's smartest smart technology is here!

Jack: So, let me try to understand this for a second. The TV showed channels I liked automatically?

Max: That's right, Jack. This is the first and finest device to pick up on *human energy*. It tailors that energy into the kind of entertainment each and every individual desires. No programming or set up necessary. That means when you get in your car and turn on the radio ~ bang, you get exactly the music you want to hear! Phones and computers turn on and you are immediately shown the sites, or downloaded the podcasts that suit whatever mood you're in!

Wilma: My goodness, you're not kidding. This is incredible! But, the channels changed …was that just for demonstration…

Max: Not at all! This device reads your energy. So when it noticed that Jack was losing interest in the nature channel, it switched automatically to the energy it read from him.

Jack and Wilma look astonished at camera. Words on screen appeared: IT'S NOT ABOUT THINKING ANYMORE. IT'S ABOUT FEELING!

Max: And it works on all your electronic devices at home, too. Imagine you're tired after a long day at work and you come home. What are you looking for? Comfort, right? So you walk in the door after work and the sensors pick up on tired energy, so it dims the lights for you, it warms or cools the house depending on the weather, it tunes into a station you love, and it can even open your favourite recipe app to suggest ideas for dinner. [applause]

Max then walks into another room, a display room showcasing other common devices: a car stereo, a lamp, and a desktop computer. He places the other sensors on each of the devices and starts talking to the camera.

Max: This next level of technology is brilliant, it's dynamic, it's cutting-edge, and it's the natural, inevitable step in our evolution in science and entertainment. The beauty is its simplicity. All you need is two signals in order to send and receive its reception to the owner of the device. The first signal is from your network provider, and the second signal, is YOU! Yes, we've been working tirelessly on this device, and I guarantee it is everything you've ever dreamed of, and more!

[Max saunters by each item and it magically comes to life. The stereo plays light jazz, the lamp dims to a comfortable mood lighting, and the computer uploads the MogulMedia website. Max winks at the camera.]

Max: You know, people like to use the word 'vibe' when they are speaking about human energies. When we say that we're referring to vibrations, we're referring to actual sound frequencies that we as humans actually emit. There is only one frequency that reads and understands our vibes, and we've harnessed its frequency to make life just that much more pleasant for everyone. [applause]

[Max is about to leave the condo when Jack stops him on his way out.]

Jack: But, you never even told us what this amazing technology is called!

Max: Sure I did. I said there's only *one channel* that carries our frequencies ~ Channel One!

The camera zooms back out of the condominium and through the city streets. It stops at windows across the city and you see people attaching the Channel One device to their TVs and stereos. Eventually the colored signals carry the camera shot back to the original antenna, which is now alive with energy and a dancing, animated city below it.

The voice over returned:

CHANNEL ONE: We know you're unique. Channel One knows you are unique. Your mood changes day-to-day, minute-to-minute sometimes. Why should you have to have the hassle of finding comfort that will complement your mood when Channel One can find it for you? Welcome to a world that knows how you feel!

CHAPTER FIFTY: COMMERCIAL PUPPET

Cyrus raised the lights and stood up, smiling wide. He slapped Max on the back in congratulations and they poured themselves another drink.

Me? Flabbergasted doesn't cover it. I was ready to jump out the window.

Our logo. Our company. Our gimmick.

The dread in my stomach slowly began bubbling into anger.

The king extended his giant hand in an offer of trust, and I shook it as I strained the most convincing fake smile of gratitude I could muster. "I want you and Ms. Devlin to take this idea of yours, Jester, this surprise show idea, and I want you to come up with the most unexpected spectacular your little brain can thing of. Let's take the world by surprise with this. We want to show Channel One to the world with fanfare! A live performance! It will be the first live show in twenty years! Whatever you want!"

"Wow, sir. I can't imagine a greater honour." Socially acceptable words somehow left my mouth despite my rising rage.

"I want the world to meet the man that came up with the idea. So, I want you to host the whole shebang, Jester! MogulMedia Expo. That's when we'll unveil our new multi-billion baby! Channel One!"

Samantha handed me a glass of champagne with a crooked curl in her smile. "It's good to have you aboard, Vincent. You're going to have a hand at literally revolutionizing entertainment! I can't wait to hear your ideas."

I felt dizzy. Betrayed.

My biggest dream had become my worst nightmare. We had gone mainstream. I can still picture the hundreds of billboards and banners literally punctuating the city with Jesters' exclamation marks. I couldn't even imagine what my friends would think.

Ending our lovely little surprise 'knife-in-the-back' meeting, Cyrus and Max left for their midnight tanning appointments. I hoped the tanning beds collapsed and burnt the bastards to a crisp. Ms. Devlin sat down beside me with her tiny, pursed lips holding back an immense amount of her own rage.

"I can't believe Eisenberg actually listens to you and your idiot ideas. And now he wants you to host a live event? Preposterous. It will never happen. Cyrus Eisenberg will lose face."

"Which one? It seems like all of you people have at least two. The whole reason you plagiarizers even have something to launch is because you stole it from us."

"Do you have any idea how lucky you are we didn't just hunt you and your stupid little group of merry losers down? Kill every last one of you?" Devlin kicked off her stilettos and massaged her toes, completely remorseless. A career of stepping on people has got to be hard on the feet.

"Oh that's nice," I said. "So the entertainment biz does actually kill for ratings. How charming. I'll tell you Samantha, I'd rather be six feet under than be forced to advertise for you thieves!"

My words were futile. Devlin kept yammering. "But no, we needed to keep you around to run tests on the new device. Apparently you, of all people, have the perfect amplitude to calibrate the Channel One frequency with other machinery.

Remember our little date? Nothing more than a testing sequence."

My palms began to sweat as I remembered that night in her suite. The subtle change in music, in lighting. Her blender now calibrated to my energy to know exactly how I like my chocolate milkshakes. "That's pretty cold, Samantha. I've heard of manipulation before...Are you telling me I've been a lab rat this whole week?"

Samantha laughed as she slipped her feet inside her stilettos. "Yes Vincent. All week. Just be thankful you have a job, unlike your friends."

"What the hell does that mean?"

"Don't you remember? You sold the rights to your company to us."

I grabbed a half-empty Plazma flask next to me and threw it into the fire. "No I didn't! You hired me, not the Jesters Incognito!"

"Yes, we hired you and all your lovely ideas, remember? You belong to us. And so do your friends. They were amply warned to shut down their silly secret parties, though. We spared their lives, and a lot of running around."

"What? You are a crazy witch!" The fire's white flames ignited a plume of smoke.

"Yes, yes. Here comes the angry scene. I guess it hurts a little to find out you are nothing more than a pawn. Same every time. Please, proceed at expressing your shock and bitterness in private. I find it so pathetic."

I sized the woman up from head to toe, unable to speak because of the volcano of insults I had piled up in my brain.

She had lived up the 'devil' in her name, that's for sure. Her red hair was her fiery crown.

"We'll be watching you." She leaned forward and had the nerve to kiss me on the nose. I don't know how I resisted the urge to bite hers. "You can be sure that once this is through, you'll only be known as 'that guy from the Channel One Expo,' and that's it. This is my baby. I discovered you. You're nothing more than a commercial puppet."

I wanted to cut my strings and strangle her.

CHAPTER FIFTY-ONE: REVENGE

Knock knock.

Who's there?
Jester.
Jester who?
Jester who agreed to the biggest lie known to man: 'I have read and agreed to the Terms and Conditions of this Contract.'

No sleep that night.

What happened?

I got out of bed and walked over to the bedroom windows, staring down below at the muted city lights to quiet my mind. Rolling, round, sky-giant clouds threatened a storm just beyond the crest of the city.

The last thing in the world I wanted to be was the king's jester. That was it. Give me my taxi job back, I thought. Cabbing beats money and fame any day.

I was alone. I was trapped. It was all my fault.

I was just a pawn.

I had given MogulMedia yet another gadget to placate the masses with. I was the reason they had Channel One ~ MogulMedia's next mega-product was completely my fault! I would never live this down! Their Channel One devices were going to be the worst brainwashing devices of all! Imagine if they hooked it up to billboards downtown. Every single person would get an advertisement tailored specifically to how they were feeling as they walked by. What a nightmare!

And I thought TV was bad? The Outerweb? Channel One gives the king total power! The more I stewed, the more I realized how much worse Channel One could be.

If the device did actually give accurate programming based on peoples' vibes, MogulMedia could take that information and tailor all their advertising, all their newscasts, all their 'suggested sites', so that the consumer spent more and more time in front of media. And, ultimately, society would buy more and more of MogulMedia's endless line of products. Supposing Eisenberg didn't like the kinds of digital footprints that Channel One left behind, he'd easily be able to over-ride the device and go back to output-centered programming. Which means they convince you what to watch, what to wear, what websites to trust, and you'll think it's what your 'mood' needs.

Could I have been any more clueless? Eisenberg said it himself that very first night! 'People are rats in a very lucrative experiment. Media and technology is the drug.'

MogulMedia is not in the business of entertainment. Its business is mind control.

And I was a part of it all.

I heard the toilet flush in the en suite bathroom, running a trickle of paranoia inside me. Who the hell was in my suite? I stepped away from the windows and got down on all fours alongside of the bed. Did Devlin have someone spying on me already? Am I about to be royally 'offed'? I heard the bathroom door open, and the spy inside started whistling, carefree. I needed to act fast. I wasn't about to let them steal my ideas *and* what little grain of pride I had left. Reaching behind me, I picked up my foolstaff, hopped on to my feet and rolled across the other side of the bed toward the bathroom with my weapon raised above my head, ready to strike…until

Chester strolled out of the washroom wearing a flub-blunder smile on his face.

I should have known.

Confetti fell out of his pockets, and an extra tall, red top hat bounced upon his head as he walked. Party streamers clung to his purple motley like spaghetti.

"Biggitybooo!" Chester shouted, blowing on a bugle and throwing a handful of confetti in the air. He stopped and looked around the room for something he clearly expected to be there. "What? Party's over?"

"Right. Funny. What a joke." I flipped on the lights and fell back on the bed. I would have preferred bludgeoning someone to death than talk to Chester.

"Jokes! Yes! I've got one for you! What's worse than finding a worm in your apple?"

"I give up."

"The Holocaust! Ha!"

"Followed closely by working at MogulMedia," I added, killing his punchline.

Chester playfully tossed confetti in my face. "What's the matter old friend? The truth pill a little too big for you to swallow? Are you choking on it, Mr. Surprise?"

"No, I'm not surprised, you ridiculous putz!" I hated how he always went straight for the jugular. "I'm totally shocked! That promo video sucked the soul right out of me! My ideas, my logo, my company! Everything?"

"I'd be a wee bit pissed myself, Vince. Cyrus picked you off the grapevine and tossed you inside his giant slobbery gob before you even knew what happened. The only word for you is sucker."

"Thanks. That makes feel me so much better." I sat up on the bed and reached for a stack of the digital business cards at my bedside, shuffling them despondently. 'Jester', they read. Singular. My thoughts shifted to my friends. I couldn't even imagine what they were thinking. "You think this is all my fault?"

"I didn't say it was your fault." Chester traipsed over to the study and spun around on the armchair, his goofy top hat bouncing about like a spring. "But I'm blaming you. Ha!" He suddenly had his bag of popcorn in his hands again, the same from my first vision.

I turned my back to him, looking out the window at the clouds amassing above. "Piss off, would you? You are such a useless dinkus!"

"Oh! Good word!" Chester clapped excitedly. "You're a slap happy wapper jaw!"

"Trouser chocolate!" I barked back.

"Pestilence!"

"You are the slimy, cheesy, geriatric filth left on an unwanted set of dentures, so vile not even rats would eat you."

Chester didn't retaliate. He pretended to cry, stuffing popcorn into his mouth for comfort. "Go ahead and insult me, I'm you anyway!" His tears turned to laughs in a snap.

True. Unbelievably. I'd love a lobotomy to get him extracted from my brain forevermore. He made me livid. If it weren't for the thoughts he put in my head, I wouldn't be in this mess at all. I wanted to set the whole building aflame!

Then it hit me. Eisenberg had paid me a lot of money already, I thought, which set me up for life. So what did anything matter? I could torch the whole empire and live the rest of my life in a tropical luxury. Yes! Perhaps I could start by setting Chester on fire…

I charged into the room, lit like a roman candle myself, and tried to tackle the smug jester to the ground, but he vanished as I hit the chair. I knew full well it was pointless, but I had had enough. He was too cocky – too preachy. Picking myself off the floor of the study I looked around the room for him. He appeared again on the top of the TV, shaking his finger at me like a displeased mother.

"Why don't you relax yourself with some music, old friend? Soothe the soul?" Chester double clicked the virtual console on the stereo. Disco boomed out of the speakers. He busted out his best moves, trying to get me to dance with him. "You dig on disco, don't you? Relax and get into, man!"

"I'm done with it all, Chester! They shafted me! Don't you see I have a valid reason to hate this place? My mind is on loop: I'm such an idiot, I'm such an idiot, I'm such and idiot!"

"If you don't like the programming on LifeTV now, then you need to change the channel!"

"Change it? I want to shut it down. All I want is to shut everything off! I want to shut MogulMedia down! I wish there was a switch I could flip to turn it off!"

Chester stopped dancing and clicked the music off. "Sounds like vengeance to me, sir, a very intriguing piece of music indeed." He took a seat in the leather armchair, crossed his legs, and folded his hands, purposefully. The words that came out of his mouth sounded not unlike a dare. "Then do it. Flip the switch, Vincent. Flip the switch. It's can be as easy as one, two, three!"

Chester took a big breath, blew his bugle garishly, and vanished in a billow of confetti.

All I was left with were his three words, lingering in my mind.

Flip the switch.

My heartbeat slowed as I tried to mute the rumbling thunder in my skull.

Flip the switch. I became fixated on Chester's phrase.

I leaned up against the windows again and peered east at the city's distant edge, which was all but consumed by the blackened sky. I could barely make out the tip of the forest leading to the periphery of Roger's farm before the darkness swallowed it. I imagined our old mood globes here and there, still buzzing with vibrancy. *Did they ever lose their power?*

Flip the switch.

My head in my hands, I turned those three little words over and over in my mind.

The storm's first bolt of lightening burst out of the clouds, jostling a distant memory awake in me.

On the night Roger unveiled the Frequencifier to all of us, he walked us through the properties inherent to vibes and the Mood Globe signals. I remembered that Roger said the vault was only functional on an INPUT level only. It could only receive frequencies. I can still see it very clearly. Roger walked over to the Frequencifier, pointed to the dial, and told us all to *never* turn it to OUTPUT. It would trigger a 'reverse signal' on the output of the Channel One Frequencifier units. Once that dial was turned, the input signal from the storage unit fed from all the mini-data globes would be directed back out into the units. He said the amount of quantum force released back into the Channel One frequency might dangerously distort other signals, and may even cause serious residual damage.

Roxy had already experienced a taste of that distortion. I had felt it rip through my skull like a heat seeking missile.

Why distort when you can destroy, right? Cyrus stole from me! He deserved it!

I jumped up from the floor and pressed my face up against the glass eagerly scanning the city. If the hundreds of globes could cause small pockets of localized distortion, then thousands of them were going to do way more damage than that! A powerful wave of pure, unadulterated human 'vibe' energy would be sure to distort Eisenberg's tacky Channel One knock-offs.

Flip the Switch! Shut MogulMedia down! Overthrow the king! I danced around my suite like a maniac.

Sitting back down in the study, I crossed my legs and folded my hands purposefully, just as Chester had done, ready to hatch a plan. I had to figure out a way to…

"Hang on a second," I said to myself. "How the hell did Cyrus get his hands on Channel One in the first place?"

FLIP THE SWITCH

CHAPTER FIFTY-TWO: THE WIZARD ALL ALONG

What about Roger's work in all of this? I asked myself.

It took him years to discover the Channel One frequency, so there's no way MogulMedia could have perfected it so quickly. If Cyrus was manufacturing Channel One on site, he would need Roger, too. Of course!

How could I have forgotten my favourite quantum physicist? My fame-fuelled self-centeredness blocked him out of mind completely. Roger had been hoodwinked just like me, I was sure of it, and that meant the source had to be near here, too. The Frequencifier could be here at MogulMedia!

And if the vibes were here, there was a chance I could get away with flipping the switch! Vengeance could be a lot closer than I thought!

I just needed to find Roger. I paced around the study doing my best Einstein impression.

Everything Chester says is code for something else, I'd learned. Replaying our conversation, the insults, the dancing, the advice, I finally settled upon Chester telling me that flipping the switch was as easy as one, two, three. What did that mean?

The WonderWall in my study activated, displaying Devlin's gigantic head on an incoming call.

"Vincent. Do not forget we have our first Expo planning meeting this morning at eleven. I expect you to be a well-behaved pet jester, as we discussed, and keep the king happy. I will layout how the event will unfold, and all you are going to do is nod and agree. Do you understand?"

"No, actually, I don't. Is that a British accent you're trying out, or a 'Bitchish' one?" I picked up my foolstaff off the floor and threw it against her face.

Devlin rolled her eyes and ended the call; the wall cleared to its default wallpaper. In the bottom right corner, as always, was the square window mapping application of the building. I expanded the window, and scrolled through the kingdom with new eyes. The towers looked more like a factory to me than before, even though I had come to know the people there so well. How could I have actually thought my 'old school' jester act was going to have any positive effect on MogulMedia? I had jested the whole place fifty times over, top to bottom, and for what?

Well, not the whole place, I guess. I never went into any of the three basement levels.

And there it was.

It's as easy one, two, three.

Level One, Level Two, and Level Three! Eureka! Chester, you creepy visual modification, you're a genius!

Of all the people I'd befriended at MogulMedia, there were only two who could help find out if Roger was down in the secret sub-layers of the central spire. Only two who could get me access. With my eyes glued to the WonderWall mapping application in my suite, I finally spotted Kevin and Keith's avatars (two multi-coloured overalls) walking toward the elevators on the 9th floor. I picked up my things, bolted out the door and into the elevator, and rocketed down 73 floors to intercept them. The doors opened moments before they reached the elevator.

I could hear them singing in unison without a care in the world. As soon as they saw me waiting for them, they opened their arms for a giant hug. "Jesty! Long time no see!" Grabbing them by their overalls, I pulled them into the elevator, and pushed the basement button. "You two are taking me downstairs. The third level below. Right now!" I demanded.

Keith gulped. "We can't do that, Jesty, it's super confidential, and the security cameras are..."

"There is no debating this, gentlemen. I want to see this right NOW! You must help me or you are going to see a very scary psychopathic jester, very soon! I'll find out where you live. I'll de-organize you lives! Now follow my lead."

We got off the elevators on the second floor and I ushered the two of them into the first men's washroom down the hall. I noticed that the security guards we passed nodded their head politely, but then discreetly radioed to their fellow employees as soon they thought I wouldn't notice. Devlin wasted no time in keeping tabs on me, that horrid, power-hungry dragon witch.

Washrooms were the only non-surveillance areas in the complex, so the three of us discreetly snuck inside so Keith and I could switch clothes.

"Here's what you have to do," I said. “It’s the easiest scam in the book. You’re me now, got it Keith? Leave this washroom, get back in the elevator and ride it to the 43rd floor. Just walk around the floor pretending to look for something. I left a bag of hats and masks inside boardroom C, so after you've done at least three laps, pick up the bag, get back in the elevator and ride down the main floor. Go inside the men's washroom and wait for Kevin and me. Do all of this slowly, we need some time."

"This is way too much stress," Keith said, losing colour in his face. "What if a security guard stops me?"

"Put on one of the masks! Tell them you are trying a new style of jesting. And then just ask them lots of questions and kind of be a jerk."

"Ok," Keith said, zipping my motley up. "But if you really want them to think I'm you, we're going to have to trade. My Bling for your staff."

"Keith is right, Jesty. No costume switch-a-roo can trick the chip tracking system." Kevin pulled my foolstaff from my hands. I had a hard time letting go. It was as if I had a foolstaff addiction.

With the Bling on my wrist and rainbow overalls strapped on, Kevin and I got back in the elevator and rode down to the first floor where the basement access doors were located. The jumpsuit fit a little tight in certain places, but I managed.

"Just so you know, I'm dead against this," Kevin said. "But I'm actually happy to have some time away from Keith. I mean I love the guy and everything, but sometimes he's just *so* gay."

With two affirmative beeps from Kevin's Bling, we were in the basement elevator doors heading deep beneath MogulMedia. The elevator was a domed Plexiglas, quiet as air, which could carry very large cargo and travelled vertically and horizontally beneath the mega complex. Except for the tracks of industrial lighting way above us, the basement seemed to sink into bottomless, blackened shadows. We went down two levels, across one wide-open area, and then down another level before the elevator stopped and opened its doors.

Kevin opened the double doors directly ahead of us by motioning his wrist at the green sensor, and we walked out onto a stainless steal platform over-looking an expansive laboratory. The lights shone brighter than the sun; we shielded our eyes and walked down the steel stairs. Any further and I'd feel the heat coming off the earth's core.

We passed an open steel crate in an area labeled ‘shipping and storage.’ Looking closer, I saw thousands of tiny black boxes inside, each adorned with a white exclamation mark design and the words ‘CHANNEL ONE: Welcome to a world that knows how you feel.’ A raft of identical steel crates stretched back as far as my eye could see. I wanted to scream. How in the world did they manage to get this product ready for shipment so fast, I wondered.

Following Kevin in front of a wall of computers, I felt wave of familiarity wash over me as we stepped into the open area; a strange, displaced feeling of déjà-vu. I stopped and squinted through the brightness of the lights in order to take a good look around. As a towering robot might emerge from a fog, I saw a cylindrical tower just a few steps away from me, taking me aback. After a major double take I registered that it was The Frequencifier from Roger's farm! It must have tripled in size! I almost lost my balance as I looked up at its astronomical flow of shades and radiance.

"Are you ok?" Kevin asked.

I looked at him, and then back at the vibes swirling inside in disbelief at these two worlds of mine meeting. "Yeah, I'm fine, I can't believe..."

"You can't believe it's the same Frequencifier? Indeed, it is," the voice came from behind us, sounding defeated. Worn out. “I’ve harnessed a satellite signal to it as well, so the reception is much stronger. Forgive my arrogance, but I think it's some of my best work."

Appearing out from behind the computer consoles, my favourite quantum physicist walked over and shook my hand. "It's a pleasure to see you again, Vincent," Roger said with a bittersweet smile on his face. "I wish it were under more favourable circumstances." His eyes were sunken and grey, and he stood hunched over wearing an official MogulMedia lab coat. He'd had the soul sucked out of him, too.

"Roger you have no idea how happy I am you're here! With all of your stuff, too! I thought you might have died!"

"Well this is a strange place to run into someone you know," Kevin commented. "High school? Summer camp?"

"Something like that, yeah," I said, laughing. "Kevin would you mind giving us some time to talk? In private?"

"I totally understand. Nobody likes a dinner for two with a place setting for three. Just remember that the guard does his rounds every hour, and it's better we're not here. Which means you two have 45 minutes to catch up. Meet me at the elevators, Jesty! Not a minute later!"

Roger hurried me the other way around the back of the lab and walked me away from its illuminated centre. We walked up a narrow corridor away from the Frequencifier, into what seemed to be the back of the basement. "Your friend is right," Roger said. "The guards are rather tenacious. I have something to show you, but we'll need to hurry."

"Roger, how did all of this happen?"

"I don't remember much. I was up late one night working in the Exihertz when the laboratory was stormed. Before I knew it I was drugged, and blindfolded, and all my equipment was transplanted here. They forced me to explain my experiments, there was nothing I could do."

"But weren't you off the grid?"

"I can only presume that while you were being tracked, they followed you to me and put two and two together, completing the equation."

"Wait, Roger, this is nuts. How could you have reformatted your lifetime of research on Channel One in the space of a week? It's impossible!"

The physicist stopped walking, standing stiff as a board in front of me. "A week? Vincent, when did they bring you here?"

I shrugged my shoulders, dismissively. "Last Saturday. On Hallowe'en."

Roger took off his letterbox glasses and held his forehead as if seeing a ghost. "My friend, I'm afraid you have been here longer than seven days. Tomorrow is the first of June. You've been here for seven months!"

CHAPTER FIFTY-THREE: TELEXCELERATOR

Roger slapped my face to focus me, his panicked whispers sounding miles away in my shocked state. "Vincent, there's only one way this could have happened. Cyrus must have hypnotized you!"

My head throbbed as though it had been dramatically resized. It felt as if a dense layer of marshmallow lining the space between my brain and my skull had been diminished. *Seven months? Impossible! I was sure it was only seven days...*

Roger slapped me again. "Did he give you anything? A charm? A gift of any kind? Surely he must have given you something..."

"The only thing Cyrus gave me was..." I patted my pockets for my foolstaff that wasn't there. "The Green Light. Woa. Roger. Do you mean…Oh my god, I'm such a fool!"

Roger pulled me over against a wall and spoke in hurried whispers. "There is digital witchery at MogulMedia of very potent proportions. The Green Light, I have deduced, is the reason why any performer stays at MogulMedia. Its hypnotic glow gives a person the allusion of freewill, yet they are in fact trapped in a time warp, brainwashed into performing at the king's whim. We must get you out of here before he realizes you are no longer in his grip."

Crouching down in front of the wall, Roger, with a microscopic drill he carried in his palm, removed the four screws on one of the wall's square panels. He proceeded to crawl inside.

Standing in the pitch black belly of Eisenberg's empire at that moment, realizing seven months of my life had been stolen from me in the blink of an eye, made me feel like I'd been swallowed whole.

Roger's hands popped out of the opening, and he pulled my pant leg to follow him inside. "Vincent, there isn't much time!"

We shuffled through what could barely be called a tunnel; metal tubing stuck out at odd angles along the floor, and nests of wires hung down, hitting me in the face.

"Believe me, I don't like being deceived either. But Vincent, I do believe that every worthy invention endures mistreatment. History has proven it. Greed is inevitable when new ideas are born. You and I are inventors in our own right, and even though what's happening to us now isn't right, it is a good thing. You need to believe me. Struggle creates opportunity, and as you always say, the fun is in not knowing how it's going to end up."

"Oh I know how it's going to end up! We're taking this place down! There is no way Cyrus is getting away with this!"

"Indeed," Roger said, stopping before we crawled into an open space that was big enough for us to stand up. The makeshift walls and ceiling were still riddled with the back ends of equipment we were hiding behind; the lights that blinked on the outside gave off a pulsating Christmas hue.

"I've been forced to keep my private research extremely private here. I can't imagine what Cyrus would do with this in his hands, too."

Roger pulled out a black, oval shaped container about the size of a steering wheel that he had hidden behind an opening in the jungle of electronics. He flipped the container over to display a shiny steel gizmo on its opposite side, encased in a glass dome.

"Remember the teleportation device I had sketched out in my notebook so many months ago?" he asked. "The one you asked me about? Well, voila!" Roger lifted the glass dome and picked up the device, which looked like a wide silver headband with small golden discs it. "The Telexcelerator."

He handed the device to me and I squeezed it around my frazzled head of hair. "Like this?"

"Correct! It's not yet complete, however. I still require more time to install the sound wave receptors in each of the discs before it can run on quantum energy. After that, the user places the Telexcelerator on their head, imagines where they want to be, and then...teleportation!"

"Roger, that's incredible! It's the perfect way out of here!"

"Indeed. I just need more time to finish my work."

"I have an idea," I said.

We could hear Kevin's voice from across the lab. "Let's make like bananas here people! Twelve minutes!"

"I know you do."

"You know I do?"

Roger put the Telexcelerator back into hiding and we began crawling back through the wires. "I'm afraid I haven't been completely honest with you from the start."

"You think? You're a walking enigma, Mr. Eventually Roger. The whole research experiment is pretty out-there. Oh, and by the way, those Vizmos keep happening, which is doing nothing for my sanity!"

“Indeed, yes, well, their effect is only temporary."

“Great. It gets more reassuring each time you tell me that.”

“More important is the role you've played in my quantum findings. You see, my research belongs to a much larger body of studies. If you think MogulMedia is able to produce their technology alone, without significant data, you are mistaken. And the data you and your friends have helped me collect needs to be shared in order to further…”

“Roger, let’s cut to the chase, ok? I want to reverse the signal on the Frequencifier.”

Keith shouted again, slightly more hysterical. “Jesty, this train is leaving the station in six minutes!”

“Agreed. Society is not yet ready for the level of technology in Channel One. The device will only end up adding to the already crippling case of the Doldrums society suffers from. You have my permission to reverse the signal on the Frequencifier,” the quantum physicist said, glancing at the Frequencifier worryingly.

“Ok, then let’s do it right now!” I squirmed my way out of the crawl space and brushed myself off. “Let’s take this place down!”

"It's not that easy," Roger whispered, drilling the wall panel into place. "If you really want to topple his empire, we're going to need a lot more vibes in the Frequencifier.”

"Whatever it takes. How many are we talking?"

"I predict 10,000. At least."

I looked up at the Frequencifier again. Impossible. Even by Hallowe'en, we had only collected 7,000 vibes, tops. And that was over the period of a year.

Still. I couldn't believe the vibes were at MogulMedia all this time, right below my feet. Cyrus had unknowingly made this step a lot easier, at least. I was a fool to get tricked by him. I'd be an idiot not to at least try to return the favour.

"Midnight on the night of the Expo," I said, completely unsure it could be done. "I'll be back here to flip the switch, and then we can teleport our asses out of here."

"Don't let them know you know about the Green Lights. And whatever you do, do not look into them again. You might wake up a few years later." I shook Roger's hand and ran back to the elevators.

"None of this would have been possible without you, Vincent," he shouted.

"Yeah. I feel like I should apologize about that."

CHAPTER FIFTY-FOUR: CARTWHEELS OF DOOM

Minutes later I was back in my motley rocketing up the central spire's elevator, a tremor of very pointed intent boiled in my belly as I turned the foolstaff over in my hands. I would never let the toy hoodwink me again. Tossing the talisman to the floor, I smashed the monitor with the heel of my foot. A thin crack spread along the glass, its system spraying sparks, short-circuited. I breathed a sigh of relief to see the staff still expanded, but the gems no longer glowed as bright. My gaze wasn't transfixed upon the Green Lights. I knew I had terminated its hallucinogenic lure, free from the time-sucking spell.

Seeing Roger locked up against his will like that, stories below the earth, was the final crack for me. We didn't sign up to have our ideas ransacked, or to have months of precious life stolen from us. I didn't get back in the entertainment scene to trick anybody into consuming entertainment, either. I'm not that big of a fool.

But I was still a fool. Not only that, I was the king's fool! And while I knew the redheaded devil-queen had her thumb planted firmly on me, I still held a chess piece powerful enough to set a plan in motion. For I, not she, was the king's trusted advisor.

The doors whooshed open and I ran up the hallway gaining as much speed as I possibly could. Then, with a series of zippy cartwheels straight into Eisenberg's master boardroom, I landed halfway through Ms. Devlin's lecture on her plans for the Expo and hopped onto the table, legs folded, directly in front of her. I fixed my cap, straightened my collar and smiled as insincerely as I could.

These were not cartwheels of superficiality, no sir. They were born from the very core, the very zenith of my anger. Cartwheels of determination. Cartwheels of vengeance. Cartwheels of doom.

"Your Excellency, with all do respect, I think a bit of advising is needed at this juncture by yours truly, pet Jester." I pulled my foolstaff from my pocket, expanded it, and balanced it on my nose. Neither of them seemed to notice the change in the glow of the Green Lights. I kept my eyes on Devlin, but spoke to Eisenberg, my energy thumping well over a million mega-hertz.

"Our esteemed Chief Operating Officer, Queen Devlin, is going to ruin the launch. She's wiping her butt with the budget, and all we're going to be left with is the skid mark of failure. In fact, I can't say I like any of her ideas yet ~ by the sounds of things, I've attended more exciting funerals. I think she has as much creativity as a bloated tick on a dog's back."

Queen Devlin let her tablet drop from her hands, utterly insulted. I saw her left eyelid quiver. "Who the hell do you think you are?"

I stepped it up a notch and rolled backwards into standing position on the table. I looked over to the king and silently mimicked an exaggerated Devlin saying 'who-the-hell-do-you-think-you-are?' His drunken giggles moved me further up the chessboard.

"You mean you still don't know who I am? I'm the guy who made all of this possible! I'm the only one who is going to plan this party! Now start taking notes before I shove that tablet up your proverbial port!"

Her eyes shot laser beams, but I didn't budge.

"You get your ideas from useless factoids and pretty pictures you find in Vidzines and Infinoogle searches. That's like reading off the teleprompter…your whole life! Not an inch of you is original. I'm the real deal honey, and I'm telling you that the party you are planning, SUCKS! I guarantee you're going to recycle every tired awards show cliché, and somehow, incredibly, make it worse! I didn't think that was possible. Let it be original for once! This show is going live across the country, and you want to shovel the same old crap down people's throats that they've been choking on for years! If you want to really 'wow' people, you've got to surprise the hell out them! This should be the party of the century, and I'm sorry honey, I just don't have time to teach you how to do that!"

Man that felt good. You know when you have a blow out argument, and you wish that you had said something more after the fact? It wasn't one of those. I laid it all out. I had released a metric ton of pent up emotion.

She had no comeback whatsoever. Devlin pursed her lips and marched out of the room, the queen's piece keeled over. Part one of my plans, complete!

I slid towards my gainful spot beside the king, tucking the staff into my belt. "I'm going to map out my ideas for the launch, Eisenberg. Guaranteed to be the Expo of a lifetime, you have my word."

"You're the jester, Jester." Cyrus leaned back in his chair with his hands behind his head. "It's a good thing, too. She gets so obnoxious after a while."

The second part of my plan was nowhere as simple: 10,000 vibes into the Frequencifier by midnight of the Channel One unveiling. Oh, my kingdom for a genie-in-a-bottle. I needed help. I had to contact my friends, but I knew I was too heavily monitored to try it from inside the empire. Devlin, I was sure, had set a drone on my foolstaff and OuterWeb account from the very start.

I needed a way to talk to them offline. I needed out of MogulMedia. And the only way that was going to happen was if I brought the big man with me. He needed some more loosening up if that was going to happen, however.

"Cyrus, would you do me a favour and step in front of the bathroom MagicMirror with me?"

The king had just poured himself a black flask of Plazma, and promptly dropped the ice cubes he was about to place in the glass.

"Jester. Please. Whatever it is you want to do in there we can do perfectly well out here."

"With all do respect, your Excellency, this conversation requires a mirror. It will be in vanity, otherwise."

"Very amusing, Jester, but bathrooms are for earthly deposits, not conversations."

"Not where I come from! Look, if it would relax you at all, call that loser Max in with us."

Eisenberg swigged his Plazma, refusing to budge on the matter.

"Ok. Forget it. I just don't know how much energy I'll have for story time with all the Expo planning happening now."

Five minutes later, the king, Max and I stood in front of a MagicMirror in the bathroom.

"Why am I here?" Max asked.

"I bet you ask yourself that every morning, don't you Max?" I jested. "Just do us a favour and shut your snooznatch."

I put my arm around the lard-assed, lying king, and the two of us looked at our reflections in the mirror. Switching off the MagicMirror program, we were left with the uncluttered images of our faces looking back at us. My reflection had never been clearer.

"I realized the other day that you and I are very similar," I said to Cyrus. "I think we even look the same."

"I think you need another drink," Max said.

"Shut it, Max. I swear I could give your plastic surgeon more work."

"Make your point Jester," Eisenberg said. "You know I don't like to stand for too long."

"My point is that you and I are one in the same! We both love the entertainment business. We both like being entertained, but I think we both like entertaining, too. Am I right?" I took a breath and held it, waiting for his response. I was 100% sure he had no idea I snooped in his hope chest, that I knew about his theatrical past, his brief foray into the music world on the clarinet, but the way in which Eisenberg finished his Plazma and passed the vial to Max, wiping his mouth with the back of his hand, and giving my reflection a careful look in the process, made me think he might have known.

A long moment passed before he said anything, this time looking squarely at his own reflection. "We're entertaining people everyday, Jester, you've taught me that."

"Exactly!" I shouted, finally exhaling. "But I'm talking about *really* doing it. Really pulling a jest! You and me! No more of this castle-in-the-sky crap. You should have some fun for free instead of paying other people to have fun for you! Do you feel me?"

Cyrus' eyes flashed. If there had been a piano in that bathroom, a thrilling trill would have begun at that very moment. It was electrifying to see the twinkle ignite inside the king's eyes, something I hadn't seen yet. There was music in his soul after all.

Cyrus Eisenberg was dark, thumping techno. And a bit of tango.

"I've told you all the stories of my jester friends," I continued. "The Dingleberry Brothers and their finger puppets, the mysterious shadow painter, Fitch and his pockets, Murphy and…"

"His Masks. Yes, and the tall one who eats only breakfast all the time. Yes. Yes. I see now what you proposing, Jester." Eisenberg continued looking at himself in the mirror. I imagined him peeling back the years from his fleshy face and staring deep within to find the former him, connecting with his performing past. The laughs he had. The energy. The places and people I'm sure he remembered fondly were locked inside.

I, on the other side of the mirror, could not have cared any less about Eisenberg's longing for his precious past. It was merely my fare back Uptown. Whatever sympathy I had had for that fat bastard was now spun on its head and spat back at him. My long shot plan suddenly had motion! I put the jester's cap on Eisenberg's head and laughed, pointing at the mirror. "See? We're not so different really. Let's just do it! Let's go out tonight! Blow off some steam! Together we can be jesters incognito!"

Eisenberg swiftly turned and gripped me by my shoulders, at arms length like a proud father.
His words came out not like a father, but squeaked out like a child begging permission.

"Can we go to Cosmos?"

The two-faced king was sold.

"You bet we can, big guy!" I took my hat back from his head and in the same motion bopped Max over his head with my foolstaff. "Make yourself useful, monkey, and have the car pulled around! We're heading out on the town!"

CHAPTER FIFTY-FIVE: MOOTS NO MORE

"Let's do it all!" Cyrus bellowed from the backseat.

I resumed my role as cabby, this time at the helm of the titanic SUV, and shipped the merry king across the city. The king held his flask out of the open window, joyfully singing and saluting the city. "The clubs, the pubs and that place you told me about with the twenty-foot subs!"

The king was having the time of his life. I, on the other hand, was ready to drive the hefty sack of blubber off the SkyBridge to drown a watery death. If I died in the process, so be it. If not, then I could salvage whatever was left of my former life. Either way, it would be better than the hell I was living. The whole scheme of mine was turning out to be a much farther fetch than the most spry dog could pull off.

"His wish is your command, freak-o," said the guard next to me. The muscle man was assigned to accompany us by none other than our fun loving queen. Involving the gossiping Max Hype was a terrible idea after all.

"You need to understand something," I said to the guard, flatly. "That sub place he wants to go to? I made it up. I also made up the underground venue for beard competitions he wants to see. And the enticing tattoo shop where the tattoo artists tattoo you as a completely different person from head to toe? I lied about that, too. The king wanted stories, so that's what I gave him."

The guard pulled out a gun from his inside vest pocket and began polishing it. "Well, take him somewhere, kid. You've got an hour. Mr. Eisenberg has never left the SUV before, so no joking around."

"Don't worry. There's only one place we need to go." I shouted as best I could over Cyrus' hooting and hollering. "Start getting changed, your Excellency! We're almost there!"

Cosmos was packed that night. And as soon as I entered that blessed restaurant full of grace - full of grease - I felt a pang of nostalgia, distracting briefly me from my mission at hand. Regular people living regular lives, albeit addicted to bubblegum entertainment. The old jesting days were suddenly another lost, another better life away. Seven months…

Being on the outside made me feel puny again. Insignificant. It truth, it felt freeing to feel small.

I shook my head to clear the emotional haze from my mind. My goal that night was to find at least one of my friends. I didn't care which. Preferably not Fitch, though. I wasn't sure he would be able to keep it together. There was too much at stake.

Nobody.

Empty on a Saturday night before a Moot?

Not even Nelly was waiting tables.

"No script, no sets, no prisoners! Planning kills the spark! Am I right, Jester?" Cyrus stumbled in the entranceway, finally joining me after wasting a ridiculous amount of time getting into costume. I was dressed in baggy hip hop attire, which we had both agreed to wear in the spirit of keeping our presence discreet, but his boozy brain had decided differently. The king dressed, instead, as a wizard. Florescent green robes adorned with glimmering silver stars, a long white beard, and a wizard's hat so high it knocked the lights about as we followed our waitress to our seats. Customers' heads had no choice but to turn as we walked through the restaurant, their attention drawn toward us like magnets.

I rolled my eyes. “Nice, your Excellency. You blend in real nice. Seamless, like a Technicolor cartoon in a black and white film. Maybe we should just sit apart from each other. That way you can jest however you want.” I desperately scanned the restaurant for my friends.

“What? Jester, I wouldn’t know where to begin. No, don’t leave my side! I need you to give me ideas! Some motivation.”

He was making my head pound. “I’m not sure you’d want to hear my ideas at the moment,” I remarked. It would take a lot longer than the thirty measly minutes we had left to fasten the bloated king into a Ziplinc and leave him stranded on the Lower East end. Dressed as a wizard, no less.

I was doomed. Doomed to watch Cyrus inhale the Lumberjack breakfast special.

Cursed to see him attempt pathetic magic shows for customers, and pull out his clarinet to serenade the cook. At one point the cook actually gave him a tip to stop playing.

And I was condemned to find no help in Cosmos before our regular Saturday night Moot.

“Nothing for you tonight, sir?” The waitress asked me, waving the menu in front of me.

“No. Thanks.” I didn’t even look at her. I was plenty full on misery.

“Not even a coffee?”

“I’m fine,” I grumbled.

“Well, could I interest you in a coffee haiku?" The woman said with a lively turn in her demeanour.

“That sounds delightful!” Cyrus wiped his mouth with his neon robes, and poured some Plazma from a flask in his coffee. “This city is so random, I love it!”

I couldn't stop her. She was on a mission to irritate me.

"Beans ground south in mouth
Flavourful cure constipate
Liquid, social hot.

See? Just as satisfying in your imagination as it is in your mouth! Words can be pretty tasty!"

I wasn’t in the mood for cutesy ‘randomness’ at all, and she could tell that from my angered expression. "Alright, alright. Just trying to have a little fun."

The guard rapped at our window with his fist, and pointed to his watch.

“Well, that’s it your anus, I mean highness” I sighed. “Did you have a nice time tonight?” I looked back at the waitress who was standing at the register, and waved my hand for the bill. We locked eyes actually, as if she had been waiting for me to look over, and then she ‘faced’ me!

A ridiculous silly fact in fact; a bloated cross-eyed chipmunk-looking something or other. I was so taken aback. The absurdity of seeing a woman make such a face, in public, in my predicament no less, was jarring. But when she did it a second time, it finally registered. Our jester code! How could I have been so stupid? Court jesting had brainwashed me from my very own roots! The waitress was LaRose! I got the giggles immediately and shot one back at her. At last! Some hope!

“What in the world are you doing?” Cyrus asked as he tried to squeeze himself out of the booth.

“Nothing, nothing. Strong coffee. Um, I’ll take care of the bill. Meet you in the car, sir?"

“Very well,” and the king farted thrice as he waddled out of the restaurant.

"I can't believe I jested *the* jester without him even knowing!” LaRose hugged me as I rushed over to the counter. I could feel the good energy coursing off of her, so long overdue. “It’s great to see you again, Mr. Meister. We all thought you were dead!”

“Not dead. Just drugged. You have no idea how good it is to see you too, LaRose. What are you doing working here?”

“Are you kidding? It’s the plight of the struggling artist. I lost my call centre job and had to make ends meet. Or have you forgotten about that?”

“Please. I crave it. Look LaRose, time is of the essence. At the Moot tonight, I need you to…”

“The Moot?” LaRose looked at me as if I’d grown another head. “Honey, the Noize have been on us like cobras. There’s hasn’t been a Moot in months. And maybe you know something about that…would you like to explain what the hell is going on out there? The banners? The commercials? Did you sell out and cut us off?"

“What? No! Absolutely not! It's the exact opposite. Look, do me a favour and pretend I'm just jesting you, ok?" I took out some money and motioned ever so subtly to the guard waiting out the window. "Just laugh a lot and play along, even though everything I’m about to tell you is far from funny.”

I held nothing back. I owed it to my friends to explain the situation. And with no communication to the outside world, LaRose was my link to the Jesters. She, like an angel sent to aid us, was how I could choreograph our takedown of MogulMedia.

HA!
HA!
HA!
HA!
HA!

CHAPTER FIFTY-SIX: OPERATION LAST LAUGH

And so the silly faces spread. Like nutty peanut butter across Roxy City.

LaRose silly faced Vixtrix at the bank who silly faced The Man Whose Scarf was Too Long down at the mall who silly faced Scalliwag at the cafe who silly faced Humdinger in the hospital who silly faced Smallfries at the skateboarding park who silly faced Feathertip at the library who silly faced Breakfast working overtime at Shmitty's, who silly faced Underplum on duty who silly faced NorthWest Wind Esquire at the airport who silly faced Crumb at the arcade who silly faced Harrington at the Ziplinc switch and on and on.

As word of the king's transgression got out, so were passwords shouted down flushed toilets, then launching jesters into the Forbid Den once more. It was the start of an upgraded underground mission, and I took great delight in imagining my fellow actors and musicians join force.

Leave it to Fitch to give our mission a name. He called it Operation Last Laugh. He said he saw a nature program about hyenas once, and that after scavenging for food, hyenas have a laughing contest to see who can laugh the longest. They all take a big breath at the same time, and the hyena that laughs last, wins the biggest piece of meat.

Later he told us he made the whole story up.

Everything except seeing it on a nature program.

Operation Last Laugh was simple, in theory: 10,000 Mood Globes. MogulMedia Expo. Steal the show. Literally.

I convinced Cyrus that if he wanted to stay authentic to the signature style our fans loved, I would need clearance to throw the biggest live, citywide extravaganza Roxy had ever seen. Live was what the city wanted, I told him. That was the only reasonably unsuspicious thing I could ask for to secure so many thousands of vibes trapped in one night.

After seven flasks of near-black Plazma, he consented. Max and Ms. Devlin would arrange the entertainment, including big Green Lit stars like The Black Nosed Poops, Toasterhead, Skrxkrttzvmkz, Mauve!, Brad Canyon, 25 Bucks, Jessica Shellbyville, and what's his face from that show: Whatever, I So Don't Even Like Care.

Without a doubt, the Jesters would find a way to make that night their own. Sneak in, take over, and paint the town crazy. I could picture the explosion of energy in the Den as plans hatched giddily. Fizzlestick would go overtime into mask making. Murphy would move truckloads of Mood Globes across the city in his Lucky van. And Apropos would code a new website deep in the sub-layers of the OuterWeb so our chapters across the country could get word.

Not to mention our fans.

Smakdabber
Crates full of snow globes in the pickup. See all you party people there! #OLL

UncleSlim
I HAVE to go to the expo this year. It's going off y'all! #OLL

Balloons.com
Planning a function? Have you considered balloons to wow the crowd? #OLL

Gizamundo
Fools rush in. #OLL #applicablequotes

ChibbyGaz
You can't stream soul this sonic, kids.

Undergroundin'
Need to hook up with my peeps. I quit my job to make this happen. I'm hardcore like that. #OLL

HighTech
I lost my job making nanoids at MogulMedia. For nothing. You're damn right I feel like going to Expo this year. #OLL

Prettysilverbullet
One minivan. Nine fans. Party of the century. #OLL #epicliving

Pign'twist
I'm bringing pizza cupcakes. That is not a metaphor. #OLL

RoxyTimesArts
Would someone please tell me what this group is all about? #OLL

Sheeppies
Wrapped up invitation kiddies! Block party styles! #OLL

Daniella
YES! I've got the car that night! Scores! #OLL #can'tfrickenwait

Penny Trix
Throwing a party on a budget sucks. Throwing one without, does not. #OLL

BrianMills
I'm coming by boat. No joke. #OLL

Doug
Inflatable Palm Tree Beer/Soda Cooler Anyone? #OLL

Youngblood
Weeeeeeeeeeeeeeeeee!!! #OLL

GangStars
If I miss the train I'm going to lose it. Anyone coming in from Biggstown? #OLL

MoonSunTreeLove
Some guys we know are coming back out of retirement. Whoever could they be? #OLL

Gungho
I'd love to come, but I've got to research this paper on anti-corporations. Wait a second…#OLL

The Paige
Bringing the tuba out. I don't even care. #OLL

OliviaSmalls
Finally! I've been dying for some good music FOREVER!! #OLL

Chump
It's funny how I just said brb to my friend, but I'm never coming back! Bring it on people! #OLL

BeeSting
Colour me there, it's large and out loud redemption time! #OLL

Pahtay Problems
Think customs will let me fly with my mood globe? #OLL

Fablines
I've been practicing, yo! I'm primed to bust out the sickest dance moves at expo! #OLL

As the Expo approached hundreds of people helped put Operation Last Laugh into effect. Our fans on Critter and

YouBoob responded in droves, being led by our neighbouring jesters, too. Apropos worked overtime to keep our plans undetected on a secure feed, and #operationlastlaugh appeared on Critter in no time. At the last Moot before Expo, the jesters received hundreds of requests from people looking to become members of the Jesters. Not all of them claimed to have any particular 'jesting' talent, however, but the troupe needed every bit of good-willingness. Past customers even volunteered to help our cause. I imagined jesters running about Hyde Park distributing Mood Globes in every nook and cranny they could find. Under park benches, behind marquees, up trees, underneath sidewalk grates, inside mailboxes, inside parked cars, you name it. Dressed in black, looking more like ninjas running back and forth to Breakfast's limo to fill up their sacs.

More than this however, more than the Jesters and followers in Roxy however, and more than any independent performance group had ever expected, was the response that blazed across the country, like an aggravated rash, once word had spread that the king of all media ripped off our beloved troupe. In a matter of days, the Jesters found themselves managing a colossal anti-mainstream media movement set to take place outside the king's very castle.

A reverse surprise party. Everyone but the host was in on it.

CHAPTER FIFTY-SEVEN: AMPHITHEATRE AH-HA

Life for me inside the empire blurred in fast forward. The only thing that gave me the oomph to keep me bouncing across my royal jester duties was in knowing the Jesters united outside. From costume fittings and set design meetings, and through sound-checks and countless rehearsals, my life became a kaleidoscope.

MogulMedia's 'less is more' advertising campaign was an overwhelming success. Multi-colored exclamation marks covered the windows of MogulMedia to keep our preparations private, and let the city's curiosity generate interest. Surprise, it worked! For the first time in MogulMedia's history, Eisenberg did not cave to the pressure of the paparazzi, those sly buggers. Not being allowed to come anywhere near MM premises, they sat like windows snipers with meter-long zoom lenses trying to snatch a shot. Critter boasted a new post every .0007 seconds in anticipation of the Mogul Expo.

Kevin and Keith became two of my closest allies. I didn't divulge a word of my real plan knowing full well how quickly Keith's mouth would ruin them, but the pair were very effective in helping us execute them.

"Eisenberg has thrown a lot of cash at this," Kevin said to me after a sound and lighting run through. "He obviously has a soft spot for you, Jesty."

"We've never seen anyone so new get treatment so good before," Keith said. "Oh my god that sounded like a commercial slogan."

"Yes, for a spa!" Kevin squealed. "You need to write that down!"

“I’m flattered, really. The set design is incredible you guys! You have no idea what it’s like to see my Exclamation Box in real life like this; it’s like I’m standing in my imagination, as corny as that sounds.”

Kevin nodded in agreement with his hands on his hips, walking across stage toward the boxes’ purple and green awesomeness.

“Yeah, we did pretty great on that. Did you know it’s 12-storeys high? There are five doors that open just like you asked Jesty, including the top. That’s where the bands and all the exhibitionists are going to come in and out of.”

“The inside has a hydraulic system working the ups and downs and opening of doors. It’s kind of like a massive Rubic’s cube with multi-platformed dynamics,” Keith added.

“We built it on top of the floor elevator that usually lifts pianos and heavy stuff on stage. We can lift any sized prop up into the bottom of the box.”

“It’s amazing engineering you guys, you’ve done an incredible job. People are going to be asking for your autograph when this is over.”

Keith slapped me on the arm, giggling. “Oh Jesty, you’re making me blush!”

“And how cool are the chandeliers?” Kevin asked. “They even constructed them in the shape of exclamation marks!”

It truly was a spectacular sight. The lighting crew perfected the spotlight mechanics to reflect off the diamond chandeliers just so. It was shaping up to be a dream come true, oddly enough.

Which is why it was such a tragedy that the whole event was basically a preview of a way over-budgeted commercial for

Channel One. I was breaking the fifth rule of the Jester code! I tried not to let it get to me, but being a glorified advertiser made me feel cheap. In fact, I think doing commercials is just a step above being a game show host, and that's saying something. Game show hosts make me puke in my mouth a little bit every time I see them. At least commercials are 30 seconds each. Much easier to stomach.

The Expo was going to be three hours long, so I did my best to pack as much variety as possible into the show.

"Say, guys, how easy would it to be to hide tablets under, say, ten random seats so I could video-jest audience members throughout the evening?"

"That's a cool idea!" Keith squealed. "Super easy!"

"Awesome! Whoever said a little cyber couldn't spice up this space? And I was thinking we should set up a Critter group that's live throughout the night so I can make a better bond with the audience. Maybe the wittiest post on Critter gets to choose which door to open next on the Exclamation Box. What about that?"

"It's all too risky. Too much can go wrong." Ms. Devlin's unmistakable voice accompanied the unmistakable clip clop clip of her tall stilettos. Even before she crossed the length of the stage I could see her lips were pursed so tightly they throbbed blue.

"Nice of you to join us, Samantha." I stepped toward her and titled my cap forward. "Risky ideas are good, by the way, when are you going to figure that out?"

"What's your plan if something goes wrong?" The look in her eyes told me she hoped with all her might that something would go wrong.

“We’ll improvise, which I know is not part of your repertoire. You’re the kind of tight-ass who knows exactly when, how long, and where you’re going to crap, six months in advance.”

Kevin and Keith snickered like children behind me. “If anything can get through,” one of them whispered.

“Just remember that your legacy starts and ends after the unveiling. You and your mob of renegade misfits will be remembered as nothing more than glorified monkeys whose entire career amounted to making money for us. Don’t forget it.”

“Great, thanks for the dollop of negativity. When you win this year’s award for most anal, discouraging and uninspiring creative visionary, I and my ‘misfit mob’ will be in attendance, cheering you on. We’ll show our support of your agonizingly limited scope of the human condition by playing funk music and stabbing hundreds of voodoo dolls in your image.”

Ms. Devlin turned and marched off stage, sufficiently dissed. As I watched her leave, I felt an unexpected, quiet pang of guilt for my hurtful words. I knew I shouldn’t have felt bad for her at that moment, but I did. She’d made my life hell, treated me like a guinea pig. But there was clearly something underneath that made her that way. At least Cyrus had an excuse...he could blame it on his Plazma...

“That woman is such a witch,” Keith said, blowing her a kiss. “Not an ounce of creativity in her, so what gives her the right to boss us artists around?’

“You said it buddy. If she were a band, she’d be The Pits.” Mulling over Keith’s comment, I brushed my hair into a do tall enough to pick up ideas from the Signal Fields. Maybe if Samantha had her creativity encouraged a little…

"Well, we should probably give you some alone time before the big day," Kevin said. "Is there anything else we can do to help before we go, Jesty?"

"Let's see. Cameraman Stu's promised to keep filming me no matter what. And Cinnamon and Butterscotch have promised to get the king so sauced that he won't be able to move. I'll tell you what. Can you guys do me one last favour?" I pulled out a wad of hundred dollar bills and gave a handful to each of them. "Can you buy me a medium size black box, some white paint, and then go crazy at the Shebang store? Some candy, a couple toys, pick up some music, some sexy jazz/pop fusion stuff, and an instrument, maybe? I don't know, like a mini hand drum. Some card stock and markers, too. The rest of the cash is for putting together the best Expo ever. Cool?"

"Very cool," Keith said. "You're going to be great tomorrow Jesty! Break a leg!"

I sat on the edge of the stage and looked out into the emptiness of the amphitheater. I couldn't see the back rows, even with all the lights on. I needed that quiet moment of meditation before the biggest night of my life. Breathing in deep I tried to exhale the butterflies floating around in my stomach. With the Exclamation Box behind me, and a vastness of empty space in front, I felt poised on the brink of a lifelong dream. To perform live for thousands.

It was hard to believe that the amphitheatre would be full in less than 24 hours, and even harder to believe I was the host. Before I finished my escape plan, I had one last box to deliver.

CHAPTER FIFTY-EIGHT: HOLOGRAPHIX

The holographic recording took a few hours to perfect. Because I hadn't written exactly what I was going to say, and it was the middle of the night before the extravaganza, it's an understatement to say my brain felt like it was going to ooze out of my ears in runny rivers of anxiousness. I spent a long time on multiple takes of me in my motley. I pre-recorded a Magnodot with the Holographix to project a virtual me at the end of my closing remarks, just before the end of the show. Clear lighting. Life sized.

My escape plan was simple enough, I hoped.

During the last commercial break I'd tell the lighting crew to keep the stage dark, for dramatic effect of course. While dark, I'd slip down into the Exclamation Box elevator shaft unseen, and then activate my holographic recording. I figured I needed to buy myself about a twelve-minute window of opportunity to get down to the lowest level, flip the switch and then, fingers crossed, teleport to freedom.

Teleport to Freedom. It'd make a good title to the autobiography of the second half of my life, wouldn't it?

"Where in god's name have you been, you fool? I've been trying to get inside your head all day!" Chester appeared in my suite. He made the oddest entrance I yet, wearing a checkerboard motley and carrying a glowing blue staff with a rusty trumpet slung around his shoulder. All while riding a massive yellow rabbit.

"What in the world?" I scrambled to my feet and backed away, pointing at the rabbit with a trembling finger. The rabbit made feel as big as a peanut. “Chester, get out of here!”

“Now, now. Guests are the bests, remember. Say, whatchya got there, buddy? Looks like it could suck the soul right out of ya!”

Keeping a careful eye on the yellow beast, I sat back down to my work at hand. “Don’t bother me, seriously, I’m recording myself.”

“Oooh, well done, Vincent. You’ve reached a whole new level of vanity. I’ll call wardrobes and get them to retro-fit elastics to your hats. Accommodate your ego.”

“Egos are healthy. Besides, you’re the one who told me to ‘go for the red fish.’ That’s what I’ve done. Now I want out.”

“Sure blame it on me. Whatever you say. I’m smart enough not to argue with an idiot. You’ll only drag me down to your level and beat me with experience.”

“What? Where’s this punishment coming from? How can you think I’m an idiot?”

“You’re not an idiot. You are idiotic, though. History has proven it.” Chester twirled his staff between his fingers and climbed off his yellow friend. I could see in his smile he completely enjoyed adding to my stress. “I used to be indecisive, but now I’m not sure. That I’m indecisive, that is. Bah! But I’ve made up my mind about all of this, though.” Chester opened his arms and motioned to the lavishness of the suite. “Have you, Vincent?”

The rabbit thumped loudly as it hopped into the kitchen, sniffing about the floor for crumbs. It would have been cute if it didn’t make me feel like I had taken drugs. “What’s with the rabbit, Chester? I really don’t even want to know.”

“He’s my new ‘sick’ ride. His name’s Yorick, and yes, he is rather unworldly, isn’t he?”

“You mean unwieldy.”

“No, I mean unworldly. Not of this earth. Mythological.” Chester tapped his staff twice, producing a radiating blue window at its top. A series of photos began to play in rapid slideshow succession. First a picture of Little Red Riding Hood, then Batman, Rumplestiltskin, a wizard, a werewolf...

“Have you forgotten all those years playing piano and drawing and dreaming? When we talked for so long about how great life is going to be? Don’t you remember? And here we are, where all the magic happens! La di doo da dippity la doo. We’ve come a long way, but really we’re just where we started, no?”

Man, jesters can be annoying. I needed to tune him out. He was only there to distract me, I thought. I positioned the Holographix perfectly to film my whole body. With my bed sheet up against the wall, I had a neutral backdrop so the camera would pick up my image only. I started to change into the motley I would wear the following night while my imagination yammered on in the background.

“Think about it Vincent. You’ve got the money. You’ve got the fame. You’ve got more techno-toys than you know what to do with. So, what’s after this? Are you going to just run away from here and fart around with your friends again? Do you know who you are anymore now than you did when you were younger?”

Chester pulled his trumpet around and played a jazz riff that sounded like a dying duck. He was mocking me with it. “Change is inevitable, Vincent, except from a vending machine. Ha! So, do you want change, or what?”

“Shut up Chester! Honestly! I’m in front of the world tomorrow night and my whole life depends on it! If I were any more stressed out I’d be crapping pickles right here on the floor!”

“Well if your shit’s already pickled, I guess you’re already too old to change.”

“Why in the world are you asking me about change?! Why should I change? This is my only chance to get back to my normal life!”

“Yes, now you’ve hit the proverbial rabbit on its metaphorical tail. Normal. Life. Let’s meditate on this for a moment, shall we?” Chester hopped on top of Yorick and struck a cross-legged meditative pose. He closed his eyes and hummed.

I did my best to ignore him. If he was really part of my psyche, which he sadly is, I was embarrassing myself. I put the Holographix aside and finished getting dressed, from belled cap to belled foot, and then took a still shot. I wanted to look exactly like I would on stage, because I planned not to be on stage at all by the end of the show.

Chester opened one eye and nearly fell over at the sight of me. “Well, well, well! Nostalgia isn’t what it used to be! Vincent! You have changed already, my man!”

Chester hopped off the rabbit and stood in front of me with his arms wide open, his smile as big as a house. Just as I realized what he was talking about, I hung my head and started laughing in defeat. Somehow I had missed this punch line the whole time. In my final motley outfit I was dressed exactly like Chester, checkerboard design and all!

“See! You think you’ll leave here and go back to a normal life? Are you kidding? Vincent you idiot, you’re me! I’m you! You’ve become the myth you wanted to be! You didn’t even know it, did you? You jungerflop, there is no more normal life for you!"

In a snap, Chester was on Yorick again, kicking his sides, and I watched them hop out the window and into invisibility, gone as quickly as they had come.

The jester inside my head was right, again. He might not have been real, but he made some great points.

What am I going to do after this, I wondered. What's life like after prancing about the entertaining industry? And then shutting it down? What will I do after everyone knows the surprise is through?

CHAPTER FIFTY-NINE: MOGULMEDIA EXPO

MogulMedia Expo. Game on.

In my green room, draped over the comfy velvet armchair, flipping channels on the TV Wall, I tried not to lose my cool while I watched every major television network that had a piece of MogulMedia's Gala Exposition.

Click: The Jesters Incognito have already punctuated this year. Punctuated it with an exclamation mark! And if the rumours online are true, there will be no shortage of surprises tonight!

Click: People are predicting this to be the most out-of-the-box starts to the Expo in history. Break-dancers, circus performers, there is talk of Gollywood stars dropping in. The rumours abound!

Click: The street parties are the Jesters' signature performance style, of course. For those who aren't familiar with the Jesters Incognito, they are a group of underground entertainers who have successfully carved themselves a niche in the city's arts scene with their unique blend of 'anonymity art'. They've given us everything from performance art to visual art, installations, and spoken word. The Jesters are responsible for the buzz surrounding this city.

Click: MogulMedia hasn't disclosed any information on their extravaganza planned at the MogulMedia Amphitheater either, but there is no doubt they have something very big in store for us! Mr. Eisenberg, the undisputed king of media and entertainment, has profited immensely from having his own personal jester. Rumour has it other companies are building business models around jesters-as-advisors, too. Who would have thought it?

Click: The scene at the MogulMedia amphitheatre rivals Times Square here tonight. We can see an aerial shot of the dome; there isn't an empty seat! And that's just the party at the main stage. MogulMedia TV is live across the city at five enormous street parties; throngs of partygoers are filling the streets at each. The sight is unreal!

Click: Every walk of life, every age, neighbours and co-workers, family and friends; this city is ready to get their groove on! This is the most anticipated affair the city, and perhaps even the country, has ever seen!

"It's the big night!" Cyrus bellowed, hovering into my dressing room with smoke frothing from his cup. Cinnamon and Butterscotch were right behind, keeping his throne steady. "Are you ready to change your life forever, Jester?"

I stood up and bowed to the king. "Sure I'm ready, Cyrus. Are you?"

"Most definitely! Channel One is a guaranteed money maker!" I watched in disgust as the king almost toppled backward as he polished off his drink. Cinnamon immediately poured him another one. My mind was on getting out of MogulMedia alive. Eisenberg's mind was on drowning himself in Plazma. "Did you think you'd ever make it this far, boy? You are a true success story."

"It is remarkable," I said, not referring to Channel One in the least. "I do believe we'll be giving the world a story to tell for years and years, your Excellency."

9:00 pm Curtain call.

I took a deep breath to prepare myself as I walked down the back stairs and awaited my official signal at starting position.

Peeping through the curtains I saw the throngs of people outside. Much more nerve racking in real life. Was I scared? More than an obese bungee jumper.

Twisting my blonde Afro into a tight ball, I squeezed it into my hat. As I released, my hair filled the hat into a veritable poof, standing tall for my national debut. I had dreamed of doing this since the dumbwollop ice cream flavour was invented. And we all know how long ago that was.

Mahler's 2nd Symphony began. My fave. Immediate tension and intrigue with Mahler. The video jumbotron showed animations that mimicked the music with intricate visualizations first, beautiful designs and vibrant colours that captivated the audience. And just as the music changed with the sustained trumpet and violin tremolos, they started the retrospective video on the year. The long legato lines accompanied images from the past year: political upheavals and natural disasters, awards and celebrities. The audience was enthralled, applauding and laughing in all the right spots. The orchestra hung onto that middle section with such craft. It was whimsical, melancholic, the whole bag.

The music changed again, descending brass, back to intensity and then, behind the ascending double bass aggression, animated words and phrases spun across the screen: Future. Hope. Trust. Innovation. Technology.

They were giving the audience hints toward Channel One. MogulMedia, they'll sell you on anything without you knowing it.

The music shifted again, this time to brilliant intrigue. An animated exclamation mark bounced in synch with the tympani and brass, large and in charge in the middle of the screen. The crowd went wild! That was my design in front of the world! My nervousness changed form right then, from anxious fear to pride and confidence. The ball turned to show its face, grinning and giggling. Then it separated from its stem and grew a jester's body! The jester ran across an animated replica of the city, leaping over buildings and dropping Exclamation Boxes wherever he liked. Just as the music simmered down again, the cartoon jester came back to the stem, which was now a crafty box, reached and pulled out a…

Boom! The lights were thrown on, the music shifted to some bass heavy funk - my cue to run onto the stage. What an opening!

I came running out of one of the Exclamation Box's doors and the crowd went absolutely mental at the sights and sounds of it all; their energy was so infectious I couldn't contain myself either! I was supposed to just stand at centre stage and let the crowd calm down. But I couldn't! Instead I signaled to the band to keep playing so I could break out my best dance moves. I couldn't help it! Once in a lifetime!

After a few more repeats on the B-section, the band turned it around and finished up. My cue to start my opening monologue was when the massive amphitheatre lights dimmed and three spotlights lit me up on centre stage. I took a B-I-G breath.

"Now this is what I call a party! From the magnificent city of Roxy, welcome to the most anticipated extravaganza of the year, MogulMedia's 32nd Annual Entertainment and Technology Expo!" [thunderous applause]

Backflipping across the stage, I then froze while standing on one leg, twirling my foolstaff and then catching it in my mouth. [more applause]

"Ladies and gentlemen, let me begin by thanking all of you for not only being here, but also for bringing me here. You see, it is really because of all of you that I'm standing on this stage tonight as your host. You have decreed to the king of MogulMedia that you can't download live entertainment! And live entertainment is what you want! For those who don't know, my name is Vincent, around here they call me Jester, and I started a little group called the Jesters Incognito." [Applause, cheering]

As the audience's went on for what felt like forever, I stole a moment of reflection and looked over to the piano I played my very first night with Cyrus. I could almost see myself there again on the night I became a court jester.

I still held the foolstaff, but it wasn't holding me any longer.

Maintaining my smile, I stepped forward motioned to the band behind me for some backbeat on drums. I needed a little pepper on the monologue to give it some flavour.

"So yes, it was you, you blessed consumers of the latest and greatest, who launched me to the top of MogulMedia. You guys made jesters in vogue, again. Like eight centuries later, how wild is that? There's a fad no one saw coming! And I won't lie, it is a major rush to be a star! Sure beats, well, everything else I've ever done! [Applause, laughter]

"Really, there isn't any difference between who I was before, and who I am now. For example, I still have beautiful women feed me. That's the same. I still laugh and point at people when it's totally inappropriate to do so. I still send my dry cleaning to the dump and buy new clothes instead. I still think everyone in the world is dumber than me, and I still hide pizza in my hat just in case conversation goes dry." [Applause, laughter]

I could make out Eisenberg beyond the harsh glare of the lights in my eyes. He sat in his glass booth above the masses, laughing with a frothy beverage in his hand, completely unaware everything I said was a mockery of him. I couldn't wait to smack that clueless smile off his face.

Breakfast and the boys would be at their locations by now, I thought. Go for it boys, get the globes out there! No time to waste! If the energy pumped as hard in the city as it was in the amphitheatre, they wouldn't have a problem.

"But who really cares about jesters, anyway? That's what you're thinking, right? It is ironic that Cyrus Eisenberg hired a jester for a company that is, in fact, the cutting edge of the future. Is there any place in this century for old-fashioned jesters? The answer is yes, obviously! Pop culture has always needed a jester, and my friends, I am proud to say it is my job to present to you the latest in devices, in movie and TV for this year's Expo. And what's even better, I get to make fun of all of it!"

I narrated along with the teaser slideshow featuring the Expo's headlining products. All except for Channel One, of course, the showstopper. I ridiculed the new telekinesis app for the power phones, and the parabolic, waterproof TV for bored scuba-divers. I thoroughly enjoyed pointing out to the audience that if you removed the actors from all of the newly released films, the special effects would still be able to carry the plot. Immediately following my monologue the distant verve of hip-hop music began to pump out of the colossal sound-system as two MCs came out of the Exclamation Box, hit the stage with their Green Lights hanging off their necks, and got the crowd on their feet again. I stepped backstage to take a breather and splash some water on my face. The show had been on for almost an hour already. Ten o'clock. The nerves were gone completely. Despite the circumstances, I was having the time of my life.

I ran back on stage and followed the hip-hop act with a few two-way video jests that went over perfectly. I got one of the bass players from the symphony to lay down a walking bass line to help move mood's momentum.

"Let's meet some real people from this town, shall we? Let's see who makes this town tick, the real reality shows of Roxy!"

Luckily, the people I chose were excellent sports. The first guy was a young dude who worked on the Ziplinc. He who wore his pants so low that he was forced to walk like a constipated monkey. I told him, in jest of course, that he was the first evidence of our species taking a step back in evolution, and that I should get a DNA sample. Some other gems, live and on air: a woman from the Beaches who sang a French folk duet with me, a Taiwanese elderly couple who finished each other's sentences with hilarious broken English, a sausage-salesmen with a nose so snout-like I had to ask him what it was like to be a cannibal. And on and on. As always, real conversations making great entertainment! You can't script that stuff!

We took a few minutes to stop in on each street party to see what was going on, via video. Max, that human nightmare, was hosting the event in Corksville. I was happy to roast him on live television!

"Hello Vincent! And hello all you party people down at the Mogul amphitheatre! As you can see from the festivities behind me, we are having a great time down here!"

"So we see. Do you always like to state the obvious, Max? We can clearly see you're having a good time, so why not tell us something different? Or do you enjoy walking around wasting other peoples' time? The sky is blue! I am wearing shoes! My mother still thinks I have a university degree!"

The crowd liked that one. Max didn't. I knew I'd never see him again, so who cares?

Another commercial break at 10:30. Seven minutes to eat something fast and go over the stage notes.

The Magnodots and Holographix were securely in my pockets.

Everything was cool.

CHAPTER SIXTY: UNLEASH THE JESTERS

At street level, the Jesters unleashed.

As the acts came out of the Exclamation Box, I watched the jumbo screens over the amphitheatre, which gave me a clear picture of the scene across the city. It looked as though Roxy was about to burst at its seams.

Jugglers, street musicians of every genre imaginable, mimes, giant marionettes, over-sized masks, sculptors, magicians and actors turned the legendary town upside down. Murphy led a twenty-jester cast who told warped stories of 'almost historical events' to a massive audience on the Plateau. Across town at the Market Square, an 'instant art' crew accompanied Twisty and Turnstylz with their rapid-fire beat boxing and graffiti styling. Humdinger and Woozle, paired up with Yoink and Scalliwag to lead a group of a thousand in a Latin dance routine. The camera caught a band of waiters running into oncoming traffic, stopping each car to take their order. Four marching bands, one disco, one military, one pop and one Asian-opera, got into a traffic jam at an intersection and just kept jamming; a fusion of very heavy-duty proportions. The city had transformed into a carnival, and the vibes pulsed spectacularly.

DJ Breakfast raised the volume another few notches on his deck in Corkville, and let the groove ripple through the crowd a little while longer before he got on the microphone. The Sonic Sticks below his deck radiated deep green and the vibrations from the beats he spun shook windowpanes all the way down the entertainment district. He had never heard such an exotic mash-up of music before. The crowd dancing crazily in front, losing themselves in the thrill of it all, probably hadn't either. Every road downtown was painted with thousands of partygoers dancing to the unique rhythms of its district; every avenue and boulevard pulsated with electricity. Like a life elixir, the city drank in the Jesters jaw-dropping spectacle brewing the city's true energy.

"This town will never be the same!" Breakfast boomed his voice over the system to the roaring response of the crowd. "DJ Breakfast is frying you up some eggs and bacon with brand new spice, these beats don't ever come out the same way twice!" Breakfast turned off his decks at those words, which cued Fitch's slap-together band, the Delivery Boyz, to launch into their set down at Ryde Park. Eight horns, three guitarists, two keyboardists, five didgeridoos, eleven percussionists, four Tablas, twenty-five dancers, three drummers and two bassists blasted out a fusion of funk-drenched world-music that turned the crowd crazy.

The Noize were forced to park their cruisers and watch as the partygoers made merry. What were they going to do? Start murdering everyone on national broadcast?

11:21 pm

At eleven-thirty I was introducing the world to Channel One. At midnight I was flipping the switch. We were so close.

There was barely any time to change into my final motley for the night before going back on stage, forcing me to hop around frantically, shoving my legs and arms into the suit and zipping myself in while trying to stay focused. I pulled out my Magnodot and tapped 'standby' on the Holographix; the tiny dot shone effervescent blue in the palm of my hand. Once it was in place on stage and I was making my escape, there was no turning back. I pulled out a stick of gum and sneaked on the darkened stage.

Tiptoed to my starting spot, marked with an x just at the base of the Exclamation box. I stuck my gum on the spot and then pressed the Magnodot securely on top to fasten it in place. Tiptoeing backstage again I positioned myself in the Exclamation Box's elevator and waited. My hands shook holding the Holographix as I watched for the musical cue on the teleprompter.

The Channel One teaser trailer began at the conductor's down beat to start the third movement of Mahler's 2nd. The third movement is called 'Schnell', meaning 'quickly'. Ironic, because I needed all the energy I could get.

It started off with a bang. The stage exploded in a burst of colour and the screen showed a nicely tweaked version of the promo Cyrus had shown to me just weeks prior. The Channel One logo was sharper, and the animations more fluid. Their version of the vibe flew through a city's streets. The choreography between the images and the music were, I admit, eye-catching.

Splash titles like, "TOMORROW'S TECHNOLOGY TODAY", "ONE WORLD, ONE FREQUENCY", and "A DEVICE THAT KNOWS HOW YOU FEEL" spun large between shiny sci-fi like images of the pulsating Channel One hues. The audience watched, captivated. People probably felt like this gala unveiling was an historic event. They couldn't have been more right.

The video transitioned back to the Jester logo, and the stage lights came up gradually for the crowd to focus on me, standing center stage. Anticipating this by a fraction of a second, I hit the hologram launch button and my holographic self was live in front of the world. I pressed the play button, followed by the elevator basement button.

CHAPTER SIXTY-ONE: PING! PING! PING! PING! PING!

"Ladies and gentlemen, it is with immense pride to stand before you tonight to introduce MogulMedia's latest technological breakthrough, Channel One. Channel One is cutting edge smart technology that could revolutionize our lives! It reads people's emotions, our human energy, and then it adjusts and accommodates our favourite devices to each individual person. This isn't smart technology, folks. This is genius technology!"

Thunderous applause. I imagined the king's ballooned palms sweating with greed with my every word.

"You come home after work, and there's nothing on TV. You're sitting there hitting the remote control like a Pavlovian chicken tapping a button for food. "Dog Swap." Crap show. Don't feel like watching that. "Foreign movie." Don't speak the language. Ugh! Another crime show! Useless drivel! Lame. Commercial, commercial, commercial. Let's face it, most of what's on is junk anyway ~ no offence to the man cutting my check though!"

Laughs. A few uncomfortable ones.

"And the same goes for the Net, right? Buttbook, Buttbook, Buttbook. Always end up on the same sites. Corporate site, lame blog, weak amateur photography, dating site, cheesy jokes, pop-up ads…it's never been easy to find anything that suits us! And the nuisance of having to press buttons and search! Pffft! I sure hope our grandkids will appreciate the struggles we had to endure to get our entertainment!"

Applause and laughter: I had them in the palm of my holographic hand.

11:40 pm

I touched down on the basement level and the doors opened. In front of me were two corridors. The left corridor was labeled 'Do Not Enter', and the right corridor, 'Security Personnel Only.' I wished I could have had a second hologram to scout out one of the corridors to save me time. Knowing I didn't have such luxury, I chose the corridor on the left and ran down it in blind faith.

"But you know folks, I am not here to sell you anything tonight. I wouldn't do that to you. Mr. Eisenberg has asked me, his faithful all-joking, all-singing, all-dancing Jester, to sell something to you tonight, but it's just not in my nature. Jesters entertain, but they don't advertise for nobody. Surely, by now, if people want to buy something, the last thing they want is it shoved down their throat. Am I right? You are all very welcome to buy Channel One, by all means! It is an amazing device. Just keep in mind that the money you are spending is only glorified toilet paper for Mr. Eisenberg's fat ass."

Massive laughter, and a huge shift in the amphitheatre's energy. They couldn't tell if I was joking or not.

"That's right, I said it! Cyrus Eisenberg has more money than most small countries! And that's about all he's interested in. Can we blame him? No! Hell, we're all interested in money. If it grew on trees we'd all be farmers. Or lumberjacks. And please, ladies and gentlemen, don't get me wrong! I love Eisenberg, I love technology, I love entertainment, too! Why else do you think I became a jester?"

There was a boom of cheering and applause that came out loud and clear on my Holographix. I was at the end of the corridor, taking a deep breath before I scanned my chip into the door's scan pad. It opened. The relief of a million marathon runners at the finish line washed over me.

Flip the switch. Get out.

Mogul Labs was lit up white and bright just as it was the first time I had been down. All of Roger's equipment was intact, which was a good sign, but I couldn't see the cryptic scientist anywhere. I tried calling his name, but my voice bounced around the laboratory, unfruitful. My heart started pounding. If something happened to Roger, the final puzzle piece, I wasn't teleporting anywhere. The words that were about to come out of my holograms mouth would bury me. Quite literally.

The WonderWall beside me blinked alive, displaying the floor-by-floor map of the entire basement. Strange, I thought. I didn't double click anything.

My eyes scanned down to the level I was on, and I located my star avatar right away.

Centimeters away, five knight's head avatars moved toward me. Up in the elevator! Guards!

11:47 pm

Murphy laughed to himself with pure glee as he hopped into the Lucky van, my voice being broadcast over the radio. He was having the night of his life, too. He had already changed costumes three times, and was there to change out of the costume he had been wearing (a bird with a fear of heights), and into his next (a fish with a fear of water). He got down to boxers and was rummaging around in the costume box for his gills when he heard a familiar metallic 'cling' that stopped him in his tracks. A Mood Globe rolled out from underneath a chair and rolled lazily near Murphy's feet.

That's odd, he thought, picking the lone globe up. He was sure they got rid of all 10,000.

Two more globes followed right behind it.

11:48 pm

"Well I'm glad you've enjoyed the ride as much as I have, my friends. It's been a wild one! I've introduced earth-shattering technology, and you've seen some amazing music and incredible showmanship across the city. I hope you all enjoy the Expo this weekend and have your minds sufficiently blown away by all that MogulMedia has to offer.

"But before I go, I want to let you in on a little secret.

"A truth we all know but no one really talks about.

"The truth is, I don't love technology and entertainment when it's owned by MogulMedia. The MogulMedia Empire is an oversized, soul-sucking vacuum of greed, lies and deception. And that's only on the first two floors! It get's worse the higher you get to the top! Fifth floor, mind control!

"Yes, mind control, kids! I know you think I'm joking, but believe me I'm not! MogulMedia has been controlling what you watch, what you download, what you buy, and what you wear for a long, long time. We haven't made an independent choice since the advent of mass media! It has actually been admitted to me that media is purposely regulated and under constant surveillance in order to make sure that we remain its faithful customers; buying what they want us to buy, watching what they want us to watch. If you're not careful the media will suck the creative soul right out of you. Channel One, sadly, is yet another happy brainwashing device for the whole family!"

11:49 pm

Roger was nowhere to be found.

The guard's in the elevator were only a floor above the real me, and I could see more knight's heads on the map storming the holographic me on stage! How in the world did they know which one was which?

The elevator doors whooshed open and the rush of the guards' heavy feet stormed down the steel steps.

Panic, engaged.

I dashed across the laboratory toward the Frequencifier, knowing that my escape was now beside the point. My part of the operation was to flip the switch. That was the whole point. All the hard work my friends had done was not going to be lost. Real heroes wouldn't think twice about sacrificing themselves for a cause this important.

But I could hear Chester in my head, laughing at me. *'A hero, huh? You're just a jester! If you don't hurry up you'll be a quickly forgotten urban myth!'*

The Frequencifier was heaving with vibes. There were more colours and galaxies of energy than ever before, and I could feel actual heat coming off of the machine.

11:50 pm

"So? What's three extra Mood Globes?" Fitch asked. Murphy had sent an emergency text to the other Blabbermouths. All three met back at the van at once.

Murphy pulled out the VPS and showed it to his friends. The screen showed 9,997 in large black numbers. "How are we going to get three more vibes in the next ten minutes when everyone in the city is already at our party?" Murphy shouted, shoving the device in Breakfast's chest. "I can't take the pressure. After everything we've done..."

Breakfast tossed his headphones to the side, and closed his eyes. "Ok, hang on, let's keep it real here. We just need three more vibes? That's it?" He turned on the satellite view on the

VPS and reviewed their target areas. The glow of the vibration markers covered the city in an even, pulsating rhythm. Their distribution seemed to be impeccable, except for a tiny strip a few blocks from where they were in Little Israel.

"There!" he exclaimed. In an instant Breakfast jumped out of the van and lifted himself up on top of it to get a better look at the area. He spotted a synagogue along the far side of the park. Silhouettes showed a large group of people inside.

"What day is today?" Breakfast shouted down below.

"It's Friday." Murphy answered. "Why?"

"Friday is Jewish Sabbath. Jewish people don't party on Fridays."

"Unless there's a wedding. Or a bar mitzvah."

"The sharp dressed dudes with the funny hats?" Fitch asked.

"Yes, Fitch. Those dudes," Breakfast said. The deejay crouched down on the top of the van and swung his head inside, hanging upside down. "Do we have any hats like that, Murph?"

11:52 pm

"And as if mind control isn't bad enough, get this! The patent for Channel One was stolen! MogulMedia stole the Channel One technology from a very good friend of mine, just as he stole my concept for the Jesters. Friendly guy that he is, Cyrus even forced me to be the image for this whole Channel One campaign! Well, I had an option. I could have been murdered. Tough call."

11:53 pm

Hanging off the switch was a green velvet bag and a sealed envelope. Roger's handwriting was scrawled on the front of the envelope. His message was distinctly his.

Reverse the signal, then go.
Read note later.
Indeed, Roger

p.s. Don't forget to allow for an approximate five-minute delay for the wave particles to reassemble before they disperse and potentially shatter their host frequencies.

Stuffing the note in my jacket pocket, I pulled the chord on the velvet bag and had Roger's single most incredible invention, the Telexcelerator, in my hand. I was in business!

The guards approached, yelling now, guns drawn. The first shot fired, ricochetting off the Frequencifier and nearly blasting me a Mohawk.

I had to grip the switch on the Frequencifier with both hands and push all my weight back with my legs because it was so heavy. With four heaves it finally flipped from INPUT to OUTPUT and the machine groaned with audible dissatisfaction. The colours began to slow and I paused long enough to see the vibes inside meld in motion like thick jello, and then gradually reverse their flow.

11:54 pm

More shots fired and I jumped behind the Frequencifier. The guards were less than ten steps away.

The Teleporter fit snugly around my head. I simply turned it on, and slipped my hat overtop.

More rapid fire banged out less than a metre from where I hid, sparks flying, and I heard the groans of fallen men just before their bodies hit the floor with heavy thuds. Then, silence.

"Vincent. It's clear. You can come out." It was Ms. Devlin's voice. She stepped around the Frequencifier and stood over me with a smoking pistol in her hand. Not an ounce of remorse showed on her face for taking down those guards, in fact, she smiled and helped me to my feet.

With trepidation, I gave her my hand. She pulled me close. "Do you specialize in plot twists, Samantha? Because I'm entirely puzzled over here."

Brushing back a crimson lock of her hair with her pistol, she smiled at me. "The foolstaff fooled you again, Vincent. It's positioning system gave you away. I figured you needed my help."

"Your help? Samantha, all you've ever done is hate me." I cursed that hexed foolstaff, shoving it into my pocket. Yet I loved to hate it so much I couldn't throw it away.

"You've made me laugh since the moment you got here, Vincent." I spotted a single tear roll down her cheek. "I got a little jealous of the attention you were getting, I guess."

"Ha! Jealous of what? Of being manipulated and pimped out? I don't think such soulless scandal is anything to envy! You might want to think of that next time you hallucinate your talent."

Samantha hung her head as she wiped the tears away. Her curled smirked had been replaced with an honest to goodness expression of humility. "This is my way of apologizing, ok? I got the box you left for me in the elevator last night. It was…really thoughtful of you. It really moved me…I finally get what you are all about, now. What you are trying to say. And you're right. I've needed to express myself for a long time…"

I put my hand on her shoulder. I had felt what she was feeling once upon a time, too. "Creativity is powerful energy, Samantha. To deny one's self of it is to suffocate one's soul."

Her hair tumbled across our faces as she stepped forward and kissed me. A juicy, sultry smack of the lips knocking me off balance. "Thank you, Vincent. For everything. I'll make sure things change around here."

"Start by getting Cyrus some anti-flatulence medication. Sitting next to him on the throne was torture." I straightened my hat, making sure the Telexcelerator was squarely around my head. A bolt from the Frequencifer suddenly shot past us in a squeal of pressurized steam. "Make sure you get out of the empire soon, Samantha. This thing is going to blow quantum any minute."

"What about you, Vincent? Do you have a way out?"

"You bet! Creativity is powerful, honey, which makes imagination pure rocket fuel!"

I closed my eyes and imagined the central party downtown. In a heartbeat, I landed smack dab in the middle of Roxy.

CHAPTER SIXTY-TWO: VANISHING ACT

11:55 pm

Teleporting is a lot like flying, actually. Except without the plane, the food, the uncomfortable seats, the jet lag, the passenger next to you whose feet smell worse than the washrooms, the copious bags of peanuts, the in-flight d-list movies, or any recollection of having left at all.

Ok, it's nothing like flying. It's more of a swift slap in the face. A slap so hard it results in total geographical relocation.

And the look of shock on my face at actually escaping MogulMedia and reappearing at Ryde Park didn't even come close to the look of shock on the face of the short frumpy woman I appeared next to. A single popcorn kernel hung at the edge of her bottom lip as her mouth dropped at the sight of me. She scanned me from head to toe, looking back and forth between the hologram me on the outdoor video screen and the real me. The hologram me was heading into its sentimental ending.

"The funny thing, friends, is that none of this is a new story, right? Ideas are stolen all the time, and corporations will always go to extremes to get our business. That's life, I guess. Greed and deceit are as much part of the human condition as burping and farting. And look, I'm just one tiny jester, so what can I possibly do about it? Well, actually, I've given it some thought, and I figure there is something I can do."

Behind the scenes, a growing army of the king's guards ran toward the stage prepared to terminate the program, and me. The gala's musicians and comedians were shoved aside, and behind the cameras operators were held at gunpoint, their broadcasts swiftly shut down. But Stu the cameraman held fast, and the helicopters above the amphitheatre were beyond the guard's reach. Undoubtedly, the audience filmed the whole speech on their personal devices, too.

The king had passed out on his throne, a baby drugged on his favourite milk, and slept through everything to follow.

11:56 pm

The crowd surrounding me was fixated on my speech; it was pretty inspiring if I don't say so myself. To be honest, I'd forgotten almost everything I recorded the night before because I had been so over-tired, so even I was hanging on my every word.

"The best I can do is give you a brief vacation from the brainwashing you've unknowingly endured. I know, I know, it's a wacky idea! But can you imagine what would happen if we took a break from information overload, even if just for a day? What if we were to just take a breather for a little while? What if we put away all the gadgets, the movies, the music, the channels, the phones, the news, the computers, the online life? What if we turned media off long enough to just hangout and make our own entertainment?"

Slowly though, more people clued into the fact that I was standing among them, and the atmosphere shifted from wonder to suspicion as their focus shifted onto me. Mumblings and murmuring grew louder. I had to get out of there.

I smiled politely and backed up behind a nearby Johnny on the Spot to take the brief window of privacy to teleport out of there. I wanted to find my friends. Imagining Murphy's face, I closed my eyes and teleported.

To my surprise, I materialized across from two Hassidic Jews in front of a narrow alleyway.

11:57 pm

Murphy was nowhere to be seen. Nobody was. I figured the Teleporter was on the fritz. At least it got me this far, I thought. It was futile to search any more for my fellow conspirators before the Frequencifier blew; there wasn't time. I was about to walk away when I noticed the two Hassids happened to be watching my broadcast on a power phone, so I casually stole a moment and leaned over their shoulder to watch the end of my speech. I didn't expect to end such a momentous evening with strangers in an alleyway, but life never ceases to surprise.

"Could we let ourselves be creative? Are we willing to tell a story, or sing a song, or pick up a brush and paint something? I don't know about all of you, but some of the best laughs I've ever had were from real situations with friends, not from movies or TV. And the great thing is that those scenes are ours. There is no way a Media Mogul could take it away! My philosophy is that if we allowed ourselves to turn off the gizmos and tune in to our inner vibes once in a while, life would be a lot more surprising. Inspiring even! We wouldn't be watching life through a screen all the time, would we? *We* are living entertainment! It's real, it's always live, and it's completely unpredictable!"

11:58 pm

Out of the blue, one of the Hassids pulled out a VPS, looked at it, and then shouted at the power phone.

"Vincent, how much longer are you going to draw this out? Get out of there!"

The voice was unmistakable. These were no Hassidic Jews!

"Shouldn't be too much longer," I said calmly, behind them.

Murphy and Breakfast looked like frightened bearded turtles when they turned and saw me standing there behind them. Murphy glanced at the phone and then back at me. I put my hand on his shoulder to comfort him.

"Just a bit of nifty tech from the empire, buddy. You're watching a pre-taped hologram."

Breakfast shook his head, shaken and confused. "Holograms? They weren't part of the plan, Vince. You've gone cyber-jester on us!"

"True. But is adopting a new religion part of your plan?"

"We were three measly globes short with nobody left to jest. Me, Breakfast and Fitch hit the synagogue undercover."

"And? Did you do it? Where's Fitch?"

"He's still inside. But the VPS says the Frequencifier's full, so we should be good to go."

It was too close for comfort. My holographic self was heading for his big finish.

11:59 pm

"Anyway, ladies and gentlemen, I could go on all night, but I must disappear. Pun intended. You'll get that joke in a minute. I'm sure I'll never work in this town again, but, you know what, it's been worth it! Eisenberg, when you hire a jester, you should expect some advice you don't want to hear! I hope you enjoy the surprise!"

At that moment Fitch came around the corner, running down the alleyway holding his black hat on his head with a dastardly smile on his face.

"The vibes are alive in there now, boys!"

A mob of irate Hassids followed just behind, quickly gaining on him. They all looked extremely offended.

Looking back at the power phone we saw that the holographic me was standing on stage with my hands in the air, frozen. I fumbled for the Holographix, punched ‘end program’ as quickly as I could and watched myself vanish from the stage.

yo. did you hear that?

CHAPTER SIXTY-THREE: MIDNIGHT

12:00 am

It was a hilarious sight, in retrospect. Three Hassidic Jews at the entrance of an alleyway without a clue. One gripped the Exclamation Box under his arm, shrugged his shoulders at the rest of us as if to say, "what else can we do?" and so we all ran as fast as we could away from the angry mob when the Frequencifier erupted at last.

At first there was no sound. A vacuum of silence blanketed the square. We braced ourselves, not knowing what to expect. Then, a distant, high-pitched blast picked up speed and intensity and shot through the streets. The partygoers ducked and covered their ears and people immediately started screaming at the top of their lungs in fear. We heard Mood Globes cracking and exploding from the force of the output, forcing us to shield our faces and cover our ears. For a fraction of a second the streetlights went out, which was our ever-so-narrow window of opportunity to run toward the van for protection.

Murphy shouted over to me as we ran; he showed me his phone blinked 'no signal'.

The rest of what happened is pandemonium muddle. I remember deafening screams and people yelling 'bomb' and 'terrorist'. All at once we felt and heard a dense wave of reverberation that emptied out over the city in a swift, cacophonous, force of sound.

The Frequencifier had emptied its 10,000 vibes back into the airwaves.

Its boom unleashed a rush of sonic-sized music that felt as though it pushed us forward as we ran and lifted us up off the ground as well. We jumped in the back of Murphy's van, slammed the doors shut and shouted at LaRose, who was ready and had the van already running, to drive as fast and as far as possible.

Judging by the enormity of the quantum blast, none of us were sure if Operation Last Laugh was going to be as amusing as we had hoped. In fact, we were pretty sure our operation scared the crap out of the city, and maybe worse. Hell, it scared the hell out of us! We wouldn't be sure until the next morning to what extent our mission was a success.

For the time being we knew we had done something legendary, our band of laughing scallywags.

CHAPTER SIXTY-FOUR: AFTERBLAST

LaRose raced the Lucky van through the back streets of Little Israel like a sports car, and sent the rest of us tumbling and rolling all over one another. A trumpet nailed me in the face on a tight corner and then a bunch of fake fruit rained over our heads as we started up the Ridge toward the Skybridge out of the city. Worse than the potential harm of a magician's staff taking one of our eyes out, or the threat of a car accident even, was Fitch's incessant shouting at the top of his lungs.

"Ican'thearanythingyouguys!" He shouted, frantically wiggled his fingers in his ears. "Canyouhearme? Ican'thearyou!OhmyGod,I'mdeaf!You'reprobablydeaftoo!Ho wareyougoingtoknowyou'redeafifIcan'ttellyou?"

"The only reason you can't hear anything, you idiot, is because you've got your fingers in your ears!" I shouted. "It's great to see you again by the way, you loveable moron."

Fitch popped his fingers out of his ears. "Did you just call me a moron?"

"I sure did!"

"Ok, great. I heard that."

"So, did we do it?" I asked. "Did it work?"

"Oh, it worked alright," LaRose said, poking her head through the window hatch from the front of the van. "The radio's dead. So is my phone. And the city's gone black, too."

I couldn't contain myself. I needed to see it for myself. The window hatch was too small to squeeze through. Acting on impulse, I ran to the back of the van. "Hold on to something boys!" I shouted as I gripped a metal rung and flung the doors wide open.

"Vincent, no!" Murphy shouted, desperately hanging onto a bench leg to keep himself in the van. He watched in horror as his costumes blew into the wind and props and beards and wigs flopped out and containers of accessories scattered out of the van, rolling out onto the empty bridge behind us. The best-dressed bridge in town.

"Dude! Have you lost your mind?" Breakfast shouted as he pinned himself tight against the wall.

I balanced myself on the ledge of the van with one arm and a leg and gleefully swung outside, pointing into the distance. "Look at what we did!"

All four of us stood at the edge of the open doors as we reached the top of the Skybridge to soak up the view. Total darkness blanketed the city above and below save the sheen of a polished moon behind MogulMedia. The city was blackened with an oily brush save for the scant blinking lights alive Uptown. Every single billboard was out and streetlights spattered futilely before they died. Miraculously, we watched in amazement as the split-second flashes of the Frequencifier's energy storm that lit up the sky in overpowering vividness. Designs of multi-coloured vibes; veins of energy still recoiling from the implosion that whipped a super sonic sound wave through the city and back into the Channel One atmosphere.

"Incredible," Murphy remarked. "Our vibes are more powerful than any of them…"

“Congratulations guys!” I shouted at the end of the van. “We didn’t just shut down MogulMedia, we blacked out the whole city!”

It felt so good to teach Eisenberg a lesson and feel that rush of vindication. It felt great to be out of that circus, too.

“Jesters win!” Fitch shouted. “Turn on the radio, maybe they’re talking about us!”

Breakfast slapped him over the head. “There is no radio signal, you putz! No OuterWeb, no TV, nothing!”

We passed a man on the side of the road just as he threw his phone over the bridge in a rage of frustration. It was impossible to imagine the degree of panic that must have just set in at the amphitheater, let alone the total fury that was exploding inside Eisenberg when he realized his quick, convenient digital world had been so swiftly extinguished. That the jester had outwitted the court.

And then, appearing over the lip of the bridge, a police car ruined our moment of bliss as it sped toward us with its lights and sirens blaring. We were sitting ducks: a jester in full motley and three Hassidic Jews hanging out of a moving van after a city-wide explosion.

“You might want to take your hat off, dude.” Breakfast whispered to me. “That probably isn’t the smartest thing to be wearing right now.”

“As if it matters,” I said. “My face has been all over national broadcasts for the last three hours.”

LaRose slowed down and pulled the Lucky van over to the side of the bridge. The police officer stepped out of his cruiser and marched slowly toward us shining his flashlight in our eyes. Weird, I thought. I’m a wanted man. I remembered what Chester had said the other night. He told me I could never go back to my regular life again. Ever again. That realization rang truer than any other of the doll's predictions.

"Which one of you jokers is Vincent Meistersinger?" the officer asked.

"That's me," I said, hopping out of the van, wondering how on Earth he found me so fast.

"Don't move! Put your hands in the air!' the officer shouted. "You are under arrest! Anything you say will be held against you in a court of law."

I squinted from the light in my eyes and started to sweat. My mind raced. Had anyone been hurt in the explosion? I needed to stay calm. Get some leeway. I did, after all, have the Telexcelerator around my head.

"Don't worry about these other guys, officer," I said, looking over my shoulder at my friends, chuckling. "They were just giving me a lift. Straight to the police station, right guys?"

"Don't get us involved, Vincent!" Murphy shouted. "You're making us accomplices! It's bad enough what you made us do for you."

I couldn't believe my ears. My friends were going to watch me squirm? I had to take the blame for all of this?

"I'd lose the humour Mr. Meistersinger," the officer said, shining the light right up in my face. "People are calling you a 'terrorist', do you know that? That's some serious stuff. No doubt the Noize are out on the streets, hungry for blood, too. So what's it going to be, jester boy? Are you coming downtown with me, or do I leave you for the real criminals?"

My eyes stung from the glaring intensity of the flashlight, so I turned my head and looked out toward the darkened city to let them cool off. I could make out the charcoal silhouette of my neighbourhood on the other side of the river. I remembered my life at the beginning of this whole adventure, when I lived like the undead – depressed and ostracized from the world, void of happiness or inner spark. And now I was going to be punished for having too much happiness? For getting people connected with their vibes again? For spreading happiness? I wasn't sure if the situation was funny-ironic, or just straight up unfunny.

I didn't care at that point. I was proud of everything I had done. The Jesters were a massive success. They could throw me away for a million years and I wouldn't apologize for any of it.

"Well officer," I said, giving him back the attitude he didn't want, "those are two very limited choices. Are you sure there isn't a third for me to consider? Like a sandwich? What's a guy gotta do to get a sandwich around here?"

"Funny you should ask," he said. He tossed the flashlight to Breakfast who caught it, as if rehearsed, and turned the beam back on the officer. "Jail, the Noize, or…you could just sign my t-shirt for me…" The officer took off his coat and bulletproof vest beneath it to reveal a shirt that read: "JESTER DETHRONES KING."

I stood and stared, speechless - stunned by the scene before me. "Where in the world did that t-shirt come from? Who the hell is this cop?" Fitch snickered a bit and the laughing quickly dominoed through the other jesters, and then the cop starting laughing, too! Looking closer, I saw he was no ordinary policeman! It was Underplum!

"You bastards!" I shouted. "You guys scared the crap out of me! Holy smokes! I was ready to take a bullet for you punks and here you are serving up a prank?"

"Got you sucka!" Breakfast laughed, whipping his big black hat at me. "Whoever said you can't fool a jester?"

"We got tons of shirts made, Vince," Fitch said. "Murphy printed them all up and sold them in advance on the website."

Flabbergasted. The four of them took off what they were wearing and showed me the slogans on their t-shirts underneath.

"OPERATION LAST LAUGH"
"THE JESTER IS BESTER"
"MOGULMEDIA EXPO (crossed out) JEST FEST"
"I'M A JESTER IN DISGUISE. OR AM I?"
"JESTER DETHRONES KING"

I laughed so hard tears streamed down my face. I couldn't believe my eyes! "Oh man, I need this laugh!" I bent over holding my sides. It had been a long time since some one had made *me* laugh, and it felt great. "How…How did you?" I was laughing so hard I couldn't even form the words.

"Everybody is in on it, Mr. Meister," Murphy said, laughing with me. "And I mean everybody. At least 10,000 people down there are keeping the party going with these shirts on. They were with us every step of the way."

"So…everybody knew?" I repeated, my head spinning to catch up from all the lost oxygen.

"Jesters from across the country. And our fans, mostly. We couldn't have pulled it off without them."

"You're larger than life, bro," Breakfast said as he hopped off the van and slapped me on the back. "Do you want to see something else that's really funny?"

"Oh man, I don't know if I can't take any more surprises."

“Underplum, I assume the ‘anonymous tip’ has been made?” Breakfast asked excitedly.

“I believe so, Breakfast, and I think we’re right on time. Follow me." Underplum waved us to follow him over to the other side of the bridge, where we leaned over the railing to look at the scene down below.

Directly underneath us was a dead quiet Shmitty’s Cabs. A few cabs were parked outside the docks, and we stared in silence at my former place of employment. “I wonder if Shmitty will give me a reference,” I wondered out loud. “I’m pretty sure I’ve lost my job by now.”

From out of the darkness along the road we saw thirty, maybe forty police cruisers throw on their lights and blare their sirens as they hurtled toward Shmitty’s Cabs. Following them were two CIA armoured trucks and then the dramatic whirling of helicopter blades joined in overhead, spotlights and everything.

“What is this all about?” I shouted over the noise.

“This is Shmitty going down, baby!” Breakfast said, smiling the widest smile I had ever seen on his face.

“What? I don’t get it?”

“He’s busted for smuggling. I told Underplum all about the boxes Shmitty made me run around town. You know was in them? Shipments of illegal computer parts. For MogulMedia.”

Looking down again we saw the S.W.A.T. team rushing the cab company’s headquarters as more men circled and secured the premises. Mere moments later, Shmitty and a few other unsavoury men were ushered outside with their hands cuffed behind his back.

"Shmitty's going to jail? For real?"

"For real! That grumpy sack of flesh ain't killing nobody's buzz no more!" Breakfast and I high-fived, and from somewhere I even got the energy to cartwheel in celebration. One less Shmitty in the world makes the world less…Shmitty! Could the night get any better?

Cartwheeling back to the van, I turned toward my friends walking back toward me. They were my closest friends that ever were or will be, and we had done it. Better than any of us could have imagined. A colossal fan base. Our big moment in the spotlight. Nationwide! And we did it our way.

"It must have been pretty wild working for Cyrus, eh?" Fitch asked.

I could read Fitch's face the easiest, the big softy. His pathetic puppy dog 'I just ate the birthday cake that was on the table' eyes were in full effect. There was an obvious change in the vibe with his question that told me something was up.

"Yeah, wild is a good word for it, Fitch, for sure. Funny to think I was earning all that dough from the man who was stealing from me at the same time. He's a sad, bloated alcoholic, but he serves up a mean milkshake, I'll give him that. But who cares, now? The joke is on him, right?" The five of them stood around me as if it were an intervention meeting. The silence was killing me. "What? What's going on? Spit it out you guys!"

"Well, the joke is on Cyrus Eisenberg, you're right," Underplum said, looking at his watch. He craned his neck to look beyond the Lucky van as if expecting someone. "For now, at least."

"Shmitty worked for Cyrus, Vincent," Breakfast said. "He was one of his fingers, so to speak. That's how he knew who you were. Remember when he hired the Noize to follow you? That's how mafia works, bro. That's how they knew about Roger, too."

"Roger! Do you guys know what happened to him?" I felt in my pocket to make sure Roger's letter was still with me. There's no way Cyrus would have…

"We thought maybe you'd know."

"MogulMedia's mafia is untouchable, Vince," Murphy added, his eyebrows angled apologetically. "The police told us he's the biggest crime boss this country has ever seen."

"And you've seriously pissed him off," Breakfast said, laughing. "I know it's not funny, but it is funny. Kind of."

"He runs mobs across the country," Underplum said. "We'll never be able to take him down, or all hell will break loose. But Shmitty was a big catch, at least. The biggest take down we've ever had, and now we're just bracing ourselves to see how the crime world is going to react to all of this."

"I get it," I said. I took a big breath in and stood tall. The city's silence soothed my thoughts as they scrambled to keep up to everything they were saying. "So I'm a dead man."

I stepped over to the ledge and looked down at our city's dark reflection rippling in the water. The building's silhouettes moved up and down, side to side, as if dancing in delight. We sure gave the city something to remember us by, I thought. All the happiness we had brought to so many lives, including our own, could not be denied. I remembered the early parties. The night Fitch rented horses and catered a family reunion picnic at the Gardens. The weekend retreat when Murphy posed as a yoga instructor and used the meditation hour to try out new material. So many great memories. And they were still around, somewhere. Blowing through uptown streets and stuck between the sidewalk cracks.

If you stay in one place long enough the memories start to layer on top of one another. You swear you can see versions of your former self going about their former business.

I was through with worrying about fame and all that nonsense. In my own way, I had achieved it without even trying to. The only difference between the fame that I got, and that a lot of other artists get, is that I didn't let mine eat me up and spit me out.

"I'm sorry Mr. Meister, but you can never show your face in this town again," Underplum said. "We're going to set you up on a witness protection plan. The detectives leading this whole case are going to be here any minute to pick you up."

"Right. And Cyrus is my bad guy. Just like my grandma used to say, 'everyone's got to have a nemesis', and he's mine. I get it. But allow me to be explicit here. I am not going to let that fat sack of Plazma ruin my life any more than he already has. Furthermore, I don't want to do anything other than be a jester for the rest of my life. Which is something I know I can do!"

"You're going to have to give up the persona, Vince, it's too dangerous," Murphy said, putting his hand on my shoulder.

"What else am I supposed to do, guys?"

"Well. I don't know," LaRose said. "You can still drive cab. Just not in this city."

"Uh, not on this continent!" Murphy added.

"Then drive cab in India!" Breakfast said.

"That's a great idea!" I shouted at the top of my lungs with my arms to the sky. "I can be a waiter in Australia! I can be a mechanic in Venezuela I can *do* anything, but I want to *be* a jester!" I jumped into the back of the van and started rifling through a costume box. I had an amazing idea. "I don't have to go on the witness protection program, do I Underplum?"

"Technically, yes you do." Underplum rubbed the back of his neck. "And the detectives are on their way."

I turned and winked at Underplum. "But I can't be forced to follow their recommendations unless you actually found me, right? If I was never here, they've got no witness to protect."

"Oh geez," Breakfast said, rolling his eyes. "It's worse than I thought you guys. He's let the whole fame thing go to his head. I think you've made enough headlines for one lifetime, bro."

"Stay with me here! I have a teleportation device," I said, lifting my hat, showing off the shiny Telexcelerator to everyone. "And I've got a Holographix machine! I've got an Exclamation Box, a few changes of underwear, and a whole lot of Eisenberg's money! Do you guys hear what I'm saying?"

The shook their heads in a unified 'no'.

"I can live the rest of my life travelling the world doing whatever I want! But what I really want to do is keep jesting! I want to keep up the element of surprise, pop in and out of other people's lives. I can actually disappear and do what I love to do! I'm going to make myself into a modern myth."

There was no preparing them for that drastic right-turn of an idea.

"Whoa, let's take a quick break and think this through for a second," Breakfast said, slapping his own face to wake up. "Listen to what you just said. What you're saying is that you're going for the Disney ending here, pal? Whooshing off into the distance, into people's imaginations? *Their imaginations?"*

“Like Santa, or the Tooth fairy!” LaRose exclaimed.

“Oh for crying out loud, don’t encourage him!”

“Yes! Just like that, LaRose. I’ll become the Jester. Some people knew me, some people didn’t. It’s perfect!” I hopped into the van and found an Exclamation Box shoved behind some instrument cases and started filling it with random pieces of costumes and things I saw lying around the van floor. “Besides, what’s so weird about wanting to jest and give people random gifts just for the fun of it? It worked for us before, didn’t it? People need absurdity in their lives.”

“Oh my god. We need a lobotomy over here! Pronto!” Breakfast shouted. “And then what are you going to do? You are going to be the magical, mystery Jester that, what? Uh, visits you late at night and blares a trumpet in your ear? Have you completely lost your mind?”

“Well, you do have to keep moving, I suppose” Underplum added.

“Exactly! I'm killing two sasquatches with one kernal. Use your imaginations! All the other myths are so old already anyway. It’s time we had a modern one!” I pulled my foolstaff from my pocket and held it in front of my friends. “Best of all, I don’t need the Green Light from anyone!” Turning toward the edge of the bridge, I hauled off and just about threw it over until LaRose grabbed it from me.

“Nobody look, ok? It’s a surprise,” LaRose said, and we averted our eyes. Moments later, she held it up proudly, giving us permission to look. In place of the Green Lights, LaRose had hung the exclamation mark Vibe Vials Roger made for Hallowe’en. The new jewels gleamed purple against the night sky.

“I know they always say don’t be a stranger,” LaRose said, with a kiss on my cheek. “But it’s not a fitting farewell for you. Be a stranger, Mr. Meister, be the most colourful you can be. And come back to visit, ok?”

“I like the modern myth idea,” Murphy said, chuckling. “It’s original. And the way you disappeared on stage last night is a pretty good beginning to a myth, actually.”

The detective’s headlights rose over the crest of the bridge in the distance like a pair of nearing owl eyes, searching.

“I should go before things get more complicated,” I said, backing up further out of view.

“So, that’s it? You’re friends with Thor now?” Fitch asked.

I laughed. “Sure, why not? You can tell people I’m the guy who brings the Easter Bunny chocolate for all I care. Just start a rumour. The crazier the better. The kind of rumour that will keep the whole mystery of the Jester going for years.”

I reached into my pocket and took out the silver box Eisenberg gave me with the hundreds of Magnodots inside, and handed one to everybody.

“Something cool for another one of your pockets, Fitch. I can call you via hologram with these things.”

“I guess that means you’ll ‘holla’ at us!”

“Right, I’ll holla at ya!” We shared another laugh together. It was good to laugh with my friends again. They understood me. They always would.

“Yeah, that is pretty cool,” Murphy said, slipping his Magnodot inside his pocket. “You’re definitely one of a kind, Mr. Meister.”

“If you’re a freak here you can be a freak anywhere, I guess.” Breakfast punched me in the arm and gave me a hug. “Do what keeps you groovy, bro. Do what you're good at.”

“Much gratitude, fellow absurdists, it's been quite a trip." I stepped out onto the bridge's railing and gave one final, extra ridiculous silly face as I balanced, and bellowed, "Violins and greasy spoons!" before vanishing a moment before the detectives pulled up.

“Violins and greasy spoons,” my friends echoed.

CHAPTER SIXTY-FIVE: THE FATHOM FOUNDATION

The first place I teleported was Roger's farm. Something told me I needed to see it again. And quite honestly, I had no idea where else to go. It's all well and good to decide to become living fiction, but where does a guy start such a wacky idea? At the beginning of it all, I guess.

I appeared just on the edge of a massive hole that surrounded what was left of the farmhouse, flapping my arms backwards to keep myself from falling head first inside of it. Gaining balance, I watched as one of the bells from my hat tumbled below, tinkling as it bounced off of the sad heap of ashen wood and broken glass remnants of the physicists' abode. The whole property had been burnt to the ground. I saw one of Roger's radios poking out underneath a ceiling beam with its wired insides pouring out. Behind me, the antenna was still standing, but only on three bent legs, aiming at the forest rather than the sky, and the barn was a collapsed deck of cards. Cyrus had sure done a number on this place. All of Roger's hard work; stolen.

Roger. I remembered the envelope he left for me still stuffed in my pocket, rumpled and folded. Setting down my Exclamation Box by my feet, I sat down and read the letter by the light of the moon.

Vincent,

By now the Frequencifier is successfully destroyed, and you are contemplating your next major life move.

I would wager that the odds of you doing anything rational are a billion to one. If I have learned anything from the way a jester thinks, it is that their logic is illogical, and their actions, unpredictable. I wish you well in whatever endeavour you might decide upon. I'm glad that I could help get you where you need to be.

Thank you again for your helping with my research. The data I amassed is staggering. Before you go gallivanting across the world, I have left a small token of my appreciation for everything you have done. Go into the woods behind my farmhouse. You will find it inside an old well, where it was hidden from prying eyes.

We're both inventors in our own right, Vincent. You are an artist, creating ideas and expression; I am a scientist, creating tools to further the development of society. Art and science intersect more than people realize. Fantasy builds futures. We have a lot in common, you and I.

You see, I belong to a secret society myself. We call ourselves the Fathom Foundation. Suffice it to say that just as you long to entertain, we thirst for scientific innovation. After I share the Channel One results with my colleagues and tell them how the research was pulled off, we may call upon your assistance in future projects.

Stick with me Vincent, and you'll be a jester well into the future. As soon as I get time travel figured out.

Keep in touch, indeed,

Eventually Roger

I looked up from the note as though I had just dunked my head in ice-cold water. I always knew there was something curious about Roger, but nothing like this! Why didn't he tell me about The Fathom Foundation before? It explained the FF stamps on all of his equipment, and his sophisticated equipment. And what was this about a token of appreciation? Knowing Roger, it had to be good.

I stuffed the note back into my pocket as I walked toward the forest. The moon was mid-sky, and its light danced dreamlike between the tree branches. It took me a few minutes inside the brush before I realized I was following the same footsteps I had had in my first vision of Chester. And then, lo and behold, as I stepped down a small, grassy ridge I saw the same stone well from my vision planted crooked and squat in a clearing right in front of me! I couldn't believe my eyes! It was real! It was the same place Chester had sat enjoying his popcorn, listening to Channel One and pontificating on the virtues of living life to its fullest. I expected to see him waiting for me. Instead it was just me sitting on its edge this time.

Filling my lungs with the night air, I closed my eyes and took a moment to listen to the forest air. It was so quiet out there. Some faint music swirled past my ears on the wind. Folk. Some electronica. A French horn? People were still jamming somewhere in the city, and Channel One had them on its frequency. And I was off to live my life in the same way music is played. Isn't that the point?

I laughed to myself as I remembered Chester's words. *I will 'become the fiction I'd always dreamed of'.*

Or were they my words?

And my laugh echoed off the walls of the well as I lowered myself down inside it.

EPILOGUE

The blackout only lasted a few hours, but the communication breakdown lasted the whole weekend.

After the vibes blitzed across the Channel One radio wave, millions of other frequencies buckled and warped. Signals jammed across wires and satellite communications ruptured, shattering the billions of wireless devices across the city. Most importantly, the hardwiring in the MogulMedia Channel One devices fried, rendering them useless, and the Frequencifier imploded after output, short-circuiting and causing an electrical fire in the basement laboratory.

Of course, the communication breakdown affected everyone. You can imagine the panic the sonic explosion created. People who incessantly check Buttbook and Critter were suddenly shut out. The horror! Stocks and the news and oh god forbid the weather updates couldn't be retrieved either. It was, on one level, pure chaos by horrid inconvenience.

When the government's communications shut down, it temporarily put everyone in hysteria. Hospitals couldn't run, planes had a hard time landing. In a nutshell, Roxy City shut down, crippled without our grid of digital technologies. It took about an hour before an emergency grounded frequency was activated, thankfully. Miraculously, no one got hurt.

So, what's a weekend like without phone calls and emails and mind numbing entertainment coursing through our collective energy?

The parties we started that night just kept growing, and by the end of the blackout every neighbourhood in Roxy was completely transformed. What else were people supposed to do? Graffiti lined so many of the walls and dancers danced freely in the streets for hours and hours. Children listened to tall tales they hadn't heard before from neighbours they hadn't met. Even Green Lit actors and comedians put on spontaneous performances. Hidden talent came out of the woodwork that week and communities bonded like never before. People built sculptures out of junk they had lying around, bus drivers did impressions of their customers, cooks tried dishes they never normally have time for, artists painted murals and started spontaneous drawing collaborations.

Best of all was the music that carried the city's vibes and rejuvenated cold, hollow streets with the frequency of life. Unused instruments had the dust blown off them and pulled from their cobwebbed basement corners. People who had played when they were young strummed and tickled the ivory and banged a drum; some people who had always said they could never play an instrument even took a leap of faith and joined in the jam sessions. It was a week of spontaneous creativity that connected and inspired the citizens of Roxy, and it was all due to the unique talents of jesters that the city was shaken alive again.

A few weeks following the blackout, after an outpouring flood of support online, the mayor of Roxy declared that weekend to be a holiday: FLIP THE SWITCH DAY ~ TURN OFF AND TUNE IN. For those three days every year, the city shuts down and parties run non-stop. People are encouraged to live offline in the spirit of person-to-person creativity, taking the time to enjoy face-to-face communication.

Cyrus moved the MogulMedia Expo to another city. He was quoted as saying he would never again host such an event to a population that was so clearly ignorant of the importance of technology and media for the economy. Needless to say, he missed the point.

Making sure to withdraw the salary I had earned during my time at MogulMedia as soon as possible, I divvied up my earnings and shared it with the Blabbermouths. I wouldn't have made it to stardom without them, and they deserved my salary as much as I did. They were tickled pickles to have the cash, and I knew each of them, in their own way, worked hard at keeping the city's jesters in business.

Fitch became co-owner of Cosmos diner and expanded it over into the building behind it. He didn't want to change Cosmos, he just wanted to add to it. Gutting the rear building, he redecorated, put in more seating and a stage complete with an orchestra pit. He made a deal with the Cosmos diner that every once in a while, at no fixed schedule, Cosmos would change their menu and call it 'The Big Surprise.' That's it. No one would know what to expect because the menu read, in extra fancy font:

<u>Menu</u>
Surprise #1: $7.00
Surprise #2: $21.50
Surprise #3: $46.25

The thrill of the idea is that customers don't know what to expect! Maybe it's Italian…perhaps it's Thai…Or maybe it's a bowl of soup carried by a man dressed as a sandwich who will read you excerpts from famous books all evening. Fitch hired a number of the other jesters to help out, every so often DJ Breakfast spun beats, and Murphy hosted stand-up comedy nights. Fitch was content as a waiter. He worked best where long-term memory wasn't required.

Murphy started his own company that offered jesters-for-hire; not to parties this time, but to businesses. Having seen the effect I had had on MogulMedia, he convinced employers that a jester on staff is the best advisor money can buy. A jester will tell you what you don't want to hear but probably need to, and they'll entertain you as they do it. Can you imagine a jester sitting in the corner of an office, getting paid to jest? Well, it worked! Some got hired as jesters incognito because bosses didn't want to draw attention to them, and other jesters showed up to work in full motley. LaRose got a gig singing jazz standards down in the warehouse at a paper factory. Fizzlestick jested meetings once a week at accounting firms by painting murals by numbers. Turnstylz hung out at the City Hall water cooler, beat boxing and telling stories, and some companies hired entire groups of jesters to perform and play music in their foyers as a regular gig. Live entertainment was on the up and up! Murphy kept the jester slogan, 'Live Like a King, Hire a Jester', and could barely keep up with business.

With Shmitty convicted of more crimes than centipedes have legs, Breakfast didn't hesitate to buy the cab company and give it a well overdue facelift. Just as he had dreamed of doing for years, he renamed it Company Beats, and each cab in the fleet was no longer a cab, it was a 'mood mobile'. Breakfast salvaged as many of the old cars Roger had sitting around on his property, like the Studebaker, the Alfa Romeo, the Ford Thunderbolt, and the Volkswagon Beetle, and had them painted up in splashes of bright colours. 'Fresh Beats for Hip Streets' was his motto, and when a customer got into any of his mood mobiles they were treated to great music spun by the best deejay in town. Working as part dispatch and part radio deejay, Breakfast made sure every ride had a good vibe.

A recent online poll showed that 73% of people believe in the myth of the modern Jester. Of course, the participants of the survey were between ages 3 and 11, but, it's a good start right? I know if I give it time I can reach the mythical status of the Sandman, or Bigfoot even, one Exclamation Box at a time.

I told myself a long time ago that I'd never let myself get depressed again, and I've achieved that. What's even better is that I've helped to lift the moods of millions, too. Surprise is the spice of life, people, and if you find yourself disengaged with it, burned out and watching LifeTV from lonely isolation, turn on some music and do something different! Our vibes don't exist outside ourselves; they're inside and need to be woken up once in a while. Bake a cake. Go for a walk with live fish in your pockets. Write absurd messages and slip them under every door of every floor of your apartment building.

It doesn’t take much to reconnect with your inner vibe.

Don't let the Doldrums get you down!

See you when you least expect it,

The Jester

GLOSSARY OF TERMS

AutoPeep ~ a 10-inch tall flying robot servant and power phone accessory. The robot can make purchases for its owner and deliver them i.e. if user is hungry, the AutoPeep can purchase a burger and deliver it. The AutoPeep will also hang out with friends and update user via Critter and Buttbook

Bling ~ a personal computer worn around the wrist, like a bracelet, it activates double-clickable surfaces throughout the MogulMedia kingdom

Buttbook ~ a social networking site for friends, and enemies

Channel One ~ the radio channel on which human energy is heard as discernible music ~ also the name of MogulMedia's predictive technology using human energy to delivery media content and adjust levels on other gadgetry. (TV, radio, air conditioning etc…)

Critter ~ a social networking micro-blogging service on the OuterWeb that allows users to communicate in a limited 140 characters. Critter posts, or 'creeps' appear like ticker tape across mobile devices, or are projected onto surfaces via projection camera, resulting in a 'crawling', insect-like appearance.

Digi ~ prefix for 'digital'

DigiDecks ~ deejay turntables calibrated digitally on fiber optic records

Digipad ~ a palm-sized digital tablet used for storing signatures, fingerprints, and retina scans

Digiposter ~ a poster with touch-screen digital content

Digiscreen ~ any digital screen with short and long range communication capabilities ranging from two to twenty person conference calls

Double-clickable surfaces (DCS) ~ a surface containing hyper-text data and accessed by the Bling in the same way information is double-clicked on a computer ~ information on DCS ranges anywhere from fabric used in clothing, to food ingredients, to luggage contents, to cavity detection, to a person's recent activity

Dynamitaxi ~ elite taxis boasting top power, speed, and efficiency, as well as sound-tight air bubbles for rear passengers in which directions are communicated to the driver through a Digiscreen ~ four-dimensional TV screens and a variety of beverages are also available

Emitimotimeter ~ a palm-sized, rectangular device that reads human emotion and translates it as energy, in mega-hertz

Googles ~ Long, conical eye-wear with access to the OuterWeb and Infinoogle wherein information is controlled by sight patters and blinking

Gourdly ~ the Jester's membership to the underground performing group, a doll made from a gourd in the likeness of its owner

Green Light ~ a radish-sized green light with a hypnotic glow, issued exclusively to MogulMedia performers after having successfully auditioned for Cyrus Eisenberg, king of media

Holodots ~ penny-sized metallic satellite disks used to host holographic broadcasts

Holographix ~ a sophisticated holographic machine with a broadcasting range of over twenty-five kilometers

Infinoogle ~ the primary search-engine on the OuterWeb

LensFlare ~ a small, thin, concave data storage device resembling a contact lens placed directly on a monitor's surface whereby its data is released and transferred into the receiving device

MagicMirror ~ a mirror with computer functionality set to individual preference using its signature feature: face recognition

Magnachair ~ a large, spherical, magnetic chair that polarizes a subject's energy, enabling quantum extraction

Meanwhile ~ a computer application that accesses the location of mobile devices via satellite, allowing users to track friend's movement in real time video

mycerebellum.com ~ a top-secret website housing the collective memories of anyone who has undergone a Tellmet download and been granted access

Omnibag ~ A teardrop shaped shoulder bag that is extremely lightweight, and deceivingly smaller on the outside than on the inside. The Omnibag is only 25 inches in length, but can hold over 150 lbs without weighing heavily on its carrier

Optitron ~ a meditation-inducing visualizer used to focus and calm subjects prior to experimentation

OuterWeb ~ a global system of interconnected computer networks to serve billions of users worldwide. Once known as the Internet, a network of networks that consisted of millions of private and public networks. The OuterWeb, in contrast, is only privately owned and heavily monitored by the rich and elite

Power Phone ~ the ultimate mobile phone with capacity to read hand gestures off screen, dictate and narrate texts, help brainstorm ideas, scan foods for harmful products, and expandable, shapeable screen surfaces

Swype ~ a popular communication application, it reduces human conversation down to a basic exchange of 183 possible questions, responses and statements represented pictorially. Swype won awards for most convenient app because it worked on voice command and by literally 'swiping' on screen, rather than texting on laborious keypads

Tellmet ~ a helmet with built-in neurological sensors to record and monitor thought-patterns, dreams and memories stored in the brain

Terahertz Exitron ~ a quantum accelerator that excites and extracts quantum energy on a sub-atomic level

uScroll ~ a flexi-monitor scroll-shaped personal computer that can be rolled out 27 inches wide, and collapsed into a pocket-sized tube. The uScroll is OuterWeb ready, 4D enabled, and boasts downloadable applications that manifest physically

Vidchat ~ a console-to-console method of communication that requires physical facial expressions rather than emoticons

Vidzine ~ a physical magazine with videos embedded into its pages rather than text

Vizmo ~ a temporary, realistic visualization of either a memory or a dream that can occur while awake

VPS ~Vibrational Positioning System ~ a location system based on the vibrations released from individual or groups of human energy over the Channel One radio frequency

weFling ~ a data storage and pocket projection device

WonderWall ~ a wall-sized, touch sensitive video screen with 7D cinematic software that really puts you in the action

YellowFang ~ a power phone that is worn like an earring or other piercing

YouBoob ~ MogulMedia's video networking site on the OuterWeb, strictly showcasing Green Light performers; illegal uploading of personal videos onto YouBoob is prohibited.

Ziplinc ~ Downtown Roxy's above-city transportation system. Citizens travel in plastic spheres, 'zipping' across a complex series of cables running between skyscrapers. The Ziplinc's capacity ranges from ten person spheres down to one, and the very rich have private zip lines running straight from their condo window to their place of work.

CPSIA information can be obtained at www.ICGtesting.com
Printed in the USA
LVOW072323251012

304456LV00022B/7/P